SEVERANCE

SEVERANCE

stories

ROBERT OLEN BUTLER

CHRONICLE BOOKS
San Francisco

With special thanks to Jay Schaefer, Catherine Argand, and Isabelle Reinharez, and to David Baker, James Cummins, and David Lehman.

First Chronicle Books LLC paperback edition, published in 2008.

ISBN: 978-0-8118-6098-7

The Library of Congress has cataloged the previous edition under
ISBN-10: 0-8118-5614-3
ISBN-13: 978-0-8118-5614-0

Manufactured in Canada

Designed by Brooke Johnson
Cover photo by Keyvan Behpour

This is a work of fiction. Names, places, characters, and incidents are products of the author's imagination or are used fictionally.

The stories in this book originally appeared in *Agni Magazine, The Cincinnati Review, Five Points, The Georgia Review, Glimmer Train, The Kenyon Review, McSweeney's, Ninth Letter, Open City, Prairie Schooner, The Southern Review, Tin House, 21 Magazine, The Virginia Quarterly Review,* and *Water-Stone Review.*

10 9 8 7 6 5 4 3 2 1

Chronicle Books LLC
680 Second Street
San Francisco, California 94107

www.chroniclebooks.com

for **ELIZABETH**

This book began when I showed you my beloved Saigon and we stood before the guillotine at the War Crimes Museum, long before the fall of the blade.

After careful study and due deliberation it is my opinion the head remains conscious for one minute and a half after decapitation.

—DR. DASSY D'ESTAING, 1883

In a heightened state of emotion, we speak at the rate of 160 words per minute.

—DR. EMILY REASONER, *A Sourcebook of Speech,* 1975

MUD

man, beheaded by saber-toothed
tiger, circa 40,000 B.C.

sharp the air with cold that comes so fast, and far we all run, along water turning to rock, many suns and only short-snout and short-snout to eat between us, the old of us lagging, the cold rushing, the touchwood barely warm we blow long on the touchwood last darktime, we blow and much growling anger for the touchwood keeps its flame tight, we all will lose the flame soon, and we alone fall back to the old ones in skins but we all keep the body-grease for our ourselves to hold our heat inside while the old carry the cold inside, and one is the suckle woman, long suns past she holds us alone to her suckle and we alone sit at flame and suckle woman puts her hand upon our head alone and puts her mouth to our ear alone and makes a soft cry, but we all feel the time coming like many suns past, before suckle woman is old, and there were other old and the cold came quick and we all were drawn tight on our bones and the biting was fierce in our centers and we all were going slow and it was time to eat, to eat the old, and now the cold is upon us and now the time is again and we alone fall back to hold the suckle woman and to make cries into her ear before we all eat

MEDUSA

Gorgon and former human beauty,
beheaded by Perseus, circa 2000 B.C.

dreaming, surely I dream now: I can still shake my hair down long and billowing like waves upon the sea, how tender I am how fair I can see in the reflection of water and shield and a man's eyes, and this softer hair makes no difference I still turn a man to stone who looks at me, the part of him that snakes inside me, a clefting of stone, and my body weeps the sea, pours forth the thickest sea for my god-man Poseidon who smells of brine and the great swimming creatures who attend him scaled and heavy wet limbs about me and that bitch Athena thinks her temple defiled but it was he who came to me and leaned his trident upon her marble face and dripped upon her floor, she tries to hurt me but I love my living hair these serpents whisper when men come close each strand with a split tongue hissing my desire for them I shake my dear children my tresses down and they curl back up their black eyes flashing and the man cries out at my beauty and then his tongue and face and chest and arms and thighs and his toad-headed serpent all turn hard forever the clearing before my cave is thronged with them my admirers, but my children are my true loves rooted in my brain and gathered sleeping against my face muttering sibilant dreams of love

MARCUS TULLIUS

CICERO

orator and politician, beheaded on orders of Marc Antony, 43 B.C.

louder, Marcus Tullius, I cannot hear you cries Helvia my noble mother her forehead ringed in curls calling from the top row of the empty theater *speak louder* and my arms are leaden from a thousand apt gestures and I cannot think and I am small *stand straight* she cries I lift my upper body and the senators are packed before me like sardelles straight from the sea their eyes unblinking their mouths gaping my voice rings through the curia and I feel the comforting press of my toga over my shoulder and now the senate is empty but for Antony *speak up* he says *I cannot hear you* his centurions are nowhere in sight and I straighten and say *if, noble Antony, your nobility were made coinage for the empire its measure would be*—I falter—I adjust the toga folds about my chest, searching for an appropriately minuscule measure—but time is running quickly, I know—I have no arms to lift—*your nobility* I say *is the nobility of green flies on goat shit they glitter in the sunlight and they eat and they move their wings and fly but their life is short* and Antony lifts up on diaphanous wings and rises and vanishes and now a woman's voice says *speak up, Marcus Tullius, speak up I cannot hear you* and I say *o noble mother, Helvia, if your nobility were made coinage for the empire*

JOHN THE BAPTIST

prophet, beheaded by
King Herod, circa 30

smelling of garlic he comes to me and he is lank with long hands and I rejoice that he enjoys his food and that in my own mouth there was only the bitter crunch of locust and the sour berry and the cloying of wild honey as I waited for him and I draw my face close to his mouth as I hold him in my arms to smell his very breath and I feel the hardness of his back and his hand curls up to cup my elbow angled by his side I pull that arm closer laying it along his body feeling his ribs and the Jordan rushes about us the fish rubbing at my legs like hungry dogs and I am hungry too and I would rub against him, my Lord my face of God, his eyes dark and narrowing at me as I hesitate to press him under and he whispers to me *John you must do this* and my mouth would speak but it is so close to his now and I lift him slightly toward me this man I have waited for all my life, waited to kiss, thinking it would be his feet but now I would have him open his mouth and devour me take me in his mouth and let me disappear into his very flesh and I would be sweet to his taste I am certain and he says *John*

VALERIA

MESSALINA

wife of Emperor Claudius I of Rome,
beheaded by order of her husband, 48

I am sighted through my tongue I run the tip of my tongue through the cleft of his chin watching him and I hear through my tongue I draw my tongue across his chest and pause and listen to his heart beating, rushing faster even as I linger here, and I lift my face from the chest of my Caius Silius we are panting now we are the Circus Maximus we are the rush of wheels the wild breath of horses on the throne room floor the bright expanse of marble I shift my eyes and I see us both in the mirror of stone our flanks naked and pressed together as one I return my eyes to him, his head reclines, he sighs, I memorize his flesh the faint groove along the underside of his jaw the marble expanse of his chest this cinnamon nipple I pluck now with my lips and just below it is the red birth spot, the kiss of the goddess Voluptas: I have turned my eyes away from this too long, I will pull down her temple for this, I draw a circle around this spot on his flesh with my tongue I take it between my teeth tugging gently and he moans and I bite hard now his skin yielding his blood sudden and warm his body thrashes but I hold fast to my man I tear this other kiss from his body

DIOSCORUS

shipmaster and companion to Paul, beheaded by
Roman soldiers who mistook him for the apostle, 67

sails swell and braces hum overhead, my hand on the tiller night and day and night again and all the things of the world are beneath my feet now, all at once, the timber and the cattle and the linen and the glass, the wine, the wool, ivory and apes, olives and cheese, plums and pears and pomegranates and ginger, myrrh and incense, alabaster and amber, oysters and slaves, their dark eyes turning to me awake in the midst of the night as I hug the coast out of Aden and it's day now and still I have wind in the great middle sea and I have woodwork and statuary from Sicily and papyrus and granite and glass from Egypt, corn and fish and hides from the Black Sea and from Smyrna I have carpets rolled and bound and stacked in the hold, and passengers, a man and two others who bow to him a man with a naked head like mine bare to the sky and the wind, there is only the terrible motionlessness of my house, becalmed, my son barely drawing a breath, this man touches my son's head and speaks to his god and my son lives and the man says *leave all these things* and I am in a marketplace and I cry out the name of this man's god as if into a gale and around me are figs and linen and vessels of clay

PAUL
(SAUL OF TARSUS)

apostle, beheaded
by the Emperor Nero, 67

narrow the gate through to the warren of merchants past figs and linen and clay vessels the smells of wood fire and bodies moving in the shadows of houses I am restless in my limbs and the way turns to a square a fountain and a great and sudden flare of light, I close my eyes to the welter of it blinded and open them again, and in the center of this brilliance a woman young her hair loose radiant her forearms bare she is bent to draw water and she lifts her face to me her eyes dark in the midst of the light which roils silently all about her and within me and I would move to her now and kneel before the mysteries of her body I am tumescent with devotion but instantly she turns her face away and I hesitate gasping waiting, if she but speak if she but call me to her, for all my readiness to act I wait and my horse nickers at my restlessness the land flat to the horizons my body sucked dry by the sun Damascus ahead and heretic Jews to shackle at the wrists at the ankles and the air around me ignites I am at the center of a flame and I am tumbling down I am on my knees I lift my face to see her and instead I hear a voice, a man, and I understand

MATTHEW

tax collector and apostle, beheaded
by King Hirtacus of Ethiopia, 78

faintly bitter, the smell of this wine, the old man stands with eyes rheumy in the shade of my custom shack and he says *please honorable publican this is very low quality wine* and I say *it is wormwood wine which adds twenty-five percent to the value at thirteen percent tax you owe the Empire three drachmas for these goods* and I wait for him to appeal my application of the highest allowed duty and then I will explain the further tax on horse and cart and wheels and the bridge he must cross and I will listen and allow him to convince me to lower the rate of duty by a few points and this will still leave me ample profit my thumb sliding up and down my forefinger on my writing hand I wait and he is silent and beyond him the Sea of Galilee is bright from the sun but it is more than that, the tips of the upchurning waves are flames rising and I begin to tremble and now a day of clouds and a fine misty rain and he says *follow me* and we are at Cana, he and the others he's called and his mother, and there is no wine and he passes his hand over six jugs of water and I sniff there and it is fine aged wine at ten drachmas per jug at thirteen percent duty *be still* he says

VALENTINE

Roman priest and saint, beheaded by
Emperor Claudius II, circa 270

in she pads and crouches over me, quietly, the she-wolf, I am in her cave, not beneath the fig tree where Romulus and Remus cry in hunger, she has abandoned them to give me her tit and the cave is my jail cell and I wake ready to die for my Lord, His name on my lips, the dream a dream from my childhood before Christ and I crouch tiny in our doorway and naked men run by striking the backs of women who willingly bare their flesh to receive the lash of goatskin, receiving fertility on the day of Lupercalia, and Julia appears now at my cell door, daughter of Asterius my jailer, her eyes sightless from birth, I rise and cross to her and take the cup of water and the crust of bread and I drop them at once, knowing this time my hands are filled with the Spirit and I need only touch her eyelids and she will see, and her hair falls soft about her shoulders and I hesitate, my loins filling, and in my head the sound of naked men rushing past and we bare our backs, we priests, ready for the lash of God, and her face is lambent, turned slightly aside, and I slough off my clothes: I am naked, visibly filled with the ache of men, and I lay my thumbs lightly on her eyes so she can see her Valentine

DRAGON

beast, beheaded by Saint George, 301

fly and land and run upon the pale fleshy jitteries I breathe hot upon them their wailing comes then and in my mouth the soft flail of their limbs the pulpy oozy of them and the cracky breaking, this body I eat nice body, oozy too this blood I drink nice blood, I settle my legs and I fold my wings the quieting comes upon me now after the bodies and the blood, all the rushy sputtery in my center is gone, the flying and landing and running all done, more of the fleshies dashing off I watch them and they seem now much like my eggy littles come forth, my wings are still, I close my eyes and open them and all around are the quivery greentops and the great ball of breath above, I will fly up that high sometime but now I am in a peaceful dawdle that I don't understand, full in the center and sweet heavy in my legs and fluttery of the wingtips, and I lick the air and again and one of these I eat is before me just a dashy-run across the way I ask my center if it wants this bit more and I rise and I rush and this one looks not soft but glinty all over him with the light and he sits on a long-face creature and he makes a sign at me up and down and across

GEORGE

soldier and saint, beheaded by the
Emperor Diocletian, 303

far across the field the evil thing sits, small-seeming from here, my horse rears and frets sensing the ancient beast as all creatures of God do, while in my ears I still hear the voices of the villagers *a dragon* they cry, and so it is, I see the evil one as I have never seen him before, complacent in a meadow beneath the sun his scaled body the color of a toad his breath a faint hiss in the air wisps of smoke rising like morning mist about him the villagers cry *my daughter eaten my son eaten my husband* and I tell them of the Lord God and his own son whose body also was destroyed and they cry *that did us no good* and they wail on and I say *it did you no good because you have not eaten of your savior* and I kneel before a priest in a secret place in Rome and I eat the body and the blood and afterwards I say *father shall I leave my arms* and he says *fight in the Lord's name* and now I sit on the edge of this ignorant village and the dragon lifts his head and unfurls his wings and I thump my fist upon my breastplate and I draw my sword and in the center of me there is only the peace that passes all understanding because of the things I have eaten

THE LADY OF THE LAKE

enchantress, beheaded by Balin, the Knight of the Two Swords, circa 470

diving deep I swim in his beard my breath giving out quickly in spite of all I know to do, all that he has taught me, my Merlin, he has schooled me in the things of the pot—the dragon's blood and the mistletoe and the black willow—he has yoked my dreams to my will, he has fed me four poisons—mandrake and henbane and nightshade and his blunt-headed sword, his manthing—he has fed me these till I was safe from each till my skin no longer crawled and my muscles no longer seized and my bones no longer quaked and instead I became strong and cunning and master of the elements and he has shown me how to bare my breasts and my loins and dance silently and I dance while he sleeps and I spin and cry out and he falls deeper into sleep and his staff rolls off his fingertips and I lift his cloak and he must be dreaming of me for his sword is raised and I put my hand to it and pluck it off—he will enter no other lady now he will live out his life with the memory of me—and it grows in my hand and hardens into steel and its torn root heals into hilt and pommel and I dive deep into my black water where I will wait his summons and I call his sword Excalibur

AH BALAM

Mayan ballplayer, beheaded by custom
as captain of losing team, 803

life is held within the ball the lives of all the world's people and the sky is over us and the high walls are about us with the stone circle the gateway to heaven fixed there far above and the sun has swung from low to high as we play for the king and for our fate for the year to come, the skull of Ah Pitzlaw the Great is inside the rubber globe so it flies higher today the ring score is possible, weary I plant my foot and leap and hit the ball with my hip Ah Mun my brother sliding alongside and forward to take the next volley of the team of Ah Peku his small striker catching my volley on the knee and it flies up I am descended upon my two feet and squaring forward the ball lifting over my head and Ah Tabai behind me cries like the macaw and the ball slips low from him past my shoulder and caroms from the right wall and Ah Peku himself is running already for a mighty hip shot and I see our ancestors the first men on earth playing ball with the Lords of Death and even as Ah Peku flies toward the hanging ball I know I will end headless like the first men, my hands, useless in this game, tremble, but my heart is ready, the ball flies up and through the circle

PIERS

GAVESTON

male consort to King Edward II,
beheaded by posse of English nobles, 1312

Edward's gift at my throat my head pushed down rough and I touch my emerald brooch my king gives me emerald and sapphire and ruby we are bright color, he and I, we are fields and sky and pomegranates his mouth smeared with the ruby juice sweet and sharp and I carry his crown soft on a pillow woven of gold, his child-wife put aside for his Piers for his sweet man she watches his crowning like a cameo face of milky glass pinned against a vast cloak of a crowd and I am draped in purple velvet bestarred with pearls the barons also watching us, my Edward and me, they are drops of piss in the king's great sea they push my head roughly down and I touch my emerald hidden in my clothes holding my silken self together my secret smooth stone en cabochon polished round as the tip of the Green Man's member as green as the deep forest, my king and I riding, the heat of my horse the chuff of its breath we are in flight and I am happy my sweet Ed my sweet Ned my sweet Eddy and we run from all the others and night comes and we unbuckle we unbrooch we unburden he says my name and I say his and it is dark and now we are alone in the world we are polished stones we are orbs and scepters

GOOSENECK
(GANSNACKEN)

court jester to Duke Eberhard the Bearded,
beheaded by his master, 1494

quickly, my lord arrives soon, I tether the goat and place the crest of my lord's defeated enemy round its neck and put my oft-merrily-used floppy crown on my ass-eared hat its bells jingling as if in laughter already at my jest and I have secured the rope in the ceiling beam and I stretch and draw myself up, hanging for a moment, breathless from my own wit, my father places his hand on my shoulder and pushes me toward the Duke descended from his horse and laughing at the belt of choked geese around my waist, me wishing to keep their feet dry I say, and he laughs loud and I am excited by this sound, my jokes are my lovers thrilling me, and he takes me to Württemberg and a life of mirth and he will soon be here I begin to swing on the rope, pulling hard at it and I am swinging faster and the goat looks up at me and I wave at him whom I will, as the great Duke, shortly leap upon in antic triumph and the door opens and it is the Duke and I am a jester not a sailor the goat breaks his knot and bolts just as I leap from the rope and fly at my stricken lord and fall heavy upon him, crotch to face, and alas I am already full excited at my joke, like a lover

THOMAS

MORE

Lord Chancellor of England and saint, beheaded by King Henry VIII for opposing his divorce, 1535

arm around my neck the king leads me out among my roses the Thames sliding heavily along just beyond the rosemary hedge *you never fail me* he says, tugging me closer in the crook of his arm his breath on my face smelling of pheasant and ale from my table *let's speak now of the stars spinning round the earth* he says, and I sit in a palace hall the king and Catherine the queen beside him and the plates are of gold and the servants are backtreading softly and there is not a sound, we wait for Henry's hands to open from the fists beside his plate and the peacocks are before us their bright plumes vanished their flesh darkened by the fire and waiting, the king loosens his right hand and takes up a knife and he places his left hand on the back of the bird and the knife comes down, the body comes apart, and he lifts the meat and he says *eat,* but my hands are folded before me, I am kneeling, I wait—where now?—there is only darkness *eat* I open my mouth *Corpus Domini nostri* his arm is round my neck he twists me to him his hair a fiery crown *I am your king* he says, and it is dark again and I lift my eyes to a body torn *Jesu Christi* the bread on my tongue I eat my king

ANNE

BOLEYN

Queen of England, beheaded after the displeasure of her husband, King Henry VIII, 1536

tiny and gray is the boy and I am undone, him being no living boy and no heir to my husband, though I hold his body close and I am breathless with love for him, and the next is merely a lump of blood between my legs and he was my last chance to live, this clot this stain this wet-cleansed spot in my place of sex, but still there is my sweet girl my Elizabeth her pale face and her hair the color of the first touch of sun in the sky, the pale fire of her hair, she turns her gray eyes to me and I know I am soon to leave her and she is dressed in russet velvet and a purple satin cap with a caul of gold and the candlelight thrashes about the walls and I say to her *Lady Princess I will always be your mother* and she says in her wee voice *madam you are my Queen* and she bows as she has been taught and I ache to take her up but she is right, of course, we are who we are to each other and I am who I am to the man who must cast me off now, and I say *rise my sweet child* and she straightens and lifts her face and I bend to her, I draw near to her, I cup my daughter's head in my hands

CATHERINE
HOWARD

Queen of England, beheaded
for adultery by Henry VIII, 1542

what a tumble what a tumble rolling in the sudden dark the secret parts of my body my own body recently giving forth blood thick and fragrant and then, soon after, my first Henry, Henry the First, whose hands I whisper my secrets to who touches my hidden body my self and what sweet tumblings roll through me Henry who teaches me the flute I hold in two hands and blow into his flute and there is music and then the dark of night in Lambeth my step-grandmother somewhere far away in another room and I lie dormitoried amidst the unmarried girls with great unseen puffing all about and my own Francis, Francis the First, king of the dark, and he places his secret inside mine and what a tumble it is breaking me in two and then reuniting me turning me into him, and Henry my second, eighth to the realm, his body enormous and folded into hidden places and he has parts only I will touch, the abscess of his leg issuing forth a pale green flow *do you not find this loathsome* he asks, softly for once, *no* I say *it is our secret,* and my cousin Thomas whose pepper I am happy to cull pulled from the deep earth for me to see and it destroys me at last I walk unsteady to the block has it happened I can't remember I can't see I tumble

LADY JANE
GREY

Queen of England for nine days,
beheaded by Queen Mary Tudor, 1554

I am certain he does love me, my good John Aylmer, who teaches me Latin and Greek and French and Italian—o cara mio—he touches with his forefinger that hollow of bone beneath my throat and he says to me *Jane est omnes divisa in partes tres* and I am but fourteen years upon this earth when this love begins when John puts his fingertip beneath my throat and his face bows slightly and the men ruffle to their knees, their faces bowed, the crown on my head, and my brocade is gold and silver—I think only of the dress not of the crown, which is my husband's desire and his father's—I am not this tall but for the chopines I totter upon and I settle into the royal barge and sail upon the dark surface of the river and all the faces of London look and are silent Edward my king being dead his head bows and the sound rises from his chest he touches his mouth and upon his fingertips there is a dark red bloom and he crosses himself forehead, chest, shoulder, and then his bloody hand passes across his throat and there is only one touch upon my throat my sweet John naming the three parts of Jane: the heart, which I know now is his, and the body, which has lain down already a voiceless child upon the earth, and my head

MARY

STUART

Queen of Scots, beheaded
by Queen Elizabeth I, 1587

dark abrupt the bite at my neck gone, *sweet Jesus* I say the bite fierce upon me, my breath snarled somewhere in my chest I wait silent, my sweet Geddon inside my petticoat lays his furry throat into the bend behind my knee, the cold of the stone rises to me, hands pressing my shoulders, a veil of Corpus Christi cloth descends before my eyes, words appear about forgiveness and innocence and they are from my mouth though they might as well be from a separated head, his muzzle wetly tracing along my calf Geddon presses his wee body into my petticoat as I kneel, I stand before the stone block in the center of the Great Hall the February cold raking my breasts through my bodice scarlet the color of martyrdom, men's hands upon me roughly pulling off my gown of black satin and velvet, my throat naked now, *be gentle with the lamb* I say as he lifts the golden Agnus Dei off my neck, and my rosary, Geddon's claws clicking along at my heels I cross the stone floor refusing the arm of a man, down the great staircase my heart beating faster than Geddon's, Fotheringhay's Great Hall is below me full of upturned faces, I press him close to me his heart racing against my throat, brushing the hair from his eyes I say *there now, little man, we must see to go down these steps*

WALTER

RALEIGH

courtier and explorer,
beheaded by King James I, 1618

Bess my dear old queen my Elizabeth her lips brittle her body smelling sharply beneath the clove and cinnamon from her pomander she lies next to me in the dark still besmocked though the night is warm and she has asked me here at last and I am masted for her and her bedchamber is black as pitch so she is but a shadow *no torch* she cried as I entered *upon pain of death* and now we are arranged thus my own nakedness perhaps too quick she says *call your new-found land the place of the virgin, Virginia, to honor my lifelong state* and I flinch but her smock does rise and I find the mouth of her Amazon her long fingers scrawling upon my back a history of the world *oh sir oh sir you have found the city of gold at last* she says, knowing me well this fills my sails the jungles of ancient lands are mine my queen *oh swisser swatter* she cries and falls away and I lie beside her staring into the dark, and I am sated certainly, but the moment calls for some new thing, and I say *wait, my queen* and I am out her door to the nearest torch and I have already prepared the treasure from my new world, this sweet sotweed this tobacco, and I sail back and slip in beside her and we sit and we smoke

BRITA

GULLSMED

Swedish woman, beheaded
for alleged witchcraft, 1675

night has come and curls about my head and stays and sleeps a long sleep, for months here on the edge of the taiga I rise to trim the lamp and Margit leaps silently up and rubs her chin on my knuckle she is not an imp of Satan my black cat but she is not of these others either, these humans I am one of, I lie down in the darkness of my bed and once again there is a man and I am safely that to the world, the woman beside him, he lies heavy upon me raking my face with his beard and beating my loins and cursing the ashen soil he turns and cursing my barren womb and I am of him he says but I cannot draw a breath and I do not know him and he is gone to molder in the ground and now Margit leaps upon my chest and she tramps softly there drooling and murmuring to me and I lay my hands upon her fur and we purr together and I am this cat and through her I am the spruce and the pine standing all about and I am the moon-glint of the ice and the drifting of the snow and the cry of the wolf and she lays her face against mine and I am the scattered white fire of the stars and I am the long long night

LOUIS XVI

King of France, guillotined by order
of the French Revolutionary Tribunal, 1793

thrash and flurry in the undergrowth a bird a boar a stag the rush of wings of legs I lift a Charleville to my shoulder the musket cool to my hands I squeeze the trigger and feel heavily that half heartbeat of silence and then the cry and the kick of her, the night my bed I shudder the trees nearby I am alone at wood's edge *be a man* the king my father says but I am not a man and I feel the beast there invisible in the dark—the Beast of Gévaudan—he is far from Paris but he steps from the woods before me a wolf as big as a lion a hundred dead in the countryside he has passed by the animals of the field to savage a man or woman or child and he faces me and he lifts his ragged muzzle to the sky and howls *liberty to kill, equality of death, fraternity of beasts* and I wake and I am still a child my king's horsemen are off slogging through the marshes of the Auvergne to find him but he is with me and I am king now and I pass the smoking musket to my man who hands me another and I shoot and shoot again and again and the bird falls and the boar and the stag but behind me is the beast and he seizes me by the head

MARIE ANTOINETTE

Queen of France, guillotined by order
of the French Revolutionary Tribunal, 1793

softly on the arm he touches his wife and they hesitate in the dim corridor I a few steps behind holding tight to nurse's petticoat and I know how never never again will I be present in a moment like this because there is always the great goose-flock of my brothers and sisters and always there are courtiers and ladies-in-waiting and I am but a little girl a little little girl with a lute I can play and satin shoes with such elegant thin soles I feel the cold stone on my toes and he touches his wife's arm, he who is Emperor of Austria, King of Jerusalem, Hungary, Bohemia, Dalmatia, Croatia, and even more, that's as far as I can remember, I am small as small can be I could crawl into the belly of my lute and stay there looking between the strings he touches his wife's arm and he is my father and she is my mother the Empress of Austria and Queen of Jerusalem and Hungary and so forth and her skirts are bright and enormous I could live inside them and bring my three dogs and my pony too and all my clothes and the skirts are a problem for my father who has touched my mother's arm because he leans far over far across them and nearly falls but she turns her face to him knowing he is her beloved and he kisses her

MARIE-JEANNE

BÉCU

(COMTESSE DU BARRY)

mistress to King Louis xv, guillotined
by order of the French Revolutionary Tribunal, 1793

snow is falling the Seine runs with ice and I come in from the cold my face tingling I climb the narrow stairs Monsieur Gluck pushing past me descending and humming some bit of sad music and I am led by the elbow and now I am beside his bed, Monsieur Voltaire, and he takes my hand and draws it to his face and the tip of his long nose touches my knuckle as his lips kiss my fingers and his breath is labored like my King I sit beside Louis and I cannot see the pox upon him in the dark but his breath drags itself heavily through his body and I bend to him and whisper *my Lord the child you lately took to your bed has done this to you* and my hand falls upon his wrist and squeezes hard and Monsieur Voltaire lifts his face from my hand and there is a faint stain of blood at the corner of his lip and he narrows his eyes at me *we are merely at a play, my dear* he says and I ask *is it true there is no place beyond, where the King will hold me again* and he says *whether there is a heaven and hell or not, I am afraid you are finished with Louis* and only as I speak do I understand why it is I reply *then all is for the best*

ANTOINE-LAURENT

LAVOISIER

scientist, guillotined by order
of the French Revolutionary Tribunal, 1794

air and fire, I breathe deep upon a shore in Brittany and the sun is falling into the sea before my eyes but I am full of thoughts, the ideas of things beyond my sight—the essence of fire is matter fusing with oxygen—a flame from a candle by my bed this vast orb of sun the torch lighting the way past iron doors my wrists shackled my time come my breath guttering like a flame, these are all one, the welter of the sun the welter in my chest, I have proved this also—to burn, to breathe are the same process—the oxygen of the air rushes inside the furnace of my lungs and it flares I give off heat I dress Monsieur Seguin in a suit of taffeta and elastic gum and I seal his mouth with putty and his breath comes and goes through my instruments through my mind he lives he burns we carry our own small sun inside us and not a particle of mass is lost nothing is lost we fuse we are carried off to another state my father-in-law moves ahead of me along the corridor and now he lays down his head on the instrument and the blade falls the head falls one fire goes out and another begins and nothing is lost on a shore in Brittany the sun vanishes but the seams of cloud flare up before me

ANDRÉ

CHÉNIER

poet, guillotined by order
of the French Revolutionary Tribunal, 1794

great the minds in Mother's gilded chairs, Lavoisier and David and Suvée, and along the edge of our salon the heavy scent of women, lavender and jasmine and the smell of their bodies, and the mounting of powdered hair that falls now about the shoulders of the Duchess of Fleury who kissed Mother's cheeks and me full on the mouth and asked *are you truly a man* and *who here is a poet,* dull-eyed now she drifts near our jailer who palms her breast and she pauses as if in thought and he lets her pass, *Lavoisier is gone to the blade* whispers Suvée who has bribed for paints, and I sit for him in a slant of light from the high window and he lifts his brush and tells me to stop trembling, the stone hall full of our kind our lace filthy the turnkeys lifting their red Phrygian caps to cheer the reading of tomorrow's condemned, and in my cell my hands will not stop quaking nor my chest nor my knees when I try to stand and I pace and I wait for my own brush my own paint as words pass through my head in a death cart, iron wheels turning on the cobbles, they pass to the scaffold and are lost, but now: at last, my quill, my ink, a basket full of dirty clothes, my words are hid within, *I am* and *I am*

MAXIMILIEN

ROBESPIERRE

lawyer and revolutionary, guillotined
by the Revolutionary Convention, 1794

Father dressed immaculately his knee breeches his silk stockings his tailcoat Mother dead in the parlor her arms folded across her chest he leans against the far wall and I am trying to get my arms around Augustin and Charlotte and Henriette they seem like children to me now, my brother and my sisters, though I am myself only six years on this earth I try to hold them my arms straining and inadequate and I know already that the man leaning there is dead to us too and I am responsible and now the door shuts hard the knocker clangs he has said nothing I follow quickly and strain at the door and he is gone his horse clatters away and he is gone the Bois de Boulogne is full of citizens dressed innocently in tricolor trousers and clogs and red caps I walk among them my hound at my side the summer daylight lingering and they look to me and I want to open my arms they are children and there are many who would harm them and I am in my room above the carpentry yard the sky incarnate with dawn my words prepared at last for the Convention and I dress in white silk stockings and knee breeches and floral waistcoat and black tailcoat and red cravat and my hair is powdered and on the cobbles a scaffold and the blade, dear father, for us all

PIERRE-FRANÇOIS

LACENAIRE

criminal and memoirist,
guillotined for murder, 1836

slim at hip and thigh my lover my fiancée my guillotine but her opening is large, large enough for me to give her everything my head sliding inside her, she is tall and she is painted crimson not mere lips and cheeks but all over my sweet woman—her narrow shoulders, her arms held primly to her side, her lap that I will fling myself upon—all her thin body is rouged for me, all but her bosom which is naked and unadorned, polished bright, her sharp-edged tit that waits for me and has always waited for me, I pass her in the street in a blood dawn and she will soon give herself to another man—she is no virgin, my fiancée, I am reconciled to her past with others—and this first moment I see her I stagger to a stop I am but a boy a petty thief and my father is at my side his mustache waxed into rapier points he lifts his hand toward the lady and says *that is where you will end* and cuffs the back of my head and I am betrothed and I come to her no virgin I put my own blade deep inside a widow she moans though it is but a boy's affair to prepare me for my worldly lover: I stand before her now I bow I slide I enter her and I await her ferocious embrace

TA CHIN

Chinese wife,
beheaded by her husband, 1838

straight and whole are my feet I would rise and run as I have loved for many winkings of the moon to run with my brothers but I press my feet side by side and wiggle my toes this last time and whisper to them *goodbye* I know what is before me my mother in the courtyard singing prayers to Kuan Yin the goddess of mercy, not to spare me a life of pain but to wither my feet to perfection, the mercy of the golden lotus, the mercy of a wealthy man to keep me, I tremble I am ready to weep but for these tiny stones of anger Kuan Yin has placed in the corners of my eyes even as the foot-binder puts the soaking tub before me that first night even as my husband trembles before me in the torch light trembling always from the opium but this night he trembles from what he believes about the brushing of my sleeve by a man he himself brought to our house and my mother sings and my toes are seized and folded hard under and the wrappings wind and wind and squeeze and my arch cracks and I see Buddha in heaven sitting on his lotus but it is my naked foot the golden lotus he sits upon and hands push me down my neck made bare and I cry *please, before my head cut off my feet*

JACOB

American slave, beheaded
by his owner, 1855

sowbelly frying in the first coming-up light I smell it being only a child my Sukey-mammy whisper me about how my own from-her-body mammy done been sold away but she still loves me the morning bell ringing on some other plantation far off Sukey-mammy singing *my way's cloudy go send them angels down* our own morning bell ringing and I am a strong-back man and the driver beats me bullwhip fire, now across my right side, now across my left, and another day he beats me, and another, my back always on fire, clearing some new part of the forest for corn and for cotton the chopping done and the grubbing and the log heaps piled and burning filling the night sky with flame, and I know something burning in me and Sukey lying in the dirt the driver nudging her at the shoulder with his boot cause she tell a child how he have a soul of his own and that night I am rushing and my thumbs dig deep in the driver's throat and I lay a torch to a hayrick the sky going hot as a bullwhip lash behind me the hounds calling and I am running hard through corn row and forest and I am a child and I walk just a little ways from my Sukey to the window and I see the first fire of dawn and a bell is ringing far off somewhere

ANGRY EYES

Apache warrior, beheaded
by Mexican troops, 1880

breechcloth and moccasins only these things on my body and my head bound by a cloth band my face and chest and arms stained but I do not know the colors I do not look, my eyes are fixed on the horizon beyond mesquite and piñon and stone and I am ready to fight though I have no bow no arrow not even the rifle, I bend to the white man in dark blue, the first to die by my hand, and I listen for his spirit nearby, his hair the color of flame his face filled with tiny faded spots painted there perhaps to call upon the stars his mouth open voiceless my arrow through the center of his chest I put my hand on the stock of his rifle, still listening but there is nothing no bird no insect—*where are you, my foe?*—and the sun is setting and my hands are empty and I dance, like a woman I dance with mincing steps my elbows held close against me my face impassive before the fading light, the edge of the world is the color of old blood, my body dances stealthily all my flesh trembling to an unheard drum and I am alone in this place, but no, his spirit whispers he is beside me now, in breechcloth and moccasins, and we dance barely moving nearly touching I and this white man with hair of flame

CHIN CHIN

CHAN

student, beheaded by Chinese authorities for maintaining a romantic correspondence with an American girl he met while studying in the USA, 1882

moon no longer a blossom a pearl a lantern in a lover's door but a bodiless face, mine, in a train window, she on the platform trying not to look at me directly, as if she were there for someone else, and the train hurtles in the dark and I stare into the stars and not even a poet could find the moon in this sky not even Li Po in a boat with quill and ink in hand he searches this night sky and then looks at me from across the water and shrugs and I am the cicada, seventeen at last, my skin splits open and I emerge a perfect man ready to sing but there is so little time and the song I hear in return fades in the grind of these engines, I sit with my own quill and ink, the cicadas singing in the courtyard outside, *my dear Elizabeth my love* these words I write blur before my eyes even as she draws near, the smell of lavender the low trill of her laughter and then a sigh *you sweet boy what are we to do* she says and I put my hand on hers and I float above in the dark and I see Li Po in his boat and he leans far out over the water opening his arms to embrace the severed head of a moon and he tips forward and vanishes

DAVE

RUDABAUGH

outlaw and briefly member of Billy the Kid's gang,
beheaded by townspeople in Parral, Mexico, 1886

ready now to throw down on me some old Johnny Reb calls me out and I'm young and twitchy and into my hand comes my 1860 Colt Army my first sweet thing walnut in my palm black powder and paper-wrapped cartridges eight-inch barrel coming out and it's been around a long time and knows what to do the bluing near all rubbed off but you can see the big-masted ships etched on the cylinder the Texas navy blowing up the Mexicans their dark faces around me hands grabbing and a later Colt in my hand my Peacemaker barks like a stable dog a fat Mex flying back from the table his sombrero spattered from my bullet in his brain and Billy touches my shoulder, the Kid is dead but there are his eyes, as blue as noonday, and his tiny hand on my shoulder, he has the smallest damn hands, like a girl, Billy whispers *let's ride* and I lift my hand to touch his and I'm holding my first Colt all sassy and sweet and long and it thumps and kicks and goes hot and Johnny Reb is falling backward, my first kill, and I say to him *here's me,* and all at once I see my life ahead my hand full of pistol my trigger finger touchy as my cock and I'm riding hard and I'm lying under the stars and Billy's sleeping nearby quiet as a girl

AGNES

GWENLAN

factory girl, decapitated by elevator, 1899

quarry sounds, the thump and boom all day, the dishes rattle and Mama flinches each time with Papa out there breaking up the mountain and then he and my uncles are by the fire and they sing and I huddle into sleep *ar hyd y nos* they sing *all through the night* and I am curled on a straw mattress stacked with a hundred others belowdecks the ocean out in the dark all around us and Mama lies above me I can hear her crying for my father crushed by falling slate, a quarryman's death, Miss Liberty watches us sail by, her torch lifted in the twilight, and it suddenly flares into electric light and we gasp and cheer and we sit in the harbor, the city on one hand and Ellis Island on the other, a basket goes over the side and up comes a strange new thing bananas I would eat one skin and all but for a man with quarry hands bending near and peeling it for me and I eat and it is good and he is gone and we are in an open trolley, Mama and I, and we are carried up Broadway beneath buildings higher than mountains and harder than slate and the tenement is dark and surrounds us like the sea and he sings softly in my ear *sleep my love and peace attend thee* and I whisper *all right Papa all right*

CHARLES H.
STUART

Texas farmer, beheaded
by his two teenage daughters, 1904

underfoot the pine board cricks, I pause and let it die, I want to go in quiet, the dark and the chill are coming up under my nightshirt and I'm skittish feeling the dangle of my parts I'm moving along again bobbling and churning down there, the door is closed I come near and I palm the knob which is cool as the curve of their shoulders I turn the knob softly but now they're sitting in sunlight in the kitchen their mama working the water pump in the yard, them both side by side, my daughters, come from my flesh, and Wilhelmina is old enough to look at me that way—the stare that don't flicker—the woman-stare like her mama but without the prattle and the complaints—Valmer not yet with the stare, her eyes still restless like some other women I know—and the pine board cricks under my step and I keep on to the doorknob and I touch it and it's cold and I turn it and the pine board cricks and I slide on along and my hand goes to the doorknob and it is serious cold to the touch—no, not cold at all—it's hot it's searing hot my hand is fixing to torch up but I can't let go and from under the door comes the smell of sulphur and I know it's not them inside, it's what's next for me

ROKHEL

POGORELSKY

Jewish woman, beheaded
in Russian pogrom, 1905

taste of horseradish taste of nettle I draw the covers tight about me the trees beyond the dark window lash in the wind my brother nearby weeps against his will *sorry Papa sorry* and beneath the wind my father's voice tumbles *Pinchas be still the blood was on the doorpost* the lambs in the field raise their head to a hollow sound the soles of my feet quake *our sons were spared* father says to Pinchas but in the field I hear horses and I have my own first son on my back my Aron and I turn from the sound of hooves and I run across the field that rolls beneath me twisting at my ankles I look behind and the men on horses stay on the road a dozen Cossacks in high boots and billowing trousers and one turns his face toward me I run hard and they go on toward the village and I follow the hedge line and through a stand of water oaks and Aron begins to cry his tiny hands plucking at my ears *be still* I say and my cottage now my husband gone a lashing in my chest like trees in a wind and a basket by the step, I put my son inside, my shawl on top, for when this all is done another must find him: a scythe nearby, I cut my hand and spill my blood upon the door

JOHN

MARTIN

boy, decapitated by subway after lifting sidewalk grate and falling onto the tracks below, 1921

Babe oh Babe hit it all the way out here Babe and jumping jimjams he's done it the ball lifting up like a Fourth of July rocket but not exploding just keeping on going up and coming my way out here in the right-field bleachers and all the Polo Grounds Johnnies around me losing their bowlers falling on themselves and there's a rush from the dark and steel on my throat and the nickel rolls perfect on its edge and we're all real quiet my friends and me and down it goes into the grate and down I go into the dark after it and down I go falling to the track I can get up now but something's happened to my arms and legs they're flimsy loose and too light to lift and it's only jostling shoulders and elbows and sweat beads flying and hats tumbling and I fight clear and Babe's thirty-first of the year is falling from the sky rushing at me oh Babe the orphan boy oh Babe smoking a cigar in his tweedy cap a few weeks ago he comes out of the stadium trailing smoke and I got nothing for him to sign but the back of my hand and this time I'll take him a ball but all of a sudden it dies and falls a few rows in front of me Babe signs my skin and puts his hand on my head

HENRI
LANDRU

second-hand furniture dealer, also known as the "Bluebeard of Gambais," guillotined for the murder of ten women, 1922

parlor mirrors are hard to sell when flawed like this one, tinting my beard the color of a bruise, I clap my hand over the bristled hair and turn to this woman but her deer's eyes are blind to my beard, seeing only my sympathetic gaze, and her face is traced with age and her upper lip is furred and her husband is long dead and her hands are brittle from scrubbing and she is worse than dead as a widow, her money useless to her, the newspapers were right I am spinning from Mother Goose's mouth—the young wife choking back her disgust at my blue beard, which, however, I do not shave, and I go off giving her all the chateau's keys and warning her on pain of death not to enter the cellar room, the room where I have secretly placed the disassembled bodies of seven wives, the room that yields only to this small key, which, however, I do not simply withhold from her—my hands quicken I kiss Madame's furred lip and she cries out in pleasure and the deal is struck, a moment of passion she would never have had, for the dead man's settee and his four-poster bed and his commode and his wife's head lying upon its pillow and this cleaver in my hand and I cut through and hold it up, her eyes still blinking, and I kiss her trembling lips

PAUL

GORGULOFF

Russian immigrant to France, guillotined
for assassinating French President Paul Doumer
at charity book signing, 1932

silver rivets all around I step into the rocket Paul Gorguloff space pilot who turns to Professor Oberth and shakes his hand I am to fly his rocket to the moon and I step from the rocket the rivets scorched black and great crowds of people press in crying *tell us your story* and I sit before the window and I take up my fine pen and the pistol is on my desk and a sheaf of blank paper and I post the cap of my Mont Blanc and I write *Memoirs of Paul Gorguloff* and the pages tumble from me Paul Gorguloff the writer paces the floor the carpet worn through the desk overflowing I am in a crowd now that clamors for books and they are fools not recognizing the greatness moving among them my pen clipped in my shirt pocket and Claude Farrère—a novelist unworthy to wipe my dripping nib—sits signing and I deign to buy his *Useless Hands* about breadmakers in the distant future replaced by robot hands and he autographs my book with a cheap pen and I turn the book and I uncap my Mont Blanc before his eyes and I sign it above his name *Paul Gorguloff the man who killed the President of the French Republic* Paul Doumer at another table signing his books thinking himself a writer and the pistol is in my hand and I critique his work

BENITA

VON BERG

German baroness, beheaded
by Adolf Hitler for espionage, 1935

dying tip of one cigarette I touch to another, my cell at Plötzensee is full of tobacco smoke and I fill my lungs holding very still, woolen socks on my feet prison trousers and shirt if I could but whiten my face and trace my lips in scarlet we lean together and sing Brecht the club full of smoke and bodies the emcee in tails and white tie points at me—*welcome to Kabarett madam but free that red fox about your neck he is our comrade*—and it is Munich now a woman in a swirl of silk, her body naked beneath, she leaps onto our table and her womansmell fills my lungs I leave my cigarette in my mouth my hand falling the sound of weeping from some other cell I slip my hand inside these rough trousers to my own cleft like hers flashing above me on the table and her face is white her lips scarlet and Friedrichstrasse is ablaze with electric light passing in a cab his clumsy Polish hand between my legs I whisper *Captain, your country is in danger,* as if I loved him, and our voices swell through the smoke and we sing *there was a time and now it's all gone by* and I move down the corridor into the room of the ax and the executioner turns to greet me and he is dressed in tails and white tie *welcome*

NGUYEN VAN

TRINH

Viet Minh guerrilla leader, guillotined by French Colonial authorities, 1952

very still, I hold my rifle hard against my chest and I am careful even in the breath I draw I am folded against a mangrove tree my knees tucked close I move my eyes but I can see none of my comrades and of course I cannot hear them for we all wait on the noisy French wait till they are between the two columns of us and I should at least be able to see my friend Ky I know his place forward in a closing of vines but he is not there and I wait for the French and I think of my father in his collar and cravat and the way his head would draw down like a tortoise when he spoke of the Frenchman who ran his lycée *pull your collar off, my father, seize by the throat that man who shames you* and my father is a vase of ashes and my mother prays in the bourgeois myth that his spirit lives yet in another realm, and I hear them nearby, breaking dry leaves beneath their feet, and it is time and I make a sharp bird cry and I leap now but there is no rifle in my hands I have come from the trees onto the path and these are not Frenchmen but Vietnamese in mandarin dress and one turns his face and it is my father and he offers his hand

ALWI

SHAH

Yemeni executioner, beheaded
for a crime unrelated to his work, 1958

rising slow from a low place I see a row of heads sitting before me on a stone wall ear-to-ear arrayed beyond my sight to either side, I face them and their eyes turn to me and I hear the stirring of feet all around me, a jumbled huddling-in of bodies naked and battered with bones cracked and bulging knots and blooms of bruise and crusted lappings of blood, how I loved you all, loved righteously snapping the cords of all your lives, and so you come to taunt me but praise Allah I have done his holy work and I took as his sign the trill of sweetness that came upon me in this my work and now I turn and look into the stone-shattered face of Haleema Alsakkaf an adultering woman and she holds in her right hand the head of Akram Alshami her lover who, like the others, moves his eyes to me and I say *praise Allah you have paid righteously* and she says *praise Allah who we call the one God and who loves his creatures, we are sent as you knew us but we are restored in heaven* and I see now that my own head hangs in her left hand and I cry *praise Allah he will have mercy on me also* and she says *the mercy of God seeks sinful love before righteous hatred* and I wait for my head to fall

CHICKEN

Americauna pullet, beheaded
in Alabama for Sunday dinner, 1958

little grit things in the straw here and I peck and peck and they're gone and I go over there a wormy thing but it's a leaf stem which I always grab but it never goes mush like an actual worm which I look and look and listen for and the flying ones come down and they walk among us and they cock their heads and hear the slither in the earth and they grab and up one comes but after a rain it's good for me the worms come up and I run here and I run there and I eat and the grit is good too over there I go for grit though the soft slither is even better but it's dry now dry all around and they are vanished, wait, wait, the rest of me is gone and from beyond the wire from past the dog-leap from down the long ruts I can hear a muttery cluckering and it is like when I broke at last from the eggy wall and into the light and a fluff of feathers hovered near and made this same sound but this muckery wuckering is vast, this at last is the hen who fills the sky, and I am rushing now along the path and the clucking is for me and it is very loud and a great wide road is suddenly before me and she is beyond and I cross

VERA JAYNE

PALMER

(STAGE NAME, JAYNE MANSFIELD)

actress, decapitated in car crash, 1967

faint his face his eyes but I feel the soft run of his hand on my hair I am so tiny I am so much his little Vera that I am breathless I put my arms across his chest my father and I listen to the draw of his breath and he is gone and I am before these faces upturned I could open my arms and not get round them all I am their Jayne I am their Miss Freeway I am their Miss Electric Switch and Miss Photoflash and Miss Geiger Counter I am their Miss Pure Maple Syrup I am the wide clean road to where they want to go and I am the thing you touch to turn on the light and I am the bright caught moment and I am the crackle of invisible fire that will burn the very flesh from your bones and I am sweet beyond all bearing and pure and I am Chanel Number Five I sit in the quiet in a dressing room before the eyes will turn to me and I touch the scent to my skin and suddenly I am the smell of jasmine and of orange blossom and if you concentrate harder I am rose and iris and lily-of-the-valley and if you wait I am amber and patchouli and vanilla and he puts his face in my hair and he breathes in and he says *how sweet*

LE VAN

KY

Hue city official, beheaded
by North Vietnamese troops, 1968

blossoms floating on the Perfume River plumeria and mango and lychee the water itself smelling of mountain flowers even after the blossoms have eddied away I drag my hand in the river my father pulling at the oar and he says my name sharply *Ky* and I take up my own oar again and now we loll in the sun beside the South China Sea my father sleeping my mother huddling against my sister and speaking low and I wander away back toward the river far along the edge of the lagoon and even though there is no one in sight my heart is already beating furiously and the jungle closes in and around a bend she is crouched by the river's edge and I cut toward the tree line before she knows to look up, I circle and I creep close, her back is to me and she must be a peasant girl her skin is dark from the sun and her shirt clings to her, her naked back shines through the thin wet cloth, and she angles her head and pours the river into her long midnight hair, once, and again, and she has stolen my breath and she sits back and shakes her wet hair and I watch, never seeing her face, then she rises and goes away forever, and I understand: though the blossoms pass along in the current and vanish the river still smells sweet

KIMITAKE

HIRAOKA

(PEN NAME, YUKIO MISHIMA)

Japanese novelist, beheaded at his own request by a paramilitary colleague as he committed ritual disembowelment after failing to persuade Japan's Self-Defense Forces to overthrow the government, 1970

Tokyo roiling in flames like the sea my young man's body too frail to find a patriot's death I am a watcher shaping words already from the roof of the arsenal my wrists thin my arms a girl's arms the American bombers invisible in the scarlet smoke of the night sky, the flames now inside my body, brought there by my own hand, my own sword, my samurai arm—no, vanished now—no body at all—but words, always words, only words, which are my coward's sword—and I call the flames to return, to fill the sky with bombs, take the salary-men sleeping on commuter trains take the shops filled with breakfast cereal and French perfume and vacuum cleaners take the politicians who yield our swords, who make our Emperor the English queen, rise up, my country grown girlish and frail, my face grows hot from the flames of Tokyo and from shame at my body and then ten thousand confrontations before a gymnasium mirror and my arms thicken my thighs muscled carrying me to an act, I am breathless with power the rising sun tied round my head I stand before our warriors, our past, and they laugh at a girlish boychild and the city lies quiet against the night the horizon filling not with flame but with words, with manu-scripts, I have named myself after snow I have been cold all along I am only a writer

ROBERT

KORNBLUTH

senior partner in advertising firm,
decapitated by elevator, 1984

look I cry: SHE CLOSED, THE DOOR, RIGHT IN YOUR FACE, THE WHISKERS SIR, YOU MUST ERASE, BURMA SHAVE swept by my headlights, *there, I wrote those words,* my hands clenched tight on the wheel, the wrong thing to say she is quiet beside me quaking and weeping in rage and I yearn for a no more tears formula, *I give the best to you each morning* I say *it takes a wife to know the difference between Hanes and just underwear,* surely I'm not speaking these words to Anne the long-suffering Anne my wife once my wife long ago we are in a brand new 1952 Packard—ask the man who owns one—long before this present darkness came upon me—is it possible? panties more comfortable than wearing nothing?—Anne naked by the window in a luxury suite, affordable comfort, *no more tears* I say, *do you know me* she says, *what we have is the real thing* I say, and she is gone I dream of her and she is wearing her Maidenform Bra and my mouth brims with words that I know will do only harm—would you offer a Tiparillo to a lady?—a cigarette at least, outside the lawyer's office, mellow, an aid to digestion, we smoke and we stay silent and she sighs and is gone, DON'T LOSE, YOUR HEAD, TO GAIN A MINUTE, YOU NEED YOUR HEAD, YOUR BRAINS ARE IN IT

JENNIFER

HADLEY

marketing director,
decapitated in car crash, 1989

overhead jet engines the phone rings and a flash of landing lights outside, the chocolate mint still on my pillow, I know who it is, *hello* I say, *hello* he says, *I'm just down the hall* he says, *I know* I say, *are we going to do this* he says, a statement, my husband has called already to say goodnight and I say *your wife's call, just finished* he says, I don't say that I'm having trouble holding the phone to my ear I am so weak in the limbs breathless, overhead jet engines the phone rings a flash of light beyond the window a jet rushing back to earth from somewhere the chocolate on my pillow *hello* I say, *hello I'm just down the hall* he says, *I know* I say, *are we going to do this* he says, the phone rings a sound like ice falling from the eaves jet engines overhead my husband standing thigh-high in snow just beyond our patio his breath pluming and ice falling between us and then he waves *did it snow* I ask him tonight, *yes* he says *but the ice is worse the wires are down there is no electricity no heat,* I say *goodnight,* the line rasping with his thrown kiss, I put the receiver in the cradle, I pick up the chocolate I put it down, jet engines overhead the phone rings there is a knock at my door

NICOLE BROWN

SIMPSON

California woman,
decapitated by assailant, 1994

running hard along Venice Beach the clutch of breakers around my feet I run against the pull and I've come to this, to a place of jasmine smell and sea and car exhaust and stucco walls and Hollywood spelled across a mountain, and I run easily with the question *what can I be,* I've got great legs he says, and he should know because he runs for a living I love to see him run though he says I don't really understand but I do I run with him each time he holds something private in his arm and all the others rush to bring him down but he cuts and jukes and surges: run now, my children, run down the hall and close your doors because I cannot, his sweet slick child's face in the faces of my children, such beautiful skin I draw my hand tender along his cheek and he closes his eyes the moon out there rising I am large with her inside me, my child, and glass shatters and the bones of my face vibrate and my teeth all hurt I draw my hand along my cheek I think to try to run and he rushes up fast and I can see what's tucked there in the crook of his arm and it is me, it is my head, and I stare into my own eyes and I know the answer always was *his wife*

MOHAMMED AZIZ

NAJAFI

Iraqi Shiite cleric, beheaded
by Saddam Hussein, 1996

barren ground but holy, this plateau before me, trampled smooth by the feet of millions, the true people of Allah, but empty now though it is Hajj and the Mount of Mercy is behind me I feel its press between my shoulder blades and the pilgrims should be everywhere but the ground is beaten into silence and there is no one—*oh Allah leave me not alone*—for I have no seed but your holy words, I have no family but the family of your great people, no child but your revealed way, I would summon the millions cloaked in white so I could be among them and we would cry out as one *Allah I have responded to you* I am draped in seamless cotton I am barefoot and I am penitent, and the echo of my prayers is still in my head I have been silent only the briefest of moments and I yearn for the tumult of my brothers in Allah I would kneel and touch my face to this long-beaten ground as one with a million other faces, but no, I am standing upright and I am alone and before me now there is only a desert tamarisk, feathery pink, the merest growing thing and it catches the sun as if it is on fire and I hear a voice say to me *it is time now to take thy only son and cut his throat*

LYDIA

KOENIG

Chicago woman, decapitated
by her son, 1999

baby Mama calls me baby on my lap a lump of cloth baby doll and then a freckled face, Howdy Doody baby, I hum his name his puppet strings folded under, not a doll but I like his hard legs and arms beneath his clothes like real bones, Lake Michigan at twilight the color of tarnished brass a hand inside my lap and he asks me that night atop the Prudential Building the lake too dark to see and then my baby my own baby boy his bones deep and untouchable inside him, I dress him in pink thinking it makes no difference I hold him baby and then in plaid and he has freckles on his nose and he stinks of urine from his bed I carry the great lump of soiled cloth and the Tide waiting, the cleaning power of Tide and Oxydol and Clorox, and the man is gone and my baby cries all night through, though he is no baby he is returned and he says *help me find a vein help me tap this vein* and I cannot, I take his load of piss sheets to the Maytag in the basement and it is cool here and smells of the lake on a bad day and I wash them and dry them sitting in the dimness of the basement and I hold these sheets in my lap my baby my baby's voice is behind me

CLAUDE

MESSNER

homeless man, decapitated by Amtrak train
after laying his neck on the track, 2000

no oh no not him again from the rush of a fucking train I get the old man, what's taking that goddam train so long it was here a moment ago, maybe it's lying on its side jumped by a penny on the track I hide in the weeds and my shiny Lincoln-head is out there waiting for the Illinois Central from Chicago and I know I should be thinking about the careening of the engine the flight of the baggage car into the trees but all I've got is him whipping off his belt to do me, the sonofabitch, he disappears for a week only to come back for this, and I can't fucking believe I'm lifting my hand trying to take his, we're walking along storefronts I'm barely taller than the fire plugs and I'm trying to take that hand and it flicks like at a house-fly, and later on there's a long while, a few years, of just me and my mother and she likes her young man she runs her finger through the great front wave of my hair, and then he's back and he's about breaking my arm and I'm in a barber's chair and I can see my beautiful duck's ass of a do in the mirror and I whisper to the barber *please just a little around the edges* and my dad says *buzz him, buzz him up clean, take it all off*

LOIS
KENNERLY

systems analyst, beheaded in collapse of the south tower of the World Trade Center, 2001

oh my god oh my god Paul Anka is looking at me now even as he sings he bends down from the stage and his hand comes out asking me to rise to go up there with him and I am next to him dazzled by the lights the crowd roaring his voice near my face *squeeze me oh so tight* and his arm comes around me I am sixteen and now I am twenty and we step out the side door of the church hall and no one has noticed us go, me in my bridal dress and Sam in his tux, and we crouch flat-footed near the door like you see the Vietnamese do on TV and we smoke and I've just married him but this is the moment I know I love him for sure, us smoking outside alone, and the snow is falling beyond my window I have awakened and I know it's time for my baby she's ready though my water hasn't broken and I'm not in any pain I know this is the day and it's still snowing beyond the hospital window the flakes look big as her hands and she's taking my milk and Sam is singing *you're having my baby* and I think him a damn fool, she's mine, and I can hardly see, the lights are so bright, and an arm slips around my waist *put your head on my shoulder*

ISIOMA

OWOLABI

woman of Bani, Burkina Faso,
beheaded by fatwa, 2002

Mother I cannot see your face I walk beside you too young to veil my own but I yearn for your eyes, surely I can see my mother's eyes even in public, let the men turn their own eyes away for my sake, but behind us are the nine mosques that have risen from the earth and their veined walls are beneath our feet, the desiccated road, for father takes us east to a purer love of Allah, and his back is to me—no—he has turned round, in Nigeria, I am nearly a woman, the veil drops upon my face, he whispers that I live now where the road has ended on the cliff's edge and if I lift this thing between me and the world I will lose my balance and fall to my death, so my mother will never see my eyes again in sunlight, and there is a great rushing about me now, she lies dead and veiled and I slip into the night and the moonlight falls upon my naked eyes, my hand in the hand of a man whose body is unveiled and his part rises like a mosque of Bani, and I speak to the world a gentle truth about the prophet and the dark swims upon me I hurtle back along the road to the mosques of my home where I know that heaven is simply a shaping of the earth

HANADI TAYSEER

JARADAT

law student, beheaded by self-detonation
of shaheed-belt suicide bomb, 2003

I am heavy with child praise Allah I am at last with child my head is full of the law that I am permitted to study to serve our people but I have not forgotten my greater destiny praise Allah I am also with child, the words of the Prophet—peace be upon him—saying *Paradise lies at the feet of mothers,* I have not forgotten, I move across rubbled ground and my baby is pressed hard against my womb wait wait my face is naked my head is bare I touch where my baby is and he is very heavy ten kilos and his bones are large and hard and stacked side by side his cord winds secretly into the pocket of the jeans that bind my legs my loins I wear the clothes of harlots my hand is on his private part I am but to press there, my baby placed in me by a man with his face covered I turn my head and open my cloak to a man I do not know, an angel of Allah surely, his arms around me and my baby is suddenly holding me tight I am moving in a room full of people cursed by Allah my baby heavy against me surely he has eyes and a mouth and a heart, a woman nearby damned but large with child, I have my own, I touch him and he cries out

EARL DAGGETT

laid-off Mississippi heavy-equipment operator,
beheaded by his lover's husband, 2003

Elmer, that economy-size coon turd who is my friend, points his shotgun straight up over his dang head—and mine, if you please, I'm standing right next to him—and he goes and does this so fast I ain't got time to jump away from sharing his rightly earned fate, he pulls the trigger fixing to kill a squirrel and instead of bringing buckshot and tree limbs and small-animal guts raining down on our heads, like ought to be the outcome, he plumb misses the whole tree and falls backwards—he's got that bad a damn aim—and likewise his thumbs is always about hammered to pulp whenever it's time to tarpaper his barn or fix a porch plank, and he don't even deserve the love of Maisie who has billowy warm thighs and Elmer probably can't even manage to get it into her honey pot, not with both hands on his pecker and a red flag flying between her legs, so I figure I'm okay as I open one eye and it's only half past two and he should be at the planing mill and Maisie is still snoring like a rotary saw beside me and I jump up and grab my pants to make one clean leap: here I go right now I am so light and graceful like a greyhound at the track I'll just leap through that window and be clean plumb away from his ax

MAISIE

HOBBS

Mississippi woman,
beheaded by her husband, 2003

night that's dark as fresh tar on the county road we roll through our trailer park late from Wednesday church and I rest my chin on our Chevy's door and one lit window after another goes by Mandy Lou leaning into Henry him putting his arms around her and shadows going up and down beside the flicker of Lila's TV and I'm thinking I'm fixing to grow up and take a man inside me and I'm moving along in another tarry night through the woods out back of Stanco's Lawn Ornaments and Tombstones and he's got me by the hand saying sweet things like *you little dual-exhaust you, you little road-runner let me rev you up* and I keep on batting at him till we're on a stump at the quarry pond and this is the good part this is the part I knew I'd like, the cuddle beforehand, him knowing I'll say yes and it makes him cuddle real good cause I told him already it's the only way he's getting inside me and I say I got to have a great kiss first and then he can go down there to what he wants and he squares around and puckers and he moves in fast glancing off my nose and sliding along my cheek and he says *oopsie doops sorry there Maisie* and I say *that's okay Elmer* he's so cute being clumsy I know I'll marry him

ROBERT

DURAND

commuter, beheaded in crash
of Staten Island ferry, 2003

underneath her earlobe with its wisp of invisible fuzz the cleavage of her toes in her pointiest black stilettos the hollow of her ankle her sacral dimples each holding a tiny shadow as she sleeps in the morning light that slides beneath the shade, unawares she has sloughed off the toga of bedclothes the long indent of her spine bared and those dimples I put the tip of my tongue in one and she stirs, my wife, her shoulders her tall knuckles the lift of her arm the hollow beneath I put my face there and she bats at my ear *I'm not fresh* she says, *it's you* I say, kissing this hidden place, the round forward points of her hips that I palm as she sits upon me, my wife, my Ann, and she will not close her eyes *I want to see you in that moment* she says the knot of her wrist her brow I ruffle her brow with my lower lip the tiny arc of a scar on the back of her hand the mark of a Christmas-tree light the bruises of that childhood long gone and the father dead and the mother too just this scar remains and I turn her hand and I kiss her there and she puts her hands on my cheeks and she draws me to her and presses me down and she kisses me on the top of the head

TYLER
ALKINS

civilian truck driver, beheaded
by the Iraqi Al-Tawhid Wal-Jihad (Monotheism
and Holy Struggle) group, 2004

my name is Tyler Alkins my voice sounding far off guttering like the bleeder flames in the refineries outside Houston *my mother's name is Marietta* the red dot on the video camera a drop of blood at the corner of her mouth *my father's name is Ralph* and the old man is upon me grabbing at my shoulder *boy turn around and take this beating now* he says but I wrench my mind to him and me out with shotguns waiting for the doves to break and then he squeezes at my shoulder, but gently, the feathers of a dove fluttering still from the air the kick of the gun shuddering through me and a hand comes upon my shoulder from behind and a voice cries *allahu akbar* and it is just me and my rig driving the interstate hard at night the sodium vapor lamps coming up out of the dark like a sky full of nearby stars *I live in Lubbock Texas* and our own George is the President and he calls upon all of us and I can drive a truck and my old man grabs my shoulder and I have done something wrong and he says *in the name of Jesus* and a bite at my neck *allahu akbar* and George has prayed to God and he will kick ass and plenty of it and my father cries *take this beating now for your own good*

VASIL

BUKHALOV

Bulgarian agricultural aid worker, beheaded
by the Iraqi Salafist Brigade of Abu Bakr al-Siddiq, 2004

on my tongue the bitter bite of green walnut Baba's face in the lamp light her hands black from the peeling of the skins the nuts inside white and very soft, too young yet to be hardened, and I eat another and another until bitter is sweet to me and the cheese she gives me is soft as well and tastes like the goat's milk but after it's turned and it tastes also of the stable floor and of the rutted earth and I make a face I am very young and Baba puts her hand on mine and she says *eat more and you will find the taste is good* and then her hand touches my face *you look like your grandfather in this light* and I have seen a picture on a postcard of Diado and I will look again to see if I can find my own face and I look into my own son's face and see Diado's eyes and I make cheese and I grow pears and I give my son a curl of cheese from my fingertip and he makes a sour face and Baba lays her forearm beneath the piss-spill of the lamp and she shows me the number there, faint, in blue, *I was in Macedonia because of your grandfather and they took us* and this is all she says and we eat bitter herbs and they taste sweet to me now

ROBERT OLEN BUTLER

writer, decapitated on the job, 2010

heedless words but whispered, they begin as I stand before the guillotine and I am filled with the scent of motor exhaust and wood fire and fish sauce and jasmine in a strange country, a good scent, her hand in mine at last, the city that roars in my dreams is beyond the stucco walls a balcony the Saigon River the rim of the world bleeding from the setting sun and self-righteousness, the guillotine in the museum rises above the cannon barrels and rotor blades and unexploded bombs the blade darkened by the wet air and the voices begin to speak not in my head not in the place where I think but in my ear directly in my fingertips a computer screen before me the clatter of keys like tiny clawed feet running in a wall, come to me little ones nibble from my hands snuggle into my pockets and curl your naked tails in peace like these words already fixed and bound and tucked beneath my arm, half a dozen autographs signed tonight and thanks for buying my book I step into the elevator and I am alone and the air buzzes in silence and I consult the scrap of paper in my pocket to see where I belong and I push the button and down the hall there are voices agitated ardent full of yearning and I lean forward and I stick my head out to listen

THE HEADS

MUD, man	Northern Europe	ca. 40,000 B.C.
MEDUSA, Gorgon	Greece	ca. 2000 B.C.
Marcus Tullius CICERO, politician	Rome	43 B.C.
JOHN the BAPTIST, prophet	Roman Empire	ca. 30
Valeria MESSALINA, empress	Rome	48
DIOSCORUS, shipmaster	Pontiole	67
PAUL, apostle	Rome	67
MATTHEW, apostle	Ethiopia	78
VALENTINE, priest	Rome	ca. 270
DRAGON, beast	Libya	301
GEORGE, soldier	Palestine	303
The LADY of the LAKE, enchantress	Britain	ca. 470
AH BALAM, Mayan ballplayer	Mexico	803
Piers GAVESTON, royal consort	England	1312
GOOSENECK, court jester	Germany	1494
Thomas MORE, Lord Chancellor	England	1535
Anne BOLEYN, Queen	England	1536
Catherine HOWARD, Queen	England	1542
Lady Jane GREY, Queen	England	1554
Mary STUART, Queen of Scots	England	1587
Walter RALEIGH, courtier	England	1618

Brita GULLSMED, woman	Sweden	1675
LOUIS XVI, King	France	1793
Marie ANTOINETTE, Queen	France	1793
Marie-Jeanne BÉCU, mistress	France	1793
Antoine-Laurent LAVOISIER, scientist	France	1794
André CHÉNIER, poet	France	1794
Maximilien ROBESPIERRE, revolutionary	France	1794
Pierre-François LACENAIRE, criminal	France	1836
TA CHIN, wife	China	1838
JACOB, slave	USA (GA)	1855
ANGRY EYES, Apache warrior	Mexico	1880
Chin Chin CHAN, student	China	1882
Dave RUDABAUGH, outlaw	Mexico	1886
Agnes GWENLAN, factory girl	USA (MA)	1899
Charles H. STUART, farmer	USA (TX)	1904
Rokhel POGORELSKY, woman	Russia	1905
John MARTIN, boy	USA (NY)	1921
Henri LANDRU, furniture dealer	France	1922
Paul GORGULOFF, assassin	France	1932
Benita VON BERG, baroness	Germany	1935
Nguyen Van TRINH, guerrilla leader	Vietnam	1952

Alwi SHAH, executioner	Yemen	1958
CHICKEN, Americauna pullet	USA (AL)	1958
Vera-Jayne PALMER, actress	USA (LA)	1967
Le Van KY, city official	Vietnam	1968
Yukio MISHIMA, novelist	Japan	1970
Robert KORNBLUTH, advertising executive	USA (NY)	1984
Jennifer HADLEY, marketing director	USA (CT)	1989
Nicole Brown SIMPSON, woman	USA (CA)	1994
Mohammed Aziz NAJAFI, Shiite cleric	Iraq	1996
Lydia KOENIG, woman	USA (IL)	1999
Claude MESSNER, homeless man	USA (IL)	2000
Lois KENNERLY, systems analyst	USA (NY)	2001
Isioma OWOLABI, woman	Burkina Faso	2002
Hanadi Tayseer JARADAT, law student	Israel	2003
Earl DAGGETT, heavy-equipment operator	USA (MS)	2003
Maisie HOBBS, woman	USA (MS)	2003
Robert DURAND, commuter	USA (NY)	2003
Tyler ALKINS, truck driver	USA (TX)	2004
Vasil BUKHALOV, aid worker	Bulgaria	2004
Robert Olen BUTLER, writer	USA (FL)	2010

CHAPTER 22

The second and third days of the *Calpurnia* voyage were calm, both the weather and the first-class section of the ship. The news of the death of a passenger cast a pall over the voyagers. Mrs. Charles Boothroyd was confined to quarters under the constant supervision of the ship's doctor and attending nurses. She had gone into hysterics upon hearing the news of her husband and it had been necessary to administer large doses of sedatives.

By the third day, with revived health, the optimism of most passengers revived.

Elizabeth Wyckham Scarlatti and her young table escort made it a point to part company after each meal. By ten thirty every night, however, Matthew Canfield let himself into her quarters to take up his post lest there be a recurrence of the Boothroyd attempt. It was an unsatisfactory arrangement.

"If I were a hundred years younger, you might pass yourself off as one of those distasteful men who perform services for middle-aged adventuresses."

"If you used some of your well-advertised money to buy your own ocean liner, I might get some sleep at night."

These late-hour conversations served one good purpose, however. Their plans began to take shape. Also Canfield's responsibilities as an employee of Elizabeth Scarlatti were diplomatically discussed.

"You understand," said Elizabeth, "I wouldn't expect you to do anything detrimental to the government. Or

against your own conscience. I do believe in a man's conscience."

"But I gather you'd like to make the decision about what's detrimental and what isn't?"

"To a degree, yes. I believe I'm qualified."

"What happens if I don't agree with you?"

"We'll cross that bridge when we come to it."

"Oh, that's great!"

In essence, Matthew Canfield would continue submitting his reports to Washington's Group Twenty with one alteration—they first would be approved by Elizabeth Scarlatti. Together they would, through the field accountant, make certain requests of his office they both felt necessary. In all matters of physical well-being, the old woman would follow the instructions of the young man without argument.

Matthew Canfield would receive ten payments of ten thousand dollars each commencing with the first day in London. In small American bills.

"You realize, Mr. Canfield, that there's another way to look at this arrangement."

"What's that?"

"Your office is getting the benefit of my not inconsiderable talents for absolutely nothing. Extremely beneficial to the taxpayers."

"I'll put that in my next report."

The basic problem of the arrangement had not been resolved, however. For the field accountant to fulfill his obligations to both employers, a reason had to be found explaining his association with the old woman. It would become obvious as the weeks went by and it would be foolish to try to pass it off as either companionship or business. Both explanations would be suspect.

With a degree of self-interest, Matthew Canfield asked, "Can you get along with your daughter-in-law?"

"I assume you mean Ulster's wife. No one could stand Chancellor's."

"Yes."

"I like her. However, if you're thinking about her as a third party, I must tell you that she despises me. There are many reasons, most of them quite valid. In order to get what I want I've had to treat her quite badly. My only defense, if I felt I needed one—which I don't—is that what I wanted was for her benefit."

"I'm deeply moved, but do you think we could get her coopperation? I've met her on several occasions."

"She's not very responsible. But I suppose you know that."

"Yes. I also know that she suspects you of going to Europe on your son's account."

"I realize that. It would help to enlist her, I imagine. But I don't think I could manage it by cable, and I certainly wouldn't want to spell it out in a letter."

"I've a better way. I'll go back for her and I'll take a written . . . explanation from you. Not too involved, not too specific. I'll handle the rest."

"You must know her very well."

"Not so. I just think that if I can convince her that you—and I—are on her side . . . if someone's on her side, she'll help."

"She might be able to. She could show us places. . . ."

"She might recognize people. . . ."

"But what will I do while you're in America? I'll no doubt be dead when you come back."

Canfield had thought of that. "When we reach England, you should go into retreat."

"I beg your pardon?"

"For your immortal soul. And your son's as well, of course."

"I don't understand you."

"A convent. The whole world knows of your bereavement. It's a logical thing to do. We'll issue a statement to the press to the effect that you've gone to an undisclosed retreat in the north of England. Then send you somewhere down south. My office will help."

"It sounds positively ridiculous!"

"You'll be fetching in your black robes!"

The veiled, grieving Mrs. Boothroyd was led off with the first contingent of passengers. She was met by a man at customs who hurried her through the procedures and took her to a Rolls-Royce waiting on the street. Canfield followed the couple to the car.

Forty-five minutes later Canfield checked into the hotel. He had called his London contact from a public phone and they had agreed to meet as soon as the Lon-

doner could drive down. The field accountant then spent a half hour enjoying the stability of a dry-land bed. He was depressed at the thought of going right back on board ship but he knew there was no other solution. Janet would supply the most reasonable explanation for his accompanying the old lady and it was logical that the wife and mother of the missing Ulster Scarlett should travel together. And certainly Canfield was not unhappy at the prospect of a continued association with Janet Scarlett. She was a tramp, no question; but he had begun to doubt his opinion that she was a bitch.

He was about to doze off when he looked at his watch and realized that he was late for his meeting. He picked up the phone and was delighted by the crisp British accent answering him.

"Madame Scarlatti is in suite five. Our instructions are to ring through prior to callers, sir."

"If you'll do that, please, I'll just go right up. Thank you."

Canfield said his name quite loudly before Elizabeth Scarlatti would open the door. The old woman motioned the young man inside to a chair while she sat on a huge Victorian sofa by the window.

"Well, what do we do now?"

"I phoned our London man nearly an hour ago. He should be here shortly."

"Who is he?"

"He said his name is James Derek."

"Don't you know him?"

"No. We're given an exchange to call and a man is assigned to us. It's a reciprocal arrangement."

"Isn't that convenient." A statement.

"We're billed for it."

"What will he want to know?"

"Only what we want to tell him. He won't ask any questions unless we request something either inimical to the British government or so expensive he'd have to justify it; that's the point he'll be most concerned with."

"That strikes me as very amusing."

"Taxpayers' money." Canfield looked at his watch. "I asked him to bring along a list of religious retreats."

"You're really serious about that, aren't you?"

"Yes. Unless he has a better idea. I'll be gone for about

two and half weeks. Did you write the letter for your daughter-in-law?"

"Yes." She handed him an envelope.

Across the room on a table near the door, the telephone rang. Elizabeth walked rapidly to the table and answered it.

"Is that Derek?" asked Canfield, when she had hung up.

"Yes."

"Good. Now, please, Madame Scarlatti, let me do most of the talking. But if I ask you a question, you'll know I want an honest answer."

"Oh? We don't have signals?"

"No. He doesn't want to know anything. Believe that. Actually, we're a source of embarrassment to each other."

"Should I offer him a drink, or tea, or isn't that allowed?"

"I think a drink would be very much appreciated."

"I'll call room service and have a bar sent up."

"That's fine."

Elizabeth Scarlatti picked up the phone and ordered a complete selection of wines and liquors. Canfield smiled at the ways of the rich and lit one of his thin cigars.

James Derek was a pleasant-looking man in his early fifties, somewhat rotund, with the air of a prosperous merchant. He was terribly polite but essentially cool. His perpetual smile had a tendency to curve slowly into a strained straight line as he spoke.

"We traced the license of the Rolls at the pier. It belongs to a Marquis Jacques Louis Bertholde. French resident alien. We'll get information on him."

"Good. What about the retreats?"

The Britisher took out a paper from his inside coat pocket. "There're several we might suggest depending upon Madame Scarlatti's wishes to be in touch with the outside."

"Do you have any where contact is completely impossible? On both sides?" asked the field accountant.

"That would be Catholic, of course. There're two or three."

"Now, see here!" interrupted the imposing old lady.

"What are they?" asked Canfield.

"There's a Benedictine order and a Carmelite. They're

in the southwest, incidentally. One, the Carmelite, is near Cardiff."

"There are limits, Mr. Canfield, and I propose to establish them. I will not associate with such people!"

"What is the most fashionable, most sought after retreat in England, Mr. Derek?" asked the field accountant.

"Well, the duchess of Gloucester makes a yearly trek to the Abbey of York. Church of England, of course."

"Fine. We'll send out a story to all the wire services that Madame Scarlatti has entered for a month."

"That's far more acceptable," said the old woman.

"I haven't finished." He turned to the amused Londoner. "Then book us into the Carmelites. You'll escort Madame Scarlatti there tomorrow."

"As you say."

"Just one minute, gentlemen. I do not consent! I'm sure Mr. Derek will adhere to my wishes."

"Terribly sorry, madame. My instructions are to take orders from Mr. Canfield."

"And we have an agreement, Madame Scarlatti, or do you want to tear it up?"

"What can I possibly say to such people? I simply can not stand that voodoo mumbo jumbo coming from Rome!"

"You'll be spared that discomfort, madame," said Mr. Derek. "There's a vow of silence. You'll not hear from anyone."

"Contemplate," added the field accountant. "Good for the immortal soul."

CHAPTER 23

YORK, ENGLAND, *August 12, 1926*— The famed Abbey of York sustained a damaging explosion and fire at dawn this morning in its west wing, the residential quarters of the religious order. An undisclosed number of sisters and novices were killed in the tragic occurrence. It was believed that the explosion was due to a malfunction in the heating system recently installed by the order.

Canfield read the story in the ship's newspaper one day before arriving in New York.

They do their homework well, he thought. And although the price was painfully high, it proved two points conclusively: the press releases were read and Madame Scarlatti was marked.

The field accountant reached into his pocket and took out the old woman's letter to Janet Scarlett. He'd read it many times and thought it effective. He read it once more.

My dear Child:

I am aware that you are not particularly fond of me and I accept the fact as my loss. You have every right to feel as you do—the Scarlattis have not been pleasant people with whom to be associated. However, for whatever reasons and regardless of the pain you have been caused, you are now a Scarlatti and you have borne a Scarlatti into this world. Per-

haps you will be the one who will make us better than we are.

I do not make this statement lightly or out of sentiment. History has shown that the least expected among us often emerge splendidly because of the grave responsibilities placed upon them. I ask you to consider this possibility.

I further ask you to give deep consideration to what Mr. Matthew Canfield will tell you. I trust him. I do so because he has saved my life and nearly lost his own in so doing. His interests and ours are inextricably bound together. He will tell you what he can and he will ask of you a great deal.

I am a very, very old woman, my dear, and do not have much time. What months or years I do have (precious perhaps only to me) may well be cut short in a fashion I'd like to believe is not the will of God. Naturally, I accept this risk gladly as the head of the house of Scarlatti, and if I can spend what time I have left preventing a great dishonor upon our family, I will join my husband with a grateful heart.

Through Mr. Canfield, I await your answer. If it is as I suspect, we will be together shortly and you will have gladdened me far beyond that which I deserve. If it is not, you still have my affection and, believe me when I say, my understanding.

Elizabeth Wyckham Scarlatti

Canfield replaced the letter in the envelope. It was quite good, he thought again. It explained nothing and asked for implicit trust that the unsaid explanation was vitally urgent. If he did his job, the girl would be coming back to England with him. If he failed to persuade her, an alternative would have to be found.

The Ulster Scarlett brownstone on Fifty-fourth Street was being repainted and sandblasted. There were several scaffolds lowered from the roof and a number of workmen diligently at their crafts. The heavy Checker cab pulled up in front of the entrance and Matthew Canfield walked up the steps. He rang the bell; the door was opened by the obese housekeeper.

"Good afternoon, Hannah. I don't know if you remem-

ber, but my name's Canfield. Matthew Canfield to see Mrs. Scarlett."

Hannah did not budge or offer entrance. "Does Mrs. Scarlett expect you?"

"Not formally, but I'm sure she'll see me." He had had no intention of phoning. It would have been too easy for her to refuse.

"I don't know if madame is in, sir."

"Then I'll just have to wait. Shall it be here on the stairs?"

Hannah reluctantly made way for the field accountant to step into the hideously colored hallway. Canfield was struck again by the intensity of the red wallpaper and the black drapes.

"I'll inquire, sir," said the housekeeper as she started toward the stairs.

In a few minutes Janet came down the long staircase, followed by a waddling Hannah. She was very much composed. Her eyes were clear, aware, and devoid of the panic he had remembered. She was in command and without question a beautiful woman.

Canfield felt a sudden sting of inferiority. He was outclassed.

"Why, Mr. Canfield, this is a surprise."

He could not determine whether her greeting was meant to be pleasant or not. It was friendly, but cool and reserved. This girl had learned the lessons of the old money well.

"I hope not an unwelcome one, Mrs. Scarlett."

"Not at all."

Hannah had reached the bottom step and walked toward the dining room doors. Canfield quickly spoke again. "During my trip I ran across a fellow whose company makes dirigibles. I knew you'd be interested." Canfield watched Hannah out of the corner of his eye without moving his head. Hannah had turned abruptly and looked at the field accountant.

"Really, Mr. Canfield? Why would that concern me?" The girl was mystified.

"I understood your friends on Oyster Bay were determined to buy one for their club. Here, I've brought all the information. Purchase price, rentals, specifications, the works. . . . Let me show you."

The field accountant took Janet Scarlett's elbow and led her swiftly toward the living room doors. Hannah hesitated ever so slightly but, with a glance from Canfield, retreated into the dining room. Canfield then closed the living room doors.

"What are you doing? I don't want to buy a dirigible."

The field accountant stood by the doors, motioning the girl to stop talking.

"What?"

"Be quiet for a minute. Please." He spoke softly.

Canfield waited about ten seconds and then opened the doors in one swinging motion.

Directly across the hallway, standing by the dining room table, was Hannah and a man in white overalls, obviously one of the painters. They were talking while looking over toward the living room doors. They were now in full view of Canfield's stare. Embarrassed, they moved away.

Canfield shut the door and turned to Janet Scarlett. "Interesting, isn't it?"

"What are you doing?"

"Just interesting that your help should be so curious."

"Oh, that." Janet turned and picked up a cigarette from a case on the coffee table. "Servants will talk and I think you've given them cause."

Canfield lit her cigarette. "Including the painters?"

"Hannah's friends are her own business. They're no concern of mine. Hannah's barely a concern of mine. . . ."

"You don't find it curious that Hannah nearly tripped when I mentioned a dirigible?"

"I simply don't understand you."

"I admit I'm getting ahead of myself."

"Why didn't you telephone?"

"If I had, would you have seen me?"

Janet thought for a minute. "Probably. . . . Whatever recriminations I had over your last visit wouldn't be any reason to insult you."

"I didn't want to take that gamble."

"That's sweet of you and I'm touched. But why this very odd behavior?"

There was no point in delaying any longer. He took the envelope out of his pocket. "I've been asked to give you this. May I sit down while you read it?"

Janet, startled, took the envelope and immediately rec

ognized her mother-in-law's handwriting. She opened the envelope and read the letter.

If she was astonished or shocked, she hid her emotions well.

Slowly she sat down on the sofa and put out her cigarette. She looked down at the letter and up at Canfield, and then back to the letter. Without looking up, she asked quietly, "Who are you?"

"I work for the government. I'm an official . . . a minor official in the Department of the Interior."

"The government? You're not a salesman, then?"

"No, I'm not."

"You wanted to meet me and talk with me for the government?"

"Yes."

"Why did you tell me you sold tennis courts?"

"We sometimes find it necessary to conceal our employment. It's as simple as that."

"I see."

"I assume you want to know what your mother-in-law means in the letter?"

"Don't assume anything." She was cold as she continued. "It was your job to meet me and ask me all those amusing questions?"

"Frankly, yes."

The girl rose, took the necessary two steps toward the field accountant, and slapped him across the face with all her strength. It was a sharp and painful blow. "You son of a bitch! Get out of this house!" She still did not raise her voice. "Get out before I call the police!"

"Oh, my God, Janet, will you stop it!" He grabbed her shoulders as she tried to wriggle away. "Listen to me! I said listen or I'll slap you right back!"

Her eyes shone with hatred and, Canfield thought, a touch of melancholy. He held her firmly as he spoke. "Yes, I was assigned to meet you. Meet you and get whatever information I could."

She spat in his face. He did not bother to brush it away.

"I got the information I needed and I used that information because that's what I'm paid for! As far as my department is concerned, I left this house by nine o'clock after you served me two drinks. If they want to pick you

up for illegal possession of alcohol, that's what they can get you for!"

"I don't believe you!"

"I don't give a good God damn whether you do or not! And for your further information I've had you under surveillance for weeks! You and the rest of your playmates. . . . It may interest you to know that I've omitted detailing the more . . . ludicrous aspects of your day-to-day activities!"

The girl's eyes began to fill with tears.

"I'm doing my job as best I can, and I'm not so sure you're the one who should scream 'violated virgin'! You may not realize it, but your husband, or former husband, or whatever the hell he is, could be very much alive. A lot of nice people who never heard of him—women like you and young girls—were burned to death because of him! Others were killed, too, but maybe they should have been."

"What are you saying?" He relaxed his grip on her but still held her firmly.

"I just know that I left your mother-in-law a week ago in England. It was a hell of a trip over! Someone tried to kill her the first night out on the ship. Oh, you can bet your life it would have been suicide! They would have said she had tearfully thrown herself overboard. No trace at all. . . . A week ago we let out a story to the newspapers saying she'd gone to a retreat in a place called York, in England. Two days ago the heating system blew up and killed Christ knows how many people! An accident, of course!"

"I don't know what to say."

"Do you want me to finish, or do you still want me to go?"

There was a sadness about Ulster Scarlett's wife as she tried to smile. "I guess you'd better stay and . . . finish."

They sat on the sofa and Canfield talked.

He talked as he had never talked before.

CHAPTER 24

Benjamin Reynolds sat forward in his chair, clipping a week-old article from the Sunday supplement of the *New York Herald*. It was a photograph of Janet Saxon Scarlett being escorted by "sportingoods executive, M. Canfield" to a dog show at Madison Square Garden. Reynolds smiled as he recalled Canfield's remark on the telephone.

"I can stand everything but the God damn dog shows. Dogs are for the very rich or the very poor. Not for anyone in between!"

No matter, thought Group Twenty's head. The newspapers were doing an excellent job. Washington had ordered Canfield to spend an additional ten days in Manhattan thoroughly establishing his relationship with Ulster Scarlett's wife before returning to England.

The relationship was unmistakable and Benjamin Reynolds wondered if it was really a public facade. Or was it something else? Was Canfield in the process of trapping himself? The ease with which he had engineered a collaboration with Elizabeth Scarlatti bore watching.

"Ben"—Glover walked briskly into the office—"I think we've found what we've been looking for!" He closed the door firmly and approached Reynolds's desk.

"What have you got? About what?"

"A link with the Scarlatti business. I'm sure of it."

"Let me see."

Glover placed several pages on top of the spread-out newspaper. "Nice coverage, wasn't it?" he said, indicating the photograph of Canfield and the girl.

"Just what us dirty old men ordered. He's going to be the toast of society if he doesn't spit on the floor."

"He's doing a good job, Ben. They're back on board ship now, aren't they?"

"Sailed yesterday. . . . What is this?"

"Statistics found it. From Switzerland. Zurich area. Fourteen estates all purchased within the year. Look at these latitude and longitude marks. Every one of the properties is adjacent to another one. A borders on B, B on C, C on D, right down the line. Hundreds of thousands of acres forming an enormous compound."

"One of the buyers Scarlatti?"

"No. . . . But one of the estates was bought in the name of Boothroyd. Charles Boothroyd."

"You're sure? What do you mean 'bought in the name of'?"

"Father-in-law bought it for his daughter and her husband. Named Rawlins. Thomas Rawlins. Partner in the brokerage house of Godwin and Rawlins. His daughter's name is Cecily. Married to Boothroyd."

Reynolds picked up the page with the list of names. "Who are these people? How does it break down?"

Glover reached for the other two pages. "It's all here. Four Americans, two Swedes, three English, two French, and three German. Fourteen in all."

"Do you have any rundowns?"

"Only on the Americans. We've sent for information on the rest."

"Who are they? Besides Rawlins."

"A Howard Thornton, San Francisco. He's in construction. And two Texas oilmen. A Louis Gibson and Avery Landor. Between them they own more wells than fifty of their competitors combined."

"Any connections between them?"

"Nothing so far. We're checking that out now."

"What about the others? The Swedes, the French? . . . The English and the Germans?"

"Only the names."

"Anyone familiar?"

"Several. There's an Innes-Bowen, he's English, in textiles, I think. And I recognize the name of Daudet, French. Owns steamship lines. And two of the Germans. Kindorf—he's in the Ruhr Valley. Coal. And von Schritz-

er, speaks for I. G. Farben. Don't know the rest, never heard of the Swedes, either."

"In one respect they're all alike—"

"You bet your life they are. They're all as rich as a roomful of Astors. You don't buy places like these with mortgages. Shall I contact Canfield?"

"We'll have to. Send the list by courier. We'll cable him to stay in London until it arrives."

"Madame Scarlatti may know some of them."

"I'm counting on it. . . . But I see a problem."

"What's that?"

"It's going to be a temptation for the old girl to head right into Zurich. . . . If she does, she's dead. So's Canfield and Scarlett's wife."

"That's a pretty drastic assumption."

"Not really. We're presuming that a group of wealthy men have bought fourteen estates all adjoining one another because of a common interest. And Boothroyd—courtesy of a generous father-in-law—is one of them."

"Which ties Zurich to Scarlatti. . . ."

"We think so. We believe it because Boothroyd tried to kill her, right?"

"Of course."

"But the Scarlatti woman is alive. Boothroyd failed."

"Obviously."

"And the property was purchased before that fact."

"It must have been—"

"Then if Zurich is tied to Boothroyd, Zurich wants Scarlatti dead. They want to stop her. Also . . . Zurich presumed success. They expected Boothroyd to succeed."

"And now that he's gone," interrupted Glover, "Zurich will figure the old woman found out who he was. Maybe more. . . . Ben, perhaps we've gone too far. It might be better to call it off. Make a report to Justice and get Canfield back."

"Not yet. We're getting close to something. Elizabeth Scarlatti's the key right now. We'll get them plenty of protection."

"I don't want to make an alibi in advance, but this is your responsibility."

"I understand that. In our instructions to Canfield make one thing absolutely clear. He's to stay out of Zurich. Under no condition is he to go to Switzerland."

"I'll do that."

Reynolds turned from his desk and stared out the window. He spoke to his subordinate without looking at him. "And . . . keep a line open on this Rawlins. Boothroyd's father-in-law. He's the one who may have made the mistake."

CHAPTER 25

Twenty-five miles from the ancient limits of Cardiff, set in a remote glen in a Welsh forest, stands the Convent of the Virgin, the home of the Carmelite sisters. The walls rise in alabaster purity, like a new bride standing in holy expectation in a lush but serpentless Eden.

The field accountant and the young wife drove up to the entrance. Canfield got out of the car and walked to a small arched doorway set in the wall in which was centered a viewer. There was a black iron knocker on the side of the door that he used, then waited for several minutes until a nun answered.

"May I help you?"

The field accountant drew out his indentification card and held it up for the nun to see. "My name is Canfield, sister. I'm here for Madame Elizabeth Scarlatti. Her daughter-in-law is with me."

"If you'll wait, please. May I?" She indicated that she wished to take his identification card with her. He handed it to her through the small opening.

"If course."

The viewer was closed and bolted. Canfield wandered back to the car and spoke to Janet. "They're very cautious."

"What's happening?"

"She's taking my card in to make sure the photograph's me and not someone else."

"Lovely here, isn't it? So quiet."

"It is now. I make no promises when we finally see the old girl."

"Your callous, unfeeling disregard for my well-being, to say nothing of my comforts, is beyond anything I can describe! Do you have any idea what these idiots sleep on? I'll tell you! Army cots!"

"I'm sorry—" Canfield tried not to laugh.

"And do you know the slops they eat? I'll tell you! Food I'd prohibit in my stables!"

"I'm told they grow their own vegetables," the field accountant countered gently.

"They pluck up the fertilizer and leave the plants!"

At that moment the bells of the Angelus pealed out.

"That goes on night and day! I asked that damned fool, Mother MacCree, or whoever she is, why so early in the morning—and do you what know what she said?"

"What, Mother?" asked Janet.

" 'That is the way of Christ,' that's what she said. 'Not a good Episcopal Christ!' I told her. . . . It's been intolerable! Why were you so late? Mr. Derek said you'd be here four days ago."

"I had to wait for a courier from Washington. Let's go. I'll tell you about it."

Elizabeth sat in the back seat of the Bentley reading the Zurich list.

"Know any of those people?" asked Canfield.

"Not personally. Most all of them by reputation, however."

"For instance?"

"The Americans, Louis Gibson and Avery Landor are two self-styled Texas Bunyans. They think they built the oil territories. Landor's a pig, I'm told. Harold Leacock, one of the Englishmen, is a power on the British Stock Exchange. Very bright. Myrdal from Sweden is also in the European market. Stockholm. . . ." Elizabeth looked up and acknowledged Canfield's glance in the rearview mirror.

"Anybody else?"

"Yes. Thyssen in Germany. Fritz Thyssen. Steel com-

panies. Everyone knows Kindorf—Ruhr Valley coal, and von Schnitzler. He's I. G. Farben now. . . . One of the Frenchmen, D'Almeida, has control of railroads, I think. I don't know Daudet but I recognize the name."

"He owns tankers. Steamships."

"Oh, yes. And Masterson. Sydney Masterson. English. Far East imports, I think. I don't know Innes-Bowen, but again I've heard the name."

"You didn't mention Rawlins. Thomas Rawlins."

"I didn't think I had to. Godwin and Rawlins. Boothroyd's father-in-law."

"You don't know the fourth American, Howard Thornton? He's from San Francisco."

"Never heard of him."

"Janet says your son knew a Thornton from San Francisco."

"I'm not at all surprised."

On the road from Pontypridd, on the outskirts of the Rhondda Valley, Canfield became aware of an automobile, which regularly appeared in his side mirror. It was far behind them, hardly more than a speck in the glass, but it was never out of sight except around curves. And whenever Canfield rounded one of the many turns, the automobile appeared subsequently much sooner than its previous distance would indicate. On long stretches it stayed far in the distance and whenever possible allowed other cars to come between them.

"What is it, Mr. Canfield?" Elizabeth was watching the field accountant, who kept shifting his eyes to the mirror outside his window.

"Nothing."

"Is someone following us?"

"Probably not. There aren't that many good roads leading to the English border."

Twenty minutes later Canfield saw that the automobile was drawing nearer. Five minutes after that he began to understand. There were no cars between the two vehicles now. Only a stretch of road—a very long curve—bordered on one side by the rocky slope of a small incline and on the other by a sheer drop of fifty feet into the waters of a Welsh lake.

Beyond the end of the curve, Canfield saw that the ground leveled off into a pasture or overgrown field. He accelerated the Bentley. He wanted to reach that level area.

The car behind shot forward closing the gap between them. It swung to the right on the side of the road by the rocky slope. Canfield knew that once the car came parallel it could easily force him off the road, over the edge, plunging the Bentley down the steep incline into the water. The field accountant held the pedal down and veered the car toward the center trying to cut off the pursuer.

"What is it? What are you doing?" Janet held on to the top of the dashboard.

"Brace yourselves! Both of you!"

Canfield held the Bentley in the center, crossing to the right each time the car behind him tried to squeeze between him and the solid ground. The level field was nearer now. Only another hundred yards.

There were two sharp, heavy crunches as the Bentley lurched spastically under the second car's impact. Janet Scarlett screamed. Her mother-in-law kept silent, clutching the girl's shoulders from behind, helping to brace her.

The level pasture was now on the left and Canfield suddenly swerved the car toward it, going off the road, holding to the dirt border beyond the pavement.

The pursuing car plunged forward at tremendous speed. Canfield riveted his eyes on the rapidly receding black-and-white license plate. He shouted, *"E, B . . . I* or *L!* Seven! Seven or nine! One, one, three!" He repeated the numbers again softly, quickly. He slowed the Bentley down and came to a stop.

Janet's back was arched against the seat. She held Elizabeth's arms with both her hands. The old woman sat forward, her cheek pressed against her daughter-in-law's head.

Elizabeth spoke.

"The letters you called out were *E, B, I* or *L,* the numbers, seven or nine, one, one, three."

"I couldn't tell the make of the car."

Elizabeth spoke again as she took her arms from Janet's shoulders.

"It was a Mercedes-Benz."

CHAPTER 26

"The automobile in question is a Mercedes-Benz coupé. Nineteen twenty-five model. The license is EBI nine, one, one, three. The vehicle is registered in the name of Jacques Louis Bertholde. Once again, the Marquis de Bertholde." James Derek stood by Canfield in front of Elizabeth and Janet who sat on the sofa. He read from his notebook and wondered if these curious Americans realized who the marquis was. Bertholde, too, often stayed at the Savoy and was probably as rich as Elizabeth Scarlatti.

"The same man who met Boothroyd's wife at the pier?" asked Canfield.

"Yes. Or I should say, no. We assume it was Bertholde at the pier from your description. It couldn't have been yesterday. We've established that he was in London. However, the automobile is registered to him."

"What do you think, Mr. Derek?" Elizabeth smoothed her dress and avoided looking at the Englishman. There was something about the man that disturbed her.

"I don't know what to think. . . . However, I feel I should tell you that the Marquis de Bertholde is a resident alien of considerable influence and position. . . ."

"He is the owner of Bertholde et Fils, as I recall." Elizabeth rose from the sofa and gave her empty sherry glass to Canfield. It was not that she wished more wine. She was just too wrought up to sit still. "Bertholde et Fils is an old established firm."

The field accountant went to the drinks table and poured Elizabeth's sherry.

"Then you've met the marquis, Madame Scarlatti? Perhaps you know him?"

Elizabeth didn't like Derek's insinuation. "No, I do not know the marquis. I may have met his father. I'm not sure. The Bertholdes go back many years."

Canfield handed Elizabeth her glass aware that the old woman and the British operative were playing a mental tennis game. He broke in. "What's his business?"

"Plural. Businesses. Near East oil, mining and drilling in Africa, imports—Australia and South America. . . ."

"Why is he a resident alien?"

"I can answer that," said Elizabeth, returning to the couch. "The physical plants—his offices—are, no doubt, within Empire territories or protectorates."

"Quite correct, madame," said Derek. "Since the majority of his interests lie within the borders of British possessions, he deals continuously with Whitehall. He does so, most favorably."

"Is there a government dossier on Bertholde?"

"As a resident alien, of course there is."

"Can you get it for me?"

"I'd have to have a very sound reason. You know that."

"Mr. Derek!" interrupted Elizabeth. "An attempt was made on my life aboard the *Calpurnia!* Yesterday in Wales an automobile tried to run us off the road! In both instances the Marquis de Bertholde can be implicated. I would call these sound reasons!"

"I'm afraid I must disagree. What you describe are police matters. Anything I know to the contrary is privileged information and I respect it as such. Certainly no charges are being made in either case. It's a gray area, I grant you, but Canfield knows what I'm talking about."

The field accountant looked at Elizabeth and she knew the time had come to use his ploy. He had explained that eventually they would have to. He had called it—"part of the truth." The reason was simple. British Intelligence was not going to be used as someone's personal police force. There had to be other justifications. Justifications that Washington would confirm. Canfield looked at the Englishman and spoke softly.

"The United States government wouldn't involve any agency unless there were reasons beyond police matters. When Madame Scarlatti's son—Mrs. Scarlett's husband—

was in Europe last year, large sums of money, in the form of negotiable securities on a number of American corporations, were forwarded to him. We think they were sold undercover on the European markets. The British exchange included."

"Are you telling me that someone is forming an American monopoly over here?"

"The State Department thinks that the manipulation was handled by our own embassy personnel. They're right here in London now."

"Your own embassy personnel! And you think Scarlett was a party to it?"

"We think he was used." Elizabeth's voice pierced the air. "Used and then eliminated."

"He traveled in that crowd, Derek. So does the Marquis de Bertholde."

James Derek replaced his small notebook in his breast pocket. The explanation obviously was sufficient. The British operative was also very curious. "I'll have a copy of the dossier for you tomorrow, Canfield. . . . Good evening, ladies." He went out.

"I congratulate you, young man. Embassy personnel. Really very intelligent of you."

"I think he was remarkable!" said Janet Scarlett, smiling at him.

"It'll work," mumbled the field accountant, swallowing the major portion of a Scotch. "Now, may I suggest we all need some relief. Speaking for myself, I'm tired of thinking—and I wouldn't appreciate a comment on that, Madame Scarlatti. How about dinner at one of those places you upper class always go? I hate dancing but I swear I'll dance with you both until you drop."

Elizabeth and Janet laughed.

"No, but I thank you," said Elizabeth. "You two go and romp." She looked at the field accountant fondly. "An old woman thanks you again, Mr. Canfield."

"You'll lock the doors and windows?"

"Seven stories off the ground? Of course, if you like."

"I do," said Canfield.

CHAPTER 27

"It's heaven!" shrieked Janet over the din of voices at Claridge's. "Come on, Matthew, don't look so sour!"

"I'm not sour. I just can't hear you."

"Yes, you are. You didn't like it. Let me enjoy it."

"I will. I will! Do you want to dance?"

"No. You hate dancing. I just want to watch."

"No charge. Watch. It's good whiskey."

"Good what?"

"I said whiskey."

"No, thanks. See? I can be good. You're two up on me, you know."

"I may be sixty up on you if this keeps going."

"What, darling?"

"I said I may be sixty when we get out of here."

"Oh, stop it. Have fun!"

Canfield looked at the girl opposite him and felt once again a surge of joy. There was no other word but joy. She was a delight that filled him with pleasure, with warmth. Her eyes held the immediacy of commitment that only a lover can know. Yet Canfield tried so hard to disassociate, to isolate, to objectify, and found that he could not do it.

"I love you very much," he said.

She heard him through the music, the laughter, the undercurrent hum of movement.

"I know." She looked at him and her eyes had the hint of tears. "We love each other. Isn't that remarkable?"

"Do you want to dance, now?"

The girl threw back her head ever so slightly. "Oh,

Matthew! My dear, sweet Matthew. No, darling. You don't have to dance."

"Now, look, I will."

She clasped his hand. "We'll dance by ourselves, all by ourselves later."

Matthew Canfield made up his mind that he would have this woman for the rest of his life.

But he was a professional and his thoughts turned for a moment to the old woman at the Savoy.

Elizabeth Wyckham Scarlatti at that moment got out of her bed and into a dressing gown. She had been reading the *Manchester Guardian.* Turning its thin pages, she heard two sharp metallic clicks accompanied by a muffled sound of movement from the living room. She was not at first startled by the noise; she had bolted the hallway door and presumed that her daughter-in-law was fumbling with a key unable to enter because of the latch. After all, it was two o'clock in the morning and the girl should have returned by now. She called out.

"Just one minute, my dear. I'm up."

She had left a table lamp on and the fringe of the shade rippled as she passed it causing a flickering of minute shadows on the wall.

She reached the door and began to unbolt the latch. Remembering the field accountant, she halted momentarily.

"That is you, isn't it, my dear?"

There was no reply.

She automatically snapped back the bolt.

"Janet? Mr. Canfield? Is that you?"

Silence.

Fear gripped Elizabeth. She had heard the sound; age had not impaired her hearing.

Perhaps she had confused the clicking with the unfamiliar rustling of the thin English newspaper. That was not unreasonable and although she tried to believe it, she could not.

Was there someone else in the room?

At the thought she felt pain in the pit of her stomach.

As she turned to go back into the bedroom, she saw that one of the large french windows was partially

opened, no more than one or two inches but enough to cause the silk draperies to sway slightly from the incoming breeze.

In her confusion she tried to recall whether she had closed it before. She thought she had, but it had been an uninterested motion because she hadn't taken Canfield seriously. Why should she? They were seven stories high.

Of course, she hadn't closed it. Or, if she had, she hadn't secured the catch and it had slipped off. Nothing at all unusual. She crossed to the window and pushed it closed.

And then she heard it.

"Hello, Mother."

Out of the shadows from the far end of the room walked a large man dressed in black. His head was shaved and he was deeply tanned.

For several seconds she did not recognize him. The light from the one table lamp was dim and the figure remained at the end of the room. As she became adjusted to the light and the object of her gaze, she realized why the man appeared to be a stranger. The face had changed. The shining black hair was shaved off; the nose was altered, smaller and the nostrils wider apart; the ears were different, flatter against the head; even the eyes —where before there had been a Neapolitan droop to the lids—these eyes were wide, as if no lids existed. There were reddish splotches around the mouth and forehead. It was not a face. It was the mask of a face. It was striking. It was monstrous. And it was her son.

"Ulster! My God!"

"If you die right now of heart failure, you'll make fools out of several highly paid assassins."

The old woman tried to think, tried with all her strength to resist panic. She gripped the back of a chair until the veins in her aged hands seemed to burst from the skin.

"If you've come to kill me, there's little I can do now."

"You'll be interested to know that the man who ordered you killed will soon be dead himself. He was stupid."

Her son wandered toward the french window and checked the latch. He cautiously peered through the glass and was satisfied. His mother noticed that the grace with which he had always carried himself remained but there

was no softness now, no gentle relaxation, which had taken the form of a slight aristocratic slouch. Now there was a taut, hard quality in his movement, accentuated by his hands—which were encased in skintight black gloves, fingers extended and rigidly curved.

Elizabeth slowly found the words. "Why have you come here?"

"Because of your obstinate curiosity." He walked rapidly to the hotel phone on the table with the lighted lamp, touching the cradle as if making sure it was secure. He returned to within a few feet of his mother and the sight of his face, now seen clearly, caused her to shut her eyes. When she reopened them, he was rubbing his right eyebrow, which was partially inflamed. He watched her pained look.

"The scars aren't quite healed. Occasionally they itch. Are you maternally solicitous?"

"What have you done to yourself?"

"A new life. A new world for me. A world which has nothing to do with yours. Not yet!"

"I asked you what you've done."

"You know what I've done, otherwise you wouldn't be here in London. What you must understand, now, is that Ulster Scarlett no longer exists."

"If that's what you want the world to believe, why come to me of all people?"

"Because you rightly assumed it wasn't true and your meddling could prove irksome to me."

The old woman steeled herself before speaking. "It's quite possible then that the instructions for my death were not stupid."

"That's very brave. I wonder, though, if you've thought about the others?"

"What others?"

Scarlett sat on the couch and spoke in a biting Italian dialect. "La Famiglia Scarlatti! That's the proper phrase, isn't it? . . . Eleven members to be exact. Two parents, a grandmother, a drunken bitch wife, and seven children. The end of the tribe! The Scarlatti line abruptly stops in one bloody massacre!"

"You're mad! I'd stop you! Don't pit your piddling theft against what I have, my boy!"

"You're a foolish old woman! We're beyond sums. It's only how they're applied now. You taught me that!"

"I'd put them out of your reach! I'd have you hunted down and destroyed!"

The man effortlessly sprang up from the couch.

"We're wasting time. You're concerning yourself with mechanics. That's pedestrian. Let's be clear. I make one phone call and the order is sent to New York. Within forty-eight hours the Scarlattis are snuffed out! Extinguished! It will be an expensive funeral. The foundation will provide nothing but the best."

"Your own child as well?"

"He'd be the first. All dead. No apparent reason. The mystery of the lunatic Scarlattis."

"You are mad." She was hardly audible.

"Speak up, Mother! Or are you thinking about those curly headed moppets romping on the beach at Newport, laughing in their little boats on the sound. Tragic, isn't it? Just one of them! Just one out of the whole lot might make it for you, and the Scarlatti tribe continues in glory! Shall I make my call? It's a matter of indifference to me."

The old woman, who had not moved, walked slowly toward one of the armchairs. "Is what you want from me so valuable that the lives of my family depend upon it?"

"Not to you. Only to me. It could be worse, you know. I could demand an additional one hundred million."

"Why don't you? Under the circumstances you know I'd pay it."

The man laughed. "Certainly you'd pay it. You'd pay it from a source that'd cause a panic in the ticker rooms. No, thank you. I don't need it. Remember, we're beyond sums."

"What is it you want?" She sat in the chair, crossing her thin arms on her lap.

"The bank letters for one. They're no good to you anyway, so there should be no struggle with your conscience."

She had been right! The concept had been right! Always trace the practical. The money.

"Bank letters?"

"The bank letters Cartwright gave you."

"You killed him! You knew about our agreement?"

"Come, Mother. A Southern ass is made vice-president of Waterman Trust! Actually given responsibility. We fol-

lowed him for three days. We have your agreement. At least his copies. Let's not fool each other. The letters, please."

The old lady rose from the chair and went into her bedroom. She returned and handed him the letters. He rapidly opened the envelopes and took them out. He spread them on the couch and counted them.

"Cartwright earned his money."

He gathered them up and casually sat down on the sofa.

"I had no idea those letters were so important."

"They're not, really. Nothing could be accomplished with them. All the accounts have been closed and the money . . . dispersed to others, shall we say."

"Then why were you so anxious to get them?" She remained standing.

"If they were submitted to the banks, they could start a lot of speculation. We don't want a great deal of talk right now."

The old woman searched her son's confident eyes. He was detached, pleased with himself, almost relaxed.

"Who is 'we'? What are you involved in?"

Again that grotesque smile from the crooked mouth underneath the unnatural nostrils. "You'll know in good time. Not by name, of course, but you'll know. You might even be proud but you'll never admit it." He looked at his wristwatch. "Down to business."

"What else?"

"What happened on the *Calpurnia*? Don't lie!" He riveted his eyes on the old woman's and they did not waver.

Elizabeth strained the muscles in her abdomen to help her conceal any reaction to the question. She knew that the truth might be all she had left. "I don't understand you."

"You're lying!"

"About what? I received a cablegram from a man named Boutier concerning Cartwright's death."

"Stop it!" He leaned forward. "You wouldn't have gone to the trouble of throwing everyone off with that York Abbey story unless something happened. I want to know where he is."

"Where who is? Cartwright?"

"I warn you!"

"I have no idea what you're talking about!"

"A man disappeared on that ship! They say he fell overboard."

"Oh, yes. I recall. . . . What has that to do with me?" Her look personified innocence.

Neither moved.

"You know nothing about the incident?"

"I didn't say that."

"What did you say, then?"

"There were rumors. Reliable sources."

"What rumors?"

The old woman weighed several replies. She knew that her answer had to have the ring of authenticity without any obvious errors in character or behavior. On the other hand, whatever she said had to reflect the sketchy extremes of gossip.

"That the man was drunk and belligerent. There'd been a struggle in the lounge. . . . He had to be subdued and carried to his stateroom. He tried to return and fell over the rail. Did you know him?"

A cloud of detachment covered Scarlett's answer. "No, he was no part of us." He was dissatisfied but he did not dwell on it. For the first time in several minutes he looked away from her. He was deep in thought. Finally he spoke. "One last item. You started out to find your missing son . . ."

"I started out to find a thief!" she interrupted sharply.

"Have it your way. From another point of view I simply moved up the calendar."

"That's not true! You stole from Scarlatti. What was assigned to you was to be used in conjunction with the Scarlatti Industries!"

"We're wasting time again."

"I wanted the point cleared up."

"The point is that you set out to find me and you succeeded. We agree on that fact?"

"Agreed."

"Now I'm telling you to say nothing, do nothing, and return to New York. Furthermore, destroy any letters or instructions you may have left concerning me."

"Those are impossible demands!"

"In that event my orders go out. The Scarlattis are dead! Go to your church and let them tell you how they've been washed in the blood of the lamb!"

Ulster Scarlett sprang up from the Victorian couch and before the old woman could adjust her eyes to his movement, he had reached the telephone. There wasn't the slightest hesitation on his part. He picked up the telephone without looking at her and waited for the switchboard to answer.

The old woman rose unsteadily. "Don't!"

He turned to face her. "Why not?"

"I'll do as you ask!"

He replaced the phone. "Are you sure?"

"I'm sure." He had won.

Ulster Scarlett smiled with his misshapen lips. "Then our business is concluded."

"Not quite." Elizabeth now would try, realizing that the attempt might cost her her life.

"Oh?"

"I'd like to speculate, for just a minute."

"On what?"

"For the sake of argument, supposing I decided to abandon our understanding?"

"You know the consequences. You couldn't hide from us, not for any length of time."

"Time, however, could be the factor on my side."

"The securities have been disposed of. No sense in thinking about that."

"I assumed they had been, or else you wouldn't have come here."

"This is a good game. Go on."

"I'm sure that if you hadn't thought of it yourself, someone would have told you that the only intelligent way of selling those securities would be on a currency basis in exchange for diminished value."

"No one had to tell me."

"Now it's my turn to ask a question."

"Go ahead."

"How difficult do you think it is to trace deposits, gold or otherwise, of that magnitude? I'll make it two questions. Where are the only banks in the world willing or even capable of such deposits?"

"We both know the answer. Coded, numbered, impossible."

"And in which of the great banking concerns of Switzerland is there the incorruptible man?"

Her son paused and squinted his lidless eyes. "Now you're the one who's insane," he answered quietly.

"Not at all. You think in small blocks, Ulster. You use large sums but you think in small blocks. . . . Word goes out in the marble halls of Bern and Zurich that the sum of one million American dollars can be had for the confidential exchange of information. . . ."

"What would you gain by it?"

"Knowledge! . . . Names! People!"

"You make me laugh!"

"Your laughter will be short-lived! . . . It's obvious that you have associates; you need them. Your threats make that doubly clear, and I'm sure you pay them well. . . . The question is—once they're known to me and I to them—will they be able to resist my price? Certainly you can never match it! In this we are not beyond sums!"

The grotesque face distorted itself further as a thick, drawlish laugh came forth from the misshapen mouth. "I've waited years to tell you that your slide-rule theories smell! Your stinking buy-me, sell-me manipulations are finished! You've had your way! It's finished! Dead! Gone! . . . Who are you to manipulate? With your conniving bankers! Your stinking little Jews! You're finished! I've watched you! Your kind is dead! . . . Don't talk to me about my associates. They wouldn't touch you or your money!" The man in black was in a rage.

"You believe that?" Elizabeth did not move. She asked a simple question.

"Completely!" Ulster Scarlett's unhealed flesh was red with the blood rushing to his head. "We have something else! And you can't touch us! Any of us! *There is no price for us!*"

"However, you'll grant—as with the bank letters—I could prove irksome. Only to a far greater degree. Do you wish to take that gamble?"

"You sign eleven death warrants! A mass burial! Is that what you want, Mother?"

"The answer to both our questions would seem to be no. This is now a more reasonable understanding."

The man-mask in black paused and spoke softly, precisely. "You're not my equal. Don't for one minute think you are!"

"What happened, Ulster? What happened? . . . Why?"

"Nothing and everything! I'm doing what none of you

are capable of doing! What has to be done! But you can't do it!"

"Would I . . . or we . . . want to?"

"More than anything in the world? But you haven't the stomachs! You're weak!"

The telephone rang, piercing the air.

"Don't bother to answer it," Ulster said. "It'll ring only once. It's merely a signal that my wife—the devoted whore—and her newest bedmate have left Claridge's."

"Then I assume our meeting is adjourned." She saw to her great relief that he accepted the statement. She noted also that, in such a position he was dangerous. A tick was developing on the surface of his skin above his right eye. He again stretched his fingers in a slow deliberate motion.

"Remember what I say. You make one mistake . . ."

She interrupted before he could finish. "Remember who I am, young man! You're speaking to the wife of Giovanni Merighi Scarlatti! There is no need to repeat yourself. You have your agreement. Go about your filthy business. I have no further interest in you!"

The man in black strode rapidly to the door. "I hate you, Mother."

"I hope you benefit as much from those you hold less dear."

"In ways you'd never understand!"

He opened the door and slipped out, slamming it harshly behind him.

Elizabeth Scarlatti stood by the window and pulled apart the drapes. She leaned against the cold glass for support. The city of London was asleep, and only a scattering of lights dotted its concrete facade.

What in God's name had he done?

More important, who was paying attention to him?

What might have been mere horror turned into terror for he had the weapon. The weapon of power—which she and Giovanni innocently, productively provided.

They were, indeed, beyond sums.

Tears fell from her old eyes and that inner consciousness, which afflicts all human beings, was taken by surprise. She had not cried in over thirty years.

Elizabeth pushed herself away from the window and slowly wandered about the room. She had a great deal of thinking to do.

CHAPTER 28

In a room in the Home Office, James Derek took out a file. "Jacques Louis Bertholde, The Fourth Marquis of Chatellerault."

The dossier custodian entered the room. "Hello, James. Late hours tonight, I see."

"I'm afraid so, Charles. I'm taking out a copy. Did you get my request?"

"Right here. Fill me in and I'll sign for it. But please make it short. I've a card game in my office."

"Short and simple. The Americans suspect their embassy personnel of selling Yank securities undercover over here. This Bertholde travels in the diplomatic circles. There could be a connection with the Scarlatti fellow."

The dossier custodian made his appropriate notes. "When did this all take place?"

"About a year ago, as I understand it."

The custodian stopped writing and looked at James Derek. "A year ago?"

"Yes."

"And this American chap wants to confront embassy personnel *now? Over here?*"

"That's right."

"He's on the wrong side of the Atlantic. All American embassy personnel were transferred four months ago. There's no one there now—not even a secretary—who was in London a year ago."

"That's very strange," said Derek quietly.

"I'd say your American friend has a rather poor connection with his State Department."

"Which means he's lying."

"Which means he is."

Janet and Matthew, laughing, got off on the seventh floor and started down the corridor toward Elizabeth's suite. The length of their walk was approximately one hundred feet and they stopped four times to embrace and exchange kisses.

The girl took a key out of her purse and handed it to the field accountant.

He inserted it and simultaneously turned the knob before making any lateral motion with the key. The door opened and in a split second the field accountant was more sober than drunk.

He practically fell into the room.

Elizabeth Scarlatti was sitting on the Victorian couch in the dim light emanating from the single lamp. She did not move other than to look up at Canfield and her daughter-in-law.

"I heard you in the hallway."

"I told you to lock these doors!"

"I'm sorry, I forgot."

"The hell you did! I waited until I heard the latch and the bolt!"

"I ordered some coffee from room service."

"Where's the tray?"

"In my bedroom, which I presume to be private."

"Don't you believe it!" The field accountant ran toward the bedroom door.

"I apologize again! I called to have it taken away. I'm quite confused. Forgive me."

"Why? What's the matter?"

Elizabeth Scarlatti thought quickly and looked at her daughter-in-law as she spoke. "I had a most distressing telephone call. A business matter completely unrelated to you. It entails a great deal of money and I must make a decision before the British exchange opens." She looked at the field accountant.

"May I ask what's so important that you don't follow my instructions?"

"Several million dollars. Perhaps you'd care to help me. Should the Scarlatti Industries conclude the purchase

of the remaining convertible debentures in Sheffield Cutlery and by exercising the conversions gain control of the company or not?"

Still uncertain, the field accountant asked, "Why is that so . . . distressing?"

"Because the company constantly loses money."

"Then you don't buy. That shouldn't keep you up all night."

The old woman eyed him coldly. "Sheffield Cutlery is one of the oldest, finest firms in England. Their product is superb. The problem is neither management nor labor conditions but a heavy influx of Japanese imitations. The question is, Will the purchasing public learn in time to reverse the trend?"

Elizabeth Scarlatti rose from the couch and went into her bedroom, closing the door behind her. The field accountant turned to Janet Scarlett. "Does she do this sort of thing all the time? Doesn't she have advisers?"

But Janet was still staring at the bedroom door. She took off her wrap and approached the field accountant. She spoke quietly. "She's not telling the truth."

"How do you know?"

"The way she looked at me when she was talking to you. She was trying to tell me something."

"Like what?"

The girl shrugged impatiently and continued in a hushed whisper. "Oh, I don't know, but you know what I mean. You're with a group of people, and you start to tell a whopper or exaggerate something, and while you do, you look at your husband or a friend who knows better . . . and they know they shouldn't correct you. . . ."

"Was she lying about that company she spoke of?"

"Oh, no. That's the truth. Chancellor Drew's been trying to persuade her to buy that firm for months."

"How do you know?"

"She's already turned it down."

"Then why did she lie?"

As Canfield started to sit down, his attention was drawn to the linen antimacassar on the back of the chair. At first he dismissed it and then he looked again. The material was crumpled as if it had been mangled or bunched together. It was out of place in an immaculate suite. He looked closer. There were breaks in the threads

and the imprint of fingertips was unmistakable. Whoever had gripped the chair had done so with considerable force.

"What is it, Matthew?"

"Nothing. Get me a drink, will you?"

"Of course, darling." She went to the dry bar as Canfield walked around the chair in front of the french window. For no particular reason, he pulled apart the curtains and inspected the window itself. He turned the latch and pulled the left side open. He saw what he had begun to look for. The wood around the clasp was scratched. On the sill he could see where the paint had been discolored by the impression of a heavy coarse object, probably a rubber-soled boot or a crepe-soled shoe. Not leather; there were no scratches on the enamel. He opened the right side and looked out. Below were six stories straight down; above two floors to what he recalled was an acutely slanting roof. He pushed the window shut and locked it.

"What on earth are you doing?"

"We've had a visitor. An uninvited guest, you might say."

The girl stood absolutely still. "Oh, my God!"

"Don't be frightened. Your mother-in-law wouldn't do anything foolish. Believe that."

"I'm trying to. What are we going to do?"

"Find out who it was. Now get hold of yourself. I'll need you."

"Why didn't she say something?"

"I don't know, but you may be able to find out."

"How?"

"Tomorrow morning she'll probably bring up the Sheffield business. If she does, tell her you remember she refused to buy it for Chancellor. She'll have to give you an explanation of some kind."

"If Mother Scarlatti doesn't want to talk, she just won't. I know."

"Then don't press it. But she'll have to say something."

Although it was nearly three o'clock, the lobby had a flow of stragglers from late parties. They were mostly in evening dress, a great many were unbalanced and giggling, all were happily tired.

Canfield went to the desk clerk and spoke in a gentle, folksy tone. "Say, fella, I've got a little problem."

"Yes, sir. May we be of service?"

"Well, it's a bit touchy. . . . I'm traveling with Madame Elizabeth Scarlatti and her daughter. . . ."

"Oh, yes indeed. Mr. . . . Canfield, isn't it?"

"Sure. Well, the old girl's getting on, you know, and the people above her keep pretty late hours."

The clerk, who knew the legend of the Scarlatti wealth, was abject in apology. "I'm dreadfully sorry, Mr. Canfield. I'll go up myself at once. This is most embarrassing."

"Oh, no, please, everything's quiet now."

"Well, I can assure you it won't happen again. They must be loud, indeed. As I'm sure you're aware, the Savoy is the soundest of structures."

"Well, I guess they keep the windows open, but, please, don't say anything. She'd be pretty sore at me if she thought I talked to you about it. . . ."

"I don't understand, sir."

"Just tell me who they are and I'll talk to them myself. You know, friendly-like, over a drink."

The clerk couldn't have been happier with the American's solution. "Well, if you insist, sir. . . . In eight west one is the Viscount and Viscountess Roxbury, charming couple and quite elderly, I believe. Most unusual. However, they could be entertaining."

"Who's above them?"

"Above them, Mr. Canfield? I don't think . . ."

"Just tell me, please."

"Well in nine west one is . . ." The clerk turned the page. "It's not occupied, sir."

"Not occupied? That's unusual for this time of year, isn't it?"

"I should say unavailable, sir. Nine west one has been leased for the month for business conferences."

"You mean no one stays there at night?"

"Oh, they're certainly entitled to but that hasn't been the case."

"Who leased it?"

"The firm is Bertholde et Fils."

CHAPTER 29

The telephone beside James Derek's bed rang harshly, waking him.

"It's Canfield. I need help and it can't wait."

"That may possible be only your judgment. What is it?"

"Scarlatti's suite was broken into."

"What! What does the hotel say?"

"They don't know about it."

"I do think you should tell them."

"It's not that simple. She won't admit it."

"She's your problem. Why call me?"

"I think she's frightened. . . . It was a second-story."

"My dear fellow, her rooms are on the seventh floor! You're too fantastic! Or do the nasty men fly by themselves?"

The American paused just long enough to let the Englishman know he wasn't amused. "They figured she wouldn't open the door, which, in itself, is interesting. Whoever it was, was lowered from one of the rooms above and used a blade. Did you learn anything about Bertholde?"

"One thing at a time." Derek began to take Canfield seriously.

"That's the point. I think they are the same thing. Bertholde's company leased the rooms two floors above."

"I beg your pardon?"

"That's right. For a month. Daily business conferences, no less."

"I think we'd better have a talk."

"The girl knows about it and she's frightened. Can you put a couple of men on?"

"You think it's necessary?"

"Not really. But I'd hate to be wrong."

"Very well. The story will be anticipated jewel theft. Not uniformed, of course. One in the corridor, one in the street."

"I appreciate it. You beginning to wake up?"

"I am, confound you. I'll be with you in a half hour. With everything I've been able to dig up on Bertholde. And I think we'd better get at look at their suite."

Canfield left the phone booth and started back to the hotel. His lack of sleep was beginning to take effect and he wished he was in an American city where such institutions as all-night diners provided coffee. The English, he thought, were wrong in thinking themselves so civilized. No one was civilized without all-night diners.

He entered the opulent lobby and noted that the clock above the desk read quarter to four. He walked toward the ancient elevators.

"Oh, Mr. Canfield, sir!" The clerk rushed up.

"What is it?" Canfield could only think of Janet and his heart stopped.

"Just after you left, sir! Not two minutes after you left! . . . Most unusual this time of night. . . ."

"What the hell are you talking about?"

"This cablegram arrived for you." The clerk handed Canfield an envelope.

"Thank you," said a relieved Canfield as he took the cablegram and entered the open-grill elevator. As he rose from the ground floor he pressed the cable between his thumb and forefinger. It was thick. Benjamin Reynolds had either sent a long abstract lecture or there would be a considerable amount of decoding to be done. He only hoped he could finish it before Derek arrived.

Canfield entered his room, sat down in a chair near a floor lamp, and opened the cable.

No decoding was necessary. It was all written in simple business language and easily understood when applied to the current situation. Canfield separated the pages. There were three.

SORRY TO INFORM YOU RAWLINS THOMAS AND LILLIAN IN AUTOMOBILE ACCIDENT REPEAT ACCIDENT POCONO MOUNTAINS STOP BOTH ARE DEAD STOP KNOW THIS WILL UPSET YOUR DEAR FRIEND E S STOP SUGGEST YOU CARE FOR HER IN HER DISTRESS STOP TO WIMBLEDON BUSINESS STOP WE HAVE SPARED NO EXPENSE AGAIN SPARED NO EXPENSE WITH OUR ENGLISH SUPPLIERS TO OBTAIN MAXIMUM QUOTAS OF MERCHANDISE STOP THEY ARE SYMPATHETIC WITH OUR PROBLEMS OF SCANDINAVIAN EXPORTS STOP THEY ARE PREPARED TO AID YOU IN YOUR NEGOTIATIONS FOR FAIR REDUCTIONS ON MAXIMUM PURCHASES STOP THEY HAVE BEEN TOLD OF OUR COMPETITORS IN SWITZERLAND AGAIN SWITZERLAND AND THE COMPANIES REPEAT COMPANIES INVOLVED STOP THEY KNOW OF THE THREE BRITISH FIRMS IN COMPETITION STOP THEY WILL GIVE YOU ALL ASSISTANCE AND WE EXPECT YOU TO CONCENTRATE AGAIN CONCENTRATE ON OUR INTERESTS IN ENGLAND STOP DO NOT AGAIN DO NOT ATTEMPT TO UNDERBID OUR COMPETITORS IN SWITZERLAND STOP STAY OUT OF IT STOP NOTHING CAN BE ACCOMPLISHED STOP

J. HAMMER WIMBLEDON NEW YORK

Canfield lit a thin cigar and placed the three pages on the floor between his outstretched legs. He peered down at them.

Hammer was Reynolds's code name for messages sent to field accountants when he considered the contents to be of the utmost importance. The word *again* was for positive emphasis. The word *repeat* a simple inversion. It denoted the negative of whatever it referred to..

So the Rawlinses—Canfield had to think for a minute before he remembered that the Rawlinses were Boothroyd's in-laws—had been murdered. Not an accident. And Reynolds feared for Elizabeth Scarlatti's life. Washington had reached an agreement with the British government to gain him unusual cooperation—no expense spared—and in return had told the English of the Swedish securities and the land purchases in Switzerland, which were presumed to be related. However, Reynolds did not specify who the men in Zurich were. Only that they existed and three upstanding Englishmen were on the list. Canfield recalled their names—Masterson of India fame;

Leacock of the British Stock Exchange; and Innes-Bowen, the textile magnate.

The main points Hammer made were to protect Elizabeth and stay out of Switzerland.

There was a light tapping on his door. Canfield gathered the pages together and put them in his pocket. "Who is it?"

"Goldilocks, confound you! I'm looking for a bed to sleep in." The crisp British accent belonged, of course, to James Derek. Canfield opened the door and the Englishman walked in without further greeting. He threw a manila envelope on the bed, placed his bowler on the bureau, and sat down in the nearest stuffed chair.

"I like the hat, James."

"I'm just praying that it may keep me from being arrested. A Londoner prowling around the Savoy at this hour has to have the look of immense respectability."

"You have it, take my word."

"I wouldn't take your word for a damn thing, you insomniac."

"Can I get you a whiskey?"

"God, no! . . . Madame Scarlatti didn't mention a thing to you?"

"Nothing. Less than nothing. She tried to divert my attention. Then she just shut up and locked herself in her bedroom."

"I can't believe it. I thought you two were working together." Derek withdrew a hotel key attached to the usual wooden identification tag. "I had a chat with the hotel bobby."

"Can you trust him?"

"It doesn't matter. It's a master key and he thinks I'm covering a party on the second floor."

"Then I'll get going. Wait for me, please. Grab some sleep."

"Hold on. You're obviously connected with Madame Scarlatti. I should do the reconnoitering."

The field accountant paused. There was merit in what Derek said. He presumed the British operative was far more adept at this kind of sleuthing than he was. On the other hand, he could not be sure of the man's confidence. Neither was he prepared to tell him very much and have the British government making decisions.

"That's brave of you, Derek, but I wouldn't ask it."

"Not brave at all. Numerous explanations under the Alien Order."

"Nevertheless, I'd prefer going myself. Frankly, there's no reason for you to be involved. I called you for help, not to do my work."

"Let's compromise. In my favor."

"Why?"

"It's safer."

"You've won a point."

"I'll go in first while you wait in the corridor by the lift. I'll check the rooms and then signal you to join me."

"How?"

"With as little energy as possible. Perhaps a short whistle."

Canfield heard the short, shrill whistle and walked quickly down the hallway to nine west one.

He closed the door and went to the source of the flashlight. "Everything all right?"

"It's a well-kept hotel suite. Perhaps not so ostentatious as the American variety, but infinitely more homelike."

"That's reassuring."

"More than you know. I really don't like this sort of work."

"I thought you people were famous for it."

This small talk covered the start of their rapid but thorough search of the premises. The floor plan of the rooms was identical to the Scarlatti suite two stories below. However, instead of similar furniture there was a long table in the center of the main room with perhaps a dozen chairs around it.

"Conference table, I presume," said Derek.

"Let's take a look at the window."

"Which one?"

Canfield thought. "Over here." He went toward the french windows directly in line with those of Elizabeth Scarlatti.

"Good point. Here." The Englishman edged Canfield out of the way as he directed the light.

On the wooden sill was a freshly made valley, which had gone through the paint to the wood grain. Where

the wood met the outer stone there was a similar semicircle, which had cut through the layers of dirt and turned that small portion of blackish stone to light gray. The ridge was approximately an inch and a half thick and obviously caused by the friction of a wide rope.

"Whoever it was is a cat," said Canfield.

"Let's look around." The two men walked first through the left bedroom door and found a double bed fully made up. The bureaus were empty and nothing but the usual stationery and corked pens were on the desk. The closets held nothing but hangers and cloth shoe repositories. The bathroom was spotless, the fixtures gleaming. The second bedroom to the right was the same except that the bedspread was mussed. Someone had slept or rested on it.

"Large frame. Probably six feet or over," said the Englishman.

"How can you tell?"

"Imprint of the buttocks. See here, below the half point of the bed."

"I wouldn't have thought of that."

"I have no comment."

"He could have been sitting."

"I said probably."

The field accountant opened the closet door. "Hey, shine the light here."

"There you are."

"Here it is!"

On the closet floor was a sloppily coiled pile of rope. Through the coils at the bottom were three wide straps of leather attached to the rope by metal clasps.

"It's an Alpine rig," said the English agent.

"For mountain climbing?"

"Precisely. Very secure. The professionals won't use it. Unsporting. Used for rescues, mainly."

"God bless 'em. Would it scale a wall at the Savoy?"

"Beautifully. Very quick, very safe. You were correct."

"Let's get out of here," said Canfield.

"I'll take that drink now."

"My pleasure." Canfield rose from the bed with difficulty. "Scotch whiskey and soda, friend?"

"Thanks."

The American walked to a table by the window that served as his bar and poured two large quantities of whiskey into glasses. He handed one to James Derek and half raised his own in a toast.

"You do good work, James."

"You're quite competent yourself. And I've been thinking, you may be right about taking that rig."

"All it can do is cause confusion."

"That's what I mean. It could be helpful. . . . It's such an American device."

"I don't understand."

"Nothing personal. Just that you Americans are so equipment conscious, if you know what I mean. When you shoot birds in Scotland, you carry heavy millimeter cannon with you into the field. . . . When you fish in the Lowlands, you have six-hundred artifices in your tackle box. The American's sense of sportsmanship is equated with his ability to master the sport with his purchases, not his skill."

"If this is hate-the-American hour, you should get a radio program."

"Please, Matthew. I'm trying to tell you that I think you're right. Whoever broke into the Scarlatti suite was an American. We can trace the rig to someone at your embassy. Hasn't that occurred to you?"

"We can do what?"

"Your embassy. If it is someone at your embassy. Someone who knows Bertholde. The men you suspect of having been involved with the securities. . . . Even an Alpine rig has to be manipulated by a trained mountain climber. How many climbers can there be in your embassy? Scotland Yard could check it in a day."

"No. . . . We'll handle it ourselves."

"Waste of time, you know. After all, embassy personnel have dossiers just as Bertholde has. How many are mountain climbers?"

The field accountant turned away from James Derek and refilled his glass. "That puts it in a police category. We don't want that. We'll make the interrogations."

"Just as you say. It shouldn't be difficult. Twenty to thirty people at most. You should track it down quickly."

"We will." Canfield walked to his bed and sat down.

"Tell me," said the Englishman, finishing the last of

his whiskey, "do you have a current list of your embassy personnel? Up-to-date, that is?"

"Of course."

"And you're absolutely sure that members of the staff working there now were part of this securities swindle last year?"

"Yes. I've told you that. At least, the State Department thinks so. I wish you'd stop harping on it."

"I shan't any longer. It's late and I have a great deal of work on my desk which I've neglected." The British operative rose from the chair and went to the bureau where he had put his hat. "Good night, Canfield."

"Oh, you're leaving? . . . Was there anything in the Bertholde file? I'll read it but right now I'm bushed."

James Derek stood by the door looking down at the exhausted field accountant. "One item I'm sure you'll be interested in. . . . Several probably, but one comes to mind."

"What's that?"

"Among the marquis's athletic pursuits is mountain climbing. The imminent sportsman is, in fact, a member of the Matterhorn Club. He's also one of the few hundred who've scaled the north side of the Jungfrau. No mean feat, I gather."

Canfield stood up angrily and shouted at the Englishman. "Why didn't you say so, for Christ's sake?"

"I frankly thought you were more interested in his associations with your embassy. That's really what I was looking for."

The field accountant stared at Derek. "So it was Bertholde. But why? . . . Unless he knew she wouldn't open the door for anyone."

"Perhaps. I really wouldn't know. Enjoy the dossier, Canfield. It's fascinating. . . . However, I don't think you'll find much in it related to the American embassy. . . . But that's not why you wanted it, is it?"

The Britisher let himself out the door, closing it sharply behind him. Canfield stared after him, confused but too tired to care.

CHAPTER 30

The telephone awoke him.

"Matthew?"

"Yes, Jan?" He held the phone and the blood drained from his arm and it hurt.

"I'm in the lobby. I told Mother Scarlatti I had some shopping to do."

The field accountant looked at his watch. It was eleven thirty. He had needed the sleep. "What happened?"

"I've never seen her like this, Matthew. She's frightened."

"That's new. Did she bring up the Sheffield business?"

"No. I had to. She brushed it aside and said the situation had changed."

"Nothing else? Just that?"

"Yes. . . . There was something else. She said she was going to talk with you this afternoon. She says there are problems back in New York that have to be attended to. I think she's going to tell you that she's decided to leave England and go home."

"That's impossible! What did she say exactly?"

"She was vague. Just that Chancellor was a fool and that it was senseless throwing away time on a wild-goose chase."

"She doesn't believe that!"

"I know she doesn't. She wasn't convincing either. But she means it. What are you going to do?"

"Take her by surprise, I hope. Stay out shopping for at least two hours, will you?"

They made plans for a late lunch and said good-bye.

Thirty minutes later the field accountant walked across the Savoy lobby into the grill and ordered breakfast. It was no time to go without food. Without energy.

He carried the Bertholde file with him. He promised himself that he'd read through it, or most of it, at the table. He opened it and placed it to the left of his plate and started at the top of the first page.

Jacques Louis Aumont Bertholde, fourth marquis of Chatellerault.

It was a dossier like so many other dossiers on the very wealthy. Exhaustive details about the family lineage. The positions and titles held by each member for several generations in business, government, and society—all impressive sounding, all meaningless to anyone else. The Bertholde holdings—enormous—mainly, as Elizabeth Scarlatti had said, within British territories. The specific education of the subject in question and his subsequent rise in the world of commerce. His clubs—all very correct. His hobbies—automobiles, horse breeding, dogs—also correct. The sports he excelled in—polo, sailing, the Matterhorn and the Jungfrau—not only correct, but colorful, fitting. And finally the character estimates elicited from his contemporaries. The most interesting part and yet the part many professionals disregarded. The flattering contributions were generally supplied by friends or associates hoping to gain. The unflattering, by enemies or competitors with a wish to undermine.

Canfield withdrew a pencil and made two notations in the dossier.

The first was on page 18, paragraph 5.

No particular reason other than the fact that it seemed out of place—unattractive—and it contained the name of a city Canfield recalled was on Ulster Scarlett's European itinerary.

> The Bertholde family had extensive interests in the Ruhr Valley, which were sold to the German Ministry of Finance several weeks before the assassination at Sarajevo. The Bertholde offices in Stuttgart and Tassing were closed. The sale caused considerable comment in French business circles and the Bertholde family was criticized by the States General and in numerous newspaper editorials. No collusion accused, however, due to explanation that the

German Finance Ministry was paying exorbitant prices. Explanation proved out. Following the war, the Ruhr Valley interests repurchased from the Weimar government. Offices in Stuttgart and Tassing reopened.

The second, on page 23, paragraph 2, referred to one of Bertholde's more recently formed corporations and included the following information.

> The Marquis de Bertholde's partners in the importing firm are Mr. Sydney Masterson and Mr. Harold Leacock. . . .

Masterson and Leacock.

Both were on the Zurich list. Each owned one of the fourteen properties in Switzerland.

No surprise. They tied Bertholde to the Zurich contingent.

No surprise at all. Just comforting—in a professional way—to know that another piece of the puzzle fitted.

As he finished his coffee, an unfamiliar man in a Savoy waistcoat approached the field accountant.

"Front desk, sir. I have two messages."

Canfield was alarmed. He reached for the notes extended to him. "You could have had me paged."

"Both parties requested that we not do that, sir."

"I see. Thank you."

The first message was from Derek. "Imperative you contact me."

The second was from Elizabeth Scarlatti. "Please come to my suite at two thirty. It is most urgent. I cannot see you before then."

Canfield lit one of his thin cigars and settled back into the curved Savoy dining chair. Derek could wait. The Englishman probably had gotten word of Benjamin Reynolds's new arrangement with the British government and was either furious or apologetic. He'd postpone Derek.

Scarlatti, on the other hand, had made a decision. If Janet was right, she was folding up. Forgetting for the moment his own potential loss, he could never explain her reversal to Reynolds, or Glover, or anyone else at Group Twenty, for that matter. He had spent thousands

of dollars on the premise that he had Elizabeth's cooperation.

The field accountant thought about the old woman's visitor, the fourth marquis of Chatellerault, veteran of the Matterhorn and the Jungfrau, Jacques Louis Bertholde. Why had he broken into the Scarlatti suite the way he had? Was it simply the locked door and the knowledge that it would remain locked? Was it to terrify Elizabeth? Or was he searching for something?

Just as he and Derek had searched in the darkness two floors above.

Once confronting her what could Bertholde have said to bend her will? What could he possibly say that would frighten Elizabeth Scarlatti?

He could promise the death of her son if he were still alive. That might do it. . . . But would it? Her son had betrayed her. Betrayed the Scarlatti Industries. Canfield had the unnatural feeling that Elizabeth would rather see her son dead than let him continue that betrayal.

Yet now she was retreating.

Again Canfield felt the inadequacy he had begun to feel aboard the *Calpurnia*. An assignment conceived of as theft had been complicated by extraordinary occurrences, extraordinary people.

He forced his mind back to Elizabeth Scarlatti. He was convinced she could "not see" him before two thirty because she was completing arrangements to return home.

Well, he had a shock in store for her. He knew she had had an early-morning visitor. And he had the Bertholde dossier.

The dossier she could refuse. The Alpine rig would be irresistible.

"I wrote in my note that I couldn't see you before two thirty! Would you please respect my wishes?"

"It can't wait. Let me in quickly!"

She opened the door in disgust, leaving it ajar as she walked back into the center of the room. Canfield closed it, loudly inserting the bolt. He spoke before she turned around to face him. "I've read the dossier. I know now why your visitor didn't have to open the door."

It was as if a pistol had been fired in front of her an-

cient face. The old woman turned and sprang her back forward and arched her neck. Had she been thirty years younger, she would have leapt upon him in fury. She spoke with an intensity he had never heard from her before.

"You unconscionable bastard! You're a liar! A thief! Liar! Liar! I'll have you spend the rest of your life in prison!"

"That's very good. Attack for attack! You've pulled it before but not this time. Derek was with me. We found the rig. An Alpine rig, he called it—which your visitor let down the side of the building."

The old woman lurched toward him, unsteady on her feet.

"For Christ's sake, relax! I'm on your side." He held her thin shoulders.

"You've got to buy him! Oh, my God! You've got to buy him! Get him here!"

"Why? Buy him how? Who?"

"Derek. How long have you known? Mr. Canfield, I ask you in the name of all that's holy, how long have you known?"

"Since about five o'clock this morning."

"Then he's talked to others! Oh, my God, he's talked to others!" She was beside herself, and Canfield was now frightened for her.

"I'm sure he has. But only to his immediate superiors and I gather he's pretty superior himself. What did you expect?"

The old woman tried with what strength she had left to regain control of herself. "You may have caused the murder of my entire family. If you've done that, I'll see you dead!"

"That's pretty strong language! You'd better tell me why!"

"I'll tell you nothing until you get Derek on that telephone."

The field accountant crossed the room to the telephone and gave the operator Derek's number. He talked urgently, quietly, for a few moments and turned to the old woman. "He's going in to a meeting in twenty minutes. He has a full report and they'll expect him to read it."

The old woman walked rapidly toward Canfield. "Give me that phone!"

He handed her both the stand and the receiver. "Mr. Derek! Elizabeth Scarlatti. Whatever this meeting is, do not go to it! I am not in the habit of begging, sir, but I implore you, do not go! Please, please do not speak to a soul about last night! If you do, you will be responsible for the deaths of a number of innocent people. I can say no more now. . . . Yes, yes, whatever you like. . . . I'll see you, of course. In an hour. Thank you. Thank you!"

She replaced the receiver on the hook and slowly, with great relief, put the telephone back on the table. She looked at the field accountant. "Thank God!"

The field accountant watched her as she spoke. He began to walk toward her. "Sweet mother of Jesus! I'm beginning to see. That crazy Alpine thing. The acrobatics at two in the morning. It wasn't just to scare you half to death—it was necessary!"

"What are you talking about?"

"Since early this morning I've thought it was Bertholde! And he'd come to you like that to scare hell out of you! But it didn't make sense. It wouldn't accomplish anything. He could have stopped you in the lobby, in a store, in the dining room. It had to be someone who couldn't do that! Someone who couldn't take a chance anywhere!"

"You're babbling! You're incoherent!"

"Sure, you're willing to call the whole thing off! Why not? You did what you'd set out to do! You found him! You've found your missing son, haven't you?"

"That's a lie!"

"Oh, no, it's not. It's so clear I should have thought of it last night. The whole damn thing was so weird I looked for insane explanations. I thought it was persuasion by terror. It's been used a lot these past few years. But it wasn't that at all! It was our celebrated war hero come back to the land of the living! Ulster Stewart Scarlett! The only one who couldn't risk stopping you outside. The only one who couldn't take a chance that you might not unlatch that bolt!"

"Conjecture! I deny it!"

"Deny all you like! Now I'm giving you a choice! Derek will be here in less than an hour. Either we straighten this out between us before then, or I walk out that door

and cable my office that in my highly regarded professional opinion we've found Ulster Scarlett! And, incidentally, I'm taking your daughter-in-law with me."

The old woman suddenly lowered her voice to nearly a whisper. She walked haltingly toward the field accountant. "If you have any feeling whatsoever for that girl, you'll do as I ask. If you don't, she'll be killed."

It was now the field accountant's turn to raise his voice. It was no longer the shout of the angry debater, it was the roar of an angry man. "Don't you make any pronouncements to me! Don't you or your rotten bastard son make any threats to me! You may buy part of me, but you don't buy all of me! You tell him I'll kill him if he touches that girl!"

Pleading without shame, Elizabeth Scarlatti touched his arm. He withdrew it swiftly from her. "It's not my threat. Please, in the name of God, listen to me. Try to understand. . . . I'm helpless. And I can not be helped!"

The field accountant saw the tears roll down her wrinkled cheeks. Her skin was white and the hollows of her eyes were black with exhaustion. He thought, quite out of context with the moment, that he was looking at a tear-stained corpse. His anger ebbed.

"Nobody has to be helpless. Don't let anybody tell you that."

"You love her, don't you?"

"Yes. And because I do, you don't have to be quite so afraid. I'm a committed public servant. But far more committed to us than the public."

"Your confidence doesn't change the situation."

"You won't know that until you tell me what it is."

"You leave me no choice? No alternative?"

"None."

"Then God have mercy on you. You have an awesome responsibility. You are responsible for our lives."

She told him.

And Matthew Canfield knew exactly what he would do. It was time to confront the Marquis de Bertholde.

CHAPTER 31

Fifty-seven miles southeast of London is the seaside resort of Ramsgate. Near the town, on a field set back from the main road, stood a wooden shack no more than twenty feet by twenty. It had two small windows and in the early-morning mist a dim light could be seen shining through them. About a hundred yards to the north was a larger building—once a barn—five times the size of the shack. It was now a hangar for two small monoplanes. One of them was being wheeled out by three men in gray overalls.

Inside the shack, the man with the shaved head sat at a table drinking black coffee and munching bread. The reddish splotch above his right eye was sore and inflamed and he touched it continually.

He read the message in front of him and looked up at the bearer, a man in a chauffeur's uniform. The contents of the message infuriated him.

"The marquis has gone too far. The instructions from Munich were clear. The Rawlinses were *not* to be killed in the States. They were to be brought to Zurich! They were to be killed in *Zurich!*"

"There's no need for concern. Their deaths, the man and his wife, were engineered above suspicion. The marquis wanted you to know that. It has appeared as an accident."

"To whom? God damn it, to *whom?* Go shag, all of you! Munich doesn't want risks! In *Zurich* there would have been no risk!" Ulster Scarlett rose from the chair and walked to the small window overlooking the field.

His plane was nearly ready. He hoped his fury would subside before takeoff. He disliked flying when he was angry. He made mistakes in the air when he was angry. It had been happening more frequently as the pressures mounted.

God damn Bertholde! Certainly Rawlins had to be killed. In his panic over Cartwright's discovery Rawlins had ordered his son-in-law to kill Elizabeth Scarlatti. A massive error! It's funny, he reflected. He no longer thought of the old woman as his mother. Simply Elizabeth Scarlatti. . . . But to have Rawlins murdered three thousand miles away was insanity! How could they know who was asking questions? And how easily might the order be traced back to Bertholde?

"Regardless of what happened . . ." Labishe started to speak.

"What?" Scarlett turned from the window. He had made up his mind.

"The marquis also wanted you to know that regardless of what happened to Boothroyd, all associations with him are buried with the Rawlinses."

"Not quite, Labishe. Not quite." Scarlett spoke softly but his voice was hard. "The Marquis de Bertholde was ordered . . . commanded by Munich to have the Rawlinses brought to Switzerland. He disobeyed. That was most unfortunate."

"Pardon, monsieur?"

Scarlett reached for his flying jacket, which hung over the back of his chair. Again he spoke quietly, simply. Two words.

"Kill him."

"Monsieur!"

"Kill him! Kill the Marquis de Bertholde and do it today!"

"Monsieur! I do not believe what I hear!"

"Listen to me! I don't give explanations! By the time I reach Munich I want a cable waiting for me telling me that stupid son of a bitch is dead! . . . And, Labishe! Do it so there's no mistake who killed him. You! We can't have any investigations now! . . . Get back here to the field. We'll fly you out of the country."

"Monsieur! I have been with *le marquis* for fifteen years! He has been good to me! . . . I can not . . ."

"You what?"

"Monsieur . . ." The Frenchman sunk to one knee. "Do not ask me. . . ."

"I don't ask. I command! Munich commands!"

The foyer on the third floor of Bertholde et Fils was enormous. In the rear was an impressive set of white Louis XIV doors that obviously led to the sanctum sanctorum of the Marquis de Bertholde. On the right side were six brown leather armchairs in a semicircle—the sort that might be found in the study of a wealthy country squire—with a thick rectangular coffee table placed in front. On the table were neatly stacked piles of chic magazines—chic socially and chic industrially. On the left side of the room was a large white desk trimmed in gold. Behind the desk sat a most attractive brunet with spit curls silhouetted against her forehead. All this Canfield took in with his second impression. It took him several moments to get over his first.

Opening the elevator door, he had been visually overpowered by the color scheme of the walls.

They were magenta red and sweeping from the ceiling moldings were arcs of black velvet.

Good Christ! he said to himself. I'm in a hallway thirty-five hundred miles away!

Seated in the chairs beside one another were two middle-aged gentlemen in Savile Row clothes reading magazines. Standing off to the right was a man in a chauffeur's uniform, his hat off, his hands clasped behind his back.

Canfield approached the desk. The spit-curled secretary greeted him before he could speak. "Mr. Canfield?"

"Yes."

"The marquis would like you to go right in, sir." The girl spoke as she rose from the chair and started toward the large white doors. Canfield saw that the man seated on the left was upset. He uttered a few "Damns!" and went back to his magazine.

"Good afternoon, Mr. Canfield." The fourth marquis of Chatellerault stood behind his large white desk and extended his hand. "We have not met, of course, but an emissary from Elizabeth Scarlatti is a welcome guest. Do sit down."

Bertholde was almost what Canfield expected him to

be, except, perhaps, shorter. He was well-groomed, relatively handsome, very masculine, with a voice resonant enough to fill an opera house. However, in spite of his exuding virility—bringing to mind the Matterhorn and the Jungfrau—there was something artificial, slightly effete about the man. Perhaps the clothing. It was almost too fashionable.

"How do you do?" Canfield smiled, shaking the Frenchman's hand. "Is it Monsieur Bertholde? Or *Monsieur le Marquis?* I'm not sure which I should use."

"I could tell you several unflattering names given me by your countrymen." The marquis laughed. "But please, use the French custom—so scorned by our proper Anglicans. Plain Bertholde will do. Marquises are such an out-of-date custom." The Frenchman smiled ingenuously and waited until Canfield sat in the chair in front of his desk before returning to his seat. Jacques Louis Aumont Bertholde, fourth marquis of Chatellerault, was immensely likable and Canfield recognized the fact.

"I appreciate your interrupting your schedule."

"Schedules are made to be broken. Such a dull existence otherwise, yes?"

"I won't waste time, sir. Elizabeth Scarlatti wants to negotiate."

Jacques Bertholde leaned back in his chair and looked startled. "Negotiate? . . . I'm afraid I don't comprehend, monsieur. . . . Negotiate what?"

"She knows, Bertholde. . . . She knows as much as she needs to know. She wants to meet you."

"I'd be delighted—at any time—to meet Madame Scarlatti but I can't imagine what we have to discuss. Not in a business sense, monsieur, which I presume to be your . . . errand."

"Maybe the key is her son. Ulster Scarlett."

Bertholde leveled his gaze intently on the field accountant. "It is a key for which I have no lock, monsieur. I have not had the pleasure. . . . I know, as most who read newspapers know, that he vanished a number of months ago. But that is all I know."

"And you don't know a thing about Zurich?"

Jacques Bertholde abruptly sat up in his chair. *"Quoi?* Zurich?"

"We know about Zurich."

"Is this a joke?"

"No. Fourteen men in Zurich. Maybe you've got the fifteenth. . . . Elizabeth Scarlatti."

Canfield could hear Bertholde's breathing. "Where did you get this information? What do you refer to?"

"Ulster Scarlett! Why do you think I'm here?"

"I don't believe you! I don't know what you are talking about!" Bertholde got out of his chair.

"For God's sake! She's interested. . . . Not because of him! Because of you! And the others! She's got something to offer, and if I were you, I'd listen to her."

"But you are not me, monsieur! I'm afraid I must ask you to leave. There is no business between Madame Scarlatti and the Bertholde companies."

Canfield did not move. He remained in the chair and spoke quietly. "Then I'd better put it another way. I think you'll have to see her. Talk with her. . . . For your own good. For Zurich's good."

"You threaten me?"

"If you don't, it's my opinion that she'll do something drastic. I don't have to tell you she's a powerful woman. . . . You're linked with her son. . . . And she met with her son last night!"

Bertholde stood motionless. Canfield couldn't decide whether the Frenchman's look of disbelief was over the revelation of Scarlett's visit or his—the field accountant's—knowledge of it.

After a few moments Bertholde replied, "I know nothing of what you speak. It has nothing to do with me."

"Oh, come on! I found the rig! The Alpine rig! I found it at the bottom of a closet in your conference suite at the Savoy!"

"You what?"

"You heard me! Now, let's stop kidding each other!"

"You broke into my firm's private quarters?"

"I did! And that's just the beginning. We've got a list. You might know some of the names on it. . . . Daudet and D'Almeida, fellow countrymen, I think. . . . Olaffsen, Landor, Thyssen, von Schnitzler, Kindorf. . . . And, oh yes! Mr. Masterson and Mr. Leacock! Current partners of yours, I believe! There are several others, but I'm sure you know their names better than I do!"

"Enough! Enough, monsieur!" The Marquis de Bertholde sat down again, slowly, deliberately. He stared at Canfield. "I will clear my office and we will talk further.

People have been waiting. It does not look good. Wait outside. I will dispense with them quickly."

The field accountant got out of the chair as Bertholde picked up the telephone and pressed the button for his secretary.

"Monsieur Canfield will remain. I wish to finish the afternoon's business as rapidly as possible. With each person interrupt me in five minutes if I have not concluded by then. What? Labishe? Very well, send him in. I'll give them to him." The Frenchman reached into his pocket and withdrew a set of keys.

Canfield crossed to the large white double doors. Before his hand touched the brass knob, the door on his left opened swiftly, with great force.

"So sorry, monsieur," the man in uniform said.

"Voici les clefs, Labishe."

"Merci, Monsieur le Marquis! Je regrette. . . . J'ai un billet . . ."

The chauffeur closed the door and Canfield smiled at the secretary.

He wandered over to the semicircle of chairs, and as the two gentlemen looked up, he nodded pleasantly. He sat down on the end chair nearest the entrance to Bertholde's office and picked up the *London Illustrated News*. He noted that the man nearest him was fidgeting, irritable, quite impatient. He was turning the pages of *Punch*, but he was not reading. The other man was engrossed in an article in the *Quarterly Review*.

Suddenly, Canfield was diverted by an insignificant action on the part of the impatient man. The man extended his left hand through his coat sleeve, turned his wrist, and looked at the watch. A perfectly normal occurrence under the circumstances. What startled the field accountant was the sight of the man's cuff link. It was made of cloth and it was square with two stripes running diagonally from corner to corner. The small stripes were deep red and black. It was a replica of the cuff link that had identified the hulking, masked Charles Boothroyd in Elizabeth Scarlatti's stateroom on board the *Calpurnia*. The colors were the same as the paper on the marquis' walls and the black velvet drapes arcing from the ceiling.

The impatient man noticed Canfield's stare. He abruptly withdrew his hand into his jacket and placed his arm at his side.

"I was trying to read the time on your watch. Mine's been running fast."

"Four twenty."

"Thanks."

The impatient gentleman folded his arms and leaned back, looking exasperated. The other man spoke.

"Basil, you'll have a stroke if you don't relax."

"Well and good for you, Arthur! But I'm late for a meeting! I told Jacques it was a hectic day, but he insisted I come over."

"He can be insistent."

"He can be bloody rude, too!"

There followed five minutes of silence except for the rustling of papers at the secretary's desk.

The large left panel of the white double doors opened and the chauffeur emerged. He closed the door, and Canfield noticed that once it was shut, the chauffeur twisted the knob to make sure it was secure. It was a curious motion.

The uniformed man went to the secretary and leaned over her desk, whispering. She reacted to his information with resigned annoyance. He shrugged his shoulders and walked quickly to a door to the right of the elevator. Canfield saw through the slowly closing door the flight of stairs he had presumed to be there.

The secretary placed some papers into a manila folder and looked over at the three men. "I'm sorry, gentlemen, the Marquis de Bertholde can not see anyone further this afternoon. We apologize for any inconvenience."

"Now see here, young lady!" The impatient gentleman was on his feet. "This is preposterous! I've been here for three-quarters of an hour at the explicit request of the Marquis! . . . Request be damned! At his instructions!"

"I'm sorry, sir, I'll convey your displeasure."

"You'll do more than that! You'll convey to Monsieur Bertholde that I am waiting right here until he sees me!" He sat down pompously.

The man named Arthur rose and walked toward the elevator.

"For heaven's sake, man, you'll not improve French manners. People have been trying for centuries. Come along, Basil. We'll stop at the Dorchester and start the evening."

"Can't do it, Arthur. I'm staying right where I am."

"Have it your way. Be in touch."

Canfield remained in his seat next to the impatient Basil. He knew only that he would not leave until Bertholde came out. Basil was his best weapon.

"Ring the marquis again, please, miss," said Basil.

She did so.

A number of times. And there was no response.

The field accountant was alarmed. He rose from his chair and walked to the large double doors and knocked. There was no answer. He tried opening both doors; they were locked.

Basil unfolded his arms and got out of his chair. The spit-curled secretary stood up behind her white desk. She automatically picked up the phone and started pressing the buzzer, finally holding her finger down upon it.

"Unlock the door," commanded the field accountant.

"Oh, I don't know . . ."

"I do! Get me a key!"

The girl started to open the top drawer of her desk and then looked up at the American. "Perhaps we should wait. . . ."

"Damn it! Give me the key!"

"Yes, sir!" She picked up a ring of keys and selecting one, separated it from the others, and gave the key to Canfield. He rapidly unlocked the doors and flung them open.

There in front of them was the Frenchman sprawled across the top of his white desk, blood trickling from his mouth; his tongue was extended and swollen; his eyes bulged from their sockets; his neck was inflated and lacerated just below the chin line. He had been expertly garroted.

The girl kept screaming but did not collapse—a fact that Canfield wasn't sure was fortunate. Basil began to shake and repeated "Oh, my God!" over and over again. The field accountant approached the desk and lifted the dead man's wrist by the coat sleeve. He let it go and the hand fell back.

The girl's screams grew louder and two middle-aged executives burst through the staircase doorway into the outer room. Through the double doors the scene was clear to both men. One ran back to the stairway, shouting at the top of his voice, while the other slowly, fearfully walked into Bertholde's room.

"Le bon Dieu!"

Within a minute, a stream of employees had run down and up the staircase, log-jamming themselves in the doorway. As each group squeezed through, subsequent screams and oaths followed. Within two minutes twenty-five people were shouting instructions to nonexistent subordinates.

Canfield shook the spit-curled secretary in an attempt to stop her screaming. He kept telling her to phone the police, but she could not accept the order. Canfield did not want to make the call himself because it would have required separate concentration. He wished to keep his full attention on everyone in sight, especially Basil, if that was possible.

A tall, distinguished-looking, gray-haired man in a double-breasted pin-stripe suit came rushing through the crowd up to the secretary and Canfield. "Miss Richards! Miss Richards! What in God's name happened?"

"We opened his door and found him like this! That's what happened," shouted the field accountant over the growing din of excited voices.

And then Canfield looked closely at the questioner. Where had he seen him before? Or had he? The man was like so many in the Scarlatti world. Even to the perfectly waxed moustache.

"Have you phoned the police?" asked the gentleman.

Canfield saw Basil pushing his way through the hysterical mob gathered by the office doors. "No, the police haven't been called," yelled the American as he watched Basil making headway through the crowd. "Call them! . . . It might be a good idea to close these doors." He started after Basil as if to push the doors shut. The distinguished-looking man with the waxed moustache held him firmly by the lapel.

"You say you found him?"

"Yes. Let go of me!"

"What's your name, young man?"

"What?"

"I asked you your name!"

"Derek, James Derek! Now, phone the police!"

Canfield took the man's wrist and pressed hard against the vein. The arm withdrew in pain and Canfield ran into the crowd after Basil.

The man in the pin-striped suit winced and turned to

the secretary. "Did you get his name, Miss Richards? I couldn't hear."

The girl was sobbing. "Yes, sir. It was Darren, or Derrick. First name, James."

The man with the waxed moustache looked carefully at the secretary. She had heard. "The police, Miss Richards. Phone the police!"

"Yes, sir, Mr. Poole."

The man named Poole pushed his way through the crowd. He had to get to his office, he had to be by himself. *They* had done it! The men of Zurich had ordered Jacques' death! His dearest friend, his mentor, closer to him than anyone in the world. The man who'd given him everything, made everything possible for him.

The man he'd killed for—willingly.

They'd pay! They'd pay and pay and pay!

He, Poole, had never failed Bertholde in life. He'd not fail him in death either!

But there were questions. So many questions.

This Canfield who'd just lied about his name. The old woman, Elizabeth Scarlatti.

Most of all the misshapen Heinrich Kroeger. The man Poole knew beyond a doubt was Elizabeth Scarlatti's son. He knew because Bertholde had told him.

He wondered if anyone else knew.

On the third-floor landing, which was now completely filled with Bertholde employees in varying stages of hysteria, Canfield could see Basil one floor below pulling himself downward by the railing. Canfield began yelling.

"Get clear! Get clear! The doctor's waiting! I've got to bring him up! Get clear!"

To some degree the ruse worked and he made swifter headway. By the time he reached the first-floor lobby, Basil was no longer in sight. Canfield ran out the front entrance onto the sidewalk. There was Basil about half a block south, limping in the middle of Vauxhall Road, waving, trying to hail a taxi. The knees of his trousers were coated with mud where he had fallen in his haste.

Shouts were still coming from various windows of Bertholde et Fils, drawing dozens of pedestrians to the foot of the company's steps.

Canfield walked against the crowd toward the limping figure.

A taxi stopped and Basil grabbed for the door handle.

As he pulled the door open and climbed in, Canfield reached the side of the cab and prevented the Englishman from pulling the door shut. He moved in alongside Basil, pushing him sideway to make room.

"I say! What are you doing?" Basil was frightened but he did not raise his voice. The driver kept turning his head back and forth from the street in front of him to the gathering crowds receding behind him. Basil did not wish to draw additional attention.

Before Basil could think further, the American grasped the Englishman's right hand and pulled the coat above his wrist. He twisted Basil's arm revealing the red and black cuff link.

"Zurich, Basil!" the field accountant whispered.

"What are you talking about?"

"You damn fool, I'm with you! Or I will be, if they let you live!"

"Oh, my God! Oh, my God!" Basil babbled.

The American released Basil's hand by throwing it downward. He looked straight ahead as if ignoring the Englishman. "You're an idiot. You realize that, don't you?"

"I don't know you, sir! I don't know you!" The Englishman was near collapse.

"Then we'd better change that. I may be all you have left."

"Now see here. I had nothing to do with it! I was in the waiting room with you. I had nothing to do with it!"

"Of course, you didn't. It's pretty damned obvious that it was the chauffeur. But a number of people are going to want to know why you ran. Maybe you were just making sure the job was done."

"That's preposterous!"

"Then why did you run away?"

"I . . . I . . ."

"Let's not talk now. Where can we go where we'll be seen for about ten or fifteen minutes? I don't want it to look as though we dropped out of sight."

"My club . . . I suppose."

"Give him the address!"

CHAPTER 32

"What the devil do you mean I was there?" James Derek shouted into the phone. "I've been here at the Savoy since midafternoon! . . . Yes, of course I am. Since three or thereabouts. . . . No, she's here with me." The Englishman suddenly caught his breath. When he spoke again his words were barely audible, drawn out in disbelief. "Good Lord! . . . How horrible. . . . Yes. Yes, I heard you."

Elizabeth Scarlatti sat across the room on the Victorian couch, absorbed in the Bertholde dossier. At the sound of Derek's voice she looked up at the Englishman. He was staring at her. He spoke again into the phone.

"Yes. He left here roughly at three thirty. With Ferguson, from our office. They were to meet Mrs. Scarlett at Tippin's and he was to proceed from there to Bertholde's. . . . I don't know. His instructions were that she remain in Ferguson's custody until he returned. Ferguson's to call in. . . . I see. For heaven's sake, keep me posted. I'll phone you if there're any developments here."

He replaced the telephone receiver on the hook and remained at the table. "Bertholde's been killed."

"Good God! Where's my daughter?"

"With our man. She's all right. He reported in an hour ago."

"Canfield! Where's Canfield?"

"I wish I knew."

"Is he all right?"

"How can I answer that if I don't know where he is?

We can presume he's functioning. He identified himself as me and left the scene!"

"How did it happen?"

"He was garroted. A wire around his throat."

"Oh!" Elizabeth suddenly, vividly recalled the picture of Matthew Canfield thrusting the cord in her face after Boothroyd's attempt on her life aboard the *Calpurnia*. "If he killed him, he must have had a reason!"

"What?"

"For killing him. He must have had to!"

"That's most interesting."

"What is?"

"That you would think Canfield had to kill him."

"It couldn't have happened otherwise! He's no killer."

"He didn't kill Bertholde either, if it's any comfort to you."

Her relief was visible. "Do they know who did?"

"They believe so. Apparently it was Bertholde's chauffeur."

"That's odd."

"Very. The man's been with him for years."

"Perhaps Canfield's gone after him."

"Not likely. The man left some ten to twelve minutes before they found Bertholde."

James Derek walked from the telephone table toward Elizabeth. It was obvious that he was upset. "In the light of what's just happened, I'd like to ask you a question. But, of course, you needn't answer. . . ."

"What is it?"

"I'd like to know how—or perhaps why—Mr. Canfield received a full clearance from the British Foreign Office."

"I don't know what that is."

"Come, madame. If you don't care to answer, I respect that. But since my name's been used in the killing of an influential man, I believe I'm entitled to something more than another . . . falsehood."

"Another . . . falsehood? That's insulting, Mr. Derek."

"Is it? And are you and Mr. Canfield still setting elaborate traps for embassy personnel who returned to the United States over four months ago?"

"Oh." Elizabeth sat down again on the couch. She was not concerned with the Englishman's complaint; she only wished Canfield was there to answer him. What she

was concerned with was the agent's reference to the Foreign Office. "An unfortunate necessity."

"Most unfortunate. . . . I gather, then, that you don't care to answer."

"On the contrary, I have answered you." Elizabeth looked up at the Britisher. "I wish you'd explain. What is full clearance?"

"Extraordinary cooperation from the highest echelons of our government. And such decisions from the British Foreign Office are generally reserved for major political crises! Not a stocks-and-bonds struggle between squabbling millionaires. . . . Or, if you'll pardon me, a private citizen's personal tragedy."

Elizabeth Scarlatti froze.

What James Derek had just said was abhorrent to the head of Scarlatti. More than anything else she had to operate outside the boundaries of "highest echelon" scrutiny. For the sake of Scarlatti itself. Canfield's minor agency had seemed heaven-sent. Her arrangement with him gave her the facilities of official cooperation without answering to anyone of consequence. If she had wanted it otherwise, she would have commanded any number of men in either or both the legislative and executive branches of the United States government. It would not have been difficult. . . . Now, it seemed, Canfield's relatively unimportant department had grown in significance. Or perhaps her son had involved himself in an undertaking far more ominous than she had conceived.

Was the answer in the Bertholde dossier? Elizabeth wondered. "I gather from your tone that this full clearance is a new development."

"I was informed this morning."

Then it must be in the Bertholde dossier, thought Elizabeth. . . . Of course it was! Even Matthew Canfield had begun to perceive it! Only his perception had been based solely on the recognition of certain words, names. He had marked the pages. Elizabeth picked up the file.

"Following the war, the Ruhr Valley interests repurchased. . . . Offices in Stuttgart and Tassing . . ."

Tassing.

Germany.

An economic crisis.

The Weimar Republic.

A series of economic crises! A major and constant political crisis!

". . . partners in the importing firm are Mr. Sydney Masterson and Mr. Harold Leacock. . . ."

Masterson and Leacock. Zurich!

Tassing!

"Does the city of Tassing mean anything to you?"

"It's not a city. It is an outlying district of Munich. In Bavaria. Why do you ask?"

"My son spent a good deal of time and money there . . . among other places. Does it have any special meaning for you?"

"Munich?"

"I suppose so."

"Hotbed of radicalism. Breeding ground of malcontents."

"Malcontents? . . . Communists?"

"Hardly. They'd shoot a Red on sight. Or a Jew. Call themselves *Schutzstaffel*. Go around clubbing people. Consider themselves a race apart from the rest of the world."

A race apart.

Oh, God!

Elizabeth looked at the dossier in her hands. Slowly she replaced it in the manila envelope and stood up. Without saying a word to the Englishman, she crossed to her bedroom door and let herself in. She closed the door behind her.

James Derek remained in the center of the room. He didn't understand.

Inside her bedroom Elizabeth went to her writing desk where papers were scattered across the top. She sorted them out until she found the Zurich list.

She read each name carefully.

AVERY LANDOR, U.S.A.—*Oil.*
LOUIS GIBSON, U.S.A.—*Oil.*
THOMAS RAWLINS, U.S.A.—*Securities.*
HOWARD THORNTON, U.S.A.—*Industrial Construction.*
SYDNEY MASTERSON, GREAT BRITAIN—*Imports.*
DAVID INNES-BOWEN, GREAT BRITAIN—*Textiles.*
HAROLD LEACOCK, GREAT BRITAIN—*Securities.*
LOUIS FRANÇOIS D'ALMEIDA, FRANCE—*Railroads.*
PIERRE DAUDET, FRANCE—*Ship lines.*
INGMAR MYRDAL, SWEDEN—*Securities.*

CHRISTIAN OLAFFSEN, SWEDEN—*Steel.*
OTTO VON SCHNITZLER, GERMANY—*I. G. Farben.*
FRITZ THYSSEN, GERMANY—*Steel.*
ERICH KINDORF, GERMANY—*Coal.*

One might say that the Zurich list was a cross-section of the most powerful men in the Western hemisphere.

Elizabeth put the list down and reached for a leather-bound notebook in which she kept telephone numbers and addresses. She thumbed to the letter *O.*

Ogilvie and Storm, Ltd., Publishers, Bayswater Road, London.

She would phone Thomas Ogilvie and have him send her whatever information he could unearth on the *Schutzstaffel.*

She knew something about it already. She remembered reading its political name was the National Socialists and they were led by a man named Adolph Hitler.

CHAPTER 33

The man's name was Basil Hawkwood, and Canfield quickly pictured the trademark *hawkwood*—small letter *h*—as it appeared on a variety of leather goods. Hawkwood Leather was one of the largest firms in England, only a short distance behind Mark Cross.

The nervous Basil led Canfield into the huge reading room of his club, Knights. They chose two chairs by the Knightsbridge window, where there were no other members within earshot.

Basil's fear caused him to stutter, and when his words came, the phrases tumbled over one another. He assumed, because he wanted to assume, that the young man facing him would help him.

Canfield sat back in the comfortable chair and listened with incredulity to Hawkwood's story.

The chairman of Hawkwood Leather had been sending shipment after shipment of "damaged" leather goods to a little-known firm in Munich. For over a year the directors of Hawkwood accepted the losses on the basis of the "damaged" classification. Now, however, they had ordered a complete report on the excess malfunctions of the plants. The Hawkwood heir was trapped. There could be no more shipments for an indeterminate time.

He pleaded with Matthew Canfield to understand. He begged the young man to report and confirm his loyalty, but the boots, the belts, the holsters would have to come from someone else.

"Why do you wear the cuff links?" asked Canfield.

"I wore them today to remind Bertholde of my contribution. He presented them to me himself. . . . You're not wearing yours."

"My contribution doesn't call for them."

"Well, damn it, mine does! I haven't stinted in the past and I won't in the future!" Hawkwood leaned forward in his chair. "The present circumstances don't change my feelings! You can report that. God damn Jews! Radicals! Bolsheviks! All over Europe! A conspiracy to destroy every decent principle good Christian men have lived by for centuries! They'll murder us in our beds! Rape our daughters! Pollute the races! I've never doubted it! I'll help again. You have my word! Soon there'll be millions at our disposal!"

Matthew Canfield suddenly felt sick. What in God's name had he done? He got out of the chair and his legs felt weak.

"I'll report what you said, Mr. Hawkwood."

"Good fellow. Knew you'd understand."

"I'm beginning to." He walked rapidly away from the Englishman toward the arch to the outer hallway.

As he stood on the curb under the Knights' canopy waiting for a taxi, Canfield was numb with fear. He was no longer dealing with a world he understood. He was dealing with giants, with concepts, with commitments beyond his comprehension.

CHAPTER 34

Elizabeth had the newspaper and magazine articles spread over the couch. Ogilvie and Storm, publishers, had done an excellent job. There was more material here than Elizabeth or Canfield could digest in a week.

The National Socialist German Workers party emerged as ragtail fanatics. The *Schutzstaffel* were brutes but no one took them seriously. The articles, the photographs, even the short headlines were slanted in such a way as to give a comic-opera effect.

Why Work in the Fatherland
if You Can Dress Up
and Pretend It's Wagner?

Canfield picked up a portion of a Sunday supplement and read the names of the leaders. Adolf Hitler, Erich Ludendorff, Rudolf Hess, Gregor Strasser. They read like a team of vaudeville jugglers. Adolf, Erich, Rudolf, and Gregor. However, toward the end of the article his amusement waned. There were the phrases.

"... conspiracy of Jews and Communists ..."

"... daughters raped by Bolshevik terrorists! ..."

"... Aryan blood soiled by scheming Semites! ..."

"... a plan for a thousand years! ..."

Canfield could see the face of Basil Hawkwood, owner of one of the largest industries in England, whispering with great intensity many of these same words. He thought of the shipments of leather to Munich. The leather without the trademark *hawkwood,* but the leather

that became part of the uniforms in these photographs. He recalled the manipulations of the dead Bertholde, the road in Wales, the mass murders at York.

Elizabeth was sitting at the desk jotting down notes from an article. A picture was beginning to emerge for her. But it was incomplete, as if part of a background was missing. It bothered her, but she'd learned enough.

"It staggers your imagination, doesn't it?" said Elizabeth, rising from her chair.

"What do you make of it?"

"Enough to frighten me. An obscure but volatile political organization is being quietly, slowly financed by a number of the wealthiest men on earth. The men of Zurich. And my son is part of them."

"But why?"

"I'm not sure yet." Elizabeth walked to the window. "There's more to learn. However, one thing is clear. If this band of fanatics make solid progress in Germany—in the Reichstag—the men of Zurich could control unheard-of economic power. It's a long-range concept, I think. It could be brilliant strategy."

"Then I've got to get back to Washington!"

"They may already know or suspect."

"Then we've got to move in!"

"You can't move in!" Elizabeth turned back to Canfield, raising her voice. "No government has the right to interfere with the internal politics of another. No government has that right. There's another way. A far more effective way. But there's an enormous risk and I must consider it." The old woman brought her cupped hands up to her lips and walked away from Canfield.

"What is it? What's the risk?"

Elizabeth, however, did not hear him. She was concentrating deeply. After several minutes she spoke to him from across the room.

"There is an island in a remote lake in Canada. My husband, in a rash moment, bought it years and years ago. There are several dwellings on it, primitive but habitable. . . . If I put at your disposal whatever funds were necessary, could you have this island so guarded that it would be impregnable?"

"I think so."

"That's not good enough. There can be no element of doubt. The lives of my entire family would depend on

total isolation. The funds I mention are, frankly, limitless."

"All right, then. Yes, I could."

"Could you have them taken there in complete secrecy?"

"Yes."

"Could you set all this up within a week?"

"Yes, again."

"Very well. I'll outline what I propose. Believe me when I tell you it is the only way."

"What's your proposal?"

"Put simply, the Scarlatti Industries will economically destroy every investor in Zurich. Force them into financial ruin."

Canfield looked at the prepossessing, confident old woman. For several seconds he said nothing, merely sucked breath through his teeth as if trying to formulate a reply.

"You're a lunatic," he said quietly. "You're one person. They're fourteen . . . no, now thirteen stinking rich fatcats. You're no match for them."

"It's not what one's worth that counts, Mr. Canfield. Not after a point. It's how rapidly one can manipulate his holdings. The time factor is the ultimate weapon in economics, and don't let anyone tell you otherwise. In my case, one judgment prevails."

"What does that mean?"

Elizabeth stood motionless in front of Canfield. Her speech was measured. "If I were to liquidate the entire Scarlatti Industries, there is no one on earth who could stop me."

The field accountant wasn't sure he understood her implication. He looked at her for a few seconds before speaking. "Oh? So?"

"You fool! . . . Outside of the Rothschilds and, perhaps a few Indian maharajas, I doubt there's another person in my position, or in our civilization, who can say that!"

"Why not? Why can't any of the men in Zurich do the same thing?"

The old woman was exasperated. She clasped her hands and brought the clenched fingers to her chin. "For a man whose imagination far exceeds his intelligence,

you astonish me. Or is it only fear that provokes your perception of larger things?"

"No question for a question! I want an answer!"

"It's all related, I assure you. The primary reason why the operation in Zurich can not and will not do as I can do is their own fear. Fear of the laws binding their commitments; fear of the investments, investors; fear of extraordinary decisions; fear of the panic which always results from such decisions. Most important of all, fear of financial ruin."

"And none of that bothers you? Is that what you're saying?"

"No commitments bind Scarlatti. Until I die, there is only one voice. I *am* Scarlatti."

"What about the rest of it? The decisions, the panics, the ruin?"

"As always my decisions will be executed with precision and foresight. Panic will be avoided."

"And so will financial ruin, huh? . . . You are the God damnedest, self-confident old lady!"

"Again you fail to understand. At this juncture I anticipate the collapse of Scarlatti as inevitable should I be called. There will be no quarter given."

Matthew Canfield now understood. "I'll be damned."

"I must have vast sums. Amounts inconceivable to you, which can be allocated by a single command. Money which can purchase massive holdings, inflate or depress entire markets. Once that kind of manipulation has been exercised, I doubt that all the capital on earth could put Scarlatti back together. It would never be trusted again."

"Then you'd be finished."

"Irrevocably."

The old woman moved in front of Canfield. She looked at him but not in the manner to which he was accustomed. She might have been a worried grandmother from the dry plains of Kansas asking the preacher if the Lord would allow the rains to come.

"I have no arguments left. Please allow me my last battle. My final gesture, as it were."

"You're asking an awful lot."

"Not when you think of it. If you return, it'll take you a week to reach Washington. Another week to compile everything we've been through. Days before you reach

those in government who should listen to you, if you can get them to listen to you at all. By my calculations that would be at least three or four weeks. Do you agree?"

Canfield felt foolish standing in front of Elizabeth. For no reason other than to increase the distance between them, he walked to the center of the room. "God damn it, I don't know what I agree with!"

"Give me four weeks. Just four weeks from today. . . . If I fail we'll do as you wish. . . . More than that I'll come to Washington with you. I'll testify, if need be, in front of one of those committees. I'll do whatever you and your associates think necessary. Further, I'll settle our personal account three times above that agreed upon."

"Suppose you fail?"

"What possible difference can it make to anyone but myself? There's little sympathy in this world for fallen millionaires."

"What about your family then? They can't spend the rest of their lives in some remote lake in Canada?"

"That won't be necessary. Regardless of the larger outcome, I'll destroy my son. I shall expose Ulster Scarlett for what he is. I'll sentence him to death at Zurich."

The field accountant fell silent for a moment and looked at Elizabeth. "Have you considered the fact that you might be killed?"

"I have."

"You'd risk that. . . . Sell out Scarlatti Industries. Destroy everything you've built. Is it worth that to you? Do you hate him that much?"

"Yes. As one hates a disease. Magnified because I'm responsible for its flourishing."

Canfield put his glass down, tempted to pour himself another drink. "That's going a little far."

"I didn't say I invented the disease. I said that I'm responsible for spreading it. Not simply because I provided the money but infinitely more important, because I implanted an idea. An idea which has become warped in the process of maturing."

"I don't believe that. You're no saint, but you don't think like that." He pointed toward the papers on the couch.

The old woman's weary eyes closed.

"There's a little of . . . that in each of us. It's all part of the idea. . . . The twisted idea. My husband and I de-

voted years to the building of an industrial empire. Since his death, I've fought in the marketplace—doubling, redoubling, adding, building—always acquiring. . . . It's been a stimulating, all-consuming game. . . . I've played it well. And sometime during all those years, my son learned what many observers failed to learn—that it was never the acquisition of profits or material gain that mattered—they were merely the by-products. It was the acquisition of power. . . . I wanted that power because I sincerely believed that I was equipped for the responsibility. The more convinced I became, it had to follow that others were not equipped. . . . The quest for power becomes a personal crusade, I think. The more success one has, the more personal it becomes. Whether he understood it or not, that's what my son saw happening. . . . There may be similarities of purpose, even of motive. But a great gulf divides us—my son and me."

"I'll give you the four weeks. Jesus Christ only knows why. But you still haven't made it clear to me why you want to risk all this. Throw away everything."

"I've tried to. . . . You're slow at times. If I offend, it's because I think you do understand. You're deliberately asking me to spell out an unpleasant reality." She carried her notes to the table by her bedroom door. As the light had grown dim, she turned on the lamp, causing the fringe on the shade to shimmy. She seemed fascinated by the movement. "I imagine that all of *us*—the Bible calls us the rich and mighty—wish to leave this world somewhat different from the way it was before us. As the years go by, this vague, ill-defined instinct becomes really quite important. How many of us have toyed with the phrases of our own obituaries?" She turned from the lamp and looked at the field accountant. "Considering everything we now know, would you care to speculate on my not-too-distant obituary?"

"No deal. That's another question."

"It's a snap, you know. . . . The wealth is taken for granted. Every agonizing decision, every nerve-racking gamble—they become simple, expected accomplishments. Accomplishments more to be scorned than admired because I'm both a woman and a highly competitive speculator. An unattractive combination. . . . One son lost in the Great War. Another rapidly emerging as a pompous incompetent, sought after for every wrong reason, dis-

carded and laughed at whenever feasible. And now this. A madman leading or at least a part of a growing band of psychopathic malcontents. . . . This is what I bequeath. What Scarlatti bequeaths, Mr. Canfield. . . . Not a very enviable sum, is it?"

"No, it isn't."

"Consequently, I'll stop at nothing to prevent this final madness . . ." She picked up her notes and went into the bedroom. She closed the door behind her, leaving Canfield in the large sitting room by himself. He thought for a moment that the old woman was on the verge of tears.

CHAPTER 35

The monoplane's flight over the channel had been uneventful—the wind calm, the visibility excellent. It was fortunate for Scarlett that such was the case, for the stinging irritation of his unhealed surgery coupled with the pitch of his fury would have made a difficult trip a disastrous one. He was hardly capable of keeping his mind on the compass bearings and when he first saw the Normandy coast, it looked unfamiliar to him. Yet he had made these very same sightings a dozen times.

He was met at the small airfield outside of Lisieux by the Paris contingent, consisting of two Germans and a French Gascon, whose guttural dialect nearly matched that of his associates.

The three Europeans anticipated that the man—they did not know his name—would instruct them to return to Paris. To await further orders.

The man had other intentions, insisting that they all sit uncomfortably together in the front seat while he occupied the entire space in the back. He ordered the car to Vernon, where two got out and were told to make their own way back to Paris. The driver was to remain.

The driver vaguely protested when Scarlett ordered him to proceed west to Montbéliard, a small town near the Swiss border.

"*Mein Herr!* That's a four-hundred-kilometer trip! It will take ten hours or more on these abysmal roads!"

"Then we should be there by dinner time. And be quiet!"

"It might have been simpler for *mein Herr* to refuel and fly . . ."

"I do not fly when I am tired. Relax. I'll find you some 'seafood' in Montbéliard. Vary your diet, Kircher. It excites the palate."

"Jawohl, mein Herr!" Kircher grinned, knowing the man was really a fine *Oberführer.*

Scarlett reflected. The misfits! One day they'd be rid of the misfits.

Montbéliard was not much more complex than an oversized village. The principal livelihood of its citizens was farm produce, much of which was shipped into Switzerland and Germany. Its currency, as in many towns on the border, was a mixture of francs, marks, and Swiss francs.

Scarlett and his driver reached it a little after nine in the evening. However, except for several stops for petrol and a midafternoon lunch, they had pushed forward with no conversation between them. This quiet acted as a sedative to Scarlett's anxiety. He was able to think without anger, although his anger was ever present. The driver had been right when he had pointed out that a flight from Lisieux to Montbéliard would have been simpler and less arduous, but Scarlett could not risk any explosions of temper brought on by exhaustion.

Sometime that day or evening—the time was left open—he was meeting with the Prussian, the all-important man who could deliver what few others could. He had to be up to that meeting, every brain cell working. He couldn't allow recent problems to distort his concentration. The conference with the Prussian was the culmination of months, years of work. From the first macabre meeting with Gregor Strasser to the conversion of his millions to Swiss capital. He, Heinrich Kroeger, possessed the finances so desperately needed by the National Socialists. His importance to the party was now acknowledged.

The problems. Irritating problems! But he'd made his decisions. He'd have Howard Thornton isolated, perhaps killed. The San Franciscan had betrayed them. If the Stockholm manipulation had been uncovered, it had to

e laid at Thornton's feet. They'd used his Swedish contacts and obviously he maneuvered large blocks of securities back into his own hands at the depressed price.

Thornton would be taken care of.

As was the French dandy, Jacques Bertholde.

Thornton and Bertholde! Both misfits! Greedy, stupid misfits!

What had happened to Boothroyd? Obviously killed on the *Calpurnia*. But how? Why? Regardless, he deserved to die! So did his father-in-law. Rawlins' order to kill Elizabeth Scarlatti was stupid! The timing had been insane! Couldn't Rawlins understand that she would have left letters behind, documents? She was far more dangerous dead than alive. At least until she'd been reached—he had reached her, threatened her precious Scarlattis. Now, she could die! Now it wouldn't matter. And with Bertholde gone, Rawlins gone, and Thornton about to be killed, there'd be no one left who knew who he was. No one! He was Heinrich Kroeger, a leader of the new order!

They pulled up at L'Auberge des Moineaux, a small restaurant with a *buvette* and lodgings for the traveler or for those desiring privacy for other reasons. For Scarlett it was the appointed meeting place.

"Take the car down the road and park it," he told Kircher. "I'll be in one of the rooms. Have dinner. I'll call for you later. . . . I haven't forgotten my promise." Kircher grinned.

Ulster Scarlett got out of the car and stretched. He felt better, his skin bothered him less, and the impending conference filled him with a sense of anticipation. This was the kind of work he should always do! Matters of vast consequences. Matters of power.

He waited until the car was far enough down the street to obscure Kircher's rear-mirror view of him. He then walked back, away from the door, to the cobblestone path and turned into it. Misfits were never to be told anything that wasn't essential to their specific usefulness.

He reached an unlighted door and knocked several times.

The door opened and a moderately tall man with thick, wavy black hair and prominent, dark eyebrows stood in the center of the frame as if guarding an entrance, not welcoming a guest. He was dressed in a Bavarian-cut gray

coat and brown knickers. The face was darkly cherubic, the eyes wide and staring. His name was Rudolf Hess.

"Where have you been?" Hess motioned Scarlett to enter and close the door. The room was small; there was a table with chairs around it, a sideboard, and two floor lamps, which gave the room its light. Another man who had been looking out the window, obviously to identify the one outside, nodded to Scarlett. He was a tiny, ugly man with birdlike features, even to the hawknose. He walked with a limp.

"Joseph?" said Scarlett to him. "I didn't expect you here."

Joseph Goebbels looked over at Hess. His knowledge of English was poor. Hess translated Scarlett's words rapidly and Goebbels shrugged his shoulders.

"I asked you where you have been!"

"I had trouble in Lisieux. I couldn't get another plane so I had to drive. It's been a long day so don't aggravate me, please."

"*Ach!* From Lisieux? A long trip. I'll order you some food, but you'll have to be quick. Rheinhart's been waiting since noon."

Scarlett took off his flying jacket and threw it on the sideboard shelf. "How is he?"

Goebbels understood just enough to interrupt. "Rheinhart? . . . Im-pa-tient!" He mispronounced the word, and Scarlett grinned. Goebbels thought to himself that this giant was a horrible-looking creature. The opinion was mutual.

"Never mind the food. Rheinhart's been waiting too long. . . . Where is he?"

"In his room. Number two, down the corridor. He went for a walk this afternoon but he keeps thinking someone will recognize him so he came back in ten minutes. I think he's upset."

"Go get him. . . . And bring back some whiskey." He looked at Goebbels wishing that this unattractive little man would leave. It wasn't good that Goebbels be there while Hess and he talked with the Prussian aristocrat. Goebbels looked like an insignificant Jewish accountant.

But Scarlett knew he could do nothing. Hitler was taken with Goebbels.

Joseph Goebbels seemed to be reading the tall man's thoughts.

"Ich werde dabei sitzen während Sie sprechen." He pulled a chair back to the wall and sat down.

Hess had gone out the corridor door and the two men were in the room alone. Neither spoke.

Four minutes later Hess returned. Following him was an aging, overweight German several inches shorter than Hess, dressed in a black double-breasted suit and a high collar. His face was puffed with excess fat, his white hair cropped short. He stood perfectly erect and in spite of his imposing appearance, Scarlett thought there was something soft about him, not associated with his bulk. He strutted into the room. Hess closed the door and locked it.

"Gentlemen. General Rheinhart." Hess stood at attention.

Goebbels rose from the chair and bowed, clicking his heels.

Rheinhart looked at him unimpressed.

Scarlett noticed Rheinhart's expression. He approached the elderly general and held out his hand.

"Herr General."

Rheinhart faced Scarlett, and although he concealed it well, his reaction to Scarlett's appearance was obvious. The two men shook hands perfunctorily.

"Please sit down, *Herr General.*" Hess was enormously impressed with their company and did not hide the fact. Rheinhart sat in a chair at the end of the table. Scarlett was momentarily upset. He had wanted to sit in that particular chair for it was the commanding position.

Hess asked Rheinhart if he preferred whiskey, gin, or wine. The general waved his hand, refusing.

"Nothing for me, either," added Ulster Scarlett as he sat in the chair to the left of Rheinhart. Hess ignored the tray and also took his seat. Goebbels retreated with his limp to the chair by the wall.

Scarlett spoke. "I apologize for the delay. Unforgivable but, I'm afraid, unavoidable. There was pressing business with our associates in London."

"Your name, please?" Rheinhart interrupted, speaking English with a thick Teutonic accent.

Scarlett looked briefly at Hess before replying. "Kroeger, *Herr General*. Heinrich Kroeger."

Rheinhart did not take his eyes off Scarlett. "I do not

think that is your name, sir. You are not German." His voice was flat.

"My sympathies are German. So much so that Heinrich Kroeger is the name I have chosen to be known by."

Hess interrupted. "Herr Kroeger has been invaluable to us all. Without him we would never have made the progress we have, sir."

"*Amerikaner*. . . . He is the reason we do not speak German?"

"That will be corrected in time," Scarlett said. In fact, he spoke nearly flawless German, but still felt at a disadvantage in the language.

"I am not an American, General. . . ." Scarlett returned Rheinhart's stare and gave no quarter. "I am a citizen of the new order! . . . I have given as much, if not more than anyone else alive or dead to see it come to pass. . . . Please remember that in our conversation."

Rheinhart shrugged. "I'm sure you have your reasons, as I have, for being at this table."

"You may be assured of that." Scarlett relaxed and pulled his chair up.

"Very well, gentlemen, to business. If it is possible, I should like to leave Montbéliard tonight." Rheinhart reached into his jacket pocket and took out a page of folded stationery. "Your party has made certain not inconsequential strides in the Reichstag. After your Munich fiasco, one might even say remarkable progress . . ."

Hess broke in enthusiastically. "We have only begun! From the ignominy of treacherous defeat, Germany will rise! We will be masters of all Europe!"

Rheinhart held the folded paper in his hand and watched Hess. He replied quietly, authoritatively. "To be masters of but Germany itself would be sufficient for us. To be able to defend our country is all we ask."

"That will be the least of your guarantees from us, General." Scarlett's voice rose no higher than Rheinhart's.

"It is the only guarantee we wish. We are not interested in the excesses your Adolf Hitler preaches."

At the mention of Hitler's name, Goebbels sat forward in his chair. He was angered by the fact that he could not comprehend.

"Was gibt's mit Hitler? Was sagen sie über ihn?"

Rheinhart answered Goebbels in his own tongue. "Er ist ein sehr storener geriosse."

"Hitler ist der Weg! Hitler ist die Hoffnung für Deutschland!"

"Vielleicht für Sie."

Ulster Scarlett looked over at Goebbels. The little man's eyes shone with hatred and Scarlett guessed that one day Rheinhart would pay for his words. The general continued as he unfolded the paper.

"The times our nation lives through call for unusual alliances. . . . I have spoken with von Schnitzler and Kindorf. Krupp will not discuss the subject as I'm sure you are aware. . . . German industry is no better off than the army. We are both pawns for the Allied Controls Commission. The Versailles restrictions inflate us one minute, puncture us the next. There is no stability. There is nothing we can count on. We have a common objective, gentlemen. The Versailles treaty."

"It is only one of the objectives. There are others." Scarlett was pleased, but his pleasure was short-lived.

"It is the only objective which has brought me to Montbéliard! As German industry must be allowed to breathe, to export unencumbered, so must the German army be allowed to maintain adequate strength! The limitation of one hundred thousand troops with over sixteen hundred miles of borders to protect is ludicrous! . . . There are promises, always promises—then threats. Nothing to count on. No comprehension. No allowance for necessary growth."

"We were betrayed! We were viciously betrayed in nineteen eighteen and that betrayal continues! Traitors still exist throughout Germany!" Hess wanted more than his life to be counted among the friends of Rheinhart and his officers. Rheinhart understood and was not impressed.

"*Ja.* Ludendorff still holds to that theory. The Meuse-Argonne is not easy for him to live with."

Ulster Scarlett smiled his grotesque smile. "It is for some of us, General Rheinhart."

Rheinhart looked at him. "I will not pursue that with you."

"One day you should. It's why I'm here—in part."

"To repeat, Herr Kroeger. You have your reasons; I have mine. I am not interested in yours but you are forced to be interested in mine." He looked at Hess and

then over at the shadowed figure of Joseph Goebbels by the wall.

"I will be blunt, gentlemen. It is, at best, an ill-kept secret. . . . Across the Polish borders in the lands of the Bolshevik are thousands of frustrated German officers. Men without professions in their own country. They train the Russian field commanders! They discipline the Red peasant army. . . . Why? Some for simple employment. Others justify themselves because a few Russian factories smuggle us cannon, armaments prohibited by the Allied Commission. . . . I do not like this state of affairs, gentlemen. I do not trust the Russians. . . . Weimar is ineffectual. Ebert couldn't face the truth. Hindenburg is worse! He lives in a monarchial past. The politicians must be made to face the Versailles issue! We must be liberated from within!"

Rudolf Hess placed both his hands, palms down, on the table.

"You have the word of Adolf Hitler and those of us in this room that the first item on the political agenda of the National Socialist German Workers party is the unconditional repudiation of the Versailles treaty and its restrictions!"

"I assume that. My concern is whether you are capable of effectively uniting the diverse political camps of the Reichstag. I will not deny that you have appeal. Far more than the others. . . . The question we would like answered, as I'm sure would our equals in commerce, Do you have the staying power? Can you last? Will you last? . . . You were outlawed a few years ago. We can not afford to be allied with a political comet which burns itself out."

Ulster Scarlett rose from his chair and looked down at the aging German general. "What would you say if I told you that we have financial resources surpassing those of any political organization in Europe? Possibly the Western hemisphere."

"I would say that you exaggerate."

"Or if I told you that we possess territory—land—sufficiently large enough to train thousands upon thousands of elite troops beyond the scrutiny of the Versailles inspection teams."

"You would have to prove all this to me."

"I can do just that."

Rheinhart rose and faced Heinrich Kroeger.

"If you speak the truth . . . you will have the support of the imperial German generals."

CHAPTER 36

Janet Saxon Scarlett, eyes still shut, reached under the sheets for the body of her lover. He was not there, so she opened her eyes and raised her head, and the room spun around. Her lids were heavy and her stomach hurt. She was still exhausted, still a bit drunk.

Matthew Canfield sat at the writing desk in his undershorts. His elbows were on the desk, his chin cupped in his hands. He was staring down at a paper in front of him.

Janet watched him, aware that he was oblivious to her. She rolled onto her side so that she could observe him.

He was not an ordinary man, she thought, but on the other hand neither was he particularly outstanding, except that she loved him. What, she wondered, did she find so attractive about him? He was not like the men from her world—even her recently expanded world. Most of the men she knew were quick, polished, overly groomed and only concerned with appearances. But Matthew Canfield could not fit into this world. His quickness was an intuitive alertness not related to the graces. And in other respects there was a degree of awkwardness; what confidence he had was born of considered judgment, not simply born.

Others, too, were far more handsome, although he could be placed in the category of "good-looking" in a rough-hewn way. . . . That was it, she mused; he gave the appearance both in actions and in looks of secure independence, but his private behavior was different. In private he was extraordinarily gentle, almost weak. . . .

She wondered if he was weak. She knew he was deeply upset and she suspected that Elizabeth had given him money to do her bidding. . . . He didn't really know how to be at ease with money. She'd learned that during their two weeks together in New York. He'd obviously been told to spend without worrying about sums in order to establish their relationship—he'd suggested as much—and they'd both laughed because what they were doing on government funds was, in essence, spelling out the truth. . . . She would have been happy to pay the freight herself. She'd paid for others, and none were as dear to her as Matthew Canfield. No one would ever be so dear to her. He didn't belong to her world. He preferred a simpler, less cosmopolitan one, she thought. But Janet Saxon Scarlett knew she would adjust if it meant keeping him.

Perhaps, when it was all over, if it was ever to be all over, they would find a way. There had to be a way for this good, rough, gentle young man who was a better man than any she had ever known before. She loved him very much and she found herself concerned for him. That was remarkable for Janet Saxon Scarlett.

When she had returned the night before at seven o'clock, escorted by Derek's man Ferguson, she found Canfield alone in Elizabeth's sitting room. He'd seemed tense, edgy, even angry, and she didn't know why. He'd made feeble excuses for his temper and finally, without warning, he had ushered her out of the suite and out of the hotel.

They had eaten at a small restaurant in Soho. They both drank heavily, his fear infecting her. Yet he would not tell her what bothered him.

They'd returned to his room with a bottle of whiskey. Alone, in the quiet, they had made love. Janet knew he was a man holding on to some mythical rope, afraid to let go for fear of plunging downward.

As she watched him at the writing desk, she also instinctively knew the truth—the unwanted truth—which she had suspected since that terrible moment more than a day ago when he had said to her, "Janet. I'm afraid we've had a visitor."

That visitor had been her husband.

She raised herself on her elbow. "Matthew?"

"Oh. . . . Morning, friend."

"Matthew . . . are you afraid of him?"

Canfield's stomach muscles grew taut.

She knew.

But, of course, she knew.

"I don't think I will be . . . when I find him."

"That's always the way, isn't it? We're afraid of someone or something we don't know or can't find." Janet's eyes began to ache.

"That's what Elizabeth said."

She sat up, pulling the blanket over her shoulders, and leaned back against the headrest. She felt cold, and the ache in her eyes intensified. "Did she tell you?"

"Finally. . . . She didn't want to. I didn't give her an alternative. . . . She had to."

Janet stared straight ahead, at nothing. "I knew it," she said quietly. "I'm frightened."

"Of course you are. . . . But you don't have to be. He can't touch you."

"Why are you so sure? I don't think you were so sure last night." She was not aware of it, but her hands began to shake.

"No, I wasn't. . . . But only because he existed at all. . . . The unholy specter alive and breathing. . . . No matter how much we expected it, it was a shock. But the sun's up now." He reached for his pencil and made a note on the paper.

Suddenly Janet Scarlett flung herself down across the bed. "Oh, God, God, God!" Her head was buried in the pillow.

At first Canfield did not recognize the appeal in her voice, for she did not scream or shout out and his concentration was on his notes. Her muffled cry was one of agony, not desperation.

"Jan," he began casually. "Janet!" The field accountant threw down his pencil and rushed to the bed. "Janet! . . . Honey, please don't. Don't, please. Janet!" He cradled her in his arms, doing his best to comfort her. And then slowly his attention was drawn to her eyes.

The tears were streaming down her face uncontrollably, yet she did not cry out but only gasped for breath. What disturbed him were her eyes.

Instead of blinking from the flow of tears, they remained wide open, as if she were in a trance. A trance of horror.

He spoke her name over and over again.

"Janet. Janet. Janet. Janet. . . ."

She did not respond. She seemed to sink deeper and deeper into the fear which controlled her. She began to moan, at first quietly, then louder and louder.

"Janet! Stop it! Stop it! Darling, stop it!"

She did not hear him.

Instead she tried to push him away, to disengage herself from him. Her naked body writhed on the bed; her arms lashed out, striking him.

He tightened his grip, afraid for a moment that he might hurt her.

Suddenly she stopped. She threw her head back and spoke in a choked voice he had not heard before.

"God damn you to hell! . . . God damn you to hellll!"

She drew out the word "hell" until it became a scream.

Her legs spread slowly, reluctantly, apart on top of the sheet.

In that same choked, guttural voice she whispered, "You pig! Pig! Pig! Pig!"

Canfield watched her in dread. She was assuming a position of sexual intercourse, steeling herself against the terror which had enveloped her and which would progressively worsen.

"Janet, for God's sake, Jan. . . . Don't! Don't! No one's going to touch you! Please, darling!"

The girl laughed horridly, hysterically.

"You're the *card*, Ulster! You're the God damn jack of . . . jack of . . ." She quickly crossed her legs, one emphatically on top of the other, and brought her hands up to cover her breasts. "Leave me alone, Ulster! Please, dear God, Ulster! Leave me alone! . . . You're going to leave me alone?" She curled herself up like an infant and began to sob.

Canfield reached down to the foot of the bed and pulled the blanket over Janet.

He was afraid.

That she could suddenly, without warning, reduce herself to Scarlett's unwilling whore was frightening.

But it was there, and he had to accept it.

She needed help. Perhaps far more help than he could provide. He gently stroked her hair and lay down beside her.

Her sobs evened off into deep breathing as she closed

her eyes. He hoped she was sleeping but he could not be sure. At any rate, he would let her rest. It would give him the time to figure out a way to tell her everything she had to know.

The next four weeks would be terrible for her.

For the three of them.

But now there was an element which had been absent before, and Canfield was grateful for it. He knew he shouldn't have been, for it was against every professional instinct he had.

It was hate. His own personal hate.

Ulster Stewart Scarlett was no longer the quarry in an international hunt. He was now the man Matthew Canfield intended to kill.

CHAPTER 37

Ulster Scarlett watched the flushed, angry face of Adolf Hitler. He realized that in spite of his fury, Hitler had a capacity for control that was nothing short of miraculous. But then the man himself was a miracle. A historic man-miracle who would take them into the finest world imaginable on earth.

The three of them—Hess, Goebbels, and Kroeger—had driven through the night from Montbéliard to Munich, where Hitler and Ludendorff awaited a report of their meeting with Rheinhart. If the conference had gone well, Ludendorff's plan was to be set in motion. Each faction of the Reichstag possessing any serious following would be alerted that a coalition was imminent. Promises would be made, threats implied. As the Reichstag's sole member of the National Socialist party and its candidate for president the previous year, Ludendorff would be listened to. He was the soldier-thinker. He was slowly regaining the stature he had thrown away in defeat at the Meuse-Argonne.

Simultaneously and in twelve different cities anti-Versailles demonstrations would be staged, where the police had been paid handsomely not to interfere. Hitler was to travel to Oldenburg, in the center of the northwest Prussian territory, where the great military estates were slowly going to seed—massive remembrances of past glories. A huge rally would be mounted and it was planned that Rheinhart himself would make an appearance.

Rheinhart was enough to give credence to the party's military support. It was more than enough; it would be a

momentary climax fitting their current progress. Rheinhart's recognition of Hitler would leave no room for doubt as to where the generals were leaning.

Ludendorff looked upon the act as a political necessity. Hitler looked upon it as a political coup. The Austrian lance corporal was never unmoved by the anticipation of Junker approval. He knew that it was his destiny to have it—demand it!—but nonetheless it filled him with pride, which was why he was furious now.

The ugly little Goebbels had just finished telling Ludendorff and Hitler of Rheinhart's remarks about the Austrian.

In the large rented office overlooking the Sedlingerstrasse, Hitler gripped the arms of his chair and pushed himself up. He stood for a moment glaring at Goebbels, but the thin cripple knew that Hitler's anger was not directed at him, only at his news.

"Fettes Schwein! Wir werden ihn zu seinen Landsort zurück senden! Lass ihm zu seinen Kühen zurück gehen!"

Scarlett was leaning against the wall next to Hess. As usual when the conversations taking place were in German, the willing Hess turned to Ulster and spoke quietly.

"He's very upset. Rheinhart may be an obstacle."

"Why?"

"Goebbels doesn't believe Rheinhart will openly support the movement. He wants all the advantages without getting his tunic dirty!"

"Rheinhart said he would. In Montbéliard he said he would! What's Goebbels talking about?" Scarlett found it necessary to watch himself. He really didn't like Goebbels.

"He's just told them what Rheinhart said about Hitler. Remember?" Hess whispered with his hand cupped in front of his mouth.

Scarlett raised his voice. "They should tell Rheinhart—no Hitler, no marbles! Let him go shag!"

"Was ist los?" Hitler glowered at Hess and Scarlett. "Was sagt er, Hess?"

"Lass Rheinhart zum Teufel gehen!"

Ludendorff laughed out of the corner of his mouth. "Das ist naiv!"

"Tell Rheinhart to do as we say or he's out! No troops! No weapons! No uniforms! No one to pay for it all! I don't pay! No place to train them without the inspection

teams on his back! He'll listen!" Scarlett ignored Hess, who was rapidly translating everything the former said.

Ludendorff broke in on Hess as he finished interpreting.

"Man kann einen Mann wie Rheinhart nicht drohen. Er ist ein einflussreich Preusse!"

Hess turned to Ulster Scarlett. "Herr Ludendorff says that Rheinhart will not be threatened. He is a Junker."

"He's a frightened, overstuffed tin soldier, that's what he is! He's running scared. He's got the Russian shakes! He needs us and he knows it!"

Hess repeated Scarlett's remarks. Ludendorff snapped his fingers in the Heidelberg fashion, as if mocking a ridiculous statement.

"Don't laugh at me! I talked with him, not you! It's my money! Not yours!"

Hess did not need to translate. Ludendorff rose from his chair, as angry as Scarlett.

"Sag dem Amerikaner dass sein Gelt gibt ihm noch lange nicht das Recht uns Befehle zu geben."

Hess hesitated. "Herr Ludendorff does not believe that your financial contributions . . . as welcome as they are . . ."

"You don't have to finish! Tell him to go shag, too! He's acting just the way Rheinhart expects!" Scarlett, who had not moved from his position against the wall, pushed himself away and sprang forward effortlessly to his full height.

For a moment the aging, intellectual Ludendorff was physically afraid. He did not trust the motives of this neurotic American. Ludendorff had often suggested to Hitler and the others that this man who called himself Heinrich Kroeger was a dangerous addition to their working circle. But he had been consistently overruled because Kroeger not only possessed what appeared to be unlimited financial resources, but seemed to be able to enlist the support, or at least the interest, of incredibly influential men.

Still, he did not trust him.

Essentially because Ludendorff was convinced that this Kroeger was stupid.

"May I remind you, Herr Kroeger, that I possess a . . . working knowledge of the English language!"

"Then why don't you use it?"

"I do not feel it is—how is it said?—entirely necessary."

"It is now, damn it!"

Adolf Hitler suddenly clapped his hands twice, signifying an order of silence. It was an irksome gesture to Ludendorff, but his respect for Hitler's talents—which bordered on awe—made him accept such aggravations.

"Halt! Beide!"

Hitler stepped away from the table, turning his back on all of them. He stretched his arms, then clasped his hands behind him. He said nothing for several moments, yet no one interrupted his silence. For it was his silence, and Goebbels, whose love of theatrics was paramount, watched with satisfaction the effect Hitler was having on the others.

Ludendorff, on the other hand, played the game but remained annoyed. The Hitler he knew well was capable of poor judgment. Great vision, perhaps, but often slipshod in decisions of everyday practical realities. It was unfortunate that he also resented debate on such matters. It made it difficult for Rosenberg and himself, who knew they were the true architects of the new order. Ludendorff hoped that this particular instance was not going to be another case when Hitler overrode his sound analysis. Like himself, Rheinhart was a Junker, proud and unbending. He had to be handled artfully. Who could know this better than the former field marshal of the imperial army who was forced to maintain his dignity in the midst of tragic defeat. Ludendorff understood.

Adolf Hitler spoke quietly. "Wir werden wie Herr Kroeger sagt tun."

"Herr Hitler agrees with you, Kroeger!" Hess touched Scarlett's sleeve, delighted. He was forever being condescended to by the arrogant Ludendorff, and this was not a small victory over him. Rheinhart was a prize. If Kroeger was correct, Ludendorff would look foolish.

"Warum? Es ist sehr gefährlich."

Ludendorff had to argue although he knew at once it was no use.

"Sie sind zu Vorsichtig die unruhigen Zieten, Ludendorff. Kroeger hat recht. Aber wir werden einen Schritt weiter gehen."

Rudolf Hess expanded his chest. He looked pointedly at Ludendorff and Goebbels as he nudged Scarlett with his elbow.

"Herr Hitler says that our friend Ludendorff is mis-

ıkenly cautious. He is right. Ludendorff is always cau-
.ous. . . . But Herr Hitler wishes to elaborate on your
ıggestion. . . ."

Adolf Hitler began speaking slowly but firmly, lending finality to each German phrase. As he continued he ·atched with satisfaction the faces of those listening. Vhen he reached the end of his diatribe he spat out the ·ords.

"Da ist Montbéliard!"

For each it was a different evaluation with an underly-
ıg common denominator—the man was a genius.

For Hess, Hitler's conclusion was equated with a star-
ing flash of political insight.

For Goebbels, Hitler had once again demonstrated his bility to capitalize on an opponent's fundamental weak-
ess.

For Ludendorff, the Austrian had taken a mediocre lea, added his own boldness, and emerged with a piece f brilliant strategy.

Heinrich Kroeger—Scarlett—spoke. "What did he say, Iess?"

But it was not Rudolf Hess who answered. It was Erich .udendorff, who did not take his eyes off Adolf Hitler. Herr Hitler has just . . . solidified the military for us, Kroeger. In a brief statement he has won us the reluctant russians."

"What?"

Rudolf Hess turned to Scarlett. "General Rheinhart will e told that unless he does as we demand, the Versailles fficials will be informed that he is secretly negotiating legal procurements. It is the truth. Montbéliard can ot be denied!"

"He is a Junker!" Ludendorff added. "Montbéliard is he key because it is the truth! Rheinhart can not dis-
vow what he has done! Even if he should be tempted, here are too many who know—von Schnitzler, Kindorf. Even Krupp! Rheinhart has broken his word." And then .udendorff laughed harshly. "The holy word of a Jun-
er!"

Hitler smiled briefly and spoke rapidly to Hess, ges-
ıring his head toward Ulster Scarlett.

"*Der Führer* admires and appreciates you, Heinrich," aid Hess. "He asks what of our friends in Zurich?"

"Everything is proceeding on schedule. Several errors

have been corrected. We may lose one of the remaining thirteen. . . . It's no loss; he's a thief."

"Who is that?" Ludendorff exercised his very acceptable working knowledge of English.

"Thornton."

"What of his land?" Ludendorff again.

Scarlett, now Kroeger, looked at the academic Ludendorff, the military intellectual, with the contempt born of money. "I intend to buy it."

"Is that not dangerous?" Hess was watching Ludendorff, who had quietly translated what Scarlett said to Hitler. Both men showed signs of alarm.

"Not at all."

"Perhaps not to you personally, my dashing young friend." Ludendorff's tone was blandly incriminating. "Who knows where your sympathies will lie six months from now?"

"I resent that!"

"You're not a German. This isn't your battle."

"I don't have to be a German! And I don't have to justify myself to you! . . . You want me out? Fine! I'm out! . . . And with me go a dozen of the richest men on earth. . . . Oil! Steel! Industry! Steamship lines!"

Hess no longer tried to be tactful. He looked toward Hitler, throwing his arms up in exasperation.

Hitler did not need to be prompted for he knew exactly what to do. He crossed rapidly to the former general of the imperial German army and struck the old man lightly across the mouth with the back of his hand. It was an insulting action—the very lightness of the blow was akin to disciplining a small child. The two men exchanged words and Scarlett knew the old Ludendorff had been severely, cruelly rebuked.

"My motives seem to be questioned, Herr Kroeger. I was merely—how is it said?—testing you." He lifted his hand to his mouth. The memory of Hitler's insult was difficult for him. He struggled to suppress it.

"I was quite sincere, however, about the Swiss property. Your . . . work with us has been most impressive and undoubtedly noticed by many. Should the purchase be traced through you to the party, it might—how is it said—make useless the whole arrangement."

Ulster Scarlett answered with confident nonchalance

He enjoyed putting the thinkers in their place. "No problems. . . . The transaction will be made in Madrid."

"Madrid?" Joseph Goebbels did not fully understand what Scarlett said, but the city of Madrid had a special connotation for him.

The four Germans looked at each other. None was pleased.

"Why is . . . Madrid so safe?" Hess was concerned that his friend had done something rash.

"Papal attaché. Very Catholic. Very much beyond reproach. Satisfied?"

Hess automatically spoke Scarlett's words in German.

Hitler smiled while Ludendorff snapped his fingers, now in sincere applause.

"How is this accomplished?"

"Very simple. Alfonso's court will be told that the land is being bought with White Russian money. Unless it's done quickly, the capital could be manipulated back into Moscow. The Vatican is sympathetic. So is Rivera. This won't be the first time such an arrangement's been made."

Hess explained to Adolf Hitler as Joseph Goebbels listened intently.

"My congratulations, Herr Kroeger. Be . . . cautious." Ludendorff was impressed.

Suddenly Goebbels began chattering, waving his hands in exaggerated gestures. The Germans all laughed and Scarlett wasn't sure whether the unattractive little fascist was making fun of him or not.

Hess translated. "Herr Goebbels says that if you tell the Vatican you can keep four hungry Communists from having a loaf of bread, the pope will let you repaint the Sistine Chapel!"

Hitler broke in on the laughter. "Was hörst du aus Zürich?"

Ludendorff turned to Scarlett. "You were saying about our friends in Switzerland?"

"On schedule. By the end of next month . . . five weeks say, the buildings will be completed. . . . Here, I'll show you."

Kroeger approached the table, taking a folded map from his jacket pocket. He spread it on the table. "This heavy blue line is the perimeter of the adjacent properties. This

section . . . in the south is Thornton's. We extend west to here, north here to Baden, east to the outskirts of Pfäffikon. Approximately every mile and a quarter is a structure which can house fifty troops—eighteen in all. Nine hundred men. The water lines are down, the foundations are in. Each structure looks like a barn or a granary. You couldn't tell the difference unless you were inside."

"Excellent!" Ludendorff inserted a monocle in his left eye and looked closely at the map. Hess translated for a curious Hitler and a skeptical Goebbels. "This . . . perimeter between the . . . *Keserne* . . . barracks . . . is it fenced?"

"Twelve feet high. Wired by generators in each building for alarms. Patrols will be maintained twenty-four hours a day. Men and dogs. . . . I've paid for everything."

"Excellent. Excellent!"

Scarlett looked over at Hitler. He knew that Ludendorff's approval was never granted easily and in spite of their unpleasant encounter a few moments ago, Scarlett also realized that Hitler valued Ludendorff's opinion, perhaps above all others. It seemed to Scarlett that Hitler's penetrating stare, which was now directed at him, was a look of admiration. Kroeger controlled his own elation and quickly continued.

"The indoctrinations will be concentrated—each lasting four weeks with several days between sessions for transportation and housing. Each contingent has nine hundred men. . . . At the end of one year . . ."

Hess interrupted. "Prachtvoll! At the end of a year ten thousand trained men!"

"Ready to spread throughout the country as military units. Trained for insurgency!" Scarlett was fairly bursting with energy.

"No longer rabble, but the basis of an elite corps! Perhaps the elite corps itself!" Ludendorff himself was catching the younger man's enthusiasm. "Our own private army!"

"That's it! A skilled machine capable of moving fast, hitting hard, and regrouping swiftly and secretly."

As Kroeger spoke, it was Ludendorff who now turned his phrases into the German language for the benefit of Hitler and Goebbels.

But Goebbels was bothered. He spoke quietly, as if

this Kroeger might somehow catch the shaded meaning of his observations. Goebbels was still suspicious. This huge, strange American was too glib, too casual in spite of his fervor. In spite of the power of his money. Adolf Hitler nodded his head in agreement.

Hess spoke. "Quite rightly, Heinrich, Herr Goebbels is concerned. These men in Zurich, their demands are so . . . nebulous."

"Not to them they're not. They're very specific. These men are businessmen. . . . And besides, they're sympathetic."

"Kroeger is correct." Ludendorff looked at Ulster Scarlett, knowing that Hess would use the German tongue for the others. He was thinking as he spoke, not wishing Kroeger to have any time to formulate answers or comments. This Kroeger, although he did not speak their language fluently, understood far more than he let on, Ludendorff believed. "We have gone so far as to sign agreements, have we not? . . . Pacts, if you like, that with the emergence of our power on the political scene in Germany, our friends in Zurich will be given . . . certain priorities. . . . Economic priorities. . . . We are committed, are we not." There was no hint of a question in Ludendorff's last remark.

"That's right."

"What happens, Herr Kroeger, if we do not honor those commitments?"

Ulster Scarlett paused, returning Ludendorff's now questioning gaze. "They'd yell like sons of bitches and try to ruin us."

"How?"

"Any means they could, Ludendorff. And their means are considerable."

"Does that bother you?"

"Only if they succeeded. . . . Thornton's not the only one. They're all thieves. The difference is that the rest of them are smart. They know we're right. We'll win! Everyone likes to do business with the winner! They know what they're doing. They want to work with us!"

"I believe you're convinced."

"You're damn right I am. Between us we'll run things our way. The right way! The way we want to. We'll get rid of the garbage! The Jews, the Reds, the stinking little bourgeois bootlickers!"

Ludendorff watched the confident American closely. He was right, Kroeger was stupid. His description of the lesser breeds was emotional, not based upon the sound principles of racial integrity. Hitler and Goebbels had similar blind spots but theirs was a pyramid logic in spite of themselves—they knew because they saw; they had studied as had Rosenberg and himself. This Kroeger had a child's mentality. He was actually a bigot.

"There is much in what you say. Everyone who thinks will support his own kind. . . . Do business with his own kind." Ludendorff would watch Heinrich Kroeger's actions carefully. Such a high-strung man could do great damage. He was a fever-ridden clown.

But then, their court had need of such a jester. And his money.

As usual, Hitler was right. They dare not lose him now.

"I'm going to Madrid in the morning. I've already sent out the orders concerning Thornton. The whole business shouldn't take any longer than two or three weeks, and then I'll be in Zurich."

Hess told Hitler and Goebbels what Kroeger had said. *Der Führer* barked out a sharp question.

"Where can you be reached in Zurich?" interpreted Ludendorff. "Your schedule, if it proceeds as it has, will require communication with you."

Heinrich Kroeger paused before giving his answer. He knew the question would be asked again. It was always asked whenever he went to Zurich. Yet he was always evasive. He realized that part of his mystique, his charisma within the party, was due to his obscuring the specific individuals or firms with which he did business. In the past he had left a single phone number or a post office box, or perhaps even the name of one of the fourteen men in Zurich with instructions to ask him for a code name.

Never direct and open.

They did not understand that identities, addresses, phone numbers were unimportant. Only the ability to deliver was essential.

Zurich understood.

These Goliaths of the world's great fortunes understood. The international financiers with their tangled labyrinths of manipulations understood perfectly.

He had delivered.

Their agreements with Germany's emerging new order insured markets and controls beyond belief.

And none cared who he was or where he came from.

But now, at this moment, Ulster Stewart Scarlett realized that these titans of the new order needed to be reminded of Heinrich Kroeger's importance.

He would tell them the truth.

He would say the name of the one man in Germany sought by all who drove for power. The one man who refused to talk, refused to be involved, refused to meet with any faction.

The only man in Germany who lived behind a wall of total secrecy. Complete political isolation.

The most feared and revered man in all Europe.

"I'll be with Krupp. Essen will know where to reach us."

CHAPTER 38

Elizabeth Scarlatti sat up in her bed. A card table had been placed at her side, and papers were strewn all over the immediate vicinity—the bed, the table, the entire walking area of the room. Some were in neat piles, others scattered. Some were clipped together and labeled by index cards; others discarded, ready for the trash basket.

It was four o'clock in the afternoon and she had left her room only once. That was to let in Janet and Mathew. She noted that they looked terrible; exhausted, ill, perhaps. She knew what had happened. The pressure had become too much for the government man. He had to break out, get relief. Now that he had, he would be better prepared for her proposal.

Elizabeth gave a final look at the pages she held in her hand.

So this was it! The picture was now clear, the background filled in.

She had said that the men of Zurich might have created an extraordinary strategy. She knew now that they had.

Had it not been so grotesquely evil she might have agreed with her son. She might have been proud of his part in it. Under the circumstances, she could only be terrified.

She wondered if Matthew Canfield would understand. No matter. It was now time for Zurich.

She got up from the bed, taking the pages with her, and went to the door.

Janet was at the desk writing letters. Canfield sat in a chair nervously reading a newspaper. Both were startled when Elizabeth walked into the room.

"Do you have any knowledge of the Versailles treaty?" she asked him. "The restrictions, the reparations payments?"

"As much as the average guy, I guess."

"Are you aware of the Dawes Plan? That wholly imperfect document?"

"I thought it made the reparations livable with."

"Only temporarily. It was grasped at by the politicians who needed temporary solutions. Economically it's a disaster. Nowhere does it give a final figure. If, at any time, a final figure is given, German industry—who pays the bill—might collapse."

"What's your point?"

"Bear with me a minute. I want you to understand. . . . Do you realize who executes the Versailles treaty? Do you know whose voice is strongest in the decisions under the Dawes Plan? Who ultimately controls the internal economics of Germany?"

Canfield put the newspaper down on the floor. "Yes. Some committee."

"The Allied Controls Commission."

"What are you driving at?" Canfield got out of his chair.

"Just what you're beginning to suspect. Three of the Zurich contingent are members of the Allied Controls Commission. The Versailles treaty is being executed by these men. Working together, the men of Zurich can literally manipulate the German economy. Leading industrialists from the major powers to the north, the west, and the southwest. Completed by the most powerful financiers within Germany itself. A wolf pack. They'll make sure that the forces at work in Germany remain on a collision course. When the explosion takes place—as surely it must—they'll be there to pick up the pieces. To complete this . . . master plan, they need only a political base of operation. Believe me when I tell you they've found it. With Adolf Hitler and his Nazis. . . . With my son, Ulster Stewart Scarlett."

"My God!" Canfield spoke quietly, staring at Eliza-

beth. He had not fully understood the details of her recital, but he recognized the implications.

"It's time for Switzerland, Mr. Canfield."

He would ask his questions on the way.

CHAPTER 39

The cablegrams were all in English and except for the names and addresses of the designees, the words were identical. Each was sent to the company or corporation in which the person specified held the highest position. Time zones were respected, each cable was to arrive at its destination at twelve noon, on Monday, and each was to be hand-delivered to the individual addressee upon a signed receipt of acceptance.

Elizabeth Scarlatt wanted those illustrious corporations identified in writing. She wanted those receiving her cables to know that this was, above all, business.

Each cable read as follows:

> THROUGH THE LATE MARQUIS DE BERTHOLDE THE SCARLATTI INDUSTRIES THROUGH THE UNDERSIGNED ALONE HAVE BEEN INFORMED OF YOUR CONSOLIDATION STOP AS THE SINGLE SPOKESMAN FOR SCARLATTI THE UNDERSIGNED BELIEVES THERE EXIST AREAS OF MUTUAL INTEREST STOP THE ASSETS OF SCARLATTI COULD BE AT YOUR DISPOSAL UNDER PROPER CIRCUMSTANCES STOP THE UNDERSIGNED WILL ARRIVE IN ZURICH TWO WEEKS HENCE ON THE EVENING OF NOVEMBER 3 AT THE HOUR OF NINE O'CLOCK STOP THE CONFERENCE WILL TAKE PLACE AT FALKE HAUS
>
> ELIZABETH WYCKHAM SCARLATTI

There were thirteen reactions, all separate, in many different languages, but each with a single ingredient common to all.

Fear.

There was a fourteenth reaction, and it took place in the suite of rooms reserved for Heinrich Kroeger at Madrid's Hotel Emperador. The reaction was fury.

"I won't have it! It can't take place! They're all dead! Dead! Dead! Dead! She was warned! They're dead! Every God damned one of them! Dead. My orders go out tonight! Now!"

Charles Pennington, sent by Ludendorff to act as Kroeger's bodyguard, stood across the room looking out the balcony at the reddish, fan-shaped rays of the Spanish sun.

"Glorious! Simply glorious! . . . Don't be an ass." He didn't like to look at Heinrich Kroeger. In repose that tissued, patched face was bad enough. Angered, it was repulsive. It was now crimson with rage.

"Don't you tell me . . ."

"Oh, stop it!" Pennington saw that Kroeger continued to crush in his fist the telegram from Howard Thornton, which spelled out the Scarlatti conference in Zurich. "What bloody difference does it make to you? To any of us?" Pennington had opened the envelope and read the message because, as he told Kroeger, he had no idea when Kroeger would return from his meeting with the papal attaché. It might have been urgent. What he did not tell Kroeger was that Ludendorff had instructed him to screen all letters, phone calls—whatever—received by this animal. It was a pleasure.

"We don't want anyone else involved. We can't have anyone else! We can't! Zurich will panic! They'll run out on us!"

"They've all got the cables. If Zurich's going to run, you won't stop them now. Besides, this Scarlatti's the cat's whiskers if it's the same one I'm thinking of. She has millions. . . . Damned fortunate for us she wants to come in. I didn't think much of Bertholde—probably less than you did, smelly French Jew—but if he pulled this off, I doff my hat. Anyway, I repeat, what's it to you?"

Heinrich Kroeger glared at the stylish, effeminate Englishman who pulled at his cuffs, making sure they fell just below his jacket sleeve. The red and black cuff links were surrounded by the soft linen of his light blue shirt. Kroeger knew this appearance was deceptive. Like the social Boothroyd, Pennington was a killer who took emo-

tional sustenance from his work. He also was held in high esteem by Hitler, even more so by Joseph Goebbels. Nevertheless, Kroeger had made up his mind. He could not risk it!

"This meeting won't take place! She'll be killed. I'll have her killed."

"Then I'll have to remind you that such a decision must be multilateral. You can not make it yourself. . . . And I don't think you'll find anyone else consenting."

"You're not here to tell me what to do!"

"Oh, but I am. . . . My instructions come from Ludendorff. And, of course, he knows about your message from Thornton. I wired him several hours ago." Pennington casually looked at his wristwatch. "I'm going out for dinner. . . . Frankly, I'd prefer eating alone but if you insist upon joining me, I'll tolerate your company."

"You little prick! I could break your God damn neck!"

Pennington bristled. He knew that Kroeger was unarmed, his revolver lay on the bureau in his bedroom, and the temptation was there. He could kill him, use the telegram as proof, and say that Kroeger had disobeyed. But then there were the Spanish authorities and a hasty retreat. And Kroeger did have a job to do. Strange that it involved Howard Thornton so completely.

"That's possible, of course. But then we could, no doubt, do each other in any number of ways, couldn't we?" Pennington withdrew a thin pistol from his chest holster. "For instance, I might fire a single bullet directly into your mouth right now. . . . But I wouldn't do it in spite of your provocation because the order is larger than either of us. I'd have to answer for my action—no doubt be executed for it. You'll be shot if you take matters into your own hands."

"You don't know this Scarlatti, Pennington. I do!"

How could she have known about Bertholde? What could she have learned from him?

"Of course, you're old friends!" The Englishman put away his pistol and laughed.

How! How? She wouldn't dare challenge him! The only thing she valued was the Scarlatti name, its heritage, its future. She knew beyond a doubt that he would stamp it out! How! Why?

"That woman can't be trusted! She can't be trusted!"

Charles Pennington pulled down his blazer so the

shoulders fell correctly, the jacket cloth concealing the slight bulge of his holster. He walked to the door in calm anticipation of *chorizo.* "Really, Heinrich? . . . Can *any* of us?"

The Englishman closed the door leaving only a faint aroma of Yardley's.

Heinrich Kroeger uncrumpled the telegram in his palm.

Thornton was panic-stricken. Each of the remaining thirteen in Zurich had received identical cablegrams from Elizabeth Scarlatti. But none save Thornton knew who he was.

Kroeger had to move quickly. Pennington hadn't lied. He would be shot if he ordered Elizabeth Scarlatti's death. That did not, however, preclude such an order after Zurich. Indeed, after Zurich it would be mandatory.

But first the Thornton land. He had instructed Thornton for his own safety to let it go. The frightened Thornton had not argued, and the idiot attaché was playing right into his hands. For the glory of Jesus and another blow against atheistic communism.

The money and title would be transferred within a week. Thornton was sending his attorney from San Francisco to conclude the negotiations by signature.

As soon as the land was his, Heinrich Kroeger would issue a warrant for death that no one could deny.

And when that misfit life was snuffed out, Heinrich Kroeger was free. He would be a true light of the new order. None would know that Ulster Scarlett existed.

Except one.

He would confront her at Zurich.

He would kill her at Zurich.

CHAPTER 40

The embassy limousine climbed the small hill to the front of the Georgian house in Fairfax, Virginia. It was the elegant residence of Erich Rheinhart, attaché of the Weimar Republic, nephew of the sole imperial general who had thrown his support to the German radical movement given the name of Nazi, by philosophy, a full-fledged Nazi himself.

The well-tailored man with the waxed moustache got out of the back seat and stepped onto the driveway. He looked up at the ornate facade.

"A lovely home."

"I'm pleased, Poole," said Rheinhart, smiling at the man from Bertholde et Fils.

The two men walked into the house and Erich Rheinhart led his guest to a book-lined study off the living room. He indicated a chair for Poole and went to a cabinet, taking out two glasses and a bottle of whiskey.

"To business. You come three thousand miles at a loathsome time of year for ocean travel. You tell me I am the object of your visit. I'm flattered, of course, but what can . . ."

"Who ordered Bertholde's death?" Poole said harshly.

Erich Rheinhart was astonished. He hunched his padded shoulders, placed his glass on the small table, and extended his hands, palms up. He spoke slowly, in consternation.

"My dear man, why do you think it concerns me? I mean—in all candor—you are either deluded as to my influence or you need a long rest."

"Labishe wouldn't have killed him without having been ordered to do it. Some one of enormous authority had to issue that order."

"Well, to begin with I have no such authority, and secondly I would have no reason. I was fond of that Frenchman."

"You hardly knew him."

Rheinhart laughed. "Very well. . . . All the less reason . . ."

"I didn't say you personally. I'm asking who did and *why*." Poole was betraying his normal calm. He had good reason. This arrogant Prussian held the key if Poole was right, and he wasn't going to let him go until he found out. He would have to press nearer the truth, yet not disclose it.

"Did Bertholde know something the rest of you didn't want him to know?"

"Now, you're preposterous."

"Did he?"

"Jacques Bertholde was our London contact! He enjoyed a unique position in England that approached diplomatic immunity. His influence was felt in a dozen countries among scores of the industrial elite. His death is a great loss to us! How dare you imply that any of us was responsible!"

"I find it interesting that you haven't answered my question." Poole was exasperated. "Did he know something the men in Munich might consider dangerous?"

"If he did, I have no idea what it might be!"

But Poole knew. Perhaps he was the only one who did know. *If he could only be sure.*

"I'd like another drink, please. Forgive my temper." He smiled.

Rheinhart laughed. "You're impossible. Give me your glass. . . . You're satisfied?" The German crossed to the liquor cabinet and poured. "You travel three thousand miles for nothing. It's been a bad trip for you."

Poole shrugged. He was used to the trips—some good, some bad. Bertholde and his odd friend, the misshapen Heinrich Kroeger, had ordered him over barely six months ago. His orders had been simple then. Pick up the girl, find out what she had learned from old Scarlatti. He'd failed. The Canfield man had stopped him. The solicitous lackey, the salesman-cum-escort had prevented

it. But he hadn't failed his other orders. He'd followed the banker named Cartwright. He'd killed him and broken into the railroad station locker and gotten the banker's agreement with Elizabeth Scarlatti.

It was then that he had learned the truth of Heinrich Kroeger's identity. Elizabeth Scarlatti's son had needed an ally and Jacques Bertholde was that ally. And in return for that precious friendship, Ulster Scarlett had ordered Bertholde's death. The fanatic had commanded the death of the man who had made everything possible for him.

He, Poole, would avenge that terrible murder. But before he did, he had to confirm what he suspected was the truth. That neither the Nazi leaders nor the men in Zurich knew who Kroeger was. If that was the case, then Kroeger had murdered Bertholde to keep that identity secret.

The revelation might cost the movement millions. The Munich Nazis would know this, if they knew anything.

Erich Rheinhart stood over Poole. "A penny for your thoughts, my dear fellow? Here, a bourbon. You do not speak to me."

"Oh? . . . Yes, it's been a bad trip, Erich. You were right." Poole bent his neck back, closed his eyes, and rubbed his forehead. Rheinhart returned to his chair.

"You need a rest. . . . Do you know what I think? I think you're right. I think some damned fool *did* issue that order." Poole opened his eyes, startled by Erich Rheinhart's words. "Ja! In my opinion you are correct. And it must stop! . . . Strasser fights Hitler and Ludendorff. Ekhart rambles on like a madman. Attacking! Attacking! Kindorf screams in the Ruhr. Jodl betrays the Black Wehrmacht in Bavaria. Graefe makes a mess in the north. Even my own uncle, the illustrious Wilhelm Rheinhart, makes an idiot of himself. He speaks, and I hear the laughter behind my back in America. I tell you we are split in ten factions. Wolves at each other's throats. We will accomplish nothing! Nothing, if this does not stop!" Erich Rheinhart's anger was undisguised. He didn't care. He rose again from his chair. "What is most asinine is the most obvious! We can lose the men in Zurich. If we can not agree among ourselves, how long do you think they will stay with us? I tell you, these men are not interested in who has next week's power base in

the Reichstag—not for its own sake. They don't care a Deutschemark for the glories of the new Germany. Or the ambitions of any nation. Their wealth puts them above political boundaries. They are with us for one reason alone—their own power. If we give them a single doubt that we are not what we claim to be, that we are not the emerging order of Germany, they will abandon us. They will leave us with nothing! Even the Germans among them!"

Rheinhart's fury abated. He tried to smile but instead drained his glass quickly and crossed to the cabinet.

If Poole could only be sure. "I understand," he said quietly.

"Ja. I think you do. You've worked long and hard with Bertholde. You've accomplished a great deal . . ." He turned around facing Poole. "That's what I mean. Everything that all of us have worked for can be lost by these internal frictions. The achievements of Funke, Bertholde, von Schnitzler, Thyssen, even Kroeger, will be wiped out if we can not come together. We must unite behind one, possibly two, acceptable leaders . . ."

That was it! That was the sign. Poole was now sure. Rheinhart had said the name! Kroeger!

"Maybe, Erich, but who?" Would Rheinhart say the name again? It was not possible, for Kroeger was no German. But could he get Rheinhart to use the name, just the name, once more without the slightest betrayal of concern.

"Strasser, perhaps. He's strong, attractive. Ludendorff naturally has the aura of national fame, but he's too old now. But mark me, Poole, watch this Hitler! Have you read the transcripts of the Munich trial?"

"No. Should I?"

"Yes! He's electric! Positively eloquent! And sound."

"He has a lot of enemies. He's banned from speaking in almost every *grafshaft* in Germany."

"The necessary excesses in a march to power. The bans on him are being removed. We're seeing to that."

Poole now watched Rheinhart carefully as he spoke.

"Hitler's a friend of Kroeger, isn't he?"

"Ach! Wouldn't you be? Kroeger has millions! It is through Kroeger that Hitler gets his automobiles, his chauffeur, the castle at Berchtesgaden, God knows what else. You don't think he buys them with his royalties, do

you? Most amusing. Last year Herr Hitler declared an income which could not possibly purchase two tires for his Mercedes." Rheinhart laughed. "We managed to have the inquiry suspended in Munich, fortunately. Ja, Kroeger is good to Hitler.

Poole was now absolutely sure. The men in Zurich did not know who Heinrich Kroeger was!

"Erich, I must go. Can you have your man drive me back to Washington?"

"But of course, my dear fellow."

Poole opened the door of his room at the Ambassador Hotel. Upon hearing the sound of the key, the man inside stood up, practically at attention.

"Oh, it's you, Bush."

"Cable from London, Mr. Poole. I thought it best that I take the train down rather than using the telephone." He handed Poole the cable.

Poole opened the envelope and extracted the message. He read it.

> DUCHESS HAS LEFT LONDON STOP DESTINATION ASCERTAINED GENEVA STOP RUMORS OF ZURICH CONFERENCE STOP CABLE INSTRUCTIONS PARIS OFFICE

Poole pinched his aristocratic lips together, nearly biting into his own flesh in an attempt to suppress his anger.

"Duchess" was the code name of Elizabeth Scarlatti. So she headed for Geneva. A hundred and ten miles from Zurich. This was no pleasure trip. It was not another leg on her journey of mourning.

Whatever Jacques Bertholde had feared—plot or counterplot—it was happening now. Elizabeth Scarlatti and her son "Heinrich Kroeger" were making their moves. Separately or together, who could know.

Poole made his decision.

"Send the following to the Paris office. 'Eliminate Duchess from the market. Her bid is to be taken off our lists at once. Repeat, eliminate Duchess'."

Poole dismissed the courier and went to the telephone. He had to make reservations immediately. He had to get to Zurich.

There'd be no conference. He'd stop it. He'd kill the mother, expose the killer son! Kroeger's death would follow quickly!

It was the least he could do for Bertholde.

PART THREE

CHAPTER 41

The train clanged over the antiquated bridge spanning the Rhone River, into the Geneva station. Elizabeth Scarlatti sat in her compartment looking first down at the river barges, then at the rising banks and into the large railroad yard. Geneva was clean. There was a scrubbed look about it, which helped to hide the fact that scores of nations and a thousand score of business giants used this neutral city to further intensify conflicting interests. As the train neared the city, she thought that someone like herself belonged in Geneva. Or, perhaps, Geneva belonged to someone like herself.

She eyed the luggage piled on the seat facing her. One suitcase contained the clothes she needed, and three smaller bags were jammed with papers. Papers that contained a thousand conclusions, totaling up to a battery of weapons. The data included figures on the complete worth of every man in the Zurich group. Every resource each possessed. Additional information awaited her in Geneva. But that was a different sort of musketry. It was not unlike the *Domesday Book*. For what awaited her in Geneva was the complete breakdown of the Scarlatti interests. The legally assessed value of every asset controlled by the Scarlatti Industries. What made it deadly was her maneuverability. And opposite each block of wealth was a commitment to purchase. These commitments were spelled out, and they could be executed instantaneously by a cable to her attorneys.

And well they should be.

Each block was followed—not by the usual two col-

umns designating assessed value and sales value—but three columns. This third column was an across-the-board cut, which guaranteed the buyer a minor fortune with each transaction. Each signified a mandate to purchase that could not be refused. It was the highest level of finance, returned through the complexities of banking to the fundamental basis of economic incentive. Profit.

And Elizabeth counted on one last factor. It was the reverse of her instructions but that, too, was calculated.

In her sealed orders sent across the Atlantic was the emphatic stipulation that every contact made—to complete the task teams of administrators had to work twelve-hour shifts night and day—was to be carried out in the utmost secrecy and only with those whose authority extended to great financial commitments. The guaranteed gains absolved all from charges of irresponsibility. Each would emerge a hero to himself or to his economic constituency. But the price was consummate security until the act was done. The rewards matched the price. Millionaires, merchant princes, and bankers in New York, Chicago, Los Angeles, and Palm Beach found themselves quartered in conference rooms with their dignified counterparts from one of New York's most prestigious law firms. The tones were hushed and the looks knowing. Financial killings were being made. Signatures were affixed.

And, of course, it had to happen.

Unbelievable good fortune leads to ebullience, and ebullience is no mate for secrecy.

Two or three began to talk. Then four or five. Then a dozen. But no more than that. . . . The *price*.

Phone calls were made, almost none from offices, nearly all from the quiet seclusion of libraries or dens. Most were made at night under the soft light of desk lamps with good pre-Volstead whiskey an arm's length away.

In the highest economic circles, there was a rumor that something most unusual was happening at Scarlatti.

It was just enough. Elizabeth knew it would be just enough. After all, the *price*. . . . And the rumors reached the men in Zurich.

Matthew Canfield stretched out across the seats in his own compartment, his legs propped over his single suitcase, his feet resting on the cushions facing him. He, too, looked out the window at the approaching city of Geneva. He had just finished one of his thin cigars and the smoke rested in suspended layers above him in the still air of the small room. He contemplated opening a window, but he was too depressed to move.

It had been two weeks to the day since he had granted Elizabeth Scarlatti her reprieve of one month. Fourteen days of chaos made painful by the knowledge of his own uselessness. More than uselessness, more akin to personal futility. He could do nothing, and nothing was expected of him. Elizabeth hadn't wanted him to "work closely" with her. She didn't want anyone to work with her—closely or otherwise. She soloed. She soared alone, a crusty, patrician eagle sweeping the infinite meadows of her own particular heaven.

His most demanding chore was the purchase of office supplies such as reams of paper, pencils, notebooks, and endless boxes of paper clips.

Even the publisher Thomas Ogilvie had refused to see him, obviously so instructed by Elizabeth.

Canfield had been dismissed as he was being dismissed by Elizabeth. Even Janet treated him with a degree of aloofness, always apologizing for her manner but by apologizing, acknowledging it. He began to realize what had happened. He was the whore now. He had sold himself, his favors taken and paid for. They had very little use for him now. They knew he could be had again as one knows a whore can be had.

He understood so much more completely what Janet had felt.

Would it be finished with Janet? Could it ever be finished with her? He told himself no. She told him the same. She asked him to be strong enough for both of them, but was she fooling herself and letting him pay for it?

He began to wonder if he was capable of judgment. He had been idle and the rot inside of him frightened him. What had he done? Could he undo it? He was operating in a world he couldn't come to grips with.

Except Janet. She didn't belong to that world either. She belonged to him. She had to!

The whistle on the train's roof screeched twice and the huge metal-against-metal slabs on the wheels began to grind. The train was entering the Geneva station, and Canfield heard Elizabeth's rapid knocking on the wall between their compartments. The knocking annoyed him. It sounded like an impatient master of the house rapping for a servant.

Which is exactly what it was.

"I can manage this one, you take the other two. Let the redcaps handle the rest."

Dutifully Canfield instructed the porter, gathered up the two bags, and followed Elizabeth off the train.

Because he had to juggle the two suitcases in the small exit area, he was several feet behind Elizabeth as they stepped off the metal stairway and started down the concrete platform to the center of the station. Because of those two suitcases they were alive one minute later.

At first it was only a speck of dark movement in the corner of his eye. Then it was the gasps of several travelers behind him. Then the screams. And then he saw it.

Bearing down from the right was a massive freight dolly with a huge steel slab across the front used to scoop up heavy crates. The metal plate was about four feet off the ground and had the appearance of a giant, ugly blade.

Canfield jumped forward as the rushing monster came directly at them. He threw his right arm around her waist and pushed-pulled her out of the way of the mammoth steel plate. It crashed into the side of the train less than a foot from both their bodies.

Many in the crowd were hysterical. No one could be sure whether anyone had been injured or killed. Porters came running. The shouts and screams echoed throughout the platform.

Elizabeth, breathless, spoke into Canfield's ear. "The suitcases! Do you have the suitcases?"

Canfield found to his amazement that he still held one in his left hand. It was pressed between Elizabeth's back and the train. He had dropped the suitcase in his right hand.

"I've got one. I let the other go."

"Find it!"

"For Christ's sake!"

"Find it, you fool!"

Canfield pushed at the crowd gathering in front of them. He scanned his eyes downward and saw the leather case. It had been run over by the heavy front wheels of the dolly, crushed but still intact. He shouldered his way against a dozen midriffs and reached down. Simultaneously another arm, with a fat, uncommonly large hand thrust itself toward the crumpled piece of leather. The arm was clothed in a tweed jacket. A woman's jacket. Canfield pushed harder and touched the case with his fingers and began pulling it forward. Instinctively, amid the panorama of trousers and overcoats, he grabbed the wrist of the fat hand and looked up.

Bending down, eyes in blind fury, was a jowled face Canfield could never forget. It belonged in that hideous foyer of red and black four thousand miles away. It was Hannah, Janet's housekeeper!

Their eyes met in recognition. The woman's iron-gray head was covered tightly by a dark green Tyrolean fedora, which set off the bulges of facial flesh. Her immense body was crouched, ugly, ominous. With enormous strength she whipped her hand out of Canfield's grasp, pushing him as she did so, so that he fell back into the dolly and the bodies surrounding him. She disappeared rapidly into the crowd toward the station.

Canfield rose, clutching the crushed suitcase under his arm. He looked after her, but she could not be seen. He stood there for a moment, people pressing around him, bewildered.

He worked his way back to Elizabeth.

"Take me out of here. Quickly!"

They started down the platform, Elizabeth holding his left arm with more strength than Canfield thought she possessed. She was actually hurting him. They left the excited crowd behind them.

"It has begun." She looked straight ahead as she spoke.

They reached the interior of the crowded dome. Canfield kept moving his head in every direction, trying to find an irregular break in the human pattern, trying to find a pair of eyes, a still shape, a waiting figure. A fat woman in a Tyrolean hat.

They reached the south entrance on Eisenbahn Platz and found a line of taxis.

Canfield held Elizabeth back from the first cab. She was alarmed. She wanted to keep moving.

"They'll send our luggage."

He didn't reply. Instead he propelled her to the left toward the second car and then, to her mounting concern, signaled the driver of a third vehicle. He pulled the cab door shut and looked at the crushed, expensive Mark Cross suitcase. He pictured Hannah's wrathful, puffed face. If there was ever a female archangel of darkness, she was it. He gave the driver the name of their hotel.

"Il n'y a plus de bagage, monsieur?"

"No. It will follow," answered Elizabeth in English.

The old woman had just gone through a horrifying experience, so he decided not to mention Hannah until they reached the hotel. Let her calm down. And yet he wondered whether it was him or Elizabeth who needed the calm. His hands were still shaking. He looked over at Elizabeth. She continued to stare straight ahead, but she was not seeing anything anyone else would see.

"Are you all right?"

She did not answer him for nearly a minute.

"Mr. Canfield, you have a terrible responsibility facing you."

"I'm not sure what you mean."

She turned and looked at him. Gone was the grandeur, gone the haughty superiority.

"Don't let them kill me, Mr. Canfield. Don't let them kill me now. Make them wait till Zurich. . . . After Zurich they can do anything they wish."

CHAPTER 42

Elizabeth and Canfield spent three days and nights in their rooms at the Hotel D' Accord. Only once had Canfield gone out—and he had spotted two men following him. They did not try to take him, and it occurred to him that they considered him so secondary to the prime target, Elizabeth, that they dared not risk a call out of the Geneva police, reported to be an alarmingly belligerent force, hostile to those who upset the delicate equilibrium of their neutral city. The experience taught him that the moment they appeared together he could expect an attack no less vicious than the one made on them at the Geneva station. He wished he could send word to Ben Reynolds. But he couldn't, and he knew it. He had been ordered to stay out of Switzerland. He had withheld every piece of vital information from his reports. Elizabeth had seen to that. Group Twenty knew next to nothing about the immediate situation and the motives of those involved. If he did send an urgent request for assistance, he would have to explain, at least partially, and that explanation would lead to prompt interference by the embassy. Reynolds wouldn't wait upon legalities. He would have Canfield seized by force and held incommunicado.

The results were predictable. With him finished, Elizabeth wouldn't have a chance of reaching Zurich. She'd be killed by Scarlett in Geneva. And the secondary target would then be Janet back in London. She couldn't stay at the Savoy indefinitely. Derek couldn't continue his security precautions ad infinitum. She would eventually

leave, or Derek would become exasperated and careless. She, too, would be killed. Finally, there was Chancellor Drew, his wife, and seven children. There would be a hundred valid reasons for all to leave the remote Canadian refuge. They'd be massacred. Ulster Stewart Scarlett would win.

At the thought of Scarlett, Canfield was able to summon up what anger was left in him. It was almost enough to match his fear and depression. Almost.

He walked into the sitting room Elizabeth had converted into an office. She was writing on the center table.

"Do you remember the housekeeper at your son's house?" he said.

Elizabeth put down her pencil. It was momentary courtesy, not concern. "I've seen her on the few occasions I've visited, yes."

"Where did she come from?"

"As I recall, Ulster brought her back from Europe. She ran a hunting lodge in . . . southern Germany." Elizabeth looked up at the field accountant. "Why do you ask?"

Years later Canfield would reflect that it was because he had been trying to find the words to tell Elizabeth Scarlatti that Hannah was in Geneva that caused him to do what he did. To physically move from one place to another at that particular instant. To cross between Elizabeth and the window. He would carry the remembrance of it as long as he lived.

There was a shattering of glass and a sharp, terrible stinging pain in his left shoulder. Actually the pain seemed to come first. The jolt was so powerful that it spun Canfield around, throwing him across the table, scattering papers, and crashing the lamp to the floor. A second and third shot followed, splintering the thick wood around his body and Canfield, in panic, lurched to one side, toppling Elizabeth off her chair onto the floor. The pain in his shoulder was overpowering, and a huge splotch of blood spread across his shirt.

It was all over in five seconds.

Elizabeth was crouched against the paneling of the wall. She was at once frightened and grateful. She looked at the field accountant lying in front of her trying to hold his shoulder. She was convinced he had thrown himself over her to protect her from the bullets. He never explained otherwise.

"How badly are you hurt?"

"I'm not sure. It hurts like hell. . . . I've never been hit before. Never shot before. . . ." He was finding it difficult to speak. Elizabeth started to move toward him. "God damn it! Stay where you are!" He looked up and saw that he was out of the sight line of the window. They both were. "Look, can you reach the phone? Go on the floor. Stay down! . . . I think I need a doctor. . . . A doctor." He passed out.

Thirty minutes later Canfield awoke. He was on his own bed with the whole upper left part of his chest encased in an uncomfortable bandage. He could barely move. He could see, blurredly to be sure, a number of figures around him. As his eyes came into focus, he saw Elizabeth at the foot of the bed looking down at him. To her right was a man in an overcoat, behind him a uniformed policeman. Bending over him on his left was a balding, stern-faced man in his shirt sleeves, obviously a doctor. He spoke to Canfield. His accent was French.

"Move your left hand, please."

Canfield obeyed.

"Your feet, please."

Again he complied.

"Can you roll your head?"

"What? Where?"

"Move your head back and forth. Don't try to be amusing." Elizabeth was possibly the most relieved person within twenty miles of the Hotel D' Accord. She even smiled.

Canfield swung his head back and forth.

"You are not seriously hurt." The doctor stood erect.

"You sound disappointed," answered the field accountant.

"May I ask him questions, *Herr Doktor?*" said the Swiss next to Elizabeth.

The doctor replied in his broken English. "Yes. The bullet passed him through."

What one had to do with the other perplexed Canfield, but he had no time to think about it. Elizabeth spoke.

"I've explained to this gentleman that you're merely accompanying me while I conduct business affairs. We're totally bewildered by what's happened."

"I would appreciate this man answering for himself, madame."

"Damned if I can tell you anything, mister. . . ." And then Canfield stopped. There was no point in being a fool. He was going to need help. "On second thought, maybe I can." He looked toward the doctor, who was putting on his suit coat. The Swiss understood.

"Very well. We shall wait."

"Mr. Canfield, what can you possibly add?"

"Passage to Zurich."

Elizabeth understood.

The doctor left and Canfield found that he could lie on his right side. The Swiss *Geheimpolizist* walked around to be nearer.

"Sit down, sir," said Canfield as the man drew up a chair. "What I'm going to tell you will seem foolish to someone like you and me who have to work for our livings." The field accountant winked. "It's a private matter—no harm to anyone outside the family, family business, but you can help. . . . Does your man speak English?"

The Swiss looked briefly at the uniformed policeman.

"No, monsieur."

"Good. As I say, you can help. Both the clean record of your fair city . . . and yourself."

The Swiss *Geheimpolizist* drew up his chair closer.

He was delighted.

The afternoon arrived. They had timed the train schedules to the quarter hour and had telephoned ahead for a limousine and chauffeur. Their train tickets had been purchased by the hotel, clearly spelling out the name of Scarlatti for preferred treatment and the finest accommodations available for the short trip to Zurich. Their luggage was sent downstairs an hour beforehand and deposited by the front entrance. The tags were legibly marked, the train compartments specified, and even the limousine service noted for the Zurich porters. Canfield figured that the lowest IQ in Europe could know the immediate itinerary of Elizabeth Scarlatti if he wished to.

The ride from the hotel to the station took about twelve minutes. One-half hour before the train for Zurich departed an old woman, with a heavy black veil, ac-

companied by a youngish man in a brand-new fedora, his left arm in a white sling, got into a limousine. They were escorted by two members of the Geneva police, who kept their hands on their holstered pistols.

No incident occurred, and the two travelers rushed into the station and immediately onto the train.

As the train left the Geneva platform, another elderly woman accompanied by a youngish man, this one in a Brooks Brothers hat, and also with his left arm in a sling but hidden by a topcoat, left the service entrance of the Hotel D'Accord. The elderly woman was dressed in the uniform of a Red Cross colonel, female division, complete with a garrison cap. The man driving was also a member of the International Red Cross. The two people rushed into the back seat, and the young man closed the door. He immediately took the cellophane off a thin cigar and said to the driver, "Let's go."

As the car sped out the narrow driveway, the old woman spoke disparagingly. "Really, Mr. Canfield! Must you smoke one of those awful things?"

"Gevena rules, lady. Prisoners are allowed packages from home."

CHAPTER 43

Twenty-seven miles from Zurich is the town of Menziken. The Geneva train stopped for precisely four minutes, the time allotted for the loading of the railway post, and then proceeded on its inevitable, exact, fated ride up the tracks to its destination.

Five minutes out of Menziken, compartments D4 and D5 on Pullman car six were broken into simultaneously by two men in masks. Because neither compartment contained any passengers, and both toilet doors were locked, the masked men fired their pistols into the thin panels of the commodes, expecting to find the bodies when they opened the doors.

They found no one. Nothing.

As if predetermined, both masked men ran out into the narrow corridor and nearly collided with one another.

"Halt! Stop!" The shouts came from both ends of the Pullman corridor. The men calling were dressed in the uniforms of the Geneva police.

The two masked men did not stop. Instead they fired wildly in both directions.

Their shots were returned and the two men fell.

They were searched; no identifications were found. The Geneva police were pleased about that. They did not wish to get involved.

One of the fallen men, however, had a tattoo on his forearm: an insignia, recently given the term of swastika. And a third man, unseen, unmasked, not fallen, was first off the train at Zurich, and hurried to a telephone.

"Here we are at Aarau. You can rest up here for a while. Your clothes are in a flat on the second floor. I believe your car is parked in the rear and the keys are under the left seat." Their driver was English and Canfield liked that. The driver hadn't spoken a word since Geneva. The field accountant withdrew a large bill from his pocket and offered it to the man.

"Hardly necessary, sir," said the driver as he waved the bill aside without turning.

They waited until eight fifteen. It was a dark night with only half a moon shrouded by low clouds. Canfield had tried the car, driving it up and down a country road to get the feel of it, to get used to driving with only his right hand. The gas gauge registered *rempli* and they were ready.

More precisely, Elizabeth Scarlatti was ready.

She was like a gladiator, prepared to bleed or let blood. She was cold but intense. She was a killer.

And her weapons were paper—infinitely more dangerous than maces or triforks to her adversaries. She was also, as a fine gladiator must be, supremely confident.

It was more than her last *grande geste*, it was the culmination of a lifetime. Hers and Giovanni's. She would not fail him.

Canfield had studied and restudied the map; he knew the roads he had to take to reach Falke Haus. They would skirt the center of Zurich and head toward Kloten, turning right at the Schlieren fork and follow the central road toward Bulach. One mile to the left on the Winterthurstrasse would be the gates of Falke Haus.

He had pushed the car up to eighty-five miles an hour, and he had stopped at sixty within the space of fifty feet without causing a dislocation of the seats. The Geneva *Geheimpolizist* had done his job well. But then he was well paid. Damn near two years' wages at the going Swiss rate of Civil Service. And the car was licensed with the numbers no one would stop—for any reason—the Zurich

police. How he had done it, Canfield didn't ask. Elizabeth suggested that it might have been the money.

"Is that all?" asked Canfield as he led Elizabeth Scarlatti toward the car. He referred to her single briefcase.

"It's enough," said the old woman as she followed him down the path.

"You had a couple of thousand pages, a hundred thousand figures!"

"They're meaningless now." Elizabeth held the briefcase on her lap as Canfield shut the car door.

"Suppose they ask you questions?" The field accountant inserted the key in the ignition.

"No doubt they will. And if they do, I'll answer." She didn't wish to talk.

They drove for twenty minutes and the roads were coming out right. Canfield was pleased with himself. He was a satisfied navigator. Suddenly Elizabeth spoke.

"There is one thing I haven't told you, nor have you seen fit to bring it up. It's only fair that I mention it now."

"What?"

"It's conceivable that neither of us will emerge from this conference alive. Have you considered that?"

Canfield had, of course, considered it. He had assumed the risk, if that was the justifiable word, since the Boothroyd incident. It had escalated to pronounced danger when he realized that Janet was possibly his for life. He became committed when he knew what her husband had done to her.

With the bullet through his shoulder, two inches from death, Matthew Canfield in his own way had become a gladiator in much the same manner as Elizabeth. His anger was paramount now.

"You worry about your problems, I'll worry about mine, okay?"

"Okay. . . . May I say that you've become quite dear to me. . . . Oh, stop that little-boy look! Save it for the ladies! I'm hardly one of them! Drive on!"

On Winterthurstrasse, three-tenths of a mile from Falke Haus there is a stretch of straight road paralleled on

both sides by towering pine trees. Matthew Canfield pushed the accelerator down and drove the automobile as fast as it would go. It was five minutes to nine and he was determined that his passenger meet her appointment on time.

Suddenly in the far-off illumination of the head lamps, a man was signaling. He waved his hands, crisscrossing above his head, standing in the middle of the road. He was violently making the universal sign, stop—emergency. He did not move from the middle of the road in spite of Canfield's speed.

"Hold on!" Canfield rushed on, oblivious to the human being in his path.

As he did so, there were bursts of gunfire from both sides of the road. "Get down!" shouted Canfield. He continued to push the gas pedal, ducking as he did so, bobbing his head, watching the straight road as best he could. There was a piercing scream—pitched in a death note—from the far side of the road. One of the ambushers had been caught in the crossfire.

They passed the area, pieces of glass and metal scattered all over the seats.

"You okay?" Canfield had no time for sympathy.

"Yes. I'm all right. How much longer?"

"Not much. If we can make it. They may have gotten a tire."

"Even if they did, we can still drive?"

"Don't you worry! I'm not about to stop and ask for a jack!"

The gates of Falke Haus appeared and Canfield turned sharply into the road. It was a descending grade leading gently into a huge circle in front of an enormous flagstone porch with statuary placed every several feet. The front entrance, a large wooden door, was situated twenty feet beyond the center steps. Canfield could not get near it.

For there were at least a dozen long, black limousines lined up around the circle. Chauffeurs stood near them, idly chatting.

Canfield checked his revolver, placed it in his right-hand pocket, and ordered Elizabeth out of the car. He insisted that she slide across the seat and emerge from his side of the automobile.

He walked slightly behind her, nodding to the chauffeurs.

It was one minute after nine when a servant, formally dressed, opened the large wooden door.

They entered the great hall, a massive tabernacle of architectural indulgence. A second servant, also formally attired, gestured them toward another door. He opened it.

Inside was the longest table Matthew Canfield thought possible to build. It must have been fifty feet from end to end. And a good six to seven feet wide.

Seated around the massive table were fifteen or twenty men. All ages, from forty to seventy. All dressed in expensive suits. All looking toward Elizabeth Scarlatti. At the head of the table, half a room away, was an empty chair. It cried out to be filled, and Canfield wondered for a moment whether Elizabeth was to fill it. Then he realized that was not so. Her chair was at the foot of the table closest to them.

Who was to fill the empty chair?

No matter. There was no chair for him. He would stay by the wall and watch.

Elizabeth approached the table.

"Good evening, gentlemen. A number of us have met before. The rest of you I know by reputation, I can assure you."

The entire complement around the table rose as one body.

The man to the left of Elizabeth's chair circled and held it for her.

She sat down, and the men returned to their seats.

"I thank you. . . . But there seems to be one of us missing." Elizabeth stared at the chair fifty feet away directly in front of her eyes.

At that moment a door at the far end of the room opened and a tall man strutted in. He was dressed in the crisp, cold uniform of the German revolutionary. The dark brown shirt, the shining black belt across his chest and around his waist, the starched tan jodhpurs above the thick, heavy boots that came just below his knees.

The man's head was shaven, his face a distorted replica of itself.

"The chair is now taken. Does that satisfy you?"

"Not entirely. . . . Since I know, through one means or another, every person of consequence at this table, I should like to know who you are, sir."

"Kroeger. Heinrich Kroeger! Anything else, Madame Scarlatti?"

"Not a thing. Not a single thing . . . Herr Kroeger."

CHAPTER 44

"Against my wishes and my better judgment, Madame Scarlatti, my associates are determined to hear what you have to say." The grotesque shaven-headed Heinrich Kroeger spoke. "My position has been made clear to you. I trust your memory serves you well about it."

There were whispers around the table. Looks were exchanged. None of the men were prepared for the news that Heinrich Kroeger had had prior contact with Elizabeth Scarlatti.

"My memory serves me very well. Your associates represent an aggregate of much wisdom and several centuries of experience. I suspect far in excess of your own on both counts—collectively and individually."

Most of the men simply lowered their eyes, some pressing their lips in slight smiles. Elizabeth slowly looked at each face around the table.

"We have an interesting board here, I see. Well represented. Well diversified. Some of us were enemies in war a few short years ago, but such memories, by necessity, are short. . . . Let's see." Without singling out any one individual, Elizabeth Scarlatti spoke rapidly, almost in a cadence. "My own country has lost two members, I'm sad to note. But I don't believe prayers are in order for Messrs. Boothroyd and Thornton. If they are, I'm not the one to deliver them. But still, the United States is splendidly represented by Mr. Gibson and Mr. Landor. Between them, they account for nearly twenty percent of the vast oil interests in the American Southwest. To say nothing of a joint expansion in the Canadian North-

west Territories. Combined personal assets—two hundred and twenty-five million. . . . Our recent adversary, Germany, brings us Herr von Schnitzler, Herr Kindorf, and Herr Thyssen. I. G. Farben; the baron of Ruhr coal; the great steel companies. Personal assets? Who can really tell these days in the Weimar? Perhaps one hundred and seventy-five million, at the outside. . . . But someone's missing from this group. I trust he's successfully being recruited. I speak of Gustave Krupp. He would raise the ante considerably. . . . England sends us Messrs. Masterson, Leacock, and Innes-Bowen. As powerful a triumvirate as can be found in the British Empire. Mr. Masterson with half of the India imports, also Ceylon now, I understand; Mr. Leacock's major portion of the British Stock Exchange; and Mr. Innes-Bowen. He owns the largest single textile industry throughout Scotland and the Hebrides. Personal assets I place at three hundred million. . . . France has been generous, too. Monsieur D'Almeida; I now realize that he is the true owner of the Franco-Italian rail system, partially due to his Italian lineage, I'm sure. And Monsieur Daudet. Is there any among us who have not used some part of his merchant fleet? Personal assets, one hundred and fifty million. . . . And lastly, our neighbors to the north, Sweden. Herr Myrdal and Herr Olaffsen. Understandably"—here Elizabeth looked pointedly at the strange-faced man, her son, at the head of the table—"one of these gentlemen, Herr Myrdal, has controlling interest in Donnenfeld, the most impressive firm on the Stockholm exchange. While Herr Olaffsen's many companies merely control the export of Swedish iron and steel. Personal assets are calculated at one hundred and twenty-five million. . . . Incidentally, gentlemen, the term *personal assets* denotes those holdings which can be converted easily, quickly, and without endangering your markets. . . . Otherwise, I would not insult you by placing such meager limits on your fortunes."

Elizabeth paused to place her briefcase directly in front of her. The men around the table were aroused, apprehensive. Several were shocked at the casual mention of what they believed was highly confidential information. The Americans, Gibson and Landor, had quietly gone into the Canadian venture unannounced, without legal sanction, violating the U.S.–Canadian treaties. The Ger-

mans, von Schnitzler and Kindorf, had held secret conferences with Gustave Krupp—who was fighting desperately to remain neutral for fear of a Weimar takeover. If these conferences were made known, Krupp had sworn to expose them. The Frenchman, Louis François D'Almeida, guarded with his very life the extent of his ownership of the Franco-Italian rails. If it were known, it might well be confiscated by the republic. He had purchased the majority shares from the Italian government through plain bribery.

And Myrdal, the heavyset Swede, bulged his eyes in disbelief when Elizabeth Scarlatti spoke so knowingly about the Stockholm exchange. His own company had covertly absorbed Donnenfeld in one of the most complicated mergers imaginable, made possible by the illegal transaction of the American securities. If it became public knowledge, the Swedish law would step in, and he'd be ruined. Only the Englishmen seemed totally poised, totally proud of their achievements. But even this measure of equanimity was misleading. For Sydney Masterson, undisputed heir to the merchant domain of Sir Robert Clive, had only recently concluded the Ceylon arrangements. They were unknown in the import-export world and there were certain agreements subject to question. Some might even say they constituted fraud.

Huddled, quiet-toned conferences took place around the table in the four languages. Elizabeth raised her voice sufficiently to be heard.

"I gather some of you are conferring with your aides—I assume they are your aides. If I'd realized this meeting made provisions for second-level negotiators, I'd have brought along my attorneys. They could have gossiped among themselves while we continue. The decisions we reach tonight, gentlemen, must be our own!"

Heinrich Kroeger sat on the edge of his chair. He spoke harshly, unpleasantly. "I wouldn't be so sure of any decisions. There are none to be made! You've told us nothing which couldn't be learned by any major accounting firm!"

A number of the men around the table—specifically the two Germans, D'Almeida, Gibson, Landor, Myrdal, and Masterson—avoided looking at him. For Kroeger was wrong.

"You think so? Perhaps. But then I've overlooked you,

haven't I? . . . I shouldn't do that, you're obviously terribly important." Again, a number of the men around the table—excluding those mentioned—had traces of smiles on their lips.

"Your wit is as dull as you are." Elizabeth was pleased with herself. She was succeeding in this most important aspect of her appearance. She was reaching, provoking Ulster Stewart Scarlett. She continued without acknowledging his remark.

"Strangely obtained assets of two hundred and seventy million sold under the most questionable circumstances would necessitate a loss of at least fifty percent, possibly sixty percent of market value. I'll grant you the least, so I shall hazard an estimate of one hundred and thirty-five million dollars at the current rates of exchange. One hundred and eight, if you've been weak."

Matthew Canfield lurched from the wall, then held his place.

The men around the table were astonished. The hum of voices increased perceptibly. Aides were shaking their heads, nodding in agreement, raising their eyebrows unable to answer. Each participant thought he knew something of the others. Obviously, none were this knowledgeable of Heinrich Kroeger. They had not even been sure of his status at this table. Elizabeth interrupted the commotion.

"However, Mister Kroeger, surely you know that theft, when eminently provable, is merely subject to proper identification before steps can be taken. There are international courts of extradition. Therefore, it is conceivable that your assets might be calculated at . . . zero!"

A silence fell over the table as the gentlemen, along with their assistants, gave Heinrich Kroeger their full attention. The words *theft, courts,* and *extradition* were words they could not accept at this table. They were dangerous words. Kroeger, the man many of them vaguely feared for reasons solely associated with his enormous influence within both camps, was now warned.

"Don't threaten me, old woman." Kroeger's voice was low, confident. He sat back in his chair and glared at his mother at the opposite end of the long table. "Don't make charges unless you can substantiate them. If you're prepared to attempt that, I'm ready to counter. . . . If you or your colleagues were outnegotiated, this is no

place to cry. You won't get sympathy here! I might even go so far as to say you're on treacherous ground. Remember that!" He kept staring until Elizabeth could no longer stand the sight of his eyes. She looked away.

She was not prepared to do anything—not with him, not with Heinrich Kroeger. She would not gamble the lives of her family more than she had already. She would not wager at this table the name of Scarlatti. Not that way. Not now. There was another way.

Kroeger had won the point. It was obvious to all, and Elizabeth had to rush headlong on so that none would dwell upon her loss.

"Keep your assets. They are quite immaterial."

Around the table the phrase "quite immaterial" when applied to such millions was impressive. Elizabeth knew it would be.

"Gentlemen. Before we were interrupted, I gave you all, by national groupings, the personal assets calculated to the nearest five million for each contingent. I felt it was more courteous than breaking down each individual's specific worth—some things are sacred, after all. However, I was quite unfair, as several of you know. I alluded to a number of—shall we say, delicate negotiations, I'm sure you believed were inviolate. Treacherous to you—to use Mr. Kroeger's words—if they were known within your own countries."

Seven of the Zurich twelve were silent. Five were curious.

"I refer to my cocitizens, Mr. Gibson and Mr. Landor. To Monsieur D'Almeida, Sydney Masterson, and of course, to the brilliant Herr Myrdal. I should also include two-thirds of Germany's investors—Herr von Schnitzler and Herr Kindorf, but for different reasons, as I'm sure they realize."

No one spoke. No one turned to his aides. All eyes were upon Elizabeth.

"I don't intend to remain unfair in this fashion, gentlemen. I have something for each of you."

A voice other than Kroeger's spoke up. It was the Englishman, Sydney Masterson.

"May I ask the point of all this? All this . . . incidental intelligence? I'm sure you've been most industrious—highly accurate, too, speaking for myself. But none of us

here have entered the race for a Jesus medal. Surely, you know that."

"I do, indeed. If it were otherwise, I wouldn't be here tonight."

"Then why? Why this?" The accent was German. The voice belonged to the blustering baron of the Ruhr Valley, Kindorf.

Masterson continued. "Your cablegram, madame—we all received the same—specifically alluded to areas of mutual interest. I believe you went so far as to say the Scarlatti assets might be at our joint disposal. Most generous, indeed. . . . But now I must agree with Mr. Kroeger. You sound as though you're threatening us, and I'm not at all sure I like it."

"Oh, come, Mr. Masterson! You've never held out promises of English gold to half the minor potentates in the backwaters of India? Herr Kindorf has not openly bribed his unions to strike with pledges of increased wages once the French are out of the Ruhr? Please! You insult all of us! Of course, I'm here to threaten you! And I can assure you, you'll like it less as I go on!"

Masterson rose from the table. Several others moved their chairs. The air was hostile. "I shall not listen further," said Masterson.

"Then tomorrow at noon the Foreign Office, the British Stock Exchange, and the board of directors of the English Importers Collective will receive detailed specifics of your highly illegal agreements in Ceylon! Your commitments are enormous! The news might just initiate a considerable run on your holdings!"

Masterson stood by his chair. "Be damned!" were the only words he uttered as he returned to his chair. The table once again fell silent. Elizabeth opened her briefcase.

"I have here an envelope for each of you. Your names are typed on the front. Inside each envelope is an accounting of your individual worths. Your strengths. Your weaknesses. . . . There is one envelope missing. The . . . influential, very important Mr. Kroeger does not have one. Frankly, it's insignificant."

"I warn you!"

"So very sorry, Mr. Kroeger." Again the words were rapidly spoken, but this time no one was listening. Each

one's concentration was on Elizabeth Scarlatti and her briefcase. "Some envelopes are thicker than others, but none should place too great an emphasis on this factor. We all know the negligibility of wide diversification after a certain point." Elizabeth reached into her leather case.

"You are a witch!" Kindorf's heavy accent was now guttural, the veins stood out in his temples.

"Here. I shall pass them out. And as each of you peruse your miniature portfolios I shall continue talking, which, I know, will please you."

The envelopes were passed down both sides of the table. Some were torn open immediately, hungrily. Others, like the cards of experienced poker players, were handled carefully, cautiously.

Matthew Canfield stood by the wall, his left arm smarting badly in the sling, his right hand in his pocket, sweatily clutching his revolver. Since Elizabeth had identified Ulster Scarlett with the 270 million, he could not take his eyes off him. This man called Heinrich Kroeger. This hideous, arrogant son of a bitch was the man he wanted! This was the filthy bastard who had done it all! This was Janet's personal hell.

"I see you all have your envelopes. Except, of course, the ubiquitous Mr. Kroeger. Gentlemen, I promised you I would not be unfair and I shan't be. There are five of you who can not begin to appreciate the influence of Scarlatti unless you have, as they say in cheap merchandising, samples applicable to you alone. Therefore, as you read the contents of your envelopes, I shall briefly touch on these sensitive areas."

Several of the men who had been reading shifted their eyes toward Elizabeth without moving their heads. Others put the papers down defiantly. Some handed the pages to aides and stared at the old woman. Elizabeth glanced over her shoulder at Matthew Canfield. She was worried about him. She knew he, at last, faced Ulster Scarlett, and the pressure on him was immense. She tried to catch his eye. She tried to reassure him with a look, a confident smile.

He would not look at her. She saw only the hatred in his eyes as he stared at the man called Heinrich Kroeger.

"I shall delineate alphabetically, gentlemen. . . . Monsieur Daudet, the Republic of France would be reluctant

to continue awarding franchises to your fleet if they were aware of those ships under Paraguayan flag which carried supplies to France's enemies in time of war." Daudet remained motionless, but Elizabeth was amused to see the three Englishmen bristle at the Frenchman. The predictable, contradictory British!

"Oh, come, Mr. Innes-Bowen. You may not have run ammunition, but how many neutral ships were loaded off how many piers in India with textile cargoes bound for Bremerhaven and Cuxhaven during the same period? . . . And Mr. Leacock. You can't really forget your fine Irish heritage, can you? The Sinn Féin has prospered well under your tutelage. Monies funneled through you to the Irish rebellion cost the lives of thousands of British soldiers at a time when England could least afford them! And quiet, calm Herr Olaffsen. The crown prince of Swedish steel. Or is he the king now? He might well be, for the Swedish government paid him several fortunes for untold hundreds of tons of low-carbon ingot. However, they didn't come from his own superior factories. They were shipped from inferior mills half a world away—from Japan!"

Elizabeth reached into her briefcase once again. The men around the table were like corpses, immobile, only their minds were working. For Heinrich Kroeger, Elizabeth Scarlatti had placed the seal of approval on her own death warrant. He sat back and relaxed. Elizabeth withdrew a thin booklet from her briefcase.

"Lastly we come to Herr Thyssen. He emerges with the least pain. No grand fraud, no treason, only minor illegality and major embarrassment. Hardly a fitting tribute to the house of August Thyssen." She threw the booklet into the center of the table. "Filth, gentlemen, just plain filth. Fritz Thyssen, pornographer! Purveyor of obscenity. Books, pamphlets, even motion pictures. Printed and filmed in Thyssen warehouses in Cairo. Every government on the Continent has condemned the unknown source. There he is, gentlemen. Your associate."

For a long moment no one spoke. Each man was concerned with himself. Each calculated the damage that could result from old Scarlatti's disclosures. In every instance the loss was accompanied by degrees of disgrace. Reputations could hang in balance. The old woman had

issued twelve indictments and personally returned twelve verdicts of guilty. Somehow, no one considered the thirteenth, Heinrich Kroeger.

Sydney Masterson pierced the belligerent air with a loud, manufactured cough. "Very well, Madame Scarlatti, you've made the point I referred to earlier. However, I think I should remind you that we are not impotent men. Charges and countercharges are parts of our lives. Solicitors can refute every accusation you've made, and I can assure you that lawsuits for unmitigated slander would be in the forefront. . . . After all, when gutter tactics are employed, there are expedient replies. . . . If you think we fear disdain, believe me when I tell you that public opinion has been molded by far less money than is represented at this table!"

The gentlemen of Zurich took confidence in Masterson's words. There were nods of agreement.

"I don't for one second doubt you, Mr. Masterson. Any of you. . . . Missing personnel files, opportunistic executives—sacrificial goats. Please, gentlemen! I only contend that you wouldn't welcome the trouble. Or the anxiety which goes with such distasteful matters."

"*Non,* madame." Claude Daudet was outwardly cool but inwardly petrified. Perhaps his Zurich associates did not know the French people. A firing squad was not out of the question. "You are correct. Such troubles are to be avoided. So, then what is next? What is it you prepare for us, eh?"

Elizabeth paused. She wasn't quite sure why. It was an instinct, an intuitive need to turn around and look at the field accountant.

Matthew Canfield had not budged from his position by the wall. He was a pathetic sight. His jacket had fallen away from his left shoulder revealing the dark black sling, his right hand still plunged in his pocket. He seemed to be swallowing continuously, trying to keep himself aware of his surroundings. Elizabeth noticed that he now avoided looking at Ulster Scarlett. He seemed, in essence, to be trying to hang on to his sanity.

"Excuse me, gentlemen." Elizabeth rose from her chair and crossed to Canfield. She whispered quietly to him. "Take hold of yourself. I demand it! There's nothing to fear. Not in this room!"

Canfield spoke slowly, without moving his lips. She

could barely hear him, but what she heard startled her. Not for its content, but for the way in which he said it. Matthew Canfield was now among the ranks in this room in Zurich. He had joined them; he had become a killer, too.

"Say what you have to say and get it over with. . . . I want him. I'm sorry, but I want him. Look at him now, lady, because he's a dead man."

"Control yourself! Such talk will serve neither of us." She turned and walked back to her chair. She stood behind it while she spoke. "As you may have noticed, gentlemen, my young friend has been seriously wounded. Thanks to all of you . . . or one of you, in an attempt to prevent my reaching Zurich. The act was cowardly and provocative in the extreme."

The men looked at each other.

Daudet, whose imagination would not stop conjuring pictures of national disgrace or the firing squad, answered quickly. "Why would any here take such action, Madame Scarlatti? We are not maniacs. We are businessmen. No one sought to prevent your coming to Zurich. Witness, madame, we are all here."

Elizabeth looked at the man called Kroeger.

"One of you violently opposed this conference. We were fired upon less than a half hour ago."

The men looked at Heinrich Kroeger. Some were becoming angry. This Kroeger was, perhaps, too reckless.

"No." He answered simply and emphatically, returning their stares. "I agreed to your coming. If I'd wanted to stop you, I'd have stopped you."

For the first time since the meeting began, Heinrich Kroeger looked at the sporting goods salesman at the far end of the room, half concealed in the poor light. He had reacted with only moderate surprise when he realized Elizabeth Scarlatti had brought him to Zurich. Moderate because he knew Elizabeth's penchant for employing the unusual, both in methods and personnel, and because she probably had no one else around she could browbeat into silence as easily as this money-hungry social gadfly. He'd be a convenient chauffeur, a manservant. Kroeger hated the type.

Or was he anything else?

Why had the salesman stared at him? Had Elizabeth

told him anything? She wouldn't be that big a fool. The man was the sort who'd blackmail in a minute.

One thing was sure. He'd have to be killed.

But who had tried to kill him previously? Who had tried to stop Elizabeth? And why?

The same question was being considered by Elizabeth Scarlatti. For she believed Kroeger when he disavowed the attempts on their lives.

"Please continue, Madame Scarlatti." It was Fritz Thyssen, his cherubic face still flushed with anger over Elizabeth's disclosure of his Cairo trade. He had removed the booklet from the center of the table.

"I shall." She approached the side of her chair but did not sit down. Instead, she reached once more into her briefcase. "I have one thing further, gentlemen. With it we can conclude our business, and decisions can be made. There is a copy for each of the twelve remaining investors. Those with aides will have to share them. My apologies, Mr. Kroeger, I find I haven't one for you." From her position at the end of the table she distributed twelve slender manila envelopes. They were sealed, and as the men passed them down, the investors taking one apiece, it was apparent that each found it difficult not to rip open the top and withdraw the contents at once. But none wished to betray such obvious anxiety.

Finally, as each of the twelve held his envelope in front of him, one by one the men began to open them.

For nearly two minutes the only sound was the rustling of pages. Otherwise, silence. Even breathing was seemingly suspended. The men from Zurich were mesmerized by what they saw. Elizabeth spoke.

"Yes, gentlemen. What you hold in your hands is the scheduled liquidation of the Scarlatti Industries. . . . So that you have no illusions of doubt concerning the validity of this document, you will note that after each subdivision of holdings is typed the names of the individuals, corporations, or syndicates who are the purchasers. . . . Every one of those mentioned, the individuals as well as the organizations, are known to each of you. If not personally, then certainly by reputation. You know their capabilities, and I'm sure you're not unaware of their ambitions. Within the next twenty-four hours they will own Scarlatti."

For most of the Zurich men Elizabeth's sealed infor-

mation was the confirmation of the whispered rumors. Word had reached them that something unusual was taking place at Scarlatti. Some sort of unloading under strange circumstances.

So this was it. The head of Scarlatti was getting out.

"A massive operation, Madame Scarlatti." Olaffsen's low Swedish voice vibrated throughout the room. "But to repeat Daudet's question, what is it you prepare us for?"

"Please take note of the bottom figure on the last page, gentlemen. Although I'm quite sure you all have." The rustle of pages. Each man had turned swiftly to the final page. "It reads seven hundred and fifteen million dollars. . . . The combined, immediately convertible assets of this table, placed at the highest figure is one billion, one hundred and ten million. . . . Therefore, a disparity of three hundred and ninety-five million exists between us. . . . Another way to approach this difference is to calculate it from the opposite direction. The Scarlatti liquidation will realize sixty-four point four percent of this table's holdings—if, indeed, you gentlemen could convert your personal assets in such a manner as to preclude financial panics."

Silence.

A number of the Zurich men reached for their first envelopes. The breakdowns of their own worth.

One of these was Sydney Masterson, who turned to Elizabeth with an unamused smile. "And what you're saying, I presume, Madame Scarlatti, is that this sixty-four point plus percent is the club you hold over our heads?"

"Precisely, Mr. Masterson."

"My dear lady, I really must question your sanity . . ."

"I wouldn't, if I were you."

"Then I shall, Frau Scarlatti." I. G. Farben's von Schnitzler spoke in a disagreeable manner, lounging back in his chair as if toying verbally with an imbecile. "To accomplish what you have must have been a costly sacrifice. . . . I wonder to what purpose? You can not buy what there is not to sell. . . . We are not a public corporation. You can not force into defeat something which does not exist!" His German lisp was pronounced, his arrogance every bit as unattractive as reputed. Elizabeth disliked him intensely.

"Quite correct, von Schnitzler."

"Then, perhaps"—the German laughed—"you have been a foolish woman. I would not wish to absorb your losses. I mean, really, you can not go to some mythical *Baumeister* and tell him you have more funds than we—therefore, he must drive us out into the streets!"

Several of the Zurich men laughed.

"That, of course, would be the simplest, would it not? The appeal to one entity, negotiating with one power. It's a shame that I can't do that. It would be so much easier, so much less costly. . . . But I'm forced to take another road, an expensive one. . . . I should put that another way. I have taken it, gentlemen. It has been accomplished. The time is running out for its execution."

Elizabeth looked at the men at Zurich. Some had their eyes riveted on her—watching for the slightest waver of confidence, the smallest sign of bluff. Others fixed their stares on inanimate objects—caring only to filter the words, the tone of her voice, for a false statement or a lapse of judgment. These were men who moved nations with a single gesture, a solitary word.

"At the start of tomorrow's business, subject to time zones, enormous transfers of Scarlatti capital will have been made to the financial centers of the five nations represented at this table. In Berlin, Paris, Stockholm, London, and New York, negotiations have already been completed for massive purchases on the open market of the outstanding shares of your central companies. . . . Before noon of the next business day, gentlemen, Scarlatti will have considerable, though, of course, minority ownership in many of your vast enterprises. . . . Six hundred and seventy million dollars' worth! . . . Do you realize what this means, gentlemen?"

Kindorf roared. "*Ja!* You will drive up the prices and makes us fortunes! You will own nothing!"

"My dear lady, you are extraordinary." Innes-Bowen's textile prices had remained conservative. He was overjoyed at the prospects.

"D'Almeida, who realized she could not enter his Franco-Italian rails, took another view. "You can not purchase one share of my property, madame!"

"Some of you are more fortunate than others, Monsieur D'Almeida."

Leacock, the financier, the gentlest trace of a brogue in his cultivated voice, spoke up. "Granting what you say,

and it is entirely possible, Madame Scarlatti, what have we suffered? . . . We have not lost a daughter, but gained a minor associate." He turned to the others who, he hoped, would find humor in his analogy.

Elizabeth held her breath before speaking. She waited until the men of Zurich were once again focused on her.

"I said before noon Scarlatti would be in the position I outlined. . . . One hour later a tidal wave will form in the Kurfuerstendamm in Berlin and end in New York's Wall Street! One hour later Scarlatti will divest itself of these holdings at a fraction of their cost! I have estimated three cents on the dollar. . . . Simultaneously, every bit of information Scarlatti has learned of your questionable activities will be released to the major wire services in each of your countries. . . . You might sustain slander by itself, gentlemen. You will not be the same men when it is accompanied by financial panic! Some of you will remain barely intact. Some will be wiped out. The majority of you will be affected disastrously!"

After the briefest moment of shocked silence, the room exploded. Aides were questioned peremptorily. Answers were bellowed to be heard.

Heinrich Kroeger rose from his chair and screamed at the men. "Stop! Stop! You damn fools, stop it! She'd never do it! She's bluffing!"

"Do you really think so?" Elizabeth shouted above the voices.

"I'll kill you, you bitch!"

"You are demented, Frau Scarlatti!"

"Try it . . . Kroeger! Try it!" Matthew Canfield stood by Elizabeth, his eyes bloodshot with fury as he stared at Ulster Stewart Scarlett.

"Who the hell are you, you lousy peddler?" The man called Kroeger, hands gripping the table, returned Canfield's stare and screeched to be heard by the salesman.

"Look at me good! I'm your executioner!"

"What!"

The man called Heinrich Kroeger squinted his misshapen eyes. He was bewildered. Who was this parasite? But he could not take the time to think. The voices of the men of Zurich had reached a crescendo. They were now shouting at each other.

Heinrich Kroeger pounded the table. He had to get control. He had to get them quiet. "Stop it! . . . Listen to

me! If you'll listen to me, I'll tell you why she can't do it! She can't do it, I tell you!"

One by one the voices became quieter and finally trailed off into silence. The men of Zurich watched Kroeger. He pointed at Elizabeth Scarlatti.

"I know this bitch-woman! I've seen her do this before! She gets men together, powerful men, and frightens them. They go into panic and sell out! She gambles on *fear*, you cowards! On fear!"

Daudet spoke quietly. "You have answered nothing. Why can't she do as she says?"

Kroeger did not take his eyes off Elizabeth Scarlatti as he replied. "Because to do it would destroy everything she's ever fought for. It would collapse Scarlatti!"

Sydney Masterson spoke just above a whisper. "That would appear to be obvious. The question remains unanswered."

"She couldn't live without that power! Take my word for it! She couldn't live without it!"

"That's an opinion," said Elizabeth Scarlatti facing her son at the opposite end of the table. "Do you ask the majority of those at this table to risk everything on your opinion?"

"God damn you!"

"This Kroeger's right, honey." The Texas drawl was unmistakable. "You'll ruin yourself. You won't have a pot to piss in."

"Your language matches the crudity of your operations, Mr. Landor."

"I don't give pig piss for words, old lady. I do about money, and that's what we're talkin' about. Why do you want to pull this here crap?"

"That I'm doing it is sufficient, Mr. Landor. . . . Gentlemen, I said time was running out. The next twenty-four hours will either be a normal Tuesday or a day which will never be forgotten in the financial capitals of our world. . . . Some here will survive. Most of you will not. Which will it be, gentlemen? . . . I submit that in light of everything I've said, it's a poor fiscal decision wherein the majority allows the minority to cause its destruction."

"What is it you want of us?" Myrdal was a cautious bargainer. "A few might rather weather your threats than

accept your demands. . . . Sometimes I think it is all a game. What are your demands?"

"That this . . . association be disbanded at once. That all financial and political ties in Germany with whatever factions be severed without delay! That those of you who have been entrusted with appointments to the Allied Controls Commission resign immediately!"

"No! No! No! No!" Heinrich Kroeger was enraged. He banged his fist with all his might upon the table. "This organization has taken years to build! We will control the economy of Europe. We will control all Europe! We will do it!"

"Hear me, gentlemen! Mr. Myrdal said it's a game! Of course, it's a game! A game we expend our lives on. Our souls on! It consumes us, and we demand more and more and more until, at last, we crave our own destruction. . . . Herr Kroeger says I can't live without the power I've sought and gained. He may be right, gentlemen! Perhaps it's time for me to reach that logical end, the end which I now crave and for which I'm willing to pay the price. . . . Of course, I'll do as I say, gentlemen. I welcome death!"

"Let it be yours, then, not ours." Sydney Masterson understood.

"So be it, Mr. Masterson. I'm not overwhelmed, you know. I leave to all of you the necessity of coping with this strange new world we've entered. Don't think for a minute, gentlemen, that I can't understand you! Understand what you've done. Most horridly, why you've done it! . . . You look around your personal kingdoms and you're frightened. You see your power threatened—by theories, governments, strange-sounding concepts which eat away at your roots. You have an overpowering anxiety to protect the feudal system which spawned you. And well you should, perhaps. It won't last long. . . . But you will *not* do it this way!"

"Since you understand so, why do you stop us? This undertaking protects all of us. Ultimately yourself as well. Why do you stop us?" D'Almeida could lose the Franco-Italian rails and survive, if only the remainder could be saved.

"It always starts that way. The greater good. . . . Let's say I stop you because what you're doing is a far great-

er blemish than it is a cure. And that's all I'll say about it!"

"From you, that's ludicrous! I tell you again, she won't do it!" Kroeger pounded the flat of his hand on the table, but no one paid much attention to him.

"When you say time is running out, Madame Scarlatti, how do you mean it? From what you said, I gathered time had run out. The expensive road had been taken. . . ."

"There's a man in Geneva, Mr. Masterson, who's awaiting a phone call from me. If he receives that phone call, a cable will be sent to my offices in New York. If that cable arrives, the operation is canceled. If it doesn't, it's executed on schedule."

"That's impossible! Such complexity untangled with a cablegram? I don't believe you." Monsieur Daudet was certain of ruin.

"I assume considerable financial penalties by the action."

"You assume more than that, I would suspect, madame. You'll never be trusted again. Scarlatti will be isolated!"

"It's a prospect, Mr. Masterson. Not a conclusion. The marketplace is flexible. . . . Well, gentlemen? Your answer?"

Syndey Masterson rose from his chair. "Make your phone call. There's no other choice, is there, gentlemen?"

The men of Zurich looked at each other. Slowly they began to get out of their chairs, gathering the papers in front of them.

"It's finished. I am out of it." Kindorf folded the manila envelope and put it in his pocket.

"You're a beastly tiger. I shouldn't care to meet you in the arena with an army at my back." Leacock stood erect.

"You may be bullshitter, but I'm not gonna slip on it!" Landor nudged Gibson, who found it difficult to adjust.

"We can't be sure. . . . That's our problem. We can't be sure," said Gibson.

"Wait! Wait! Wait a minute!" Heinrich Kroeger began to shout. "You do this! You walk out! You're dead! . . . Every God damn one of you leeches is dead! Leeches! Yellow-bellied leeches! . . . You suck our blood; you make agreements with us. Then you walk out? . . . Afraid

for your little businesses? You God damn Jew bastards! We don't need you! Any of you! But you're going to need us! We'll cut you up and feed you to dogs! God damn swine!" Kroeger's face was flushed. His words spewed out, tumbling over one another.

"Stop it, Kroeger!" Masterson took a step toward the raving man with the splotched face. "It's finished! Can't you understand? It's finished!"

"Stay where you are, you scum, you English fairy!" Kroeger drew the pistol from his holster. Canfield, standing by Elizabeth, saw that it was a long-barreled forty-five and would blast half a man's body off with one shot.

"Stay where you are! . . . Finished! Nothing's finished until I say it's finished. God damn filthy pigs! Frightened little slug worms! We're too far along! . . . No one will stop us now! . . ." He waved the pistol toward Elizabeth and Canfield. "Finished! I'll tell you who's finished! She is! . . . Get out of my way." He started down the left side of the table as the Frenchman, Daudet, squealed.

"Don't do it, monsieur! Don't kill her! You do, and we are ruined!"

"I warn you, Kroeger! You murder her and you'll answer to us! We'll not be intimidated by you! We'll not destroy ourselves because of you!" Masterson stood at Kroeger's side, their shoulders nearly touching. The Englishman would not move.

Without a word, without warning, Heinrich Kroeger pointed his pistol at Masterson's stomach and fired. The shot was deafening and Sydney Masterson was jackknifed into the air. He fell to the floor, blood drenching his entire front, instantaneously dead.

The eleven men of Zurich gasped, some screamed in horror at the sight of the bloody corpse. Heinrich Kroeger kept walking. Those in his path got out of his way.

Elizabeth Scarlatti held her place. She locked her eyes with those of her killer son. "I curse the day you were born. You revile the house of your father. But know this, Heinrich Kroeger, and know it well!" The old woman's voice filled the cavernous room. Her power was such that her son was momentarily stunned, staring at her in hatred as she pronounced his sentence of execution. "Your identity will be spread across every front page of every newspaper in the civilized world after I'm dead! You will be hunted down for what you are! A madman, a murder-

er, a thief! And every man in this room, every investor in Zurich, will be branded your associate if they let you live this night!"

An uncontrollable rage exploded in the misshapen eyes of Heinrich Kroeger. His body shook with fury as he lashed at a chair in front of him sending it crashing across the floor. To kill was not enough. He had to kill at close range, he had to see the life and mind of Elizabeth Scarlatti detonated into oblivion in front of his eyes.

Matthew Canfield held the trigger of his revolver in his right-hand pocket. He had never fired from his pocket and he knew that if he missed he and Elizabeth would die. He was not sure how long he could wait. He would aim in the vicinity of the approaching man's chest, the largest target facing him. He waited until he could wait no longer.

The report of the small revolver and the impact of the bullet into Scarlett's shoulder was so much of a shock that Kroeger, for a split second, widened his eyes in disbelief.

It was enough, just enough for Canfield.

With all his strength he crashed into Elizabeth with his right shoulder sending her frail body toward the floor out of Kroeger's line of sight as he, Canfield, flung himself to the left. He withdrew his revolver and fired again, rapidly, into the man called Heinrich Kroeger.

Kroeger's huge pistol went off into the floor as he crumpled over.

Canfield staggered up, forgetting the unbearable pain in his left arm, which had been crushed under the weight of his own body. He leaped on Ulster Stewart Scarlett, wrenching the pistol from the iron grip. He began hitting the face of Heinrich Kroeger with the barrel. He could not stop.

Destroy the face! Destroy the horrible face!

Finally he was pulled off.

"*Gott!* He's dead! Halt! Stop! You can do no more!" The large, strong Fritz Thyssen held him.

Matthew Canfield felt weak and sank to the floor.

The men of Zurich had gathered around. Several helped Elizabeth, while the others bent over Heinrich Kroeger.

Rapid knocking came from the door leading to the hall.

Von Schnitzler took command. "Let them in!" he ordered in his thick German accent.

D'Almeida walked swiftly to the door and opened it. A number of chauffeurs stood at the entrance. It occurred to Canfield as he watched them that these men were not simply drivers of automobiles. He had good reason. They were armed.

As he lay there on the floor in terrible pain and shock, Canfield saw a brutish-looking blond man with close-cropped hair bent over the body of Heinrich Kroeger. He pushed the others away for the briefest instant while he pulled back the misshapen lid of one eye.

And then Canfield wondered if the agony of the last hours had played tricks with his sight, corrupted the infallible process of vision.

Or had the blond man bent his head down and whispered something into Heinrich Kroeger's ear?

Was Heinrich Kroeger still alive?

Von Schnitzler stood over Canfield. "He will be taken away. I have ordered a coup de grace. No matter, he is dead. It is finished." The obese von Schnitzler then shouted further commands in German to the uniformed chauffeurs around Kroeger. Several started to lift up the lifeless form but they were blocked by the blond man with the close-cropped hair. He shouldered them out of the way, not letting them touch the body.

He alone lifted Heinrich Kroeger off the floor and carried him out the door. The others followed.

"How's she?" Canfield gestured toward Elizabeth, who was seated in a chair. She was staring at the door through which the body had been taken, staring at the man no one knew was her son.

"Fine! She can make her call now!" Leacock was trying his best to be decisive.

Canfield rose from the floor and crossed to Elizabeth. He put his hand on her wrinkled cheek. He could not help himself.

Tears were falling down the ridges of her face.

And then Matthew Canfield looked up. He could hear the sound of a powerful automobile racing away. He was bothered.

Von Schnitzler had told him he'd ordered a coup de grace.

Yet no shot was fired.

A mile away, on the Winterthurstrasse, two men dragged the body of a dead man to a truck. They weren't sure what to do. The dead man had hired them, hired them all to stop the automobile heading to Falke Haus. He had paid them in advance, they had insisted upon it. Now he was dead, killed by a bullet meant for the driver of the automobile an hour ago. As they dragged the body over the rocky incline toward the truck, the blood from the mouth sprewed onto the perfectly matted waxed moustache.

The man named Poole was dead.

PART FOUR

CHAPTER 45

Major Matthew Canfield, aged forty-five—about to be forty-six—stretched his legs diagonally across the back of the army car. They had entered the township of Oyster Bay, and the sallow-complexioned sergeant broke the silence.

"Getting close, Major. You better wake up."

Wake up. It should be as easy as that. The perspiration streamed down his face. His heart was rhythmically pounding an unknown theme.

"Thank you, Sergeant."

The car swung east down Harbor Road toward the ocean drive. As they came closer to his home, Major Matthew Canfield began to tremble. He grabbed his wrists, held his breath, bit the front of his tongue. He could not fall apart. He could not allow himself the indulgence of self-pity. He could not do that to Janet. He owed her so much.

The sergeant blithely turned into the blue stone driveway and stopped at the path, which led to the front entrance of the large beach estate. The sergeant enjoyed driving out to Oyster Bay with his rich major. There was always lots of good food, in spite of rationing, and the liquor was always the best. No cheap stuff for the Camshaft, as he was known in the enlisted man's barracks.

The major slowly got out of the car. The sergeant was concerned. Something was wrong with the major. He hoped it didn't mean they'd have to drive back to New York. The old man seemed to have trouble standing up.

"Okay, Major?"

"Okay, Sergeant. . . . How'd you like to bunk in the boathouse tonight?" He did not look at the sergeant as he spoke.

"Sure! Great, Major!" It was where he always bunked. The boathouse apartment had a full kitchen and plenty of booze. Even a telephone. But the sergeant didn't have any signal that he could use it yet. He decided to try his luck. "Will you need me, Major? Could I call a couple of friends here?"

The major walked up the path. He called back quietly. "Do whatever you like, Sergeant. Just stay away from that radiophone. Is that understood?"

"You betcha, Major!" The sergeant gunned the engine and drove down toward the beach.

Matthew Canfield stood in front of the white, scalloped door with the sturdy hurricane lamps on both sides.

His home.

Janet.

The door opened and she stood there. The slightly graying hair, which she would not retouch. The upturned nose above the delicate, sensitive mouth. The bright, wide, brown searching eyes. The gentle loveliness of her face. The comforting concern she radiated.

"I heard the car. No one drives to the boathouse like Evans! . . . Matthew. Matthew! My darling! You're crying!"

CHAPTER 46

The plane, an Army B-29 transport, descended from the late-afternoon clouds to the airport in Lisbon. An Air Force corporal walked down the aisle.

"Please buckle all seat belts! No smoking! We'll be down in four minutes." He spoke in a monotone, aware that his passengers had to be important, so he would be more important, but courteous, when he had to tell them something.

The young man next to Matthew Canfield had said very little since their takeoff from Shannon. A number of times the major tried to explain that they were taking air routes out of range of the *Luftwaffe,* and that there was nothing to worry about. Andrew Scarlett had merely mumbled understood approval and had gone back to his magazines.

The car at the Lisbon airport was an armored Lincoln with two OSS personnel in the front. The windows could withstand short-range gunfire, and the automobile was capable of 120 miles an hour. They had to drive thirty-two miles up the Tejo River road to an airfield in Alenguer.

At Alenguer the man and boy boarded a low-flying, specially constructed Navy TBF with no markings for the trip to Bern. There would be no stops. Throughout the route, English, American, and Free French fighters were scheduled to intercept and protect to the destination.

At Bern they were met by a Swiss government vehicle, flanked by a motorcycle escort of eight men—one at the front, one at the rear, and three on each side. All were armed in spite of the Geneva pact, which prohibited such practices.

They drove to a village twenty-odd miles to the north, toward the German border. Kreuzlingen.

They arrived at a small inn, isolated from the rest of civilization, and the man and boy got out of the car. The driver sped the automobile away, and the motorcycle complement disappeared.

Matthew Canfield led the boy up the steps to the entrance of the inn.

Inside the lobby could be heard the wailing sound of an accordion, echoing from what was apparently a sparsely populated dining room. The high-ceilinged entry room was inhospitable, conveying the feeling that guests were not welcome.

Matthew Canfield and Andrew Scarlett approached the counter, which served as a front desk.

"Please, ring through to room six that April Red is here."

As the clerk plugged in his line, the boy suddenly shook. Canfield grabbed his arm and held him.

They walked up the stairs, and the two men stood in front of the door marked with the numeral six.

"There's nothing I can tell you now, Andy, except that we're here for one person. At least that's why I'm here. Janet. Your mother. Try to remember that."

The boy took a deep breath. "I'll try, Dad. Open the door! Jesus! Open the door!"

The room was dimly lit by small lamps on small tables. It was ornate in the fashion the Swiss felt proper for tourists—heavy rugs and solid furniture, overstuffed chairs and much antimacassar.

At the far end sat a man in half shadow. The spill of light angled sharply down across his chest but did not illuminate his face. The figure was dressed in brown tweeds, the jacket a combination of heavy cloth and leather.

He spoke in a throaty, harsh voice. "You are?"

"Canfield and April Red. Kroeger?"

"Shut the door."

Matthew Canfield closed the door and took several steps forward in front of Andrew Scarlett. He would cover the boy. He put his hand in his right coat pocket.

"I have a gun pointed at you, Kroeger. Not the same gun but the same pocket as last time we met. This time I won't take anything for granted. Do I make myself clear?"

"If you like, take it out of your pocket and hold it against my head. . . . There's not much I can do about it."

Canfield approached the figure in the chair.

It was horrible.

The man was a semi-invalid. He seemed to be paralyzed through the entire left portion of his body, extending to his jaw. His hands were folded across his front, his fingers extended as though spastic. But his eyes were alert.

His eyes.

His face. . . . Covered over by white splotches of skin graft below gray short-cropped hair. The man spoke.

"What you see was carried out of Sevastopol. Operation Barbarossa."

"What do you have to tell us, Kroeger?"

"First, April Red. . . . Tell him to come closer."

"Come here, Andy. By me."

"Andy!" The man in the chair laughed through his half-closed mouth. "Isn't that nice! Andy! Come here, Andy!"

Andrew Scarlett approached his stepfather and stood by his side, looking down at the deformed man in the chair.

"So you're the son of Ulster Scarlett?"

"I'm Matthew Canfield's son."

Canfield held his place, watching the father and son. He suddenly felt as though he didn't belong. He had the feeling that giants—old and infirm, young and scrawny—were about to do battle. And he was not of their house.

"No, young man, you're the son of Ulster Stewart Scarlett, heir to Scarlatti!"

"I'm exactly what I want to be! I have nothing to do with you." The young man breathed deeply. The fear was leaving him now, and in its place Canfield saw that a quiet fury was taking hold of the boy.

"Easy, Andy. Easy."

"Why? . . . For him? . . . Look at him. He's practically dead. . . . He doesn't even have a face."

"Stop it!" Ulster Scarlett's shrill voice reminded Canfield of that long-ago room in Zurich. "Stop it, you fool!"

"For what? For you? . . . Why should I? . . . I don't know you! I don't want to know you! . . . You left a long time ago!" The young man pointed to Canfield. "He took over for you. I listen to him. You're nothing to me!"

"Don't you talk to me like that! Don't you dare!"

Canfield spoke sharply. "I've brought April Red, Kroeger! What have you got to deliver! That's what we're here for. Let's get it over with!"

"He must understand first!" The misshapen head nodded back and forth. "He must be made to understand!"

"If it meant that much, why did you hide it? Why did you become Kroeger?"

The nodding head stopped, the ashen slit eyes stared. Canfield remembered Janet speaking about that look.

"Because Ulster Scarlett was not fit to represent the new order. The new world! Ulster Scarlett served his purpose and once that purpose was accomplished, he was no longer necessary. . . . He was a hindrance. . . . He would have been a joke. He had to be eliminated. . . ."

"Perhaps there was something else, too."

"What?"

"Elizabeth. She would have stopped you again. . . . She would have stopped you later, just the way she stopped you at Zurich."

At Elizabeth's name, Heinrich Kroeger worked up the phlegm in his scarred throat and spat. It was an ugly sight. "The bitch of the world! . . . But we made a mistake in twenty-six. . . . Let's be honest, I made the mistake. . . . I should have asked her to join us. . . . She would have, you know. She wanted the same things we did. . . ."

"You're wrong about that."

"Hah! You didn't know her!"

The former field accountant replied softly without inflection. "I knew her. . . . Take my word for it, she despised everything you stood for."

The Nazi laughed quietly to himself. "That's very funny. . . . I told her she stood for everything I despised. . . ."

"Then you were both right."

"No matter. She's in hell now."

"She died thinking you were dead. She died in peace because of that."

"Hah! You'll never know how tempted I was over the years, especially when we took Paris! . . . But I was waiting for London. . . . I was going to stand outside Whitehall and announce it to the world—and watch Scarlatti destroy itself!"

"She was gone by the time you took Paris."

"That didn't matter."

"I suppose not. You were just as afraid of her in death as you were when she was alive."

"I was afraid of no one! I was afraid of nothing!" Heinrich Kroeger strained his decrepit body.

"Then why didn't you carry out your threat? The house of Scarlatti lives."

"She never told you?"

"Told me what?"

"The bitch-woman always covered herself on four flanks. She found her corruptible man. My one enemy in the Third Reich. Goebbels. She never believed I'd been killed at Zurich. Goebbels knew who I was. After nineteen thirty-three she threatened our respectability with lies. Lies about me. The party was more important than revenge."

Canfield watched the destroyed man below him. As always, Elizabeth Scarlatti had been ahead of all of them. Far ahead.

"One last question."

"What?"

"Why Janet?"

The man in the chair raised his right hand with difficulty. "Him. . . . Him!" He pointed to Andrew Scarlett.

"Why?"

"I believed! I still believe! Heinrich Kroeger was part of a new world! A new order! The true aristocracy! . . . In time it would have been his!"

"But why Janet?"

Heinrich Kroeger, in exhaustion, waved the question aside. "A whore. Who needs a whore? The vessel is all we look for. . . ."

Canfield felt the anger rise inside him, but at his age and in his job, he suppressed it. He was not quick enough for the boy-man beside him.

Andrew Scarlett rushed forward to the overstuffed chair and swung his open hand at the invalid Kroeger. The

slap was hard and accurate. "You bastard! You filthy bastard!"

"Andy! Get back!" He pulled the boy away.

"Unehelich!" Heinrich Kroeger's eyes were swimming in their sockets. "It's for you! That's why you're here! You've got to know! . . . You'll understand and start us up again! Think! Think the aristocracy! For you . . . for you. . . ." He reached with his slightly mobile hand to his inside jacket pocket and withdrew a slip of paper. "They're yours. Take them!"

Canfield picked up the paper and without looking at it handed it to Andrew Scarlett.

"They're numbers. Just a lot of numbers."

Matthew Canfield knew what the numbers meant, but before he could explain, Kroeger spoke. "They're Swiss accounts, my son. My only son. . . . They contain millions! Millions! But there are certain conditions. Conditions which you will learn to understand! When you grow older, you'll know those conditions have to be met! And you'll meet them! . . . Because this power is the power to change the world! The way we wanted to change it!"

The man-boy looked at the deformed figure in the chair. "Am I supposed to thank you?"

"One day you will."

Matthew Canfield had had enough. "This is it! April Red has his message. Now I want it! What are you delivering?"

"It's outside. Help me up and we'll go to it."

"Never! What's outside? Your staff members in leather coats?"

"There's no one. No one but me."

Canfield looked at the wreck of a man in front of him and believed him. He started to help Heinrich Kroeger out of the chair.

"Wait here, Andy, I'll be back."

Major Matthew Canfield, in full uniform, helped the crippled man in brown tweeds down the stairs and onto the lobby floor. In the lobby, a servant brought over the crutches discarded by the Nazi when he first ascended the staircase to his room. The American major and the Nazi went out the front door.

"Where are we going, Kroeger?"

"Don't you think it's time you called me by my right

name? The name is Scarlett. Or, if you will, Scarlatti." The Nazi led them to the right, off the driveway, into the grass.

"You're Heinrich Kroeger. That's all you are to me."

"You realize, of course, that it was you, and you alone who caused our setback in Zurich. You pushed our timetable back a good two years. . . . No one ever suspected. . . . You were an ass!" Heinrich Kroeger laughed. "Perhaps it takes an ass to portray an ass!" He laughed again.

"Where are we going?"

"Just a few hundred yards. Hold your pistol up, if you like. There's no one."

"What are you going to deliver? You might as well tell me."

"Why not? You'll have them in your hands soon enough." Kroeger hobbled along toward an open field. "And when you have them, I'm free. Remember that."

"We have a deal. What is it?"

"The Allies will be pleased. Eisenhower will probably give you a medal! . . . You'll bring back the complete plans of the Berlin fortifications. They're known only to the elite of the German High Command. . . . Underground bunkers, rocket emplacements, supply depots, even the Führer's command post. You'll be a hero and I'll be nonexistent. We've done well, you and I."

Matthew Canfield stopped.

The plans of the Berlin fortifications had been obtained weeks ago by Allied Intelligence.

Berlin knew it.

Berlin admitted it.

Someone had been led into a trap, but it was not him, not Matthew Canfield. The Nazi High Command had led one of its own into the jaws of death.

"Tell me, Kroeger, what happens if I take your plans, your exchange for April Red, and don't let you go? What happens then?"

"Simple. Doenitz himself took my testimony. I gave it to him two weeks ago in Berlin. I told him everything. If I'm not back in Berlin in a few days, he'll be concerned. I'm very valuable. I expect to make my appearance and then . . . be gone. If I don't appear, then the whole world knows!"

Matthew Canfield thought it was the strangest of ironies. But it was no more than he had anticipated. He had

written it all down in the original file, sealed for years in the archives of the State Department.

And now a man in Berlin, unknown to him except by reputation, had reached the same conclusion.

Heinrich Kroeger, Ulster Stewart Scarlett—was expendable.

Doenitz had allowed Kroeger—bearing his false gifts—to come to Bern. Doenitz, in the unwritten rule of war, expected him to be killed. Doenitz knew that neither nation could afford this madman as its own. In either victory or defeat. And the enemy had to execute him so that no doubts existed. Doenitz was that rare enemy in these days of hatreds. He was a man his adversaries trusted. Like Rommel, Doenitz was a thorough fighter. A vicious fighter. But he was a moral man.

Matthew Canfield drew his pistol and fired twice.

Heinrich Kroeger lay dead on the ground.

Ulster Stewart Scarlett was—at last—gone.

Matthew Canfield walked through the field back to the small inn. The night was clear and the moon, three-quarters of it, shone brightly on the still foliage around him.

It struck him that it was remarkable that it had all been so simple.

But the crest of the wave is simple. Deceptively simple. It does not show the myriad pressures beneath that make the foam roll the way it does.

It was over.

And there was Andrew.

There was Janet.

Above all, there was Janet.

LUDLUM ON LUDLUM

Few writers have skyrocketed to popularity with the speed of Robert Ludlum, with each succeeding thriller becoming a bigger bestseller. The key to his success may lie in John Leonard's comment in *The New York Times*, "Mr. Ludlum stuffs more surprises into his novels than any other six-pack of thriller writers combined."

Some people claim Ludlum has secret sources for information found in his stories. In one, an early book, a key theme was CIA involvement in domestic surveillance. At that time the subject shocked many people. Later, of course, this fact proved to be correct. Other people suspect Ludlum was an agent himself during the years prior to his career as a novelist. Not true. For close to twenty years he was in show business—as an actor, producer, and as the "voice" of dozens of television commercials for products ranging from Tiparillos to Tuna Helper.

During his "voice" period, Ludlum's wife crowned him "King of the Toilet Bowls." As he tells it, "there was this product called Plunge. All I had to do was read three words: Plunge works fast. In spite of my off-hand delivery, they used my three words in over one hundred different commercials. The money from this put one of my children through two years of college."

Although none of Ludlum's novels draws on his show business background for subject matter, they all reflect techniques he learned in the theater. Ludlum says, "the theater man knows that he must involve the audience. He understands structure more than anyone else—the logical evolving of one event into another event without losing the audience's attention. Because if you lose their interest, you're closing Saturday night."

Ludlum admits, "I write primarily as an entertainer. But I find that whether you're writing comically or dramatically, you write

from a point of view of something that disturbs or outrages you. And that's what I do. I admit to being outraged—mostly by the abuse of power by the fanatics. The extremes bother me, right or left.'' Yet he adds, ''I disapprove of violence, that's why I show pain for what it is. When my characters get hit, they hurt. They don't jump back into action like John Wayne.''

All of this—and more—can be found in the published work of Robert Ludlum. Since his first novel, *THE SCARLATTI INHERITANCE*, he has amassed an enviable record of success: *THE OSTERMAN WEEKEND*, *THE MATLOCK PAPERS*, *THE RHINEMANN EXCHANGE*, *THE GEMINI CONTENDERS*; more recently, *THE CHANCELLOR MANUSCRIPT*, *THE HOLCROFT COVENANT*, *THE MATARESE CIRCLE* and *THE BOURNE IDENTITY*.

CHAPTER 22

The second and third days of the *Calpurnia* voyage were calm, both the weather and the first-class section of the ship. The news of the death of a passenger cast a pall over the voyagers. Mrs. Charles Boothroyd was confined to quarters under the constant supervision of the ship's doctor and attending nurses. She had gone into hysterics upon hearing the news of her husband and it had been necessary to administer large doses of sedatives.

By the third day, with revived health, the optimism of most passengers revived.

Elizabeth Wyckham Scarlatti and her young table escort made it a point to part company after each meal. By ten thirty every night, however, Matthew Canfield let himself into her quarters to take up his post lest there be a recurrence of the Boothroyd attempt. It was an unsatisfactory arrangement.

"If I were a hundred years younger, you might pass yourself off as one of those distasteful men who perform services for middle-aged adventuresses."

"If you used some of your well-advertised money to buy your own ocean liner, I might get some sleep at night."

These late-hour conversations served one good purpose, however. Their plans began to take shape. Also Canfield's responsibilities as an employee of Elizabeth Scarlatti were diplomatically discussed.

"You understand," said Elizabeth, "I wouldn't expect you to do anything detrimental to the government. Or against your own conscience. I do believe in a man's conscience."

"But I gather you'd like to make the decision about what's detrimental and what isn't?"

"To a degree, yes. I believe I'm qualified."

"What happens if I don't agree with you?"

"We'll cross that bridge when we come to it."

"Oh, that's great!"

In essence, Matthew Canfield would continue submitting his reports to Washington's Group Twenty with one alteration—they first would be approved by Elizabeth Scarlatti. Together they would, through the field accountant, make certain requests of his office they both felt necessary. In all matters of physical well-being, the old woman would follow the instructions of the young man without argument.

Matthew Canfield would receive ten payments of ten thousand dollars each commencing with the first day in London. In small American bills.

"You realize, Mr. Canfield, that there's another way to look at this arrangement."

"What's that?"

"Your office is getting the benefit of my not inconsiderable talents for absolutely nothing. Extremely beneficial to the taxpayers."

"I'll put that in my next report."

The basic problem of the arrangement had not been resolved, however. For the field accountant to fulfill his obligations to both employers, a reason had to be found explaining his association with the old woman. It would become obvious as the weeks went by and it would be foolish to try to pass it off as either companionship or business. Both explanations would be suspect.

With a degree of self-interest, Matthew Canfield asked, "Can you get along with your daughter-in-law?"

"I assume you mean Ulster's wife. No one could stand Chancellor's."

"Yes."

"I like her. However, if you're thinking about her as a third party, I must tell you that she despises me. There are many reasons, most of them quite valid. In order to get what I want I've had to treat her quite badly. My only defense, if I felt I needed one—which I don't—is that what I wanted was for her benefit."

"I'm deeply moved, but do you think we could get her coopperation? I've met her on several occasions."

"She's not very responsible. But I suppose you know that."

"Yes. I also know that she suspects you of going to Europe on your son's account."

"I realize that. It would help to enlist her, I imagine. But I don't think I could manage it by cable, and I certainly wouldn't want to spell it out in a letter."

"I've a better way. I'll go back for her and I'll take a written . . . explanation from you. Not too involved, not too specific. I'll handle the rest."

"You must know her very well."

"Not so. I just think that if I can convince her that you—and I—are on her side . . . if someone's on her side, she'll help."

"She might be able to. She could show us places. . . ."

"She might recognize people. . . ."

"But what will I do while you're in America? I'll no doubt be dead when you come back."

Canfield had thought of that. "When we reach England, you should go into retreat."

"I beg your pardon?"

"For your immortal soul. And your son's as well, of course."

"I don't understand you."

"A convent. The whole world knows of your bereavement. It's a logical thing to do. We'll issue a statement to the press to the effect that you've gone to an undisclosed retreat in the north of England. Then send you somewhere down south. My office will help."

"It sounds positively ridiculous!"

"You'll be fetching in your black robes!"

The veiled, grieving Mrs. Boothroyd was led off with the first contingent of passengers. She was met by a man at customs who hurried her through the procedures and took her to a Rolls-Royce waiting on the street. Canfield followed the couple to the car.

Forty-five minutes later Canfield checked into the hotel. He had called his London contact from a public phone and they had agreed to meet as soon as the Londoner could drive down. The field accountant then spent a half hour enjoying the stability of a dry-land bed. He was depressed at the thought of going right back on board ship but he knew there was no other solution. Janet would supply the most reasonable explanation for his accompanying the old lady and it was logical that the wife and mother of the missing Ulster Scarlett should travel together. And certainly Canfield was not unhappy at the prospect of a continued association with Janet Scarlett. She was a tramp, no question; but he had begun to doubt his opinion that she was a bitch.

He was about to doze off when he looked at his watch and realized that he was late for his meeting. He picked up the phone and was delighted by the crisp British accent answering him.

"Madame Scarlatti is in suite five. Our instructions are to ring through prior to callers, sir."

"If you'll do that, please, I'll just go right up. Thank you."

Canfield said his name quite loudly before Elizabeth Scarlatti would open the door. The old woman motioned the young man inside to a chair while she sat on a huge Victorian sofa by the window.

"Well, what do we do now?"

"I phoned our London man nearly an hour ago. He should be here shortly."

"Who is he?"

"He said his name is James Derek."

"Don't you know him?"

"No. We're given an exchange to call and a man is assigned to us. It's a reciprocal arrangement."

"Isn't that convenient." A statement.

"We're billed for it."

"What will he want to know?"

"Only what we want to tell him. He won't ask any questions unless we request something either inimical to the British government or so expensive he'd have to justify it; that's the point he'll be most concerned with."

"That strikes me as very amusing."

"Taxpayers' money." Canfield looked at his watch. "I asked him to bring along a list of religious retreats."

"You're really serious about that, aren't you?"

"Yes. Unless he has a better idea. I'll be gone for about

two and half weeks. Did you write the letter for your daughter-in-law?"

"Yes." She handed him an envelope.

Across the room on a table near the door, the telephone rang. Elizabeth walked rapidly to the table and answered it.

"Is that Derek?" asked Canfield, when she had hung up.

"Yes."

"Good. Now, please, Madame Scarlatti, let me do most of the talking. But if I ask you a question, you'll know I want an honest answer."

"Oh? We don't have signals?"

"No. He doesn't want to know anything. Believe that. Actually, we're a source of embarrassment to each other."

"Should I offer him a drink, or tea, or isn't that allowed?"

"I think a drink would be very much appreciated."

"I'll call room service and have a bar sent up."

"That's fine."

Elizabeth Scarlatti picked up the phone and ordered a complete selection of wines and liquors. Canfield smiled at the ways of the rich and lit one of his thin cigars.

James Derek was a pleasant-looking man in his early fifties, somewhat rotund, with the air of a prosperous merchant. He was terribly polite but essentially cool. His perpetual smile had a tendency to curve slowly into a strained straight line as he spoke.

"We traced the license of the Rolls at the pier. It belongs to a Marquis Jacques Louis Bertholde. French resident alien. We'll get information on him."

"Good. What about the retreats?"

The Britisher took out a paper from his inside coat pocket. "There're several we might suggest depending upon Madame Scarlatti's wishes to be in touch with the outside."

"Do you have any where contact is completely impossible? On both sides?" asked the field accountant.

"That would be Catholic, of course. There're two or three."

"Now, see here!" interrupted the imposing old lady.

"What are they?" asked Canfield.

"There's a Benedictine order and a Carmelite. They're

in the southwest, incidentally. One, the Carmelite, is near Cardiff."

"There are limits, Mr. Canfield, and I propose to establish them. I will not associate with such people!"

"What is the most fashionable, most sought after retreat in England, Mr. Derek?" asked the field accountant.

"Well, the duchess of Gloucester makes a yearly trek to the Abbey of York. Church of England, of course."

"Fine. We'll send out a story to all the wire services that Madame Scarlatti has entered for a month."

"That's far more acceptable," said the old woman.

"I haven't finished." He turned to the amused Londoner. "Then book us into the Carmelites. You'll escort Madame Scarlatti there tomorrow."

"As you say."

"Just one minute, gentlemen. I do not consent! I'm sure Mr. Derek will adhere to my wishes."

"Terribly sorry, madame. My instructions are to take orders from Mr. Canfield."

"And we have an agreement, Madame Scarlatti, or do you want to tear it up?"

"What can I possibly say to such people? I simply can not stand that voodoo mumbo jumbo coming from Rome!"

"You'll be spared that discomfort, madame," said Mr. Derek. "There's a vow of silence. You'll not hear from anyone."

"Contemplate," added the field accountant. "Good for the immortal soul."

CHAPTER 23

YORK, ENGLAND, *August 12, 1926*— The famed Abbey of York sustained a damaging explosion and fire at dawn this morning in its west wing, the residential quarters of the religious order. An undisclosed number of sisters and novices were killed in the tragic occurrence. It was believed that the explosion was due to a malfunction in the heating system recently installed by the order.

Canfield read the story in the ship's newspaper one day before arriving in New York.

They do their homework well, he thought. And although the price was painfully high, it proved two points conclusively: the press releases were read and Madame Scarlatti was marked.

The field accountant reached into his pocket and took out the old woman's letter to Janet Scarlett. He'd read it many times and thought it effective. He read it once more.

My dear Child:

I am aware that you are not particularly fond of me and I accept the fact as my loss. You have every right to feel as you do—the Scarlattis have not been pleasant people with whom to be associated. However, for whatever reasons and regardless of the pain you have been caused, you are now a Scarlatti and you have borne a Scarlatti into this world. Perhaps you will be the one who will make us better than we are.

I do not make this statement lightly or out of sentiment. History has shown that the least expected among us often emerge splendidly because of the grave responsibilities placed upon them. I ask you to consider this possibility.

I further ask you to give deep consideration to what Mr. Matthew Canfield will tell you. I trust him. I do so because he has saved my life and nearly lost his own in so doing. His interests and ours are inextricably bound together. He will tell you what he can and he will ask of you a great deal.

I am a very, very old woman, my dear, and do not have much time. What months or years I do have (precious perhaps only to me) may well be cut short in a fashion I'd like to believe is not the will of God. Naturally, I accept this risk gladly as the head of the house of Scarlatti, and if I can spend what time I have left preventing a great dishonor upon our family, I will join my husband with a grateful heart.

Through Mr. Canfield, I await your answer. If it is as I suspect, we will be together shortly and you will have gladdened me far beyond that which I deserve. If it is not, you still have my affection and, believe me when I say, my understanding.

Elizabeth Wyckham Scarlatti

Canfield replaced the letter in the envelope. It was quite good, he thought again. It explained nothing and asked for implicit trust that the unsaid explanation was vitally urgent. If he did his job, the girl would be coming back to England with him. If he failed to persuade her, an alternative would have to be found.

The Ulster Scarlett brownstone on Fifty-fourth Street was being repainted and sandblasted. There were several scaffolds lowered from the roof and a number of workmen diligently at their crafts. The heavy Checker cab pulled up in front of the entrance and Matthew Canfield walked up the steps. He rang the bell; the door was opened by the obese housekeeper.

"Good afternoon, Hannah. I don't know if you remember, but my name's Canfield. Matthew Canfield to see Mrs. Scarlett."

Hannah did not budge or offer entrance. "Does Mrs. Scarlett expect you?"

"Not formally, but I'm sure she'll see me." He had had no intention of phoning. It would have been too easy for her to refuse.

"I don't know if madame is in, sir."

"Then I'll just have to wait. Shall it be here on the stairs?"

Hannah reluctantly made way for the field accountant to step into the hideously colored hallway. Canfield was struck again by the intensity of the red wallpaper and the black drapes.

"I'll inquire, sir," said the housekeeper as she started toward the stairs.

In a few minutes Janet came down the long staircase, followed by a waddling Hannah. She was very much composed. Her eyes were clear, aware, and devoid of the panic he had remembered. She was in command and without question a beautiful woman.

Canfield felt a sudden sting of inferiority. He was outclassed.

"Why, Mr. Canfield, this is a surprise."

He could not determine whether her greeting was meant to be pleasant or not. It was friendly, but cool and reserved. This girl had learned the lessons of the old money well.

"I hope not an unwelcome one, Mrs. Scarlett."

"Not at all."

Hannah had reached the bottom step and walked toward the dining room doors. Canfield quickly spoke again. "During my trip I ran across a fellow whose company makes dirigibles. I knew you'd be interested." Canfield watched Hannah out of the corner of his eye without moving his head. Hannah had turned abruptly and looked at the field accountant.

"Really, Mr. Canfield? Why would that concern me?" The girl was mystified.

"I understood your friends on Oyster Bay were determined to buy one for their club. Here, I've brought all the information. Purchase price, rentals, specifications, the works. . . . Let me show you."

The field accountant took Janet Scarlett's elbow and led her swiftly toward the living room doors. Hannah hesitated ever so slightly but, with a glance from Canfield, retreated into the dining room. Canfield then closed the living room doors.

"What are you doing? I don't want to buy a dirigible."

The field accountant stood by the doors, motioning the girl to stop talking.

"What?"

"Be quiet for a minute. Please." He spoke softly.

Canfield waited about ten seconds and then opened the doors in one swinging motion.

Directly across the hallway, standing by the dining room table, was Hannah and a man in white overalls, obviously one of the painters. They were talking while looking over toward the living room doors. They were now in full view of Canfield's stare. Embarrassed, they moved away.

Canfield shut the door and turned to Janet Scarlett. "Interesting, isn't it?"

"What are you doing?"

"Just interesting that your help should be so curious."

"Oh, that." Janet turned and picked up a cigarette from a case on the coffee table. "Servants will talk and I think you've given them cause."

Canfield lit her cigarette. "Including the painters?"

"Hannah's friends are her own business. They're no concern of mine. Hannah's barely a concern of mine. . . ."

"You don't find it curious that Hannah nearly tripped when I mentioned a dirigible?"

"I simply don't understand you."

"I admit I'm getting ahead of myself."

"Why didn't you telephone?"

"If I had, would you have seen me?"

Janet thought for a minute. "Probably. . . . Whatever recriminations I had over your last visit wouldn't be any reason to insult you."

"I didn't want to take that gamble."

"That's sweet of you and I'm touched. But why this very odd behavior?"

There was no point in delaying any longer. He took the envelope out of his pocket. "I've been asked to give you this. May I sit down while you read it?"

Janet, startled, took the envelope and immediately rec

ognized her mother-in-law's handwriting. She opened the envelope and read the letter.

If she was astonished or shocked, she hid her emotions well.

Slowly she sat down on the sofa and put out her cigarette. She looked down at the letter and up at Canfield, and then back to the letter. Without looking up, she asked quietly, "Who are you?"

"I work for the government. I'm an official . . . a minor official in the Department of the Interior."

"The government? You're not a salesman, then?"

"No, I'm not."

"You wanted to meet me and talk with me for the government?"

"Yes."

"Why did you tell me you sold tennis courts?"

"We sometimes find it necessary to conceal our employment. It's as simple as that."

"I see."

"I assume you want to know what your mother-in-law means in the letter?"

"Don't assume anything." She was cold as she continued. "It was your job to meet me and ask me all those amusing questions?"

"Frankly, yes."

The girl rose, took the necessary two steps toward the field accountant, and slapped him across the face with all her strength. It was a sharp and painful blow. "You son of a bitch! Get out of this house!" She still did not raise her voice. "Get out before I call the police!"

"Oh, my God, Janet, will you stop it!" He grabbed her shoulders as she tried to wriggle away. "Listen to me! I said listen or I'll slap you right back!"

Her eyes shone with hatred and, Canfield thought, a touch of melancholy. He held her firmly as he spoke. "Yes, I was assigned to meet you. Meet you and get whatever information I could."

She spat in his face. He did not bother to brush it away.

"I got the information I needed and I used that information because that's what I'm paid for! As far as my department is concerned, I left this house by nine o'clock after you served me two drinks. If they want to pick you up for illegal possession of alcohol, that's what they can get you for!"

"I don't believe you!"

"I don't give a good God damn whether you do or not! And for your further information I've had you under surveillance for weeks! You and the rest of your playmates. . . . It may interest you to know that I've omitted detailing the more . . . ludicrous aspects of your day-to-day activities!"

The girl's eyes began to fill with tears.

"I'm doing my job as best I can, and I'm not so sure you're the one who should scream 'violated virgin'! You may not realize it, but your husband, or former husband, or whatever the hell he is, could be very much alive. A lot of nice people who never heard of him—women like you and young girls—were burned to death because of him! Others were killed, too, but maybe they should have been."

"What are you saying?" He relaxed his grip on her but still held her firmly.

"I just know that I left your mother-in-law a week ago in England. It was a hell of a trip over! Someone tried to kill her the first night out on the ship. Oh, you can bet your life it would have been suicide! They would have said she had tearfully thrown herself overboard. No trace at all. . . . A week ago we let out a story to the newspapers saying she'd gone to a retreat in a place called York, in England. Two days ago the heating system blew up and killed Christ knows how many people! An accident, of course!"

"I don't know what to say."

"Do you want me to finish, or do you still want me to go?"

There was a sadness about Ulster Scarlett's wife as she tried to smile. "I guess you'd better stay and . . . finish."

They sat on the sofa and Canfield talked.

He talked as he had never talked before.

CHAPTER 24

Benjamin Reynolds sat forward in his chair, clipping a week-old article from the Sunday supplement of the *New York Herald.* It was a photograph of Janet Saxon Scarlett being escorted by "sportingoods executive, M. Canfield" to a dog show at Madison Square Garden. Reynolds smiled as he recalled Canfield's remark on the telephone.

"I can stand everything but the God damn dog shows. Dogs are for the very rich or the very poor. Not for anyone in between!"

No matter, thought Group Twenty's head. The newspapers were doing an excellent job. Washington had ordered Canfield to spend an additional ten days in Manhattan thoroughly establishing his relationship with Ulster Scarlett's wife before returning to England.

The relationship was unmistakable and Benjamin Reynolds wondered if it was really a public facade. Or was it something else? Was Canfield in the process of trapping himself? The ease with which he had engineered a collaboration with Elizabeth Scarlatti bore watching.

"Ben"—Glover walked briskly into the office—"I think we've found what we've been looking for!" He closed the door firmly and approached Reynolds's desk.

"What have you got? About what?"

"A link with the Scarlatti business. I'm sure of it."

"Let me see."

Glover placed several pages on top of the spread-out newspaper. "Nice coverage, wasn't it?" he said, indicating the photograph of Canfield and the girl.

"Just what us dirty old men ordered. He's going to be the toast of society if he doesn't spit on the floor."

"He's doing a good job, Ben. They're back on board ship now, aren't they?"

"Sailed yesterday. . . . What is this?"

"Statistics found it. From Switzerland. Zurich area. Fourteen estates all purchased within the year. Look at these latitude and longitude marks. Every one of the properties is adjacent to another one. A borders on B, B on C, C on D, right down the line. Hundreds of thousands of acres forming an enormous compound."

"One of the buyers Scarlatti?"

"No. . . . But one of the estates was bought in the name of Boothroyd. Charles Boothroyd."

"You're sure? What do you mean 'bought in the name of'?"

"Father-in-law bought it for his daughter and her husband. Named Rawlins. Thomas Rawlins. Partner in the brokerage house of Godwin and Rawlins. His daughter's name is Cecily. Married to Boothroyd."

Reynolds picked up the page with the list of names. "Who are these people? How does it break down?"

Glover reached for the other two pages. "It's all here. Four Americans, two Swedes, three English, two French, and three German. Fourteen in all."

"Do you have any rundowns?"

"Only on the Americans. We've sent for information on the rest."

"Who are they? Besides Rawlins."

"A Howard Thornton, San Francisco. He's in construction. And two Texas oilmen. A Louis Gibson and Avery Landor. Between them they own more wells than fifty of their competitors combined."

"Any connections between them?"

"Nothing so far. We're checking that out now."

"What about the others? The Swedes, the French? . . . The English and the Germans?"

"Only the names."

"Anyone familiar?"

"Several. There's an Innes-Bowen, he's English, in textiles, I think. And I recognize the name of Daudet, French. Owns steamship lines. And two of the Germans. Kindorf—he's in the Ruhr Valley. Coal. And von Schritzer, speaks for I. G. Farben. Don't know the rest, never heard of the Swedes, either."

"In one respect they're all alike—"

"You bet your life they are. They're all as rich as a roomful of Astors. You don't buy places like these with mortgages. Shall I contact Canfield?"

"We'll have to. Send the list by courier. We'll cable him to stay in London until it arrives."

"Madame Scarlatti may know some of them."

"I'm counting on it. . . . But I see a problem."

"What's that?"

"It's going to be a temptation for the old girl to head right into Zurich. . . . If she does, she's dead. So's Canfield and Scarlett's wife."

"That's a pretty drastic assumption."

"Not really. We're presuming that a group of wealthy men have bought fourteen estates all adjoining one another because of a common interest. And Boothroyd—courtesy of a generous father-in-law—is one of them."

"Which ties Zurich to Scarlatti. . . ."

"We think so. We believe it because Boothroyd tried to kill her, right?"

"Of course."

"But the Scarlatti woman is alive. Boothroyd failed."

"Obviously."

"And the property was purchased before that fact."

"It must have been—"

"Then if Zurich is tied to Boothroyd, Zurich wants Scarlatti dead. They want to stop her. Also . . . Zurich presumed success. They expected Boothroyd to succeed."

"And now that he's gone," interrupted Glover, "Zurich will figure the old woman found out who he was. Maybe more. . . . Ben, perhaps we've gone too far. It might be better to call it off. Make a report to Justice and get Canfield back."

"Not yet. We're getting close to something. Elizabeth Scarlatti's the key right now. We'll get them plenty of protection."

"I don't want to make an alibi in advance, but this is your responsibility."

"I understand that. In our instructions to Canfield make one thing absolutely clear. He's to stay out of Zurich. Under no condition is he to go to Switzerland."

"I'll do that."

Reynolds turned from his desk and stared out the window. He spoke to his subordinate without looking at him. "And . . . keep a line open on this Rawlins. Boothroyd's father-in-law. He's the one who may have made the mistake."

CHAPTER 25

Twenty-five miles from the ancient limits of Cardiff, set in a remote glen in a Welsh forest, stands the Convent of the Virgin, the home of the Carmelite sisters. The walls rise in alabaster purity, like a new bride standing in holy expectation in a lush but serpentless Eden.

The field accountant and the young wife drove up to the entrance. Canfield got out of the car and walked to a small arched doorway set in the wall in which was centered a viewer. There was a black iron knocker on the side of the door that he used, then waited for several minutes until a nun answered.

"May I help you?"

The field accountant drew out his indentification card and held it up for the nun to see. "My name is Canfield, sister. I'm here for Madame Elizabeth Scarlatti. Her daughter-in-law is with me."

"If you'll wait, please. May I?" She indicated that she wished to take his identification card with her. He handed it to her through the small opening.

"If course."

The viewer was closed and bolted. Canfield wandered back to the car and spoke to Janet. "They're very cautious."

"What's happening?"

"She's taking my card in to make sure the photograph's me and not someone else."

"Lovely here, isn't it? So quiet."

"It is now. I make no promises when we finally see the old girl."

"Your callous, unfeeling disregard for my well-being, to say nothing of my comforts, is beyond anything I can describe! Do you have any idea what these idiots sleep on? I'll tell you! Army cots!"

"I'm sorry—" Canfield tried not to laugh.

"And do you know the slops they eat? I'll tell you! Food I'd prohibit in my stables!"

"I'm told they grow their own vegetables," the field accountant countered gently.

"They pluck up the fertilizer and leave the plants!"

At that moment the bells of the Angelus pealed out.

"That goes on night and day! I asked that damned fool, Mother MacCree, or whoever she is, why so early in the morning—and do you what know what she said?"

"What, Mother?" asked Janet.

" 'That is the way of Christ,' that's what she said. 'Not a good Episcopal Christ!' I told her. . . . It's been intolerable! Why were you so late? Mr. Derek said you'd be here four days ago."

"I had to wait for a courier from Washington. Let's go. I'll tell you about it."

Elizabeth sat in the back seat of the Bentley reading the Zurich list.

"Know any of those people?" asked Canfield.

"Not personally. Most all of them by reputation, however."

"For instance?"

"The Americans, Louis Gibson and Avery Landor are two self-styled Texas Bunyans. They think they built the oil territories. Landor's a pig, I'm told. Harold Leacock, one of the Englishmen, is a power on the British Stock Exchange. Very bright. Myrdal from Sweden is also in the European market. Stockholm. . . ." Elizabeth looked up and acknowledged Canfield's glance in the rearview mirror.

"Anybody else?"

"Yes. Thyssen in Germany. Fritz Thyssen. Steel companies. Everyone knows Kindorf—Ruhr Valley coal, and von Schnitzler. He's I. G. Farben now. . . . One of the Frenchmen, D'Almeida, has control of railroads, I think. I don't know Daudet but I recognize the name."

"He owns tankers. Steamships."

"Oh, yes. And Masterson. Sydney Masterson. English. Far East imports, I think. I don't know Innes-Bowen, but again I've heard the name."

"You didn't mention Rawlins. Thomas Rawlins."

"I didn't think I had to. Godwin and Rawlins. Boothroyd's father-in-law."

"You don't know the fourth American, Howard Thornton? He's from San Francisco."

"Never heard of him."

"Janet says your son knew a Thornton from San Francisco."

"I'm not at all surprised."

On the road from Pontypridd, on the outskirts of the Rhondda Valley, Canfield became aware of an automobile, which regularly appeared in his side mirror. It was far behind them, hardly more than a speck in the glass, but it was never out of sight except around curves. And whenever Canfield rounded one of the many turns, the automobile appeared subsequently much sooner than its previous distance would indicate. On long stretches it stayed far in the distance and whenever possible allowed other cars to come between them.

"What is it, Mr. Canfield?" Elizabeth was watching the field accountant, who kept shifting his eyes to the mirror outside his window.

"Nothing."

"Is someone following us?"

"Probably not. There aren't that many good roads leading to the English border."

Twenty minutes later Canfield saw that the automobile was drawing nearer. Five minutes after that he began to understand. There were no cars between the two vehicles now. Only a stretch of road—a very long curve—bordered on one side by the rocky slope of a small incline and on the other by a sheer drop of fifty feet into the waters of a Welsh lake.

Beyond the end of the curve, Canfield saw that the ground leveled off into a pasture or overgrown field. He accelerated the Bentley. He wanted to reach that level area.

The car behind shot forward closing the gap between them. It swung to the right on the side of the road by the rocky slope. Canfield knew that once the car came parallel it could easily force him off the road, over the edge, plunging the Bentley down the steep incline into the water. The field accountant held the pedal down and veered the car toward the center trying to cut off the pursuer.

"What is it? What are you doing?" Janet held on to the top of the dashboard.

"Brace yourselves! Both of you!"

Canfield held the Bentley in the center, crossing to the right each time the car behind him tried to squeeze between him and the solid ground. The level field was nearer now. Only another hundred yards.

There were two sharp, heavy crunches as the Bentley lurched spastically under the second car's impact. Janet Scarlett screamed. Her mother-in-law kept silent, clutching the girl's shoulders from behind, helping to brace her.

The level pasture was now on the left and Canfield suddenly swerved the car toward it, going off the road, holding to the dirt border beyond the pavement.

The pursuing car plunged forward at tremendous speed. Canfield riveted his eyes on the rapidly receding black-and-white license plate. He shouted, "*E, B . . . I* or *L!* Seven! Seven or nine! One, one, three!" He repeated the numbers again softly, quickly. He slowed the Bentley down and came to a stop.

Janet's back was arched against the seat. She held Elizabeth's arms with both her hands. The old woman sat forward, her cheek pressed against her daughter-in-law's head.

Elizabeth spoke.

"The letters you called out were *E, B, I* or *L*, the numbers, seven or nine, one, one, three."

"I couldn't tell the make of the car."

Elizabeth spoke again as she took her arms from Janet's shoulders.

"It was a Mercedes-Benz."

CHAPTER 26

"The automobile in question is a Mercedes-Benz coupé. Nineteen twenty-five model. The license is EBI nine, one, one, three. The vehicle is registered in the name of Jacques Louis Bertholde. Once again, the Marquis de Bertholde." James Derek stood by Canfield in front of Elizabeth and Janet who sat on the sofa. He read from his notebook and wondered if these curious Americans realized who the marquis was. Bertholde, too, often stayed at the Savoy and was probably as rich as Elizabeth Scarlatti.

"The same man who met Boothroyd's wife at the pier?" asked Canfield.

"Yes. Or I should say, no. We assume it was Bertholde at the pier from your description. It couldn't have been yesterday. We've established that he was in London. However, the automobile is registered to him."

"What do you think, Mr. Derek?" Elizabeth smoothed her dress and avoided looking at the Englishman. There was something about the man that disturbed her.

"I don't know what to think. . . . However, I feel I should tell you that the Marquis de Bertholde is a resident alien of considerable influence and position. . . ."

"He is the owner of Bertholde et Fils, as I recall." Elizabeth rose from the sofa and gave her empty sherry glass to Canfield. It was not that she wished more wine. She was just too wrought up to sit still. "Bertholde et Fils is an old established firm."

The field accountant went to the drinks table and poured Elizabeth's sherry.

"Then you've met the marquis, Madame Scarlatti? Perhaps you know him?"

Elizabeth didn't like Derek's insinuation. "No, I do not know the marquis. I may have met his father. I'm not sure. The Bertholdes go back many years."

Canfield handed Elizabeth her glass aware that the old woman and the British operative were playing a mental tennis game. He broke in. "What's his business?"

"Plural. Businesses. Near East oil, mining and drilling in Africa, imports—Australia and South America. . . ."

"Why is he a resident alien?"

"I can answer that," said Elizabeth, returning to the couch. "The physical plants—his offices—are, no doubt, within Empire territories or protectorates."

"Quite correct, madame," said Derek. "Since the majority of his interests lie within the borders of British possessions, he deals continuously with Whitehall. He does so, most favorably."

"Is there a government dossier on Bertholde?"

"As a resident alien, of course there is."

"Can you get it for me?"

"I'd have to have a very sound reason. You know that."

"Mr. Derek!" interrupted Elizabeth. "An attempt was made on my life aboard the *Calpurnia!* Yesterday in Wales an automobile tried to run us off the road! In both instances the Marquis de Bertholde can be implicated. I would call these sound reasons!"

"I'm afraid I must disagree. What you describe are police matters. Anything I know to the contrary is privileged information and I respect it as such. Certainly no charges are being made in either case. It's a gray area, I grant you, but Canfield knows what I'm talking about."

The field accountant looked at Elizabeth and she knew the time had come to use his ploy. He had explained that eventually they would have to. He had called it—"part of the truth." The reason was simple. British Intelligence was not going to be used as someone's personal police force. There had to be other justifications. Justifications that Washington would confirm. Canfield looked at the Englishman and spoke softly.

"The United States government wouldn't involve any agency unless there were reasons beyond police matters. When Madame Scarlatti's son—Mrs. Scarlett's husband—

was in Europe last year, large sums of money, in the form of negotiable securities on a number of American corporations, were forwarded to him. We think they were sold undercover on the European markets. The British exchange included."

"Are you telling me that someone is forming an American monopoly over here?"

"The State Department thinks that the manipulation was handled by our own embassy personnel. They're right here in London now."

"Your own embassy personnel! And you think Scarlett was a party to it?"

"We think he was used." Elizabeth's voice pierced the air. "Used and then eliminated."

"He traveled in that crowd, Derek. So does the Marquis de Bertholde."

James Derek replaced his small notebook in his breast pocket. The explanation obviously was sufficient. The British operative was also very curious. "I'll have a copy of the dossier for you tomorrow, Canfield. . . . Good evening, ladies." He went out.

"I congratulate you, young man. Embassy personnel. Really very intelligent of you."

"I think he was remarkable!" said Janet Scarlett, smiling at him.

"It'll work," mumbled the field accountant, swallowing the major portion of a Scotch. "Now, may I suggest we all need some relief. Speaking for myself, I'm tired of thinking—and I wouldn't appreciate a comment on that, Madame Scarlatti. How about dinner at one of those places you upper class always go? I hate dancing but I swear I'll dance with you both until you drop."

Elizabeth and Janet laughed.

"No, but I thank you," said Elizabeth. "You two go and romp." She looked at the field accountant fondly. "An old woman thanks you again, Mr. Canfield."

"You'll lock the doors and windows?"

"Seven stories off the ground? Of course, if you like."

"I do," said Canfield.

CHAPTER 27

"It's heaven!" shrieked Janet over the din of voices at Claridge's. "Come on, Matthew, don't look so sour!"

"I'm not sour. I just can't hear you."

"Yes, you are. You didn't like it. Let me enjoy it."

"I will. I will! Do you want to dance?"

"No. You hate dancing. I just want to watch."

"No charge. Watch. It's good whiskey."

"Good what?"

"I said whiskey."

"No, thanks. See? I can be good. You're two up on me, you know."

"I may be sixty up on you if this keeps going."

"What, darling?"

"I said I may be sixty when we get out of here."

"Oh, stop it. Have fun!"

Canfield looked at the girl opposite him and felt once again a surge of joy. There was no other word but joy. She was a delight that filled him with pleasure, with warmth. Her eyes held the immediacy of commitment that only a lover can know. Yet Canfield tried so hard to disassociate, to isolate, to objectify, and found that he could not do it.

"I love you very much," he said.

She heard him through the music, the laughter, the undercurrent hum of movement.

"I know." She looked at him and her eyes had the hint of tears. "We love each other. Isn't that remarkable?"

"Do you want to dance, now?"

The girl threw back her head ever so slightly. "Oh,

Matthew! My dear, sweet Matthew. No, darling. You don't have to dance."

"Now, look, I will."

She clasped his hand. "We'll dance by ourselves, all by ourselves later."

Matthew Canfield made up his mind that he would have this woman for the rest of his life.

But he was a professional and his thoughts turned for a moment to the old woman at the Savoy.

Elizabeth Wyckham Scarlatti at that moment got out of her bed and into a dressing gown. She had been reading the *Manchester Guardian.* Turning its thin pages, she heard two sharp metallic clicks accompanied by a muffled sound of movement from the living room. She was not at first startled by the noise; she had bolted the hallway door and presumed that her daughter-in-law was fumbling with a key unable to enter because of the latch. After all, it was two o'clock in the morning and the girl should have returned by now. She called out.

"Just one minute, my dear. I'm up."

She had left a table lamp on and the fringe of the shade rippled as she passed it causing a flickering of minute shadows on the wall.

She reached the door and began to unbolt the latch. Remembering the field accountant, she halted momentarily.

"That is you, isn't it, my dear?"

There was no reply.

She automatically snapped back the bolt.

"Janet? Mr. Canfield? Is that you?"

Silence.

Fear gripped Elizabeth. She had heard the sound; age had not impaired her hearing.

Perhaps she had confused the clicking with the unfamiliar rustling of the thin English newspaper. That was not unreasonable and although she tried to believe it, she could not.

Was there someone else in the room?

At the thought she felt pain in the pit of her stomach.

As she turned to go back into the bedroom, she saw that one of the large french windows was partially opened, no more than one or two inches but enough to cause the silk draperies to sway slightly from the incoming breeze.

In her confusion she tried to recall whether she had closed it before. She thought she had, but it had been an uninterested motion because she hadn't taken Canfield seriously. Why should she? They were seven stories high.

Of course, she hadn't closed it. Or, if she had, she hadn't secured the catch and it had slipped off. Nothing at all unusual. She crossed to the window and pushed it closed.

And then she heard it.

"Hello, Mother."

Out of the shadows from the far end of the room walked a large man dressed in black. His head was shaved and he was deeply tanned.

For several seconds she did not recognize him. The light from the one table lamp was dim and the figure remained at the end of the room. As she became adjusted to the light and the object of her gaze, she realized why the man appeared to be a stranger. The face had changed. The shining black hair was shaved off; the nose was altered, smaller and the nostrils wider apart; the ears were different, flatter against the head; even the eyes—where before there had been a Neapolitan droop to the lids—these eyes were wide, as if no lids existed. There were reddish splotches around the mouth and forehead. It was not a face. It was the mask of a face. It was striking. It was monstrous. And it was her son.

"Ulster! My God!"

"If you die right now of heart failure, you'll make fools out of several highly paid assassins."

The old woman tried to think, tried with all her strength to resist panic. She gripped the back of a chair until the veins in her aged hands seemed to burst from the skin.

"If you've come to kill me, there's little I can do now."

"You'll be interested to know that the man who ordered you killed will soon be dead himself. He was stupid."

Her son wandered toward the french window and checked the latch. He cautiously peered through the glass and was satisfied. His mother noticed that the grace with which he had always carried himself remained but there was no softness now, no gentle relaxation, which had taken the form of a slight aristocratic slouch. Now there was a taut, hard quality in his movement, accentuated by his hands—which were encased in skintight black gloves, fingers extended and rigidly curved.

Elizabeth slowly found the words. "Why have you come here?"

"Because of your obstinate curiosity." He walked rapidly to the hotel phone on the table with the lighted lamp, touching the cradle as if making sure it was secure. He returned to within a few feet of his mother and the sight of his face, now seen clearly, caused her to shut her eyes. When she reopened them, he was rubbing his right eyebrow, which was partially inflamed. He watched her pained look.

"The scars aren't quite healed. Occasionally they itch. Are you maternally solicitous?"

"What have you done to yourself?"

"A new life. A new world for me. A world which has nothing to do with yours. Not yet!"

"I asked you what you've done."

"You know what I've done, otherwise you wouldn't be here in London. What you must understand, now, is that Ulster Scarlett no longer exists."

"If that's what you want the world to believe, why come to me of all people?"

"Because you rightly assumed it wasn't true and your meddling could prove irksome to me."

The old woman steeled herself before speaking. "It's quite possible then that the instructions for my death were not stupid."

"That's very brave. I wonder, though, if you've thought about the others?"

"What others?"

Scarlett sat on the couch and spoke in a biting Italian dialect. "La Famiglia Scarlatti! That's the proper phrase, isn't it? . . . Eleven members to be exact. Two parents, a grandmother, a drunken bitch wife, and seven children. The end of the tribe! The Scarlatti line abruptly stops in one bloody massacre!"

"You're mad! I'd stop you! Don't pit your piddling theft against what I have, my boy!"

"You're a foolish old woman! We're beyond sums. It's only how they're applied now. You taught me that!"

"I'd put them out of your reach! I'd have you hunted down and destroyed!"

The man effortlessly sprang up from the couch.

"We're wasting time. You're concerning yourself with mechanics. That's pedestrian. Let's be clear. I make one phone call and the order is sent to New York. Within forty-eight hours the Scarlattis are snuffed out! Extinguished! It will be an expensive funeral. The foundation will provide nothing but the best."

"Your own child as well?"

"He'd be the first. All dead. No apparent reason. The mystery of the lunatic Scarlattis."

"You are mad." She was hardly audible.

"Speak up, Mother! Or are you thinking about those curly headed moppets romping on the beach at Newport, laughing in their little boats on the sound. Tragic, isn't it? Just one of them! Just one out of the whole lot might make it for you, and the Scarlatti tribe continues in glory! Shall I make my call? It's a matter of indifference to me."

The old woman, who had not moved, walked slowly toward one of the armchairs. "Is what you want from me so valuable that the lives of my family depend upon it?"

"Not to you. Only to me. It could be worse, you know. I could demand an additional one hundred million."

"Why don't you? Under the circumstances you know I'd pay it."

The man laughed. "Certainly you'd pay it. You'd pay it from a source that'd cause a panic in the ticker rooms. No, thank you. I don't need it. Remember, we're beyond sums."

"What is it you want?" She sat in the chair, crossing her thin arms on her lap.

"The bank letters for one. They're no good to you anyway, so there should be no struggle with your conscience."

She had been right! The concept had been right! Always trace the practical. The money.

"Bank letters?"

"The bank letters Cartwright gave you."

"You killed him! You knew about our agreement?"

"Come, Mother. A Southern ass is made vice-president of Waterman Trust! Actually given responsibility. We followed him for three days. We have your agreement. At least his copies. Let's not fool each other. The letters, please."

The old lady rose from the chair and went into her bedroom. She returned and handed him the letters. He rapidly opened the envelopes and took them out. He spread them on the couch and counted them.

"Cartwright earned his money."

He gathered them up and casually sat down on the sofa.

"I had no idea those letters were so important."

"They're not, really. Nothing could be accomplished with them. All the accounts have been closed and the money . . . dispersed to others, shall we say."

"Then why were you so anxious to get them?" She remained standing.

"If they were submitted to the banks, they could start a lot of speculation. We don't want a great deal of talk right now."

The old woman searched her son's confident eyes. He was detached, pleased with himself, almost relaxed.

"Who is 'we'? What are you involved in?"

Again that grotesque smile from the crooked mouth underneath the unnatural nostrils. "You'll know in good time. Not by name, of course, but you'll know. You might even be proud but you'll never admit it." He looked at his wristwatch. "Down to business."

"What else?"

"What happened on the *Calpurnia*? Don't lie!" He riveted his eyes on the old woman's and they did not waver.

Elizabeth strained the muscles in her abdomen to help her conceal any reaction to the question. She knew that the truth might be all she had left. "I don't understand you."

"You're lying!"

"About what? I received a cablegram from a man named Boutier concerning Cartwright's death."

"Stop it!" He leaned forward. "You wouldn't have gone to the trouble of throwing everyone off with that York Abbey story unless something happened. I want to know where he is."

"Where who is? Cartwright?"

"I warn you!"

"I have no idea what you're talking about!"

"A man disappeared on that ship! They say he fell overboard."

"Oh, yes. I recall. . . . What has that to do with me?" Her look personified innocence.

Neither moved.

"You know nothing about the incident?"

"I didn't say that."

"What did you say, then?"

"There were rumors. Reliable sources."

"What rumors?"

The old woman weighed several replies. She knew that her answer had to have the ring of authenticity without any obvious errors in character or behavior. On the other hand, whatever she said had to reflect the sketchy extremes of gossip.

"That the man was drunk and belligerent. There'd been a struggle in the lounge. . . . He had to be subdued and carried to his stateroom. He tried to return and fell over the rail. Did you know him?"

A cloud of detachment covered Scarlett's answer. "No, he was no part of us." He was dissatisfied but he did not dwell on it. For the first time in several minutes he looked away from her. He was deep in thought. Finally he spoke. "One last item. You started out to find your missing son . . ."

"I started out to find a thief!" she interrupted sharply.

"Have it your way. From another point of view I simply moved up the calendar."

"That's not true! You stole from Scarlatti. What was assigned to you was to be used in conjunction with the Scarlatti Industries!"

"We're wasting time again."

"I wanted the point cleared up."

"The point is that you set out to find me and you succeeded. We agree on that fact?"

"Agreed."

"Now I'm telling you to say nothing, do nothing, and return to New York. Furthermore, destroy any letters or instructions you may have left concerning me."

"Those are impossible demands!"

"In that event my orders go out. The Scarlattis are dead! Go to your church and let them tell you how they've been washed in the blood of the lamb!"

Ulster Scarlett sprang up from the Victorian couch and before the old woman could adjust her eyes to his movement, he had reached the telephone. There wasn't the slightest hesitation on his part. He picked up the telephone without looking at her and waited for the switchboard to answer.

The old woman rose unsteadily. "Don't!"

He turned to face her. "Why not?"

"I'll do as you ask!"

He replaced the phone. "Are you sure?"

"I'm sure." He had won.

Ulster Scarlett smiled with his misshapen lips. "Then our business is concluded."

"Not quite." Elizabeth now would try, realizing that the attempt might cost her her life.

"Oh?"

"I'd like to speculate, for just a minute."

"On what?"

"For the sake of argument, supposing I decided to abandon our understanding?"

"You know the consequences. You couldn't hide from us, not for any length of time."

"Time, however, could be the factor on my side."

"The securities have been disposed of. No sense in thinking about that."

"I assumed they had been, or else you wouldn't have come here."

"This is a good game. Go on."

"I'm sure that if you hadn't thought of it yourself, someone would have told you that the only intelligent way of selling those securities would be on a currency basis in exchange for diminished value."

"No one had to tell me."

"Now it's my turn to ask a question."

"Go ahead."

"How difficult do you think it is to trace deposits, gold or otherwise, of that magnitude? I'll make it two questions. Where are the only banks in the world willing or even capable of such deposits?"

"We both know the answer. Coded, numbered, impossible."

"And in which of the great banking concerns of Switzerland is there the incorruptible man?"

Her son paused and squinted his lidless eyes. "Now you're the one who's insane," he answered quietly.

"Not at all. You think in small blocks, Ulster. You use large sums but you think in small blocks. . . . Word goes out in the marble halls of Bern and Zurich that the sum of one million American dollars can be had for the confidential exchange of information. . . ."

"What would you gain by it?"

"Knowledge! . . . Names! People!"

"You make me laugh!"

"Your laughter will be short-lived! . . . It's obvious that you have associates; you need them. Your threats make that doubly clear, and I'm sure you pay them well. . . . The question is—once they're known to me and I to them—will they be able to resist my price? Certainly you can never match it! In this we are not beyond sums!"

The grotesque face distorted itself further as a thick, drawlish laugh came forth from the misshapen mouth. "I've waited years to tell you that your slide-rule theories smell! Your stinking buy-me, sell-me manipulations are finished! You've had your way! It's finished! Dead! Gone! . . . Who are you to manipulate? With your conniving bankers! Your stinking little Jews! You're finished! I've watched you! Your kind is dead! . . . Don't talk to me about my associates. They wouldn't touch you or your money!" The man in black was in a rage.

"You believe that?" Elizabeth did not move. She asked a simple question.

"Completely!" Ulster Scarlett's unhealed flesh was red with the blood rushing to his head. "We have something else! And you can't touch us! Any of us! *There is no price for us!*"

"However, you'll grant—as with the bank letters—I could prove irksome. Only to a far greater degree. Do you wish to take that gamble?"

"You sign eleven death warrants! A mass burial! Is that what you want, Mother?"

"The answer to both our questions would seem to be no. This is now a more reasonable understanding."

The man-mask in black paused and spoke softly, precisely. "You're not my equal. Don't for one minute think you are!"

"What happened, Ulster? What happened? . . . Why?"

"Nothing and everything! I'm doing what none of you

are capable of doing! What has to be done! But you can't do it!"

"Would I . . . or we . . . want to?"

"More than anything in the world? But you haven't the stomachs! You're weak!"

The telephone rang, piercing the air.

"Don't bother to answer it," Ulster said. "It'll ring only once. It's merely a signal that my wife—the devoted whore—and her newest bedmate have left Claridge's."

"Then I assume our meeting is adjourned." She saw to her great relief that he accepted the statement. She noted also that in such a position he was dangerous. A tick was developing on the surface of his skin above his right eye. He again stretched his fingers in a slow deliberate motion.

"Remember what I say. You make one mistake . . ."

She interrupted before he could finish. "Remember who I am, young man! You're speaking to the wife of Giovanni Merighi Scarlatti! There is no need to repeat yourself. You have your agreement. Go about your filthy business. I have no further interest in you!"

The man in black strode rapidly to the door. "I hate you, Mother."

"I hope you benefit as much from those you hold less dear."

"In ways you'd never understand!"

He opened the door and slipped out, slamming it harshly behind him.

Elizabeth Scarlatti stood by the window and pulled apart the drapes. She leaned against the cold glass for support. The city of London was asleep, and only a scattering of lights dotted its concrete facade.

What in God's name had he done?

More important, who was paying attention to him?

What might have been mere horror turned into terror for he had the weapon. The weapon of power—which she and Giovanni innocently, productively provided.

They were, indeed, beyond sums.

Tears fell from her old eyes and that inner consciousness, which afflicts all human beings, was taken by surprise. She had not cried in over thirty years.

Elizabeth pushed herself away from the window and slowly wandered about the room. She had a great deal of thinking to do.

CHAPTER 28

In a room in the Home Office, James Derek took out a file. "Jacques Louis Bertholde, The Fourth Marquis of Chatellerault."

The dossier custodian entered the room. "Hello, James. Late hours tonight, I see."

"I'm afraid so, Charles. I'm taking out a copy. Did you get my request?"

"Right here. Fill me in and I'll sign for it. But please make it short. I've a card game in my office."

"Short and simple. The Americans suspect their embassy personnel of selling Yank securities undercover over here. This Bertholde travels in the diplomatic circles. There could be a connection with the Scarlatti fellow."

The dossier custodian made his appropriate notes. "When did this all take place?"

"About a year ago, as I understand it."

The custodian stopped writing and looked at James Derek. "A year ago?"

"Yes."

"And this American chap wants to confront embassy personnel *now?* Over *here?*"

"That's right."

"He's on the wrong side of the Atlantic. All American embassy personnel were transferred four months ago. There's no one there now—not even a secretary—who was in London a year ago."

"That's very strange," said Derek quietly.

"I'd say your American friend has a rather poor connection with his State Department."

"Which means he's lying."

"Which means he is."

Janet and Matthew, laughing, got off on the seventh floor and started down the corridor toward Elizabeth's suite. The length of their walk was approximately one hundred feet and they stopped four times to embrace and exchange kisses.

The girl took a key out of her purse and handed it to the field accountant.

He inserted it and simultaneously turned the knob before making any lateral motion with the key. The door opened and in a split second the field accountant was more sober than drunk.

He practically fell into the room.

Elizabeth Scarlatti was sitting on the Victorian couch in the dim light emanating from the single lamp. She did not move other than to look up at Canfield and her daughter-in-law.

"I heard you in the hallway."

"I told you to lock these doors!"

"I'm sorry, I forgot."

"The hell you did! I waited until I heard the latch and the bolt!"

"I ordered some coffee from room service."

"Where's the tray?"

"In my bedroom, which I presume to be private."

"Don't you believe it!" The field accountant ran toward the bedroom door.

"I apologize again! I called to have it taken away. I'm quite confused. Forgive me."

"Why? What's the matter?"

Elizabeth Scarlatti thought quickly and looked at her daughter-in-law as she spoke. "I had a most distressing telephone call. A business matter completely unrelated to you. It entails a great deal of money and I must make a decision before the British exchange opens." She looked at the field accountant.

"May I ask what's so important that you don't follow my instructions?"

"Several million dollars. Perhaps you'd care to help me. Should the Scarlatti Industries conclude the purchase of the remaining convertible debentures in Sheffield Cutlery and by exercising the conversions gain control of the company or not?"

Still uncertain, the field accountant asked, "Why is that so . . . distressing?"

"Because the company constantly loses money."

"Then you don't buy. That shouldn't keep you up all night."

The old woman eyed him coldly. "Sheffield Cutlery is one of the oldest, finest firms in England. Their product is superb. The problem is neither management nor labor conditions but a heavy influx of Japanese imitations. The question is, Will the purchasing public learn in time to reverse the trend?"

Elizabeth Scarlatti rose from the couch and went into her bedroom, closing the door behind her. The field accountant turned to Janet Scarlett. "Does she do this sort of thing all the time? Doesn't she have advisers?"

But Janet was still staring at the bedroom door. She took off her wrap and approached the field accountant. She spoke quietly. "She's not telling the truth."

"How do you know?"

"The way she looked at me when she was talking to you. She was trying to tell me something."

"Like what?"

The girl shrugged impatiently and continued in a hushed whisper. "Oh, I don't know, but you know what I mean. You're with a group of people, and you start to tell a whopper or exaggerate something, and while you do, you look at your husband or a friend who knows better . . . and they know they shouldn't correct you. . . ."

"Was she lying about that company she spoke of?"

"Oh, no. That's the truth. Chancellor Drew's been trying to persuade her to buy that firm for months."

"How do you know?"

"She's already turned it down."

"Then why did she lie?"

As Canfield started to sit down, his attention was drawn to the linen antimacassar on the back of the chair. At first he dismissed it and then he looked again. The material was crumpled as if it had been mangled or bunched together. It was out of place in an immaculate suite. He looked closer. There were breaks in the threads and the imprint of fingertips was unmistakable. Whoever had gripped the chair had done so with considerable force.

"What is it, Matthew?"

"Nothing. Get me a drink, will you?"

"Of course, darling." She went to the dry bar as Canfield walked around the chair in front of the french window. For no particular reason, he pulled apart the curtains and inspected the window itself. He turned the latch and pulled the left side open. He saw what he had begun to look for. The wood around the clasp was scratched. On the sill he could see where the paint had been discolored by the impression of a heavy coarse object, probably a rubber-soled boot or a crepe-soled shoe. Not leather; there were no scratches on the enamel. He opened the right side and looked out. Below were six stories straight down; above two floors to what he recalled was an acutely slanting roof. He pushed the window shut and locked it.

"What on earth are you doing?"

"We've had a visitor. An uninvited guest, you might say."

The girl stood absolutely still. "Oh, my God!"

"Don't be frightened. Your mother-in-law wouldn't do anything foolish. Believe that."

"I'm trying to. What are we going to do?"

"Find out who it was. Now get hold of yourself. I'll need you."

"Why didn't she say something?"

"I don't know, but you may be able to find out."

"How?"

"Tomorrow morning she'll probably bring up the Sheffield business. If she does, tell her you remember she refused to buy it for Chancellor. She'll have to give you an explanation of some kind."

"If Mother Scarlatti doesn't want to talk, she just won't. I know."

"Then don't press it. But she'll have to say something."

Although it was nearly three o'clock, the lobby had a flow of stragglers from late parties. They were mostly in evening dress, a great many were unbalanced and giggling, all were happily tired.

Canfield went to the desk clerk and spoke in a gentle, folksy tone. "Say, fella, I've got a little problem."

"Yes, sir. May we be of service?"

"Well, it's a bit touchy. . . . I'm traveling with Madame Elizabeth Scarlatti and her daughter. . . ."

"Oh, yes indeed. Mr. . . . Canfield, isn't it?"

"Sure. Well, the old girl's getting on, you know, and the people above her keep pretty late hours."

The clerk, who knew the legend of the Scarlatti wealth, was abject in apology. "I'm dreadfully sorry, Mr. Canfield. I'll go up myself at once. This is most embarrassing."

"Oh, no, please, everything's quiet now."

"Well, I can assure you it won't happen again. They must be loud, indeed. As I'm sure you're aware, the Savoy is the soundest of structures."

"Well, I guess they keep the windows open, but, please, don't say anything. She'd be pretty sore at me if she thought I talked to you about it. . . ."

"I don't understand, sir."

"Just tell me who they are and I'll talk to them myself. You know, friendly-like, over a drink."

The clerk couldn't have been happier with the American's solution. "Well, if you insist, sir. . . . In eight west one is the Viscount and Viscountess Roxbury, charming couple and quite elderly, I believe. Most unusual. However, they could be entertaining."

"Who's above them?"

"Above them, Mr. Canfield? I don't think . . ."

"Just tell me, please."

"Well in nine west one is . . ." The clerk turned the page. "It's not occupied, sir."

"Not occupied? That's unusual for this time of year, isn't it?"

"I should say unavailable, sir. Nine west one has been leased for the month for business conferences."

"You mean no one stays there at night?"

"Oh, they're certainly entitled to but that hasn't been the case."

"Who leased it?"

"The firm is Bertholde et Fils."

CHAPTER 29

The telephone beside James Derek's bed rang harshly, waking him.

"It's Canfield. I need help and it can't wait."

"That may possible be only your judgment. What is it?"

"Scarlatti's suite was broken into."

"What! What does the hotel say?"

"They don't know about it."

"I do think you should tell them."

"It's not that simple. She won't admit it."

"She's your problem. Why call me?"

"I think she's frightened. . . . It was a second-story."

"My dear fellow, her rooms are on the seventh floor! You're too fantastic! Or do the nasty men fly by themselves?"

The American paused just long enough to let the Englishman know he wasn't amused. "They figured she wouldn't open the door, which, in itself, is interesting. Whoever it was, was lowered from one of the rooms above and used a blade. Did you learn anything about Bertholde?"

"One thing at a time." Derek began to take Canfield seriously.

"That's the point. I think they are the same thing. Bertholde's company leased the rooms two floors above."

"I beg your pardon?"

"That's right. For a month. Daily business conferences, no less."

"I think we'd better have a talk."

"The girl knows about it and she's frightened. Can you put a couple of men on?"

"You think it's necessary?"

"Not really. But I'd hate to be wrong."

"Very well. The story will be anticipated jewel theft. Not uniformed, of course. One in the corridor, one in the street."

"I appreciate it. You beginning to wake up?"

"I am, confound you. I'll be with you in a half hour. With everything I've been able to dig up on Bertholde. And I think we'd better get at look at their suite."

Canfield left the phone booth and started back to the hotel. His lack of sleep was beginning to take effect and he wished he was in an American city where such institutions as all-night diners provided coffee. The English, he thought, were wrong in thinking themselves so civilized. No one was civilized without all-night diners.

He entered the opulent lobby and noted that the clock above the desk read quarter to four. He walked toward the ancient elevators.

"Oh, Mr. Canfield, sir!" The clerk rushed up.

"What is it?" Canfield could only think of Janet and his heart stopped.

"Just after you left, sir! Not two minutes after you left! . . . Most unusual this time of night. . . ."

"What the hell are you talking about?"

"This cablegram arrived for you." The clerk handed Canfield an envelope.

"Thank you," said a relieved Canfield as he took the cablegram and entered the open-grill elevator. As he rose from the ground floor he pressed the cable between his thumb and forefinger. It was thick. Benjamin Reynolds had either sent a long abstract lecture or there would be a considerable amount of decoding to be done. He only hoped he could finish it before Derek arrived.

Canfield entered his room, sat down in a chair near a floor lamp, and opened the cable.

No decoding was necessary. It was all written in simple business language and easily understood when applied to the current situation. Canfield separated the pages. There were three.

SORRY TO INFORM YOU RAWLINS THOMAS AND LILLIAN IN AUTOMOBILE ACCIDENT REPEAT ACCIDENT POCONO MOUNTAINS STOP BOTH ARE DEAD STOP KNOW THIS WILL UPSET YOUR DEAR FRIEND E S STOP SUGGEST YOU CARE FOR HER IN HER DISTRESS STOP TO WIMBLEDON BUSINESS STOP WE HAVE SPARED NO EXPENSE AGAIN SPARED NO EXPENSE WITH OUR ENGLISH SUPPLIERS TO OBTAIN MAXIMUM QUOTAS OF MERCHANDISE STOP THEY ARE SYMPATHETIC WITH OUR PROBLEMS OF SCANDINAVIAN EXPORTS STOP THEY ARE PREPARED TO AID YOU IN YOUR NEGOTIATIONS FOR FAIR REDUCTIONS ON MAXIMUM PURCHASES STOP THEY HAVE BEEN TOLD OF OUR COMPETITORS IN SWITZERLAND AGAIN SWITZERLAND AND THE COMPANIES REPEAT COMPANIES INVOLVED STOP THEY KNOW OF THE THREE BRITISH FIRMS IN COMPETITION STOP THEY WILL GIVE YOU ALL ASSISTANCE AND WE EXPECT YOU TO CONCENTRATE AGAIN CONCENTRATE ON OUR INTERESTS IN ENGLAND STOP DO NOT AGAIN DO NOT ATTEMPT TO UNDERBID OUR COMPETITORS IN SWITZERLAND STOP STAY OUT OF IT STOP NOTHING CAN BE ACCOMPLISHED STOP

J. HAMMER WIMBLEDON NEW YORK

Canfield lit a thin cigar and placed the three pages on the floor between his outstretched legs. He peered down at them.

Hammer was Reynolds's code name for messages sent to field accountants when he considered the contents to be of the utmost importance. The word *again* was for positive emphasis. The word *repeat* a simple inversion. It denoted the negative of whatever it referred to..

So the Rawlinses—Canfield had to think for a minute before he remembered that the Rawlinses were Boothroyd's in-laws—had been murdered. Not an accident. And Reynolds feared for Elizabeth Scarlatti's life. Washington had reached an agreement with the British government to gain him unusual cooperation—no expense spared—and in return had told the English of the Swedish securities and the land purchases in Switzerland, which were presumed to be related. However, Reynolds did not specify who the men in Zurich were. Only that they existed and three upstanding Englishmen were on the list. Canfield recalled their names—Masterson of India fame;

Leacock of the British Stock Exchange; and Innes-Bowen, the textile magnate.

The main points Hammer made were to protect Elizabeth and stay out of Switzerland.

There was a light tapping on his door. Canfield gathered the pages together and put them in his pocket. "Who is it?"

"Goldilocks, confound you! I'm looking for a bed to sleep in." The crisp British accent belonged, of course, to James Derek. Canfield opened the door and the Englishman walked in without further greeting. He threw a manila envelope on the bed, placed his bowler on the bureau, and sat down in the nearest stuffed chair.

"I like the hat, James."

"I'm just praying that it may keep me from being arrested. A Londoner prowling around the Savoy at this hour has to have the look of immense respectability."

"You have it, take my word."

"I wouldn't take your word for a damn thing, you insomniac."

"Can I get you a whiskey?"

"God, no! . . . Madame Scarlatti didn't mention a thing to you?"

"Nothing. Less than nothing. She tried to divert my attention, Then she just shut up and locked herself in her bedroom."

"I can't believe it. I thought you two were working together." Derek withdrew a hotel key attached to the usual wooden identification tag. "I had a chat with the hotel bobby."

"Can you trust him?"

"It doesn't matter. It's a master key and he thinks I'm covering a party on the second floor."

"Then I'll get going. Wait for me, please. Grab some sleep."

"Hold on. You're obviously connected with Madame Scarlatti. I should do the reconnoitering."

The field accountant paused. There was merit in what Derek said. He presumed the British operative was far more adept at this kind of sleuthing than he was. On the other hand, he could not be sure of the man's confidence. Neither was he prepared to tell him very much and have the British government making decisions.

"That's brave of you, Derek, but I wouldn't ask it."

"Not brave at all. Numerous explanations under the Alien Order."

"Nevertheless, I'd prefer going myself. Frankly, there's no reason for you to be involved. I called you for help, not to do my work."

"Let's compromise. In my favor."

"Why?"

"It's safer."

"You've won a point."

"I'll go in first while you wait in the corridor by the lift. I'll check the rooms and then signal you to join me."

"How?"

"With as little energy as possible. Perhaps a short whistle."

Canfield heard the short, shrill whistle and walked quickly down the hallway to nine west one.

He closed the door and went to the source of the flashlight. "Everything all right?"

"It's a well-kept hotel suite. Perhaps not so ostentatious as the American variety, but infinitely more homelike."

"That's reassuring."

"More than you know. I really don't like this sort of work."

"I thought you people were famous for it."

This small talk covered the start of their rapid but thorough search of the premises. The floor plan of the rooms was identical to the Scarlatti suite two stories below. However, instead of similar furniture there was a long table in the center of the main room with perhaps a dozen chairs around it.

"Conference table, I presume," said Derek.

"Let's take a look at the window."

"Which one?"

Canfield thought. "Over here." He went toward the french windows directly in line with those of Elizabeth Scarlatti.

"Good point. Here." The Englishman edged Canfield out of the way as he directed the light.

On the wooden sill was a freshly made valley, which had gone through the paint to the wood grain. Where the wood met the outer stone there was a similar semicircle, which had cut through the layers of dirt and turned that small portion of blackish stone to light gray. The ridge was approximately an inch and a half thick and obviously caused by the friction of a wide rope.

"Whoever it was is a cat," said Canfield.

"Let's look around." The two men walked first through the left bedroom door and found a double bed fully made up. The bureaus were empty and nothing but the usual stationery and corked pens were on the desk. The closets held nothing but hangers and cloth shoe repositories. The bathroom was spotless, the fixtures gleaming. The second bedroom to the right was the same except that the bedspread was mussed. Someone had slept or rested on it.

"Large frame. Probably six feet or over," said the Englishman.

"How can you tell?"

"Imprint of the buttocks. See here, below the half point of the bed."

"I wouldn't have thought of that."

"I have no comment."

"He could have been sitting."

"I said probably."

The field accountant opened the closet door. "Hey, shine the light here."

"There you are."

"Here it is!"

On the closet floor was a sloppily coiled pile of rope. Through the coils at the bottom were three wide straps of leather attached to the rope by metal clasps.

"It's an Alpine rig," said the English agent.

"For mountain climbing?"

"Precisely. Very secure. The professionals won't use it. Unsporting. Used for rescues, mainly."

"God bless 'em. Would it scale a wall at the Savoy?"

"Beautifully. Very quick, very safe. You were correct."

"Let's get out of here," said Canfield.

"I'll take that drink now."

"My pleasure." Canfield rose from the bed with difficulty. "Scotch whiskey and soda, friend?"

"Thanks."

The American walked to a table by the window that served as his bar and poured two large quantities of whiskey into glasses. He handed one to James Derek and half raised his own in a toast.

"You do good work, James."

"You're quite competent yourself. And I've been thinking, you may be right about taking that rig."

"All it can do is cause confusion."

"That's what I mean. It could be helpful. . . . It's such an American device."

"I don't understand."

"Nothing personal. Just that you Americans are so equipment conscious, if you know what I mean. When you shoot birds in Scotland, you carry heavy millimeter cannon with you into the field. . . . When you fish in the Lowlands, you have six-hundred artifices in your tackle box. The American's sense of sportsmanship is equated with his ability to master the sport with his purchases, not his skill."

"If this is hate-the-American hour, you should get a radio program."

"Please, Matthew. I'm trying to tell you that I think you're right. Whoever broke into the Scarlatti suite was an American. We can trace the rig to someone at your embassy. Hasn't that occurred to you?"

"We can do what?"

"Your embassy. If it is someone at your embassy. Someone who knows Bertholde. The men you suspect of having been involved with the securities. . . . Even an Alpine rig has to be manipulated by a trained mountain climber. How many climbers can there be in your embassy? Scotland Yard could check it in a day."

"No. . . . We'll handle it ourselves."

"Waste of time, you know. After all, embassy personnel have dossiers just as Bertholde has. How many are mountain climbers?"

The field accountant turned away from James Derek and refilled his glass. "That puts it in a police category. We don't want that. We'll make the interrogations."

"Just as you say. It shouldn't be difficult. Twenty to thirty people at most. You should track it down quickly."

"We will." Canfield walked to his bed and sat down.

"Tell me," said the Englishman, finishing the last of

his whiskey, "do you have a current list of your embassy personnel? Up-to-date, that is?"

"Of course."

"And you're absolutely sure that members of the staff working there now were part of this securities swindle last year?"

"Yes. I've told you that. At least, the State Department thinks so. I wish you'd stop harping on it."

"I shan't any longer. It's late and I have a great deal of work on my desk which I've neglected." The British operative rose from the chair and went to the bureau where he had put his hat. "Good night, Canfield."

"Oh, you're leaving? . . . Was there anything in the Bertholde file? I'll read it but right now I'm bushed."

James Derek stood by the door looking down at the exhausted field accountant. "One item I'm sure you'll be interested in. . . . Several probably, but one comes to mind."

"What's that?"

"Among the marquis's athletic pursuits is mountain climbing. The imminent sportsman is, in fact, a member of the Matterhorn Club. He's also one of the few hundred who've scaled the north side of the Jungfrau. No mean feat, I gather."

Canfield stood up angrily and shouted at the Englishman. "Why didn't you say so, for Christ's sake?"

"I frankly thought you were more interested in his associations with your embassy. That's really what I was looking for."

The field accountant stared at Derek. "So it was Bertholde. But why? . . . Unless he knew she wouldn't open the door for anyone."

"Perhaps. I really wouldn't know. Enjoy the dossier, Canfield. It's fascinating. . . . However, I don't think you'll find much in it related to the American embassy. . . . But that's not why you wanted it, is it?"

The Britisher let himself out the door, closing it sharply behind him. Canfield stared after him, confused but too tired to care.

CHAPTER 30

The telephone awoke him.

"Matthew?"

"Yes, Jan?" He held the phone and the blood drained from his arm and it hurt.

"I'm in the lobby. I told Mother Scarlatti I had some shopping to do."

The field accountant looked at his watch. It was eleven thirty. He had needed the sleep. "What happened?"

"I've never seen her like this, Matthew. She's frightened."

"That's new. Did she bring up the Sheffield business?"

"No. I had to. She brushed it aside and said the situation had changed."

"Nothing else? Just that?"

"Yes. . . . There was something else. She said she was going to talk with you this afternoon. She says there are problems back in New York that have to be attended to. I think she's going to tell you that she's decided to leave England and go home."

"That's impossible! What did she say exactly?"

"She was vague. Just that Chancellor was a fool and that it was senseless throwing away time on a wild-goose chase."

"She doesn't believe that!"

"I know she doesn't. She wasn't convincing either. But she means it. What are you going to do?"

"Take her by surprise, I hope. Stay out shopping for at least two hours, will you?"

They made plans for a late lunch and said good-bye.

Thirty minutes later the field accountant walked across the Savoy lobby into the grill and ordered breakfast. It was no time to go without food. Without energy.

He carried the Bertholde file with him. He promised himself that he'd read through it, or most of it, at the table. He opened it and placed it to the left of his plate and started at the top of the first page.

Jacques Louis Aumont Bertholde, fourth marquis of Chatellerault.

It was a dossier like so many other dossiers on the very wealthy. Exhaustive details about the family lineage. The positions and titles held by each member for several generations in business, government, and society—all impressive sounding, all meaningless to anyone else. The Bertholde holdings—enormous—mainly, as Elizabeth Scarlatti had said, within British territories. The specific education of the subject in question and his subsequent rise in the world of commerce. His clubs—all very correct. His hobbies—automobiles, horse breeding, dogs—also correct. The sports he excelled in—polo, sailing, the Matterhorn and the Jungfrau—not only correct, but colorful, fitting. And finally the character estimates elicited from his contemporaries. The most interesting part and yet the part many professionals disregarded. The flattering contributions were generally supplied by friends or associates hoping to gain. The unflattering, by enemies or competitors with a wish to undermine.

Canfield withdrew a pencil and made two notations in the dossier.

The first was on page 18, paragraph 5.

No particular reason other than the fact that it seemed out of place—unattractive—and it contained the name of a city Canfield recalled was on Ulster Scarlett's European itinerary.

> The Bertholde family had extensive interests in the Ruhr Valley, which were sold to the German Ministry of Finance several weeks before the assassination at Sarajevo. The Bertholde offices in Stuttgart and Tassing were closed. The sale caused considerable comment in French business circles and the Bertholde family was criticized by the States General and in numerous newspaper editorials. No collusion accused, however, due to explanation that the

> German Finance Ministry was paying exorbitant prices. Explanation proved out. Following the war, the Ruhr Valley interests repurchased from the Weimar government. Offices in Stuttgart and Tassing reopened.

The second, on page 23, paragraph 2, referred to one of Bertholde's more recently formed corporations and included the following information.

> The Marquis de Bertholde's partners in the importing firm are Mr. Sydney Masterson and Mr. Harold Leacock. . . .

Masterson and Leacock.

Both were on the Zurich list. Each owned one of the fourteen properties in Switzerland.

No surprise. They tied Bertholde to the Zurich contingent.

No surprise at all. Just comforting—in a professional way—to know that another piece of the puzzle fitted.

As he finished his coffee, an unfamiliar man in a Savoy waistcoat approached the field accountant.

"Front desk, sir. I have two messages."

Canfield was alarmed. He reached for the notes extended to him. "You could have had me paged."

"Both parties requested that we not do that, sir."

"I see. Thank you."

The first message was from Derek. "Imperative you contact me."

The second was from Elizabeth Scarlatti. "Please come to my suite at two thirty. It is most urgent. I cannot see you before then."

Canfield lit one of his thin cigars and settled back into the curved Savoy dining chair. Derek could wait. The Englishman probably had gotten word of Benjamin Reynolds's new arrangement with the British government and was either furious or apologetic. He'd postpone Derek.

Scarlatti, on the other hand, had made a decision. If Janet was right, she was folding up. Forgetting for the moment his own potential loss, he could never explain her reversal to Reynolds, or Glover, or anyone else at Group Twenty, for that matter. He had spent thousands of dollars on the premise that he had Elizabeth's cooperation.

The field accountant thought about the old woman's visitor, the fourth marquis of Chatellerault, veteran of the Matterhorn and the Jungfrau, Jacques Louis Bertholde. Why had he broken into the Scarlatti suite the way he had? Was it simply the locked door and the knowledge that it would remain locked? Was it to terrify Elizabeth? Or was he searching for something?

Just as he and Derek had searched in the darkness two floors above.

Once confronting her what could Bertholde have said to bend her will? What could he possibly say that would frighten Elizabeth Scarlatti?

He could promise the death of her son if he were still alive. That might do it. . . . But would it? Her son had betrayed her. Betrayed the Scarlatti Industries. Canfield had the unnatural feeling that Elizabeth would rather see her son dead than let him continue that betrayal.

Yet now she was retreating.

Again Canfield felt the inadequacy he had begun to feel aboard the *Calpurnia*. An assignment conceived of as theft had been complicated by extraordinary occurrences, extraordinary people.

He forced his mind back to Elizabeth Scarlatti. He was convinced she could "not see" him before two thirty because she was completing arrangements to return home.

Well, he had a shock in store for her. He knew she had had an early-morning visitor. And he had the Bertholde dossier.

The dossier she could refuse. The Alpine rig would be irresistible.

"I wrote in my note that I couldn't see you before two thirty! Would you please respect my wishes?"

"It can't wait. Let me in quickly!"

She opened the door in disgust, leaving it ajar as she walked back into the center of the room. Canfield closed it, loudly inserting the bolt. He spoke before she turned around to face him. "I've read the dossier. I know now why your visitor didn't have to open the door."

It was as if a pistol had been fired in front of her ancient face. The old woman turned and sprang her back forward and arched her neck. Had she been thirty years younger, she would have leapt upon him in fury. She spoke with an intensity he had never heard from her before.

"You unconscionable bastard! You're a liar! A thief! Liar! Liar! I'll have you spend the rest of your life in prison!"

"That's very good. Attack for attack! You've pulled it before but not this time. Derek was with me. We found the rig. An Alpine rig, he called it—which your visitor let down the side of the building."

The old woman lurched toward him, unsteady on her feet.

"For Christ's sake, relax! I'm on your side." He held her thin shoulders.

"You've got to buy him! Oh, my God! You've got to buy him! Get him here!"

"Why? Buy him how? Who?"

"Derek. How long have you known? Mr. Canfield, I ask you in the name of all that's holy, how long have you known?"

"Since about five o'clock this morning."

"Then he's talked to others! Oh, my God, he's talked to others!" She was beside herself, and Canfield was now frightened for her.

"I'm sure he has. But only to his immediate superiors and I gather he's pretty superior himself. What did you expect?"

The old woman tried with what strength she had left to regain control of herself. "You may have caused the murder of my entire family. If you've done that, I'll see you dead!"

"That's pretty strong language! You'd better tell me why!"

"I'll tell you nothing until you get Derek on that telephone."

The field accountant crossed the room to the telephone and gave the operator Derek's number. He talked urgently, quietly, for a few moments and turned to the old woman. "He's going in to a meeting in twenty minutes. He has a full report and they'll expect him to read it."

The old woman walked rapidly toward Canfield. "Give me that phone!"

He handed her both the stand and the receiver. "Mr. Derek! Elizabeth Scarlatti. Whatever this meeting is, do not go to it! I am not in the habit of begging, sir, but I implore you, do not go! Please, please do not speak to a soul about last night! If you do, you will be responsible for the deaths of a number of innocent people. I can say no more now. . . . Yes, yes, whatever you like. . . . I'll see you, of course. In an hour. Thank you. Thank you!"

She replaced the receiver on the hook and slowly, with great relief, put the telephone back on the table. She looked at the field accountant. "Thank God!"

The field accountant watched her as she spoke. He began to walk toward her. "Sweet mother of Jesus! I'm beginning to see. That crazy Alpine thing. The acrobatics at two in the morning. It wasn't just to scare you half to death—it was necessary!"

"What are you talking about?"

"Since early this morning I've thought it was Bertholde! And he'd come to you like that to scare hell out of you! But it didn't make sense. It wouldn't accomplish anything. He could have stopped you in the lobby, in a store, in the dining room. It had to be someone who couldn't do that! Someone who couldn't take a chance anywhere!"

"You're babbling! You're incoherent!"

"Sure, you're willing to call the whole thing off! Why not? You did what you'd set out to do! You found him! You've found your missing son, haven't you?"

"That's a lie!"

"Oh, no, it's not. It's so clear I should have thought of it last night. The whole damn thing was so weird I looked for insane explanations. I thought it was persuasion by terror. It's been used a lot these past few years. But it wasn't that at all! It was our celebrated war hero come back to the land of the living! Ulster Stewart Scarlett! The only one who couldn't risk stopping you outside. The only one who couldn't take a chance that you might not unlatch that bolt!"

"Conjecture! I deny it!"

"Deny all you like! Now I'm giving you a choice! Derek will be here in less than an hour. Either we straighten this out between us before then, or I walk out that door and cable my office that in my highly regarded professional opinion we've found Ulster Scarlett! And, incidentally, I'm taking your daughter-in-law with me."

The old woman suddenly lowered her voice to nearly a whisper. She walked haltingly toward the field accountant. "If you have any feeling whatsoever for that girl, you'll do as I ask. If you don't, she'll be killed."

It was now the field accountant's turn to raise his voice. It was no longer the shout of the angry debater, it was the roar of an angry man. "Don't you make any pronouncements to me! Don't you or your rotten bastard son make any threats to me! You may buy part of me, but you don't buy all of me! You tell him I'll kill him if he touches that girl!"

Pleading without shame, Elizabeth Scarlatti touched his arm. He withdrew it swiftly from her. "It's not my threat. Please, in the name of God, listen to me. Try to understand. . . . I'm helpless. And I can not be helped!"

The field accountant saw the tears roll down her wrinkled cheeks. Her skin was white and the hollows of her eyes were black with exhaustion. He thought, quite out of context with the moment, that he was looking at a tear-stained corpse. His anger ebbed.

"Nobody has to be helpless. Don't let anybody tell you that."

"You love her, don't you?"

"Yes. And because I do, you don't have to be quite so afraid. I'm a committed public servant. But far more committed to us than the public."

"Your confidence doesn't change the situation."

"You won't know that until you tell me what it is."

"You leave me no choice? No alternative?"

"None."

"Then God have mercy on you. You have an awesome responsibility. You are responsible for our lives."

She told him.

And Matthew Canfield knew exactly what he would do. It was time to confront the Marquis de Bertholde.

CHAPTER 31

Fifty-seven miles southeast of London is the seaside resort of Ramsgate. Near the town, on a field set back from the main road, stood a wooden shack no more than twenty feet by twenty. It had two small windows and in the early-morning mist a dim light could be seen shining through them. About a hundred yards to the north was a larger building—once a barn—five times the size of the shack. It was now a hangar for two small monoplanes. One of them was being wheeled out by three men in gray overalls.

Inside the shack, the man with the shaved head sat at a table drinking black coffee and munching bread. The reddish splotch above his right eye was sore and inflamed and he touched it continually.

He read the message in front of him and looked up at the bearer, a man in a chauffeur's uniform. The contents of the message infuriated him.

"The marquis has gone too far. The instructions from Munich were clear. The Rawlinses were *not* to be killed in the States. They were to be brought to Zurich! They were to be killed in *Zurich!*"

"There's no need for concern. Their deaths, the man and his wife, were engineered above suspicion. The marquis wanted you to know that. It has appeared as an accident."

"To whom? God damn it, to *whom?* Go shag, all of you! Munich doesn't want risks! In *Zurich* there would have been no risk!" Ulster Scarlett rose from the chair and walked to the small window overlooking the field.

His plane was nearly ready. He hoped his fury would subside before takeoff. He disliked flying when he was angry. He made mistakes in the air when he was angry. It had been happening more frequently as the pressures mounted.

God damn Bertholde! Certainly Rawlins had to be killed. In his panic over Cartwright's discovery Rawlins had ordered his son-in-law to kill Elizabeth Scarlatti. A massive error! It's funny, he reflected. He no longer thought of the old woman as his mother. Simply Elizabeth Scarlatti. . . . But to have Rawlins murdered three thousand miles away was insanity! How could they know who was asking questions? And how easily might the order be traced back to Bertholde?

"Regardless of what happened . . ." Labishe started to speak.

"What?" Scarlett turned from the window. He had made up his mind.

"The marquis also wanted you to know that regardless of what happened to Boothroyd, all associations with him are buried with the Rawlinses."

"Not quite, Labishe. Not quite." Scarlett spoke softly but his voice was hard. "The Marquis de Bertholde was ordered . . . commanded by Munich to have the Rawlinses brought to Switzerland. He disobeyed. That was most unfortunate."

"Pardon, monsieur?"

Scarlett reached for his flying jacket, which hung over the back of his chair. Again he spoke quietly, simply. Two words.

"Kill him."

"Monsieur!"

"Kill him! Kill the Marquis de Bertholde and do it today!"

"Monsieur! I do not believe what I hear!"

"Listen to me! I don't give explanations! By the time I reach Munich I want a cable waiting for me telling me that stupid son of a bitch is dead! . . . And, Labishe! Do it so there's no mistake who killed him. You! We can't have any investigations now! . . . Get back here to the field. We'll fly you out of the country."

"Monsieur! I have been with *le marquis* for fifteen years! He has been good to me! . . . I can not . . ."

"You what?"

"Monsieur . . ." The Frenchman sunk to one knee. "Do not ask me. . . ."

"I don't ask. I command! Munich commands!"

The foyer on the third floor of Bertholde et Fils was enormous. In the rear was an impressive set of white Louis XIV doors that obviously led to the sanctum sanctorum of the Marquis de Bertholde. On the right side were six brown leather armchairs in a semicircle—the sort that might be found in the study of a wealthy country squire—with a thick rectangular coffee table placed in front. On the table were neatly stacked piles of chic magazines—chic socially and chic industrially. On the left side of the room was a large white desk trimmed in gold. Behind the desk sat a most attractive brunet with spit curls silhouetted against her forehead. All this Canfield took in with his second impression. It took him several moments to get over his first.

Opening the elevator door, he had been visually overpowered by the color scheme of the walls.

They were magenta red and sweeping from the ceiling moldings were arcs of black velvet.

Good Christ! he said to himself. I'm in a hallway thirty-five hundred miles away!

Seated in the chairs beside one another were two middle-aged gentlemen in Savile Row clothes reading magazines. Standing off to the right was a man in a chauffeur's uniform, his hat off, his hands clasped behind his back.

Canfield approached the desk. The spit-curled secretary greeted him before he could speak. "Mr. Canfield?"

"Yes."

"The marquis would like you to go right in, sir." The girl spoke as she rose from the chair and started toward the large white doors. Canfield saw that the man seated on the left was upset. He uttered a few "Damns!" and went back to his magazine.

"Good afternoon, Mr. Canfield." The fourth marquis of Chatellerault stood behind his large white desk and extended his hand. "We have not met, of course, but an emissary from Elizabeth Scarlatti is a welcome guest. Do sit down."

Bertholde was almost what Canfield expected him to

be, except, perhaps, shorter. He was well-groomed, relatively handsome, very masculine, with a voice resonant enough to fill an opera house. However, in spite of his exuding virility—bringing to mind the Matterhorn and the Jungfrau—there was something artificial, slightly effete about the man. Perhaps the clothing. It was almost too fashionable.

"How do you do?" Canfield smiled, shaking the Frenchman's hand. "Is it Monsieur Bertholde? Or *Monsieur le Marquis?* I'm not sure which I should use."

"I could tell you several unflattering names given me by your countrymen." The marquis laughed. "But please, use the French custom—so scorned by our proper Anglicans. Plain Bertholde will do. Marquises are such an out-of-date custom." The Frenchman smiled ingenuously and waited until Canfield sat in the chair in front of his desk before returning to his seat. Jacques Louis Aumont Bertholde, fourth marquis of Chatellerault, was immensely likable and Canfield recognized the fact.

"I appreciate your interrupting your schedule."

"Schedules are made to be broken. Such a dull existence otherwise, yes?"

"I won't waste time, sir. Elizabeth Scarlatti wants to negotiate."

Jacques Bertholde leaned back in his chair and looked startled. "Negotiate? . . . I'm afraid I don't comprehend, monsieur. . . . Negotiate what?"

"She knows, Bertholde. . . . She knows as much as she needs to know. She wants to meet you."

"I'd be delighted—at any time—to meet Madame Scarlatti but I can't imagine what we have to discuss. Not in a business sense, monsieur, which I presume to be your . . . errand."

"Maybe the key is her son. Ulster Scarlett."

Bertholde leveled his gaze intently on the field accountant. "It is a key for which I have no lock, monsieur. I have not had the pleasure. . . . I know, as most who read newspapers know, that he vanished a number of months ago. But that is all I know."

"And you don't know a thing about Zurich?"

Jacques Bertholde abruptly sat up in his chair. *"Quoi?* Zurich?"

"We know about Zurich."

"Is this a joke?"

"No. Fourteen men in Zurich. Maybe you've got the fifteenth. . . . Elizabeth Scarlatti."

Canfield could hear Bertholde's breathing. "Where did you get this information? What do you refer to?"

"Ulster Scarlett! Why do you think I'm here?"

"I don't believe you! I don't know what you are talking about!" Bertholde got out of his chair.

"For God's sake! She's interested. . . . Not because of him! Because of you! And the others! She's got something to offer, and if I were you, I'd listen to her."

"But you are not me, monsieur! I'm afraid I must ask you to leave. There is no business between Madame Scarlatti and the Bertholde companies."

Canfield did not move. He remained in the chair and spoke quietly. "Then I'd better put it another way. I think you'll have to see her. Talk with her. . . . For your own good. For Zurich's good."

"You threaten me?"

"If you don't, it's my opinion that she'll do something drastic. I don't have to tell you she's a powerful woman. . . . You're linked with her son. . . . And she met with her son last night!"

Bertholde stood motionless. Canfield couldn't decide whether the Frenchman's look of disbelief was over the revelation of Scarlett's visit or his—the field accountant's—knowledge of it.

After a few moments Bertholde replied, "I know nothing of what you speak. It has nothing to do with me."

"Oh, come on! I found the rig! The Alpine rig! I found it at the bottom of a closet in your conference suite at the Savoy!"

"You what?"

"You heard me! Now, let's stop kidding each other!"

"You broke into my firm's private quarters?"

"I did! And that's just the beginning. We've got a list. You might know some of the names on it. . . . Daudet and D'Almeida, fellow countrymen, I think. . . . Olaffsen, Landor, Thyssen, von Schnitzler, Kindorf. . . . And, oh yes! Mr. Masterson and Mr. Leacock! Current partners of yours, I believe! There are several others, but I'm sure you know their names better than I do!"

"Enough! Enough, monsieur!" The Marquis de Bertholde sat down again, slowly, deliberately. He stared at Canfield. "I will clear my office and we will talk further.

People have been waiting. It does not look good. Wait outside. I will dispense with them quickly."

The field accountant got out of the chair as Bertholde picked up the telephone and pressed the button for his secretary.

"Monsieur Canfield will remain. I wish to finish the afternoon's business as rapidly as possible. With each person interrupt me in five minutes if I have not concluded by then. What? Labishe? Very well, send him in. I'll give them to him." The Frenchman reached into his pocket and withdrew a set of keys.

Canfield crossed to the large white double doors. Before his hand touched the brass knob, the door on his left opened swiftly, with great force.

"So sorry, monsieur," the man in uniform said.

"Voici les clefs, Labishe."

"Merci, Monsieur le Marquis! Je regrette. . . . J'ai un billet . . ."

The chauffeur closed the door and Canfield smiled at the secretary.

He wandered over to the semicircle of chairs, and as the two gentlemen looked up, he nodded pleasantly. He sat down on the end chair nearest the entrance to Bertholde's office and picked up the *London Illustrated News*. He noted that the man nearest him was fidgeting, irritable, quite impatient. He was turning the pages of *Punch*, but he was not reading. The other man was engrossed in an article in the *Quarterly Review*.

Suddenly, Canfield was diverted by an insignificant action on the part of the impatient man. The man extended his left hand through his coat sleeve, turned his wrist, and looked at the watch. A perfectly normal occurrence under the circumstances. What startled the field accountant was the sight of the man's cuff link. It was made of cloth and it was square with two stripes running diagonally from corner to corner. The small stripes were deep red and black. It was a replica of the cuff link that had identified the hulking, masked Charles Boothroyd in Elizabeth Scarlatti's stateroom on board the *Calpurnia*. The colors were the same as the paper on the marquis' walls and the black velvet drapes arcing from the ceiling.

The impatient man noticed Canfield's stare. He abruptly withdrew his hand into his jacket and placed his arm at his side.

"I was trying to read the time on your watch. Mine's been running fast."

"Four twenty."

"Thanks."

The impatient gentleman folded his arms and leaned back, looking exasperated. The other man spoke.

"Basil, you'll have a stroke if you don't relax."

"Well and good for you, Arthur! But I'm late for a meeting! I told Jacques it was a hectic day, but he insisted I come over."

"He can be insistent."

"He can be bloody rude, too!"

There followed five minutes of silence except for the rustling of papers at the secretary's desk.

The large left panel of the white double doors opened and the chauffeur emerged. He closed the door, and Canfield noticed that once it was shut, the chauffeur twisted the knob to make sure it was secure. It was a curious motion.

The uniformed man went to the secretary and leaned over her desk, whispering. She reacted to his information with resigned annoyance. He shrugged his shoulders and walked quickly to a door to the right of the elevator. Canfield saw through the slowly closing door the flight of stairs he had presumed to be there.

The secretary placed some papers into a manila folder and looked over at the three men. "I'm sorry, gentlemen, the Marquis de Bertholde can not see anyone further this afternoon. We apologize for any inconvenience."

"Now see here, young lady!" The impatient gentleman was on his feet. "This is preposterous! I've been here for three-quarters of an hour at the explicit request of the Marquis! . . . Request be damned! At his instructions!"

"I'm sorry, sir, I'll convey your displeasure."

"You'll do more than that! You'll convey to Monsieur Bertholde that I am waiting right here until he sees me!" He sat down pompously.

The man named Arthur rose and walked toward the elevator.

"For heaven's sake, man, you'll not improve French manners. People have been trying for centuries. Come along, Basil. We'll stop at the Dorchester and start the evening."

"Can't do it, Arthur. I'm staying right where I am."

"Have it your way. Be in touch."

Canfield remained in his seat next to the impatient Basil. He knew only that he would not leave until Bertholde came out. Basil was his best weapon.

"Ring the marquis again, please, miss," said Basil.

She did so.

A number of times. And there was no response.

The field accountant was alarmed. He rose from his chair and walked to the large double doors and knocked. There was no answer. He tried opening both doors; they were locked.

Basil unfolded his arms and got out of his chair. The spit-curled secretary stood up behind her white desk. She automatically picked up the phone and started pressing the buzzer, finally holding her finger down upon it.

"Unlock the door," commanded the field accountant.

"Oh, I don't know . . ."

"I do! Get me a key!"

The girl started to open the top drawer of her desk and then looked up at the American. "Perhaps we should wait. . . ."

"Damn it! Give me the key!"

"Yes, sir!" She picked up a ring of keys and selecting one, separated it from the others, and gave the key to Canfield. He rapidly unlocked the doors and flung them open.

There in front of them was the Frenchman sprawled across the top of his white desk, blood trickling from his mouth; his tongue was extended and swollen; his eyes bulged from their sockets; his neck was inflated and lacerated just below the chin line. He had been expertly garroted.

The girl kept screaming but did not collapse—a fact that Canfield wasn't sure was fortunate. Basil began to shake and repeated "Oh, my God!" over and over again. The field accountant approached the desk and lifted the dead man's wrist by the coat sleeve. He let it go and the hand fell back.

The girl's screams grew louder and two middle-aged executives burst through the staircase doorway into the outer room. Through the double doors the scene was clear to both men. One ran back to the stairway, shouting at the top of his voice, while the other slowly, fearfully walked into Bertholde's room.

"Le bon Dieu!"

Within a minute, a stream of employees had run down and up the staircase, log-jamming themselves in the doorway. As each group squeezed through, subsequent screams and oaths followed. Within two minutes twenty-five people were shouting instructions to nonexistent subordinates.

Canfield shook the spit-curled secretary in an attempt to stop her screaming. He kept telling her to phone the police, but she could not accept the order. Canfield did not want to make the call himself because it would have required separate concentration. He wished to keep his full attention on everyone in sight, especially Basil, if that was possible.

A tall, distinguished-looking, gray-haired man in a double-breasted pin-stripe suit came rushing through the crowd up to the secretary and Canfield. "Miss Richards! Miss Richards! What in God's name happened?"

"We opened his door and found him like this! That's what happened," shouted the field accountant over the growing din of excited voices.

And then Canfield looked closely at the questioner. Where had he seen him before? Or had he? The man was like so many in the Scarlatti world. Even to the perfectly waxed moustache.

"Have you phoned the police?" asked the gentleman.

Canfield saw Basil pushing his way through the hysterical mob gathered by the office doors. "No, the police haven't been called," yelled the American as he watched Basil making headway through the crowd. "Call them! . . . It might be a good idea to close these doors." He started after Basil as if to push the doors shut. The distinguished-looking man with the waxed moustache held him firmly by the lapel.

"You say you found him?"

"Yes. Let go of me!"

"What's your name, young man?"

"What?"

"I asked you your name!"

"Derek, James Derek! Now, phone the police!"

Canfield took the man's wrist and pressed hard against the vein. The arm withdrew in pain and Canfield ran into the crowd after Basil.

The man in the pin-striped suit winced and turned to

the secretary. "Did you get his name, Miss Richards? I couldn't hear."

The girl was sobbing. "Yes, sir. It was Darren, or Derrick. First name, James."

The man with the waxed moustache looked carefully at the secretary. She had heard. "The police, Miss Richards. Phone the police!"

"Yes, sir, Mr. Poole."

The man named Poole pushed his way through the crowd. He had to get to his office, he had to be by himself. *They* had done it! The men of Zurich had ordered Jacques' death! His dearest friend, his mentor, closer to him than anyone in the world. The man who'd given him everything, made everything possible for him.

The man he'd killed for—willingly.

They'd pay! They'd pay and pay and pay!

He, Poole, had never failed Bertholde in life. He'd not fail him in death either!

But there were questions. So many questions.

This Canfield who'd just lied about his name. The old woman, Elizabeth Scarlatti.

Most of all the misshapen Heinrich Kroeger. The man Poole knew beyond a doubt was Elizabeth Scarlatti's son. He knew because Bertholde had told him.

He wondered if anyone else knew.

On the third-floor landing, which was now completely filled with Bertholde employees in varying stages of hysteria, Canfield could see Basil one floor below pulling himself downward by the railing. Canfield began yelling.

"Get clear! Get clear! The doctor's waiting! I've got to bring him up! Get clear!"

To some degree the ruse worked and he made swifter headway. By the time he reached the first-floor lobby, Basil was no longer in sight. Canfield ran out the front entrance onto the sidewalk. There was Basil about half a block south, limping in the middle of Vauxhall Road, waving, trying to hail a taxi. The knees of his trousers were coated with mud where he had fallen in his haste.

Shouts were still coming from various windows of Bertholde et Fils, drawing dozens of pedestrians to the foot of the company's steps.

Canfield walked against the crowd toward the limping figure.

A taxi stopped and Basil grabbed for the door handle.

As he pulled the door open and climbed in, Canfield reached the side of the cab and prevented the Englishman from pulling the door shut. He moved in alongside Basil, pushing him sideway to make room.

"I say! What are you doing?" Basil was frightened but he did not raise his voice. The driver kept turning his head back and forth from the street in front of him to the gathering crowds receding behind him. Basil did not wish to draw additional attention.

Before Basil could think further, the American grasped the Englishman's right hand and pulled the coat above his wrist. He twisted Basil's arm revealing the red and black cuff link.

"Zurich, Basil!" the field accountant whispered.

"What are you talking about?"

"You damn fool, I'm with you! Or I will be, if they let you live!"

"Oh, my God! Oh, my God!" Basil babbled.

The American released Basil's hand by throwing it downward. He looked straight ahead as if ignoring the Englishman. "You're an idiot. You realize that, don't you?"

"I don't know you, sir! I don't know you!" The Englishman was near collapse.

"Then we'd better change that. I may be all you have left."

"Now see here. I had nothing to do with it! I was in the waiting room with you. I had nothing to do with it!"

"Of course, you didn't. It's pretty damned obvious that it was the chauffeur. But a number of people are going to want to know why you ran. Maybe you were just making sure the job was done."

"That's preposterous!"

"Then why did you run away?"

"I . . . I . . ."

"Let's not talk now. Where can we go where we'll be seen for about ten or fifteen minutes? I don't want it to look as though we dropped out of sight."

"My club . . . I suppose."

"Give him the address!"

CHAPTER 32

"What the devil do you mean I was there?" James Derek shouted into the phone. "I've been here at the Savoy since midafternoon! . . . Yes, of course I am. Since three or thereabouts. . . . No, she's here with me." The Englishman suddenly caught his breath. When he spoke again his words were barely audible, drawn out in disbelief. "Good Lord! . . . How horrible. . . . Yes. Yes, I heard you."

Elizabeth Scarlatti sat across the room on the Victorian couch, absorbed in the Bertholde dossier. At the sound of Derek's voice she looked up at the Englishman. He was staring at her. He spoke again into the phone.

"Yes. He left here roughly at three thirty. With Ferguson, from our office. They were to meet Mrs. Scarlett at Tippin's and he was to proceed from there to Bertholde's. . . . I don't know. His instructions were that she remain in Ferguson's custody until he returned. Ferguson's to call in. . . . I see. For heaven's sake, keep me posted. I'll phone you if there're any developments here."

He replaced the telephone receiver on the hook and remained at the table. "Bertholde's been killed."

"Good God! Where's my daughter?"

"With our man. She's all right. He reported in an hour ago."

"Canfield! Where's Canfield?"

"I wish I knew."

"Is he all right?"

"How can I answer that if I don't know where he is?

We can presume he's functioning. He identified himself as me and left the scene!"

"How did it happen?"

"He was garroted. A wire around his throat."

"Oh!" Elizabeth suddenly, vividly recalled the picture of Matthew Canfield thrusting the cord in her face after Boothroyd's attempt on her life aboard the *Calpurnia*. "If he killed him, he must have had a reason!"

"What?"

"For killing him. He must have had to!"

"That's most interesting."

"What is?"

"That you would think Canfield had to kill him."

"It couldn't have happened otherwise! He's no killer."

"He didn't kill Bertholde either, if it's any comfort to you."

Her relief was visible. "Do they know who did?"

"They believe so. Apparently it was Bertholde's chauffeur."

"That's odd."

"Very. The man's been with him for years."

"Perhaps Canfield's gone after him."

"Not likely. The man left some ten to twelve minutes before they found Bertholde."

James Derek walked from the telephone table toward Elizabeth. It was obvious that he was upset. "In the light of what's just happened, I'd like to ask you a question. But, of course, you needn't answer. . . ."

"What is it?"

"I'd like to know how—or perhaps why—Mr. Canfield received a full clearance from the British Foreign Office."

"I don't know what that is."

"Come, madame. If you don't care to answer, I respect that. But since my name's been used in the killing of an influential man, I believe I'm entitled to something more than another . . . falsehood."

"Another . . . falsehood? That's insulting, Mr. Derek."

"Is it? And are you and Mr. Canfield still setting elaborate traps for embassy personnel who returned to the United States over four months ago?"

"Oh." Elizabeth sat down again on the couch. She was not concerned with the Englishman's complaint; she only wished Canfield was there to answer him. What she was concerned with was the agent's reference to the Foreign Office. "An unfortunate necessity."

"Most unfortunate. . . . I gather, then, that you don't care to answer."

"On the contrary, I have answered you." Elizabeth looked up at the Britisher. "I wish you'd explain. What is full clearance?"

"Extraordinary cooperation from the highest echelons of our government. And such decisions from the British Foreign Office are generally reserved for major political crises! Not a stocks-and-bonds struggle between squabbling millionaires. . . . Or, if you'll pardon me, a private citizen's personal tragedy."

Elizabeth Scarlatti froze.

What James Derek had just said was abhorrent to the head of Scarlatti. More than anything else she had to operate outside the boundaries of "highest echelon" scrutiny. For the sake of Scarlatti itself. Canfield's minor agency had seemed heaven-sent. Her arrangement with him gave her the facilities of official cooperation without answering to anyone of consequence. If she had wanted it otherwise, she would have commanded any number of men in either or both the legislative and executive branches of the United States government. It would not have been difficult. . . . Now, it seemed, Canfield's relatively unimportant department had grown in significance. Or perhaps her son had involved himself in an undertaking far more ominous than she had conceived.

Was the answer in the Bertholde dossier? Elizabeth wondered. "I gather from your tone that this full clearance is a new development."

"I was informed this morning."

Then it must be in the Bertholde dossier, thought Elizabeth. . . . Of course it was! Even Matthew Canfield had begun to perceive it! Only his perception had been based solely on the recognition of certain words, names. He had marked the pages. Elizabeth picked up the file.

"Following the war, the Ruhr Valley interests repurchased. . . . Offices in Stuttgart and Tassing . . ."

Tassing.

Germany.

An economic crisis.

The Weimar Republic.

A series of economic crises! A major and constant political crisis!

". . . partners in the importing firm are Mr. Sydney Masterson and Mr. Harold Leacock. . . ."

Masterson and Leacock. Zurich!

Tassing!

"Does the city of Tassing mean anything to you?"

"It's not a city. It is an outlying district of Munich. In Bavaria. Why do you ask?"

"My son spent a good deal of time and money there . . . among other places. Does it have any special meaning for you?"

"Munich?"

"I suppose so."

"Hotbed of radicalism. Breeding ground of malcontents."

"Malcontents? . . . Communists?"

"Hardly. They'd shoot a Red on sight. Or a Jew. Call themselves *Schutzstaffel*. Go around clubbing people. Consider themselves a race apart from the rest of the world."

A race apart.

Oh, God!

Elizabeth looked at the dossier in her hands. Slowly she replaced it in the manila envelope and stood up. Without saying a word to the Englishman, she crossed to her bedroom door and let herself in. She closed the door behind her.

James Derek remained in the center of the room. He didn't understand.

Inside her bedroom Elizabeth went to her writing desk where papers were scattered across the top. She sorted them out until she found the Zurich list.

She read each name carefully.

AVERY LANDOR, U.S.A.—*Oil.*
LOUIS GIBSON, U.S.A.—*Oil.*
THOMAS RAWLINS, U.S.A.—*Securities.*
HOWARD THORNTON, U.S.A.—*Industrial Construction.*
SYDNEY MASTERSON, GREAT BRITAIN—*Imports.*
DAVID INNES-BOWEN, GREAT BRITAIN—*Textiles.*
HAROLD LEACOCK, GREAT BRITAIN—*Securities.*
LOUIS FRANÇOIS D'ALMEIDA, FRANCE—*Railroads.*
PIERRE DAUDET, FRANCE—*Ship lines.*
INGMAR MYRDAL, SWEDEN—*Securities.*

Christian Olaffsen, Sweden—*Steel.*
Otto von Schnitzler, Germany—*I. G. Farben.*
Fritz Thyssen, Germany—*Steel.*
Erich Kindorf, Germany—*Coal.*

One might say that the Zurich list was a cross-section of the most powerful men in the Western hemisphere.

Elizabeth put the list down and reached for a leather-bound notebook in which she kept telephone numbers and addresses. She thumbed to the letter *O.*

Ogilvie and Storm, Ltd., Publishers, Bayswater Road, London.

She would phone Thomas Ogilvie and have him send her whatever information he could unearth on the *Schutzstaffel.*

She knew something about it already. She remembered reading its political name was the National Socialists and they were led by a man named Adolph Hitler.

CHAPTER 33

The man's name was Basil Hawkwood, and Canfield quickly pictured the trademark *hawkwood*—small letter *h*—as it appeared on a variety of leather goods. Hawkwood Leather was one of the largest firms in England, only a short distance behind Mark Cross.

The nervous Basil led Canfield into the huge reading room of his club, Knights. They chose two chairs by the Knightsbridge window, where there were no other members within earshot.

Basil's fear caused him to stutter, and when his words came, the phrases tumbled over one another. He assumed, because he wanted to assume, that the young man facing him would help him.

Canfield sat back in the comfortable chair and listened with incredulity to Hawkwood's story.

The chairman of Hawkwood Leather had been sending shipment after shipment of "damaged" leather goods to a little-known firm in Munich. For over a year the directors of Hawkwood accepted the losses on the basis of the "damaged" classification. Now, however, they had ordered a complete report on the excess malfunctions of the plants. The Hawkwood heir was trapped. There could be no more shipments for an indeterminate time.

He pleaded with Matthew Canfield to understand. He begged the young man to report and confirm his loyalty, but the boots, the belts, the holsters would have to come from someone else.

"Why do you wear the cuff links?" asked Canfield.

"I wore them today to remind Bertholde of my contribution. He presented them to me himself. . . . You're not wearing yours."

"My contribution doesn't call for them."

"Well, damn it, mine does! I haven't stinted in the past and I won't in the future!" Hawkwood leaned forward in his chair. "The present circumstances don't change my feelings! You can report that. God damn Jews! Radicals! Bolsheviks! All over Europe! A conspiracy to destroy every decent principle good Christian men have lived by for centuries! They'll murder us in our beds! Rape our daughters! Pollute the races! I've never doubted it! I'll help again. You have my word! Soon there'll be millions at our disposal!"

Matthew Canfield suddenly felt sick. What in God's name had he done? He got out of the chair and his legs felt weak.

"I'll report what you said, Mr. Hawkwood."

"Good fellow. Knew you'd understand."

"I'm beginning to." He walked rapidly away from the Englishman toward the arch to the outer hallway.

As he stood on the curb under the Knights' canopy waiting for a taxi, Canfield was numb with fear. He was no longer dealing with a world he understood. He was dealing with giants, with concepts, with commitments beyond his comprehension.

CHAPTER 34

Elizabeth had the newspaper and magazine articles spread over the couch. Ogilvie and Storm, publishers, had done an excellent job. There was more material here than Elizabeth or Canfield could digest in a week.

The National Socialist German Workers party emerged as ragtail fanatics. The *Schutzstaffel* were brutes but no one took them seriously. The articles, the photographs, even the short headlines were slanted in such a way as to give a comic-opera effect.

Why Work in the Fatherland
if You Can Dress Up
and Pretend It's Wagner?

Canfield picked up a portion of a Sunday supplement and read the names of the leaders. Adolf Hitler, Erich Ludendorff, Rudolf Hess, Gregor Strasser. They read like a team of vaudeville jugglers. Adolf, Erich, Rudolf, and Gregor. However, toward the end of the article his amusement waned. There were the phrases.

"... conspiracy of Jews and Communists ..."

"... daughters raped by Bolshevik terrorists! ..."

"... Aryan blood soiled by scheming Semites! ..."

"... a plan for a thousand years! ..."

Canfield could see the face of Basil Hawkwood, owner of one of the largest industries in England, whispering with great intensity many of these same words. He thought of the shipments of leather to Munich. The leather without the trademark *hawkwood,* but the leather that became part of the uniforms in these photographs. He recalled the manipulations of the dead Bertholde, the road in Wales, the mass murders at York.

Elizabeth was sitting at the desk jotting down notes from an article. A picture was beginning to emerge for her. But it was incomplete, as if part of a background was missing. It bothered her, but she'd learned enough.

"It staggers your imagination, doesn't it?" said Elizabeth, rising from her chair.

"What do you make of it?"

"Enough to frighten me. An obscure but volatile political organization is being quietly, slowly financed by a number of the wealthiest men on earth. The men of Zurich. And my son is part of them."

"But why?"

"I'm not sure yet." Elizabeth walked to the window. "There's more to learn. However, one thing is clear. If this band of fanatics make solid progress in Germany—in the Reichstag—the men of Zurich could control unheard-of economic power. It's a long-range concept, I think. It could be brilliant strategy."

"Then I've got to get back to Washington!"

"They may already know or suspect."

"Then we've got to move in!"

"You can't move in!" Elizabeth turned back to Canfield, raising her voice. "No government has the right to interfere with the internal politics of another. No government has that right. There's another way. A far more effective way. But there's an enormous risk and I must consider it." The old woman brought her cupped hands up to her lips and walked away from Canfield.

"What is it? What's the risk?"

Elizabeth, however, did not hear him. She was concentrating deeply. After several minutes she spoke to him from across the room.

"There is an island in a remote lake in Canada. My husband, in a rash moment, bought it years and years ago. There are several dwellings on it, primitive but habitable. . . . If I put at your disposal whatever funds were necessary, could you have this island so guarded that it would be impregnable?"

"I think so."

"That's not good enough. There can be no element of doubt. The lives of my entire family would depend on total isolation. The funds I mention are, frankly, limitless."

"All right, then. Yes, I could."

"Could you have them taken there in complete secrecy?"

"Yes."

"Could you set all this up within a week?"

"Yes, again."

"Very well. I'll outline what I propose. Believe me when I tell you it is the only way."

"What's your proposal?"

"Put simply, the Scarlatti Industries will economically destroy every investor in Zurich. Force them into financial ruin."

Canfield looked at the prepossessing, confident old woman. For several seconds he said nothing, merely sucked breath through his teeth as if trying to formulate a reply.

"You're a lunatic," he said quietly. "You're one person. They're fourteen . . . no, now thirteen stinking rich fatcats. You're no match for them."

"It's not what one's worth that counts, Mr. Canfield. Not after a point. It's how rapidly one can manipulate his holdings. The time factor is the ultimate weapon in economics, and don't let anyone tell you otherwise. In my case, one judgment prevails."

"What does that mean?"

Elizabeth stood motionless in front of Canfield. Her speech was measured. "If I were to liquidate the entire Scarlatti Industries, there is no one on earth who could stop me."

The field accountant wasn't sure he understood her implication. He looked at her for a few seconds before speaking. "Oh? So?"

"You fool! . . . Outside of the Rothschilds and, perhaps a few Indian maharajas, I doubt there's another person in my position, or in our civilization, who can say that!"

"Why not? Why can't any of the men in Zurich do the same thing?"

The old woman was exasperated. She clasped her hands and brought the clenched fingers to her chin. "For a man whose imagination far exceeds his intelligence, you astonish me. Or is it only fear that provokes your perception of larger things?"

"No question for a question! I want an answer!"

"It's all related, I assure you. The primary reason why the operation in Zurich can not and will not do as I can do is their own fear. Fear of the laws binding their commitments; fear of the investments, investors; fear of extraordinary decisions; fear of the panic which always results from such decisions. Most important of all, fear of financial ruin."

"And none of that bothers you? Is that what you're saying?"

"No commitments bind Scarlatti. Until I die, there is only one voice. I *am* Scarlatti."

"What about the rest of it? The decisions, the panics, the ruin?"

"As always my decisions will be executed with precision and foresight. Panic will be avoided."

"And so will financial ruin, huh? . . . You are the God damnedest, self-confident old lady!"

"Again you fail to understand. At this juncture I anticipate the collapse of Scarlatti as inevitable should I be called. There will be no quarter given."

Matthew Canfield now understood. "I'll be damned."

"I must have vast sums. Amounts inconceivable to you, which can be allocated by a single command. Money which can purchase massive holdings, inflate or depress entire markets. Once that kind of manipulation has been exercised, I doubt that all the capital on earth could put Scarlatti back together. It would never be trusted again."

"Then you'd be finished."

"Irrevocably."

The old woman moved in front of Canfield. She looked at him but not in the manner to which he was accustomed. She might have been a worried grandmother from the dry plains of Kansas asking the preacher if the Lord would allow the rains to come.

"I have no arguments left. Please allow me my last battle. My final gesture, as it were."

"You're asking an awful lot."

"Not when you think of it. If you return, it'll take you a week to reach Washington. Another week to compile everything we've been through. Days before you reach those in government who should listen to you, if you can get them to listen to you at all. By my calculations that would be at least three or four weeks. Do you agree?"

Canfield felt foolish standing in front of Elizabeth. For no reason other than to increase the distance between them, he walked to the center of the room. "God damn it, I don't know what I agree with!"

"Give me four weeks. Just four weeks from today. . . . If I fail we'll do as you wish. . . . More than that I'll come to Washington with you. I'll testify, if need be, in front of one of those committees. I'll do whatever you and your associates think necessary. Further, I'll settle our personal account three times above that agreed upon."

"Suppose you fail?"

"What possible difference can it make to anyone but myself? There's little sympathy in this world for fallen millionaires."

"What about your family then? They can't spend the rest of their lives in some remote lake in Canada?"

"That won't be necessary. Regardless of the larger outcome, I'll destroy my son. I shall expose Ulster Scarlett for what he is. I'll sentence him to death at Zurich."

The field accountant fell silent for a moment and looked at Elizabeth. "Have you considered the fact that you might be killed?"

"I have."

"You'd risk that. . . . Sell out Scarlatti Industries. Destroy everything you've built. Is it worth that to you? Do you hate him that much?"

"Yes. As one hates a disease. Magnified because I'm responsible for its flourishing."

Canfield put his glass down, tempted to pour himself another drink. "That's going a little far."

"I didn't say I invented the disease. I said that I'm responsible for spreading it. Not simply because I provided the money but infinitely more important, because I implanted an idea. An idea which has become warped in the process of maturing."

"I don't believe that. You're no saint, but you don't think like that." He pointed toward the papers on the couch.

The old woman's weary eyes closed.

"There's a little of . . . that in each of us. It's all part of the idea. . . . The twisted idea. My husband and I devoted years to the building of an industrial empire. Since his death, I've fought in the marketplace—doubling, redoubling, adding, building—always acquiring. . . . It's been a stimulating, all-consuming game. . . . I've played it well. And sometime during all those years, my son learned what many observers failed to learn—that it was never the acquisition of profits or material gain that mattered—they were merely the by-products. It was the acquisition of power. . . . I wanted that power because I sincerely believed that I was equipped for the responsibility. The more convinced I became, it had to follow that others were not equipped. . . . The quest for power becomes a personal crusade, I think. The more success one has, the more personal it becomes. Whether he understood it or not, that's what my son saw happening. . . . There may be similarities of purpose, even of motive. But a great gulf divides us—my son and me."

"I'll give you the four weeks. Jesus Christ only knows why. But you still haven't made it clear to me why you want to risk all this. Throw away everything."

"I've tried to. . . . You're slow at times. If I offend, it's because I think you do understand. You're deliberately asking me to spell out an unpleasant reality." She carried her notes to the table by her bedroom door. As the light had grown dim, she turned on the lamp, causing the fringe on the shade to shimmy. She seemed fascinated by the movement. "I imagine that all of *us*—the Bible calls us the rich and mighty—wish to leave this world somewhat different from the way it was before us. As the years go by, this vague, ill-defined instinct becomes really quite important. How many of us have toyed with the phrases of our own obituaries?" She turned from the lamp and looked at the field accountant. "Considering everything we now know, would you care to speculate on my not-too-distant obituary?"

"No deal. That's another question."

"It's a snap, you know. . . . The wealth is taken for granted. Every agonizing decision, every nerve-racking gamble—they become simple, expected accomplishments. Accomplishments more to be scorned than admired because I'm both a woman and a highly competitive speculator. An unattractive combination. . . . One son lost in the Great War. Another rapidly emerging as a pompous incompetent, sought after for every wrong reason, discarded and laughed at whenever feasible. And now this. A madman leading or at least a part of a growing band of psychopathic malcontents. . . . This is what I bequeath. What Scarlatti bequeaths, Mr. Canfield. . . . Not a very enviable sum, is it?"

"No, it isn't."

"Consequently, I'll stop at nothing to prevent this final madness . . ." She picked up her notes and went into the bedroom. She closed the door behind her, leaving Canfield in the large sitting room by himself. He thought for a moment that the old woman was on the verge of tears.

CHAPTER 35

The monoplane's flight over the channel had been uneventful—the wind calm, the visibility excellent. It was fortunate for Scarlett that such was the case, for the stinging irritation of his unhealed surgery coupled with the pitch of his fury would have made a difficult trip a disastrous one. He was hardly capable of keeping his mind on the compass bearings and when he first saw the Normandy coast, it looked unfamiliar to him. Yet he had made these very same sightings a dozen times.

He was met at the small airfield outside of Lisieux by the Paris contingent, consisting of two Germans and a French Gascon, whose guttural dialect nearly matched that of his associates.

The three Europeans anticipated that the man—they did not know his name—would instruct them to return to Paris. To await further orders.

The man had other intentions, insisting that they all sit uncomfortably together in the front seat while he occupied the entire space in the back. He ordered the car to Vernon, where two got out and were told to make their own way back to Paris. The driver was to remain.

The driver vaguely protested when Scarlett ordered him to proceed west to Montbéliard, a small town near the Swiss border.

"*Mein Herr!* That's a four-hundred-kilometer trip! It will take ten hours or more on these abysmal roads!"

"Then we should be there by dinner time. And be quiet!"

"It might have been simpler for *mein Herr* to refuel and fly . . ."

"I do not fly when I am tired. Relax. I'll find you some 'seafood' in Montbéliard. Vary your diet, Kircher. It excites the palate."

"Jawohl, mein Herr!" Kircher grinned, knowing the man was really a fine *Oberführer*.

Scarlett reflected. The misfits! One day they'd be rid of the misfits.

Montbéliard was not much more complex than an oversized village. The principal livelihood of its citizens was farm produce, much of which was shipped into Switzerland and Germany. Its currency, as in many towns on the border, was a mixture of francs, marks, and Swiss francs.

Scarlett and his driver reached it a little after nine in the evening. However, except for several stops for petrol and a midafternoon lunch, they had pushed forward with no conversation between them. This quiet acted as a sedative to Scarlett's anxiety. He was able to think without anger, although his anger was ever present. The driver had been right when he had pointed out that a flight from Lisieux to Montbéliard would have been simpler and less arduous, but Scarlett could not risk any explosions of temper brought on by exhaustion.

Sometime that day or evening—the time was left open—he was meeting with the Prussian, the all-important man who could deliver what few others could. He had to be up to that meeting, every brain cell working. He couldn't allow recent problems to distort his concentration. The conference with the Prussian was the culmination of months, years of work. From the first macabre meeting with Gregor Strasser to the conversion of his millions to Swiss capital. He, Heinrich Kroeger, possessed the finances so desperately needed by the National Socialists. His importance to the party was now acknowledged.

The problems. Irritating problems! But he'd made his decisions. He'd have Howard Thornton isolated, perhaps killed. The San Franciscan had betrayed them. If the Stockholm manipulation had been uncovered, it had to

e laid at Thornton's feet. They'd used his Swedish con-
ıcts and obviously he maneuvered large blocks of securi-
es back into his own hands at the depressed price.

Thornton would be taken care of.

As was the French dandy, Jacques Bertholde.

Thornton and Bertholde! Both misfits! Greedy, stupid
ıisfits!

What had happened to Boothroyd? Obviously killed on
ıe *Calpurnia*. But how? Why? Regardless, he deserved
ı die! So did his father-in-law. Rawlins' order to kill
lizabeth Scarlatti was stupid! The timing had been in-
ıne! Couldn't Rawlins understand that she would have
ft letters behind, documents? She was far more danger-
us dead than alive. At least until she'd been reached—
s he had reached her, threatened her precious Scarlattis.
ow, she could die! Now it wouldn't matter. And with
ertholde gone, Rawlins gone, and Thornton about to
e killed, there'd be no one left who knew who he was.
o one! He was Heinrich Kroeger, a leader of the new
rder!

They pulled up at L'Auberge des Moineaux, a small
estaurant with a *buvette* and lodgings for the traveler or
ır those desiring privacy for other reasons. For Scarlett
was the appointed meeting place.

"Take the car down the road and park it," he told
ircher. "I'll be in one of the rooms. Have dinner. I'll
all for you later. . . . I haven't forgotten my prom-
e." Kircher grinned.

Ulster Scarlett got out of the car and stretched. He
lt better, his skin bothered him less, and the impending
onference filled him with a sense of anticipation. This
as the kind of work he should always do! Matters of
ast consequences. Matters of power.

He waited until the car was far enough down the street
ı obscure Kircher's rear-mirror view of him. He then
alked back, away from the door, to the cobblestone
ath and turned into it. Misfits were never to be told
nything that wasn't essential to their specific usefulness.

He reached an unlighted door and knocked several
mes.

The door opened and a moderately tall man with thick,
avy black hair and prominent, dark eyebrows stood in
he center of the frame as if guarding an entrance, not
elcoming a guest. He was dressed in a Bavarian-cut gray

coat and brown knickers. The face was darkly cherubic, the eyes wide and staring. His name was Rudolf Hess.

"Where have you been?" Hess motioned Scarlett to enter and close the door. The room was small; there was a table with chairs around it, a sideboard, and two floor lamps, which gave the room its light. Another man who had been looking out the window, obviously to identify the one outside, nodded to Scarlett. He was a tiny, ugly man with birdlike features, even to the hawknose. He walked with a limp.

"Joseph?" said Scarlett to him. "I didn't expect you here."

Joseph Goebbels looked over at Hess. His knowledge of English was poor. Hess translated Scarlett's words rapidly and Goebbels shrugged his shoulders.

"I asked you where you have been!"

"I had trouble in Lisieux. I couldn't get another plane so I had to drive. It's been a long day so don't aggravate me, please."

"*Ach!* From Lisieux? A long trip. I'll order you some food, but you'll have to be quick. Rheinhart's been waiting since noon."

Scarlett took off his flying jacket and threw it on the sideboard shelf. "How is he?"

Goebbels understood just enough to interrupt. "Rheinhart? . . . Im-pa-tient!" He mispronounced the word, and Scarlett grinned. Goebbels thought to himself that this giant was a horrible-looking creature. The opinion was mutual.

"Never mind the food. Rheinhart's been waiting too long. . . . Where is he?"

"In his room. Number two, down the corridor. He went for a walk this afternoon but he keeps thinking someone will recognize him so he came back in ten minutes. I think he's upset."

"Go get him. . . . And bring back some whiskey." He looked at Goebbels wishing that this unattractive little man would leave. It wasn't good that Goebbels be there while Hess and he talked with the Prussian aristocrat. Goebbels looked like an insignificant Jewish accountant.

But Scarlett knew he could do nothing. Hitler was taken with Goebbels.

Joseph Goebbels seemed to be reading the tall man's thoughts.

"Ich werde dabei sitzen während Sie sprechen." He pulled a chair back to the wall and sat down.

Hess had gone out the corridor door and the two men were in the room alone. Neither spoke.

Four minutes later Hess returned. Following him was an aging, overweight German several inches shorter than Hess, dressed in a black double-breasted suit and a high collar. His face was puffed with excess fat, his white hair cropped short. He stood perfectly erect and in spite of his imposing appearance, Scarlett thought there was something soft about him, not associated with his bulk. He strutted into the room. Hess closed the door and locked it.

"Gentlemen. General Rheinhart." Hess stood at attention.

Goebbels rose from the chair and bowed, clicking his heels.

Rheinhart looked at him unimpressed.

Scarlett noticed Rheinhart's expression. He approached the elderly general and held out his hand.

"Herr General."

Rheinhart faced Scarlett, and although he concealed it well, his reaction to Scarlett's appearance was obvious. The two men shook hands perfunctorily.

"Please sit down, *Herr General.*" Hess was enormously impressed with their company and did not hide the fact. Rheinhart sat in a chair at the end of the table. Scarlett was momentarily upset. He had wanted to sit in that particular chair for it was the commanding position.

Hess asked Rheinhart if he preferred whiskey, gin, or wine. The general waved his hand, refusing.

"Nothing for me, either," added Ulster Scarlett as he sat in the chair to the left of Rheinhart. Hess ignored the tray and also took his seat. Goebbels retreated with his limp to the chair by the wall.

Scarlett spoke. "I apologize for the delay. Unforgivable but, I'm afraid, unavoidable. There was pressing business with our associates in London."

"Your name, please?" Rheinhart interrupted, speaking English with a thick Teutonic accent.

Scarlett looked briefly at Hess before replying. "Kroeger, *Herr General*. Heinrich Kroeger."

Rheinhart did not take his eyes off Scarlett. "I do not

think that is your name, sir. You are not German." His voice was flat.

"My sympathies are German. So much so that Heinrich Kroeger is the name I have chosen to be known by."

Hess interrupted. "Herr Kroeger has been invaluable to us all. Without him we would never have made the progress we have, sir."

"*Amerikaner*. . . . He is the reason we do not speak German?"

"That will be corrected in time," Scarlett said. In fact, he spoke nearly flawless German, but still felt at a disadvantage in the language.

"I am not an American, General. . . ." Scarlett returned Rheinhart's stare and gave no quarter. "I am a citizen of the new order! . . . I have given as much, if not more than anyone else alive or dead to see it come to pass. . . . Please remember that in our conversation."

Rheinhart shrugged. "I'm sure you have your reasons, as I have, for being at this table."

"You may be assured of that." Scarlett relaxed and pulled his chair up.

"Very well, gentlemen, to business. If it is possible, I should like to leave Montbéliard tonight." Rheinhart reached into his jacket pocket and took out a page of folded stationery. "Your party has made certain not inconsequential strides in the Reichstag. After your Munich fiasco, one might even say remarkable progress . . ."

Hess broke in enthusiastically. "We have only begun! From the ignominy of treacherous defeat, Germany will rise! We will be masters of all Europe!"

Rheinhart held the folded paper in his hand and watched Hess. He replied quietly, authoritatively. "To be masters of but Germany itself would be sufficient for us. To be able to defend our country is all we ask."

"That will be the least of your guarantees from us, General." Scarlett's voice rose no higher than Rheinhart's.

"It is the only guarantee we wish. We are not interested in the excesses your Adolf Hitler preaches."

At the mention of Hitler's name, Goebbels sat forward in his chair. He was angered by the fact that he could not comprehend.

"Was gibt's mit Hitler? Was sagen sie über ihn?"

Rheinhart answered Goebbels in his own tongue. "Er ist ein sehr storener geriosse."

"Hitler ist der Weg! Hitler ist die Hoffnung für Deutschland!"

"Vielleicht für Sie."

Ulster Scarlett looked over at Goebbels. The little man's eyes shone with hatred and Scarlett guessed that one day Rheinhart would pay for his words. The general continued as he unfolded the paper.

"The times our nation lives through call for unusual alliances. . . . I have spoken with von Schnitzler and Kindorf. Krupp will not discuss the subject as I'm sure you are aware. . . . German industry is no better off than the army. We are both pawns for the Allied Controls Commission. The Versailles restrictions inflate us one minute, puncture us the next. There is no stability. There is nothing we can count on. We have a common objective, gentlemen. The Versailles treaty."

"It is only one of the objectives. There are others." Scarlett was pleased, but his pleasure was short-lived.

"It is the only objective which has brought me to Montbéliard! As German industry must be allowed to breathe, to export unencumbered, so must the German army be allowed to maintain adequate strength! The limitation of one hundred thousand troops with over sixteen hundred miles of borders to protect is ludicrous! . . . There are promises, always promises—then threats. Nothing to count on. No comprehension. No allowance for necessary growth."

"We were betrayed! We were viciously betrayed in nineteen eighteen and that betrayal continues! Traitors still exist throughout Germany!" Hess wanted more than his life to be counted among the friends of Rheinhart and his officers. Rheinhart understood and was not impressed.

"*Ja*. Ludendorff still holds to that theory. The Meuse-Argonne is not easy for him to live with."

Ulster Scarlett smiled his grotesque smile. "It is for some of us, General Rheinhart."

Rheinhart looked at him. "I will not pursue that with you."

"One day you should. It's why I'm here—in part."

"To repeat, Herr Kroeger. You have your reasons; I have mine. I am not interested in yours but you are forced to be interested in mine." He looked at Hess and then over at the shadowed figure of Joseph Goebbels by the wall.

"I will be blunt, gentlemen. It is, at best, an ill-kept secret. . . . Across the Polish borders in the lands of the Bolshevik are thousands of frustrated German officers. Men without professions in their own country. They train the Russian field commanders! They discipline the Red peasant army. . . . Why? Some for simple employment. Others justify themselves because a few Russian factories smuggle us cannon, armaments prohibited by the Allied Commission. . . . I do not like this state of affairs, gentlemen. I do not trust the Russians. . . . Weimar is ineffectual. Ebert couldn't face the truth. Hindenburg is worse! He lives in a monarchial past. The politicians must be made to face the Versailles issue! We must be liberated from within!"

Rudolf Hess placed both his hands, palms down, on the table.

"You have the word of Adolf Hitler and those of us in this room that the first item on the political agenda of the National Socialist German Workers party is the unconditional repudiation of the Versailles treaty and its restrictions!"

"I assume that. My concern is whether you are capable of effectively uniting the diverse political camps of the Reichstag. I will not deny that you have appeal. Far more than the others. . . . The question we would like answered, as I'm sure would our equals in commerce, Do you have the staying power? Can you last? Will you last? . . . You were outlawed a few years ago. We can not afford to be allied with a political comet which burns itself out."

Ulster Scarlett rose from his chair and looked down at the aging German general. "What would you say if I told you that we have financial resources surpassing those of any political organization in Europe? Possibly the Western hemisphere."

"I would say that you exaggerate."

"Or if I told you that we possess territory—land—sufficiently large enough to train thousands upon thousands of elite troops beyond the scrutiny of the Versailles inspection teams."

"You would have to prove all this to me."

"I can do just that."

Rheinhart rose and faced Heinrich Kroeger.

"If you speak the truth . . . you will have the support of the imperial German generals."

CHAPTER 36

Janet Saxon Scarlett, eyes still shut, reached under the sheets for the body of her lover. He was not there, so she opened her eyes and raised her head, and the room spun around. Her lids were heavy and her stomach hurt. She was still exhausted, still a bit drunk.

Matthew Canfield sat at the writing desk in his undershorts. His elbows were on the desk, his chin cupped in his hands. He was staring down at a paper in front of him.

Janet watched him, aware that he was oblivious to her. She rolled onto her side so that she could observe him.

He was not an ordinary man, she thought, but on the other hand neither was he particularly outstanding, except that she loved him. What, she wondered, did she find so attractive about him? He was not like the men from her world—even her recently expanded world. Most of the men she knew were quick, polished, overly groomed and only concerned with appearances. But Matthew Canfield could not fit into this world. His quickness was an intuitive alertness not related to the graces. And in other respects there was a degree of awkwardness; what confidence he had was born of considered judgment, not simply born.

Others, too, were far more handsome, although he could be placed in the category of "good-looking" in a rough-hewn way. . . . That was it, she mused; he gave the appearance both in actions and in looks of secure independence, but his private behavior was different. In private he was extraordinarily gentle, almost weak. . . .

She wondered if he was weak. She knew he was deeply upset and she suspected that Elizabeth had given him money to do her bidding. . . . He didn't really know how to be at ease with money. She'd learned that during their two weeks together in New York. He'd obviously been told to spend without worrying about sums in order to establish their relationship—he'd suggested as much—and they'd both laughed because what they were doing on government funds was, in essence, spelling out the truth. . . . She would have been happy to pay the freight herself. She'd paid for others, and none were as dear to her as Matthew Canfield. No one would ever be so dear to her. He didn't belong to her world. He preferred a simpler, less cosmopolitan one, she thought. But Janet Saxon Scarlett knew she would adjust if it meant keeping him.

Perhaps, when it was all over, if it was ever to be all over, they would find a way. There had to be a way for this good, rough, gentle young man who was a better man than any she had ever known before. She loved him very much and she found herself concerned for him. That was remarkable for Janet Saxon Scarlett.

When she had returned the night before at seven o'clock, escorted by Derek's man Ferguson, she found Canfield alone in Elizabeth's sitting room. He'd seemed tense, edgy, even angry, and she didn't know why. He'd made feeble excuses for his temper and finally, without warning, he had ushered her out of the suite and out of the hotel.

They had eaten at a small restaurant in Soho. They both drank heavily, his fear infecting her. Yet he would not tell her what bothered him.

They'd returned to his room with a bottle of whiskey. Alone, in the quiet, they had made love. Janet knew he was a man holding on to some mythical rope, afraid to let go for fear of plunging downward.

As she watched him at the writing desk, she also instinctively knew the truth—the unwanted truth—which she had suspected since that terrible moment more than a day ago when he had said to her, "Janet. I'm afraid we've had a visitor."

That visitor had been her husband.

She raised herself on her elbow. "Matthew?"

"Oh. . . . Morning, friend."

"Matthew . . . are you afraid of him?"

Canfield's stomach muscles grew taut.

She knew.

But, of course, she knew.

"I don't think I will be . . . when I find him."

"That's always the way, isn't it? We're afraid of someone or something we don't know or can't find." Janet's eyes began to ache.

"That's what Elizabeth said."

She sat up, pulling the blanket over her shoulders, and leaned back against the headrest. She felt cold, and the ache in her eyes intensified. "Did she tell you?"

"Finally. . . . She didn't want to. I didn't give her an alternative. . . . She had to."

Janet stared straight ahead, at nothing. "I knew it," she said quietly. "I'm frightened."

"Of course you are. . . . But you don't have to be. He can't touch you."

"Why are you so sure? I don't think you were so sure last night." She was not aware of it, but her hands began to shake.

"No, I wasn't. . . . But only because he existed at all. . . . The unholy specter alive and breathing. . . . No matter how much we expected it, it was a shock. But the sun's up now." He reached for his pencil and made a note on the paper.

Suddenly Janet Scarlett flung herself down across the bed. "Oh, God, God, God!" Her head was buried in the pillow.

At first Canfield did not recognize the appeal in her voice, for she did not scream or shout out and his concentration was on his notes. Her muffled cry was one of agony, not desperation.

"Jan," he began casually. "Janet!" The field accountant threw down his pencil and rushed to the bed. "Janet! . . . Honey, please don't. Don't, please. Janet!" He cradled her in his arms, doing his best to comfort her. And then slowly his attention was drawn to her eyes.

The tears were streaming down her face uncontrollably, yet she did not cry out but only gasped for breath. What disturbed him were her eyes.

Instead of blinking from the flow of tears, they remained wide open, as if she were in a trance. A trance of horror.

He spoke her name over and over again.

"Janet. Janet. Janet. Janet. . . ."

She did not respond. She seemed to sink deeper and deeper into the fear which controlled her. She began to moan, at first quietly, then louder and louder.

"Janet! Stop it! Stop it! Darling, stop it!"

She did not hear him.

Instead she tried to push him away, to disengage herself from him. Her naked body writhed on the bed; her arms lashed out, striking him.

He tightened his grip, afraid for a moment that he might hurt her.

Suddenly she stopped. She threw her head back and spoke in a choked voice he had not heard before.

"God damn you to hell! . . . God damn you to hellll!"

She drew out the word "hell" until it became a scream.

Her legs spread slowly, reluctantly, apart on top of the sheet.

In that same choked, guttural voice she whispered, "You pig! Pig! Pig! Pig!"

Canfield watched her in dread. She was assuming a position of sexual intercourse, steeling herself against the terror which had enveloped her and which would progressively worsen.

"Janet, for God's sake, Jan. . . . Don't! Don't! No one's going to touch you! Please, darling!"

The girl laughed horridly, hysterically.

"You're the *card*, Ulster! You're the God damn jack of . . . jack of . . ." She quickly crossed her legs, one emphatically on top of the other, and brought her hands up to cover her breasts. "Leave me alone, Ulster! Please, dear God, Ulster! Leave me alone! . . . You're going to leave me alone?" She curled herself up like an infant and began to sob.

Canfield reached down to the foot of the bed and pulled the blanket over Janet.

He was afraid.

That she could suddenly, without warning, reduce herself to Scarlett's unwilling whore was frightening.

But it was there, and he had to accept it.

She needed help. Perhaps far more help than he could provide. He gently stroked her hair and lay down beside her.

Her sobs evened off into deep breathing as she closed

her eyes. He hoped she was sleeping but he could not be sure. At any rate, he would let her rest. It would give him the time to figure out a way to tell her everything she had to know.

The next four weeks would be terrible for her.

For the three of them.

But now there was an element which had been absent before, and Canfield was grateful for it. He knew he shouldn't have been, for it was against every professional instinct he had.

It was hate. His own personal hate.

Ulster Stewart Scarlett was no longer the quarry in an international hunt. He was now the man Matthew Canfield intended to kill.

CHAPTER 37

Ulster Scarlett watched the flushed, angry face of Adolf Hitler. He realized that in spite of his fury, Hitler had a capacity for control that was nothing short of miraculous. But then the man himself was a miracle. A historic man-miracle who would take them into the finest world imaginable on earth.

The three of them—Hess, Goebbels, and Kroeger—had driven through the night from Montbéliard to Munich, where Hitler and Ludendorff awaited a report of their meeting with Rheinhart. If the conference had gone well, Ludendorff's plan was to be set in motion. Each faction of the Reichstag possessing any serious following would be alerted that a coalition was imminent. Promises would be made, threats implied. As the Reichstag's sole member of the National Socialist party and its candidate for president the previous year, Ludendorff would be listened to. He was the soldier-thinker. He was slowly regaining the stature he had thrown away in defeat at the Meuse-Argonne.

Simultaneously and in twelve different cities anti-Versailles demonstrations would be staged, where the police had been paid handsomely not to interfere. Hitler was to travel to Oldenburg, in the center of the northwest Prussian territory, where the great military estates were slowly going to seed—massive remembrances of past glories. A huge rally would be mounted and it was planned that Rheinhart himself would make an appearance.

Rheinhart was enough to give credence to the party's military support. It was more than enough; it would be a momentary climax fitting their current progress. Rheinhart's recognition of Hitler would leave no room for doubt as to where the generals were leaning.

Ludendorff looked upon the act as a political necessity. Hitler looked upon it as a political coup. The Austrian lance corporal was never unmoved by the anticipation of Junker approval. He knew that it was his destiny to have it—demand it!—but nonetheless it filled him with pride, which was why he was furious now.

The ugly little Goebbels had just finished telling Ludendorff and Hitler of Rheinhart's remarks about the Austrian.

In the large rented office overlooking the Sedlingerstrasse, Hitler gripped the arms of his chair and pushed himself up. He stood for a moment glaring at Goebbels, but the thin cripple knew that Hitler's anger was not directed at him, only at his news.

"Fettes Schwein! Wir werden ihn zu seinen Landsort zurück senden! Lass ihm zu seinen Kühen zurück gehen!"

Scarlett was leaning against the wall next to Hess. As usual when the conversations taking place were in German, the willing Hess turned to Ulster and spoke quietly.

"He's very upset. Rheinhart may be an obstacle."

"Why?"

"Goebbels doesn't believe Rheinhart will openly support the movement. He wants all the advantages without getting his tunic dirty!"

"Rheinhart said he would. In Montbéliard he said he would! What's Goebbels talking about?" Scarlett found it necessary to watch himself. He really didn't like Goebbels.

"He's just told them what Rheinhart said about Hitler. Remember?" Hess whispered with his hand cupped in front of his mouth.

Scarlett raised his voice. "They should tell Rheinhart—no Hitler, no marbles! Let him go shag!"

"Was ist los?" Hitler glowered at Hess and Scarlett. "Was sagt er, Hess?"

"Lass Rheinhart zum Teufel gehen!"

Ludendorff laughed out of the corner of his mouth. "Das ist naiv!"

"Tell Rheinhart to do as we say or he's out! No troops! No weapons! No uniforms! No one to pay for it all! I don't pay! No place to train them without the inspection teams on his back! He'll listen!" Scarlett ignored Hess, who was rapidly translating everything the former said.

Ludendorff broke in on Hess as he finished interpreting.

"Man kann einen Mann wie Rheinhart nicht drohen. Er ist ein einflussreich Preusse!"

Hess turned to Ulster Scarlett. "Herr Ludendorff says that Rheinhart will not be threatened. He is a Junker."

"He's a frightened, overstuffed tin soldier, that's what he is! He's running scared. He's got the Russian shakes! He needs us and he knows it!"

Hess repeated Scarlett's remarks. Ludendorff snapped his fingers in the Heidelberg fashion, as if mocking a ridiculous statement.

"Don't laugh at me! I talked with him, not you! It's my money! Not yours!"

Hess did not need to translate. Ludendorff rose from his chair, as angry as Scarlett.

"Sag dem Amerikaner dass sein Gelt gibt ihm noch lange nicht das Recht uns Befehle zu geben."

Hess hesitated. "Herr Ludendorff does not believe that your financial contributions . . . as welcome as they are . . ."

"You don't have to finish! Tell him to go shag, too! He's acting just the way Rheinhart expects!" Scarlett, who had not moved from his position against the wall, pushed himself away and sprang forward effortlessly to his full height.

For a moment the aging, intellectual Ludendorff was physically afraid. He did not trust the motives of this neurotic American. Ludendorff had often suggested to Hitler and the others that this man who called himself Heinrich Kroeger was a dangerous addition to their working circle. But he had been consistently overruled because Kroeger not only possessed what appeared to be unlimited financial resources, but seemed to be able to enlist the support, or at least the interest, of incredibly influential men.

Still, he did not trust him.

Essentially because Ludendorff was convinced that this Kroeger was stupid.

"May I remind you, Herr Kroeger, that I possess a . . . working knowledge of the English language!"

"Then why don't you use it?"

"I do not feel it is—how is it said?—entirely necessary."

"It is now, damn it!"

Adolf Hitler suddenly clapped his hands twice, signifying an order of silence. It was an irksome gesture to Ludendorff, but his respect for Hitler's talents—which bordered on awe—made him accept such aggravations.

"Halt! Beide!"

Hitler stepped away from the table, turning his back on all of them. He stretched his arms, then clasped his hands behind him. He said nothing for several moments, yet no one interrupted his silence. For it was his silence, and Goebbels, whose love of theatrics was paramount, watched with satisfaction the effect Hitler was having on the others.

Ludendorff, on the other hand, played the game but remained annoyed. The Hitler he knew well was capable of poor judgment. Great vision, perhaps, but often slipshod in decisions of everyday practical realities. It was unfortunate that he also resented debate on such matters. It made it difficult for Rosenberg and himself, who knew they were the true architects of the new order. Ludendorff hoped that this particular instance was not going to be another case when Hitler overrode his sound analysis. Like himself, Rheinhart was a Junker, proud and unbending. He had to be handled artfully. Who could know this better than the former field marshal of the imperial army who was forced to maintain his dignity in the midst of tragic defeat. Ludendorff understood.

Adolf Hitler spoke quietly. "Wir werden wie Herr Kroeger sagt tun."

"Herr Hitler agrees with you, Kroeger!" Hess touched Scarlett's sleeve, delighted. He was forever being condescended to by the arrogant Ludendorff, and this was not a small victory over him. Rheinhart was a prize. If Kroeger was correct, Ludendorff would look foolish.

"Warum? Es ist sehr gefährlich."

Ludendorff had to argue although he knew at once it was no use.

"Sie sind zu Vorsichtig die unruhigen Zieten, Ludendorff. Kroeger hat recht. Aber wir werden einen Schritt weiter gehen."

Rudolf Hess expanded his chest. He looked pointedly at Ludendorff and Goebbels as he nudged Scarlett with his elbow.

"Herr Hitler says that our friend Ludendorff is mis-

akenly cautious. He is right. Ludendorff is always cau-
ious. . . . But Herr Hitler wishes to elaborate on your
iggestion. . . ."

Adolf Hitler began speaking slowly but firmly, lending finality to each German phrase. As he continued he ratched with satisfaction the faces of those listening. Vhen he reached the end of his diatribe he spat out the ords.

"Da ist Montbéliard!"

For each it was a different evaluation with an underly-g common denominator—the man was a genius.

For Hess, Hitler's conclusion was equated with a star-ing flash of political insight.

For Goebbels, Hitler had once again demonstrated his bility to capitalize on an opponent's fundamental weak-ess.

For Ludendorff, the Austrian had taken a mediocre lea, added his own boldness, and emerged with a piece f brilliant strategy.

Heinrich Kroeger—Scarlett—spoke. "What did he say, Iess?"

But it was not Rudolf Hess who answered. It was Erich udendorff, who did not take his eyes off Adolf Hitler. Herr Hitler has just . . . solidified the military for us, Kroeger. In a brief statement he has won us the reluctant russians."

"What?"

Rudolf Hess turned to Scarlett. "General Rheinhart will e told that unless he does as we demand, the Versailles fficials will be informed that he is secretly negotiating legal procurements. It is the truth. Montbéliard can ot be denied!"

"He is a Junker!" Ludendorff added. "Montbéliard is ne key because it is the truth! Rheinhart can not dis-yow what he has done! Even if he should be tempted, here are too many who know—von Schnitzler, Kindorf. Even Krupp! Rheinhart has broken his word." And then udendorff laughed harshly. "The holy word of a Jun-er!"

Hitler smiled briefly and spoke rapidly to Hess, ges-uring his head toward Ulster Scarlett.

"Der Führer admires and appreciates you, Heinrich," aid Hess. "He asks what of our friends in Zurich?"

"Everything is proceeding on schedule. Several errors

have been corrected. We may lose one of the remaining thirteen. . . . It's no loss; he's a thief."

"Who is that?" Ludendorff exercised his very acceptable working knowledge of English.

"Thornton."

"What of his land?" Ludendorff again.

Scarlett, now Kroeger, looked at the academic Ludendorff, the military intellectual, with the contempt born of money. "I intend to buy it."

"Is that not dangerous?" Hess was watching Ludendorff, who had quietly translated what Scarlett said to Hitler. Both men showed signs of alarm.

"Not at all."

"Perhaps not to you personally, my dashing young friend." Ludendorff's tone was blandly incriminating. "Who knows where your sympathies will lie six months from now?"

"I resent that!"

"You're not a German. This isn't your battle."

"I don't have to be a German! And I don't have to justify myself to you! . . . You want me out? Fine! I'm out! . . . And with me go a dozen of the richest men on earth. . . . Oil! Steel! Industry! Steamship lines!"

Hess no longer tried to be tactful. He looked toward Hitler, throwing his arms up in exasperation.

Hitler did not need to be prompted for he knew exactly what to do. He crossed rapidly to the former general of the imperial German army and struck the old man lightly across the mouth with the back of his hand. It was an insulting action—the very lightness of the blow was akin to disciplining a small child. The two men exchanged words and Scarlett knew the old Ludendorff had been severely, cruelly rebuked.

"My motives seem to be questioned, Herr Kroeger. I was merely—how is it said?—testing you." He lifted his hand to his mouth. The memory of Hitler's insult was difficult for him. He struggled to suppress it.

"I was quite sincere, however, about the Swiss property. Your . . . work with us has been most impressive and undoubtedly noticed by many. Should the purchase be traced through you to the party, it might—how is it said—make useless the whole arrangement."

Ulster Scarlett answered with confident nonchalance

He enjoyed putting the thinkers in their place. "No problems. . . . The transaction will be made in Madrid."

"Madrid?" Joseph Goebbels did not fully understand what Scarlett said, but the city of Madrid had a special connotation for him.

The four Germans looked at each other. None was pleased.

"Why is . . . Madrid so safe?" Hess was concerned that his friend had done something rash.

"Papal attaché. Very Catholic. Very much beyond reproach. Satisfied?"

Hess automatically spoke Scarlett's words in German.

Hitler smiled while Ludendorff snapped his fingers, now in sincere applause.

"How is this accomplished?"

"Very simple. Alfonso's court will be told that the land is being bought with White Russian money. Unless it's done quickly, the capital could be manipulated back into Moscow. The Vatican is sympathetic. So is Rivera. This won't be the first time such an arrangement's been made."

Hess explained to Adolf Hitler as Joseph Goebbels listened intently.

"My congratulations, Herr Kroeger. Be . . . cautious." Ludendorff was impressed.

Suddenly Goebbels began chattering, waving his hands in exaggerated gestures. The Germans all laughed and Scarlett wasn't sure whether the unattractive little fascist was making fun of him or not.

Hess translated. "Herr Goebbels says that if you tell the Vatican you can keep four hungry Communists from having a loaf of bread, the pope will let you repaint the Sistine Chapel!"

Hitler broke in on the laughter. "Was hörst du aus Zürich?"

Ludendorff turned to Scarlett. "You were saying about our friends in Switzerland?"

"On schedule. By the end of next month . . . five weeks say, the buildings will be completed. . . . Here, I'll show you."

Kroeger approached the table, taking a folded map from his jacket pocket. He spread it on the table. "This heavy blue line is the perimeter of the adjacent properties. This section . . . in the south is Thornton's. We extend west to here, north here to Baden, east to the outskirts of Pfäffikon. Approximately every mile and a quarter is a structure which can house fifty troops—eighteen in all. Nine hundred men. The water lines are down, the foundations are in. Each structure looks like a barn or a granary. You couldn't tell the difference unless you were inside."

"Excellent!" Ludendorff inserted a monocle in his left eye and looked closely at the map. Hess translated for a curious Hitler and a skeptical Goebbels. "This . . . perimeter between the . . . *Keserne* . . . barracks . . . is it fenced?"

"Twelve feet high. Wired by generators in each building for alarms. Patrols will be maintained twenty-four hours a day. Men and dogs. . . . I've paid for everything."

"Excellent. Excellent!"

Scarlett looked over at Hitler. He knew that Ludendorff's approval was never granted easily and in spite of their unpleasant encounter a few moments ago, Scarlett also realized that Hitler valued Ludendorff's opinion, perhaps above all others. It seemed to Scarlett that Hitler's penetrating stare, which was now directed at him, was a look of admiration. Kroeger controlled his own elation and quickly continued.

"The indoctrinations will be concentrated—each lasting four weeks with several days between sessions for transportation and housing. Each contingent has nine hundred men. . . . At the end of one year . . ."

Hess interrupted. "Prachtvoll! At the end of a year ten thousand trained men!"

"Ready to spread throughout the country as military units. Trained for insurgency!" Scarlett was fairly bursting with energy.

"No longer rabble, but the basis of an elite corps! Perhaps the elite corps itself!" Ludendorff himself was catching the younger man's enthusiasm. "Our own private army!"

"That's it! A skilled machine capable of moving fast, hitting hard, and regrouping swiftly and secretly."

As Kroeger spoke, it was Ludendorff who now turned his phrases into the German language for the benefit of Hitler and Goebbels.

But Goebbels was bothered. He spoke quietly, as if

this Kroeger might somehow catch the shaded meaning of his observations. Goebbels was still suspicious. This huge, strange American was too glib, too casual in spite of his fervor. In spite of the power of his money. Adolf Hitler nodded his head in agreement.

Hess spoke. "Quite rightly, Heinrich, Herr Goebbels is concerned. These men in Zurich, their demands are so . . . nebulous."

"Not to them they're not. They're very specific. These men are businessmen. . . . And besides, they're sympathetic."

"Kroeger is correct." Ludendorff looked at Ulster Scarlett, knowing that Hess would use the German tongue for the others. He was thinking as he spoke, not wishing Kroeger to have any time to formulate answers or comments. This Kroeger, although he did not speak their language fluently, understood far more than he let on, Ludendorff believed. "We have gone so far as to sign agreements, have we not? . . . Pacts, if you like, that with the emergence of our power on the political scene in Germany, our friends in Zurich will be given . . . certain priorities. . . . Economic priorities. . . . We are committed, are we not." There was no hint of a question in Ludendorff's last remark.

"That's right."

"What happens, Herr Kroeger, if we do not honor those commitments?"

Ulster Scarlett paused, returning Ludendorff's now questioning gaze. "They'd yell like sons of bitches and try to ruin us."

"How?"

"Any means they could, Ludendorff. And their means are considerable."

"Does that bother you?"

"Only if they succeeded. . . . Thornton's not the only one. They're all thieves. The difference is that the rest of them are smart. They know we're right. We'll win! Everyone likes to do business with the winner! They know what they're doing. They want to work with us!"

"I believe you're convinced."

"You're damn right I am. Between us we'll run things our way. The right way! The way we want to. We'll get rid of the garbage! The Jews, the Reds, the stinking little bourgeois bootlickers!"

Ludendorff watched the confident American closely. He was right, Kroeger was stupid. His description of the lesser breeds was emotional, not based upon the sound principles of racial integrity. Hitler and Goebbels had similar blind spots but theirs was a pyramid logic in spite of themselves—they knew because they saw; they had studied as had Rosenberg and himself. This Kroeger had a child's mentality. He was actually a bigot.

"There is much in what you say. Everyone who thinks will support his own kind. . . . Do business with his own kind." Ludendorff would watch Heinrich Kroeger's actions carefully. Such a high-strung man could do great damage. He was a fever-ridden clown.

But then, their court had need of such a jester. And his money.

As usual, Hitler was right. They dare not lose him now.

"I'm going to Madrid in the morning. I've already sent out the orders concerning Thornton. The whole business shouldn't take any longer than two or three weeks, and then I'll be in Zurich."

Hess told Hitler and Goebbels what Kroeger had said. *Der Führer* barked out a sharp question.

"Where can you be reached in Zurich?" interpreted Ludendorff. "Your schedule, if it proceeds as it has, will require communication with you."

Heinrich Kroeger paused before giving his answer. He knew the question would be asked again. It was always asked whenever he went to Zurich. Yet he was always evasive. He realized that part of his mystique, his charisma within the party, was due to his obscuring the specific individuals or firms with which he did business. In the past he had left a single phone number or a post office box, or perhaps even the name of one of the fourteen men in Zurich with instructions to ask him for a code name.

Never direct and open.

They did not understand that identities, addresses, phone numbers were unimportant. Only the ability to deliver was essential.

Zurich understood.

These Goliaths of the world's great fortunes understood. The international financiers with their tangled labyrinths of manipulations understood perfectly.

He had delivered.

Their agreements with Germany's emerging new order insured markets and controls beyond belief.

And none cared who he was or where he came from.

But now, at this moment, Ulster Stewart Scarlett realized that these titans of the new order needed to be reminded of Heinrich Kroeger's importance.

He would tell them the truth.

He would say the name of the one man in Germany sought by all who drove for power. The one man who refused to talk, refused to be involved, refused to meet with any faction.

The only man in Germany who lived behind a wall of total secrecy. Complete political isolation.

The most feared and revered man in all Europe.

"I'll be with Krupp. Essen will know where to reach us."

CHAPTER 38

Elizabeth Scarlatti sat up in her bed. A card table had been placed at her side, and papers were strewn all over the immediate vicinity—the bed, the table, the entire walking area of the room. Some were in neat piles, others scattered. Some were clipped together and labeled by index cards; others discarded, ready for the trash basket.

It was four o'clock in the afternoon and she had left her room only once. That was to let in Janet and Matthew. She noted that they looked terrible; exhausted, ill, perhaps. She knew what had happened. The pressure had become too much for the government man. He had to break out, get relief. Now that he had, he would be better prepared for her proposal.

Elizabeth gave a final look at the pages she held in her hand.

So this was it! The picture was now clear, the background filled in.

She had said that the men of Zurich might have created an extraordinary strategy. She knew now that they had.

Had it not been so grotesquely evil she might have agreed with her son. She might have been proud of his part in it. Under the circumstances, she could only be terrified.

She wondered if Matthew Canfield would understand. No matter. It was now time for Zurich.

She got up from the bed, taking the pages with her, and went to the door.

Janet was at the desk writing letters. Canfield sat in a chair nervously reading a newspaper. Both were startled when Elizabeth walked into the room.

"Do you have any knowledge of the Versailles treaty?" she asked him. "The restrictions, the reparations payments?"

"As much as the average guy, I guess."

"Are you aware of the Dawes Plan? That wholly imperfect document?"

"I thought it made the reparations livable with."

"Only temporarily. It was grasped at by the politicians who needed temporary solutions. Economically it's a disaster. Nowhere does it give a final figure. If, at any time, a final figure is given, German industry—who pays the bill—might collapse."

"What's your point?"

"Bear with me a minute. I want you to understand. . . . Do you realize who executes the Versailles treaty? Do you know whose voice is strongest in the decisions under the Dawes Plan? Who ultimately controls the internal economics of Germany?"

Canfield put the newspaper down on the floor. "Yes. Some committee."

"The Allied Controls Commission."

"What are you driving at?" Canfield got out of his chair.

"Just what you're beginning to suspect. Three of the Zurich contingent are members of the Allied Controls Commission. The Versailles treaty is being executed by these men. Working together, the men of Zurich can literally manipulate the German economy. Leading industrialists from the major powers to the north, the west, and the southwest. Completed by the most powerful financiers within Germany itself. A wolf pack. They'll make sure that the forces at work in Germany remain on a collision course. When the explosion takes place—as surely it must—they'll be there to pick up the pieces. To complete this . . . master plan, they need only a political base of operation. Believe me when I tell you they've found it. With Adolf Hitler and his Nazis. . . . With my son, Ulster Stewart Scarlett."

"My God!" Canfield spoke quietly, staring at Elizabeth. He had not fully understood the details of her recital, but he recognized the implications.

"It's time for Switzerland, Mr. Canfield."

He would ask his questions on the way.

CHAPTER 39

The cablegrams were all in English and except for the names and addresses of the designees, the words were identical. Each was sent to the company or corporation in which the person specified held the highest position. Time zones were respected, each cable was to arrive at its destination at twelve noon, on Monday, and each was to be hand-delivered to the individual addressee upon a signed receipt of acceptance.

Elizabeth Scarlatt wanted those illustrious corporations identified in writing. She wanted those receiving her cables to know that this was, above all, business.

Each cable read as follows:

> THROUGH THE LATE MARQUIS DE BERTHOLDE THE SCARLATTI INDUSTRIES THROUGH THE UNDERSIGNED ALONE HAVE BEEN INFORMED OF YOUR CONSOLIDATION STOP AS THE SINGLE SPOKESMAN FOR SCARLATTI THE UNDERSIGNED BELIEVES THERE EXIST AREAS OF MUTUAL INTEREST STOP THE ASSETS OF SCARLATTI COULD BE AT YOUR DISPOSAL UNDER PROPER CIRCUMSTANCES STOP THE UNDERSIGNED WILL ARRIVE IN ZURICH TWO WEEKS HENCE ON THE EVENING OF NOVEMBER 3 AT THE HOUR OF NINE O'CLOCK STOP THE CONFERENCE WILL TAKE PLACE AT FALKE HAUS
>
> ELIZABETH WYCKHAM SCARLATTI

There were thirteen reactions, all separate, in many different languages, but each with a single ingredient common to all.

Fear.

There was a fourteenth reaction, and it took place in the suite of rooms reserved for Heinrich Kroeger at Madrid's Hotel Emperador. The reaction was fury.

"I won't have it! It can't take place! They're all dead! Dead! Dead! Dead! She was warned! They're dead! Every God damned one of them! Dead. My orders go out tonight! Now!"

Charles Pennington, sent by Ludendorff to act as Kroeger's bodyguard, stood across the room looking out the balcony at the reddish, fan-shaped rays of the Spanish sun.

"Glorious! Simply glorious! . . . Don't be an ass." He didn't like to look at Heinrich Kroeger. In repose that tissued, patched face was bad enough. Angered, it was repulsive. It was now crimson with rage.

"Don't you tell me . . ."

"Oh, stop it!" Pennington saw that Kroeger continued to crush in his fist the telegram from Howard Thornton, which spelled out the Scarlatti conference in Zurich. "What bloody difference does it make to you? To any of us?" Pennington had opened the envelope and read the message because, as he told Kroeger, he had no idea when Kroeger would return from his meeting with the papal attaché. It might have been urgent. What he did not tell Kroeger was that Ludendorff had instructed him to screen all letters, phone calls—whatever—received by this animal. It was a pleasure.

"We don't want anyone else involved. We can't have anyone else! We can't! Zurich will panic! They'll run out on us!"

"They've all got the cables. If Zurich's going to run, you won't stop them now. Besides, this Scarlatti's the cat's whiskers if it's the same one I'm thinking of. She has millions. . . . Damned fortunate for us she wants to come in. I didn't think much of Bertholde—probably less than you did, smelly French Jew—but if he pulled this off, I doff my hat. Anyway, I repeat, what's it to you?"

Heinrich Kroeger glared at the stylish, effeminate Englishman who pulled at his cuffs, making sure they fell just below his jacket sleeve. The red and black cuff links were surrounded by the soft linen of his light blue shirt. Kroeger knew this appearance was deceptive. Like the social Boothroyd, Pennington was a killer who took emotional sustenance from his work. He also was held in high esteem by Hitler, even more so by Joseph Goebbels. Nevertheless, Kroeger had made up his mind. He could not risk it!

"This meeting won't take place! She'll be killed. I'll have her killed."

"Then I'll have to remind you that such a decision must be multilateral. You can not make it yourself. . . . And I don't think you'll find anyone else consenting."

"You're not here to tell me what to do!"

"Oh, but I am. . . . My instructions come from Ludendorff. And, of course, he knows about your message from Thornton. I wired him several hours ago." Pennington casually looked at his wristwatch. "I'm going out for dinner. . . . Frankly, I'd prefer eating alone but if you insist upon joining me, I'll tolerate your company."

"You little prick! I could break your God damn neck!"

Pennington bristled. He knew that Kroeger was unarmed, his revolver lay on the bureau in his bedroom, and the temptation was there. He could kill him, use the telegram as proof, and say that Kroeger had disobeyed. But then there were the Spanish authorities and a hasty retreat. And Kroeger did have a job to do. Strange that it involved Howard Thornton so completely.

"That's possible, of course. But then we could, no doubt, do each other in any number of ways, couldn't we?" Pennington withdrew a thin pistol from his chest holster. "For instance, I might fire a single bullet directly into your mouth right now. . . . But I wouldn't do it in spite of your provocation because the order is larger than either of us. I'd have to answer for my action—no doubt be executed for it. You'll be shot if you take matters into your own hands."

"You don't know this Scarlatti, Pennington. I do!"

How could she have known about Bertholde? What could she have learned from him?

"Of course, you're old friends!" The Englishman put away his pistol and laughed.

How! How? She wouldn't dare challenge him! The only thing she valued was the Scarlatti name, its heritage, its future. She knew beyond a doubt that he would stamp it out! How! Why?

"That woman can't be trusted! She can't be trusted!"

Charles Pennington pulled down his blazer so the

shoulders fell correctly, the jacket cloth concealing the slight bulge of his holster. He walked to the door in calm anticipation of *chorizo*. "Really, Heinrich? . . . Can *any* of us?"

The Englishman closed the door leaving only a faint aroma of Yardley's.

Heinrich Kroeger uncrumpled the telegram in his palm.

Thornton was panic-stricken. Each of the remaining thirteen in Zurich had received identical cablegrams from Elizabeth Scarlatti. But none save Thornton knew who he was.

Kroeger had to move quickly. Pennington hadn't lied. He would be shot if he ordered Elizabeth Scarlatti's death. That did not, however, preclude such an order after Zurich. Indeed, after Zurich it would be mandatory.

But first the Thornton land. He had instructed Thornton for his own safety to let it go. The frightened Thornton had not argued, and the idiot attaché was playing right into his hands. For the glory of Jesus and another blow against atheistic communism.

The money and title would be transferred within a week. Thornton was sending his attorney from San Francisco to conclude the negotiations by signature.

As soon as the land was his, Heinrich Kroeger would issue a warrant for death that no one could deny.

And when that misfit life was snuffed out, Heinrich Kroeger was free. He would be a true light of the new order. None would know that Ulster Scarlett existed.

Except one.

He would confront her at Zurich.

He would kill her at Zurich.

CHAPTER 40

The embassy limousine climbed the small hill to the front of the Georgian house in Fairfax, Virginia. It was the elegant residence of Erich Rheinhart, attaché of the Weimar Republic, nephew of the sole imperial general who had thrown his support to the German radical movement given the name of Nazi, by philosophy, a full-fledged Nazi himself.

The well-tailored man with the waxed moustache got out of the back seat and stepped onto the driveway. He looked up at the ornate facade.

"A lovely home."

"I'm pleased, Poole," said Rheinhart, smiling at the man from Bertholde et Fils.

The two men walked into the house and Erich Rheinhart led his guest to a book-lined study off the living room. He indicated a chair for Poole and went to a cabinet, taking out two glasses and a bottle of whiskey.

"To business. You come three thousand miles at a loathsome time of year for ocean travel. You tell me I am the object of your visit. I'm flattered, of course, but what can . . ."

"Who ordered Bertholde's death?" Poole said harshly.

Erich Rheinhart was astonished. He hunched his padded shoulders, placed his glass on the small table, and extended his hands, palms up. He spoke slowly, in consternation.

"My dear man, why do you think it concerns me? I mean—in all candor—you are either deluded as to my influence or you need a long rest."

"Labishe wouldn't have killed him without having been ordered to do it. Some one of enormous authority had to issue that order."

"Well, to begin with I have no such authority, and secondly I would have no reason. I was fond of that Frenchman."

"You hardly knew him."

Rheinhart laughed. "Very well. . . . All the less reason . . ."

"I didn't say you personally. I'm asking who did and *why.*" Poole was betraying his normal calm. He had good reason. This arrogant Prussian held the key if Poole was right, and he wasn't going to let him go until he found out. He would have to press nearer the truth, yet not disclose it.

"Did Bertholde know something the rest of you didn't want him to know?"

"Now, you're preposterous."

"Did he?"

"Jacques Bertholde was our London contact! He enjoyed a unique position in England that approached diplomatic immunity. His influence was felt in a dozen countries among scores of the industrial elite. His death is a great loss to us! How dare you imply that any of us was responsible!"

"I find it interesting that you haven't answered my question." Poole was exasperated. "Did he know something the men in Munich might consider dangerous?"

"If he did, I have no idea what it might be!"

But Poole knew. Perhaps he was the only one who did know. *If he could only be sure.*

"I'd like another drink, please. Forgive my temper." He smiled.

Rheinhart laughed. "You're impossible. Give me your glass. . . . You're satisfied?" The German crossed to the liquor cabinet and poured. "You travel three thousand miles for nothing. It's been a bad trip for you."

Poole shrugged. He was used to the trips—some good, some bad. Bertholde and his odd friend, the misshapen Heinrich Kroeger, had ordered him over barely six months ago. His orders had been simple then. Pick up the girl, find out what she had learned from old Scarlatti. He'd failed. The Canfield man had stopped him. The solicitous lackey, the salesman-cum-escort had prevented it. But he hadn't failed his other orders. He'd followed the banker named Cartwright. He'd killed him and broken into the railroad station locker and gotten the banker's agreement with Elizabeth Scarlatti.

It was then that he had learned the truth of Heinrich Kroeger's identity. Elizabeth Scarlatti's son had needed an ally and Jacques Bertholde was that ally. And in return for that precious friendship, Ulster Scarlett had ordered Bertholde's death. The fanatic had commanded the death of the man who had made everything possible for him.

He, Poole, would avenge that terrible murder. But before he did, he had to confirm what he suspected was the truth. That neither the Nazi leaders nor the men in Zurich knew who Kroeger was. If that was the case, then Kroeger had murdered Bertholde to keep that identity secret.

The revelation might cost the movement millions. The Munich Nazis would know this, if they knew anything.

Erich Rheinhart stood over Poole. "A penny for your thoughts, my dear fellow? Here, a bourbon. You do not speak to me."

"Oh? . . . Yes, it's been a bad trip, Erich. You were right." Poole bent his neck back, closed his eyes, and rubbed his forehead. Rheinhart returned to his chair.

"You need a rest. . . . Do you know what I think? I think you're right. I think some damned fool *did* issue that order." Poole opened his eyes, startled by Erich Rheinhart's words. "Ja! In my opinion you are correct. And it must stop! . . . Strasser fights Hitler and Ludendorff. Ekhart rambles on like a madman. Attacking! Attacking! Kindorf screams in the Ruhr. Jodl betrays the Black Wehrmacht in Bavaria. Graefe makes a mess in the north. Even my own uncle, the illustrious Wilhelm Rheinhart, makes an idiot of himself. He speaks, and I hear the laughter behind my back in America. I tell you we are split in ten factions. Wolves at each other's throats. We will accomplish nothing! Nothing, if this does not stop!" Erich Rheinhart's anger was undisguised. He didn't care. He rose again from his chair. "What is most asinine is the most obvious! We can lose the men in Zurich. If we can not agree among ourselves, how long do you think they will stay with us? I tell you, these men are not interested in who has next week's power base in the Reichstag—not for its own sake. They don't care a Deutschemark for the glories of the new Germany. Or the ambitions of any nation. Their wealth puts them above political boundaries. They are with us for one reason alone—their own power. If we give them a single doubt that we are not what we claim to be, that we are not the emerging order of Germany, they will abandon us. They will leave us with nothing! Even the Germans among them!"

Rheinhart's fury abated. He tried to smile but instead drained his glass quickly and crossed to the cabinet.

If Poole could only be sure. "I understand," he said quietly.

"Ja. I think you do. You've worked long and hard with Bertholde. You've accomplished a great deal . . ." He turned around facing Poole. "That's what I mean. Everything that all of us have worked for can be lost by these internal frictions. The achievements of Funke, Bertholde, von Schnitzler, Thyssen, even Kroeger, will be wiped out if we can not come together. We must unite behind one, possibly two, acceptable leaders . . ."

That was it! That was the sign. Poole was now sure. Rheinhart had said the name! Kroeger!

"Maybe, Erich, but who?" Would Rheinhart say the name again? It was not possible, for Kroeger was no German. But could he get Rheinhart to use the name, just the name, once more without the slightest betrayal of concern.

"Strasser, perhaps. He's strong, attractive. Ludendorff naturally has the aura of national fame, but he's too old now. But mark me, Poole, watch this Hitler! Have you read the transcripts of the Munich trial?"

"No. Should I?"

"Yes! He's electric! Positively eloquent! And sound."

"He has a lot of enemies. He's banned from speaking in almost every *grafshaft* in Germany."

"The necessary excesses in a march to power. The bans on him are being removed. We're seeing to that."

Poole now watched Rheinhart carefully as he spoke.

"Hitler's a friend of Kroeger, isn't he?"

"Ach! Wouldn't you be? Kroeger has millions! It is through Kroeger that Hitler gets his automobiles, his chauffeur, the castle at Berchtesgaden, God knows what else. You don't think he buys them with his royalties, do you? Most amusing. Last year Herr Hitler declared an income which could not possibly purchase two tires for his Mercedes." Rheinhart laughed. "We managed to have the inquiry suspended in Munich, fortunately. Ja, Kroeger is good to Hitler.

Poole was now absolutely sure. The men in Zurich did not know who Heinrich Kroeger was!

"Erich, I must go. Can you have your man drive me back to Washington?"

"But of course, my dear fellow."

Poole opened the door of his room at the Ambassador Hotel. Upon hearing the sound of the key, the man inside stood up, practically at attention.

"Oh, it's you, Bush."

"Cable from London, Mr. Poole. I thought it best that I take the train down rather than using the telephone." He handed Poole the cable.

Poole opened the envelope and extracted the message. He read it.

DUCHESS HAS LEFT LONDON STOP DESTINATION ASCERTAINED GENEVA STOP RUMORS OF ZURICH CONFERENCE STOP CABLE INSTRUCTIONS PARIS OFFICE

Poole pinched his aristocratic lips together, nearly biting into his own flesh in an attempt to suppress his anger. "Duchess" was the code name of Elizabeth Scarlatti. So she headed for Geneva. A hundred and ten miles from Zurich. This was no pleasure trip. It was not another leg on her journey of mourning.

Whatever Jacques Bertholde had feared—plot or counterplot—it was happening now. Elizabeth Scarlatti and her son "Heinrich Kroeger" were making their moves. Separately or together, who could know.

Poole made his decision.

"Send the following to the Paris office. 'Eliminate Duchess from the market. Her bid is to be taken off our lists at once. Repeat, eliminate Duchess'."

Poole dismissed the courier and went to the telephone. He had to make reservations immediately. He had to get to Zurich.

There'd be no conference. He'd stop it. He'd kill the mother, expose the killer son! Kroeger's death would follow quickly!

It was the least he could do for Bertholde.

PART THREE

CHAPTER 41

The train clanged over the antiquated bridge spanning the Rhone River, into the Geneva station. Elizabeth Scarlatti sat in her compartment looking first down at the river barges, then at the rising banks and into the large railroad yard. Geneva was clean. There was a scrubbed look about it, which helped to hide the fact that scores of nations and a thousand score of business giants used this neutral city to further intensify conflicting interests. As the train neared the city, she thought that someone like herself belonged in Geneva. Or, perhaps, Geneva belonged to someone like herself.

She eyed the luggage piled on the seat facing her. One suitcase contained the clothes she needed, and three smaller bags were jammed with papers. Papers that contained a thousand conclusions, totaling up to a battery of weapons. The data included figures on the complete worth of every man in the Zurich group. Every resource each possessed. Additional information awaited her in Geneva. But that was a different sort of musketry. It was not unlike the *Domesday Book*. For what awaited her in Geneva was the complete breakdown of the Scarlatti interests. The legally assessed value of every asset controlled by the Scarlatti Industries. What made it deadly was her maneuverability. And opposite each block of wealth was a commitment to purchase. These commitments were spelled out, and they could be executed instantaneously by a cable to her attorneys.

And well they should be.

Each block was followed—not by the usual two columns designating assessed value and sales value—but three columns. This third column was an across-the-board cut, which guaranteed the buyer a minor fortune with each transaction. Each signified a mandate to purchase that could not be refused. It was the highest level of finance, returned through the complexities of banking to the fundamental basis of economic incentive. Profit.

And Elizabeth counted on one last factor. It was the reverse of her instructions but that, too, was calculated.

In her sealed orders sent across the Atlantic was the emphatic stipulation that every contact made—to complete the task teams of administrators had to work twelve-hour shifts night and day—was to be carried out in the utmost secrecy and only with those whose authority extended to great financial commitments. The guaranteed gains absolved all from charges of irresponsibility. Each would emerge a hero to himself or to his economic constituency. But the price was consummate security until the act was done. The rewards matched the price. Millionaires, merchant princes, and bankers in New York, Chicago, Los Angeles, and Palm Beach found themselves quartered in conference rooms with their dignified counterparts from one of New York's most prestigious law firms. The tones were hushed and the looks knowing. Financial killings were being made. Signatures were affixed.

And, of course, it had to happen.

Unbelievable good fortune leads to ebullience, and ebullience is no mate for secrecy.

Two or three began to talk. Then four or five. Then a dozen. But no more than that. . . . The *price*.

Phone calls were made, almost none from offices, nearly all from the quiet seclusion of libraries or dens. Most were made at night under the soft light of desk lamps with good pre-Volstead whiskey an arm's length away.

In the highest economic circles, there was a rumor that something most unusual was happening at Scarlatti.

It was just enough. Elizabeth knew it would be just enough. After all, the *price*. . . . And the rumors reached the men in Zurich.

Matthew Canfield stretched out across the seats in his own compartment, his legs propped over his single suitcase, his feet resting on the cushions facing him. He, too, looked out the window at the approaching city of Geneva. He had just finished one of his thin cigars and the smoke rested in suspended layers above him in the still air of the small room. He contemplated opening a window, but he was too depressed to move.

It had been two weeks to the day since he had granted Elizabeth Scarlatti her reprieve of one month. Fourteen days of chaos made painful by the knowledge of his own uselessness. More than uselessness, more akin to personal futility. He could do nothing, and nothing was expected of him. Elizabeth hadn't wanted him to "work closely" with her. She didn't want anyone to work with her—closely or otherwise. She soloed. She soared alone, a crusty, patrician eagle sweeping the infinite meadows of her own particular heaven.

His most demanding chore was the purchase of office supplies such as reams of paper, pencils, notebooks, and endless boxes of paper clips.

Even the publisher Thomas Ogilvie had refused to see him, obviously so instructed by Elizabeth.

Canfield had been dismissed as he was being dismissed by Elizabeth. Even Janet treated him with a degree of aloofness, always apologizing for her manner but by apologizing, acknowledging it. He began to realize what had happened. He was the whore now. He had sold himself, his favors taken and paid for. They had very little use for him now. They knew he could be had again as one knows a whore can be had.

He understood so much more completely what Janet had felt.

Would it be finished with Janet? Could it ever be finished with her? He told himself no. She told him the same. She asked him to be strong enough for both of them, but was she fooling herself and letting him pay for it?

He began to wonder if he was capable of judgment. He had been idle and the rot inside of him frightened him. What had he done? Could he undo it? He was operating in a world he couldn't come to grips with.

Except Janet. She didn't belong to that world either. She belonged to him. She had to!

The whistle on the train's roof screeched twice and the huge metal-against-metal slabs on the wheels began to grind. The train was entering the Geneva station, and Canfield heard Elizabeth's rapid knocking on the wall between their compartments. The knocking annoyed him. It sounded like an impatient master of the house rapping for a servant.

Which is exactly what it was.

"I can manage this one, you take the other two. Let the redcaps handle the rest."

Dutifully Canfield instructed the porter, gathered up the two bags, and followed Elizabeth off the train.

Because he had to juggle the two suitcases in the small exit area, he was several feet behind Elizabeth as they stepped off the metal stairway and started down the concrete platform to the center of the station. Because of those two suitcases they were alive one minute later.

At first it was only a speck of dark movement in the corner of his eye. Then it was the gasps of several travelers behind him. Then the screams. And then he saw it.

Bearing down from the right was a massive freight dolly with a huge steel slab across the front used to scoop up heavy crates. The metal plate was about four feet off the ground and had the appearance of a giant, ugly blade.

Canfield jumped forward as the rushing monster came directly at them. He threw his right arm around her waist and pushed-pulled her out of the way of the mammoth steel plate. It crashed into the side of the train less than a foot from both their bodies.

Many in the crowd were hysterical. No one could be sure whether anyone had been injured or killed. Porters came running. The shouts and screams echoed throughout the platform.

Elizabeth, breathless, spoke into Canfield's ear. "The suitcases! Do you have the suitcases?"

Canfield found to his amazement that he still held one in his left hand. It was pressed between Elizabeth's back and the train. He had dropped the suitcase in his right hand.

"I've got one. I let the other go."

"Find it!"

"For Christ's sake!"

"Find it, you fool!"

Canfield pushed at the crowd gathering in front of them. He scanned his eyes downward and saw the leather case. It had been run over by the heavy front wheels of the dolly, crushed but still intact. He shouldered his way against a dozen midriffs and reached down. Simultaneously another arm, with a fat, uncommonly large hand thrust itself toward the crumpled piece of leather. The arm was clothed in a tweed jacket. A woman's jacket. Canfield pushed harder and touched the case with his fingers and began pulling it forward. Instinctively, amid the panorama of trousers and overcoats, he grabbed the wrist of the fat hand and looked up.

Bending down, eyes in blind fury, was a jowled face Canfield could never forget. It belonged in that hideous foyer of red and black four thousand miles away. It was Hannah, Janet's housekeeper!

Their eyes met in recognition. The woman's iron-gray head was covered tightly by a dark green Tyrolean fedora, which set off the bulges of facial flesh. Her immense body was crouched, ugly, ominous. With enormous strength she whipped her hand out of Canfield's grasp, pushing him as she did so, so that he fell back into the dolly and the bodies surrounding him. She disappeared rapidly into the crowd toward the station.

Canfield rose, clutching the crushed suitcase under his arm. He looked after her, but she could not be seen. He stood there for a moment, people pressing around him, bewildered.

He worked his way back to Elizabeth.

"Take me out of here. Quickly!"

They started down the platform, Elizabeth holding his left arm with more strength than Canfield thought she possessed. She was actually hurting him. They left the excited crowd behind them.

"It has begun." She looked straight ahead as she spoke.

They reached the interior of the crowded dome. Canfield kept moving his head in every direction, trying to find an irregular break in the human pattern, trying to find a pair of eyes, a still shape, a waiting figure. A fat woman in a Tyrolean hat.

They reached the south entrance on Eisenbahn Platz and found a line of taxis.

Canfield held Elizabeth back from the first cab. She was alarmed. She wanted to keep moving.

"They'll send our luggage."

He didn't reply. Instead he propelled her to the left toward the second car and then, to her mounting concern, signaled the driver of a third vehicle. He pulled the cab door shut and looked at the crushed, expensive Mark Cross suitcase. He pictured Hannah's wrathful, puffed face. If there was ever a female archangel of darkness, she was it. He gave the driver the name of their hotel.

"Il n'y a plus de bagage, monsieur?"

"No. It will follow," answered Elizabeth in English.

The old woman had just gone through a horrifying experience, so he decided not to mention Hannah until they reached the hotel. Let her calm down. And yet he wondered whether it was him or Elizabeth who needed the calm. His hands were still shaking. He looked over at Elizabeth. She continued to stare straight ahead, but she was not seeing anything anyone else would see.

"Are you all right?"

She did not answer him for nearly a minute.

"Mr. Canfield, you have a terrible responsibility facing you."

"I'm not sure what you mean."

She turned and looked at him. Gone was the grandeur, gone the haughty superiority.

"Don't let them kill me, Mr. Canfield. Don't let them kill me now. Make them wait till Zurich. . . . After Zurich they can do anything they wish."

CHAPTER 42

Elizabeth and Canfield spent three days and nights in their rooms at the Hotel D' Accord. Only once had Canfield gone out—and he had spotted two men following him. They did not try to take him, and it occurred to him that they considered him so secondary to the prime target, Elizabeth, that they dared not risk a call out of the Geneva police, reported to be an alarmingly belligerent force, hostile to those who upset the delicate equilibrium of their neutral city. The experience taught him that the moment they appeared together he could expect an attack no less vicious than the one made on them at the Geneva station. He wished he could send word to Ben Reynolds. But he couldn't, and he knew it. He had been ordered to stay out of Switzerland. He had withheld every piece of vital information from his reports. Elizabeth had seen to that. Group Twenty knew next to nothing about the immediate situation and the motives of those involved. If he did send an urgent request for assistance, he would have to explain, at least partially, and that explanation would lead to prompt interference by the embassy. Reynolds wouldn't wait upon legalities. He would have Canfield seized by force and held incommunicado.

The results were predictable. With him finished, Elizabeth wouldn't have a chance of reaching Zurich. She'd be killed by Scarlett in Geneva. And the secondary target would then be Janet back in London. She couldn't stay at the Savoy indefinitely. Derek couldn't continue his security precautions ad infinitum. She would eventually leave, or Derek would become exasperated and careless. She, too, would be killed. Finally, there was Chancellor Drew, his wife, and seven children. There would be a hundred valid reasons for all to leave the remote Canadian refuge. They'd be massacred. Ulster Stewart Scarlett would win.

At the thought of Scarlett, Canfield was able to summon up what anger was left in him. It was almost enough to match his fear and depression. Almost.

He walked into the sitting room Elizabeth had converted into an office. She was writing on the center table.

"Do you remember the housekeeper at your son's house?" he said.

Elizabeth put down her pencil. It was momentary courtesy, not concern. "I've seen her on the few occasions I've visited, yes."

"Where did she come from?"

"As I recall, Ulster brought her back from Europe. She ran a hunting lodge in . . . southern Germany." Elizabeth looked up at the field accountant. "Why do you ask?"

Years later Canfield would reflect that it was because he had been trying to find the words to tell Elizabeth Scarlatti that Hannah was in Geneva that caused him to do what he did. To physically move from one place to another at that particular instant. To cross between Elizabeth and the window. He would carry the remembrance of it as long as he lived.

There was a shattering of glass and a sharp, terrible stinging pain in his left shoulder. Actually the pain seemed to come first. The jolt was so powerful that it spun Canfield around, throwing him across the table, scattering papers, and crashing the lamp to the floor. A second and third shot followed, splintering the thick wood around his body and Canfield, in panic, lurched to one side, toppling Elizabeth off her chair onto the floor. The pain in his shoulder was overpowering, and a huge splotch of blood spread across his shirt.

It was all over in five seconds.

Elizabeth was crouched against the paneling of the wall. She was at once frightened and grateful. She looked at the field accountant lying in front of her trying to hold his shoulder. She was convinced he had thrown himself over her to protect her from the bullets. He never explained otherwise.

"How badly are you hurt?"

"I'm not sure. It hurts like hell. . . . I've never been hit before. Never shot before. . . ." He was finding it difficult to speak. Elizabeth started to move toward him. "God damn it! Stay where you are!" He looked up and saw that he was out of the sight line of the window. They both were. "Look, can you reach the phone? Go on the floor. Stay down! . . . I think I need a doctor. . . . A doctor." He passed out.

Thirty minutes later Canfield awoke. He was on his own bed with the whole upper left part of his chest encased in an uncomfortable bandage. He could barely move. He could see, blurredly to be sure, a number of figures around him. As his eyes came into focus, he saw Elizabeth at the foot of the bed looking down at him. To her right was a man in an overcoat, behind him a uniformed policeman. Bending over him on his left was a balding, stern-faced man in his shirt sleeves, obviously a doctor. He spoke to Canfield. His accent was French.

"Move your left hand, please."

Canfield obeyed.

"Your feet, please."

Again he complied.

"Can you roll your head?"

"What? Where?"

"Move your head back and forth. Don't try to be amusing." Elizabeth was possibly the most relieved person within twenty miles of the Hotel D' Accord. She even smiled.

Canfield swung his head back and forth.

"You are not seriously hurt." The doctor stood erect.

"You sound disappointed," answered the field accountant.

"May I ask him questions, *Herr Doktor?*" said the Swiss next to Elizabeth.

The doctor replied in his broken English. "Yes. The bullet passed him through."

What one had to do with the other perplexed Canfield, but he had no time to think about it. Elizabeth spoke.

"I've explained to this gentleman that you're merely accompanying me while I conduct business affairs. We're totally bewildered by what's happened."

"I would appreciate this man answering for himself, madame."

"Damned if I can tell you anything, mister. . . ." And then Canfield stopped. There was no point in being a fool. He was going to need help. "On second thought, maybe I can." He looked toward the doctor, who was putting on his suit coat. The Swiss understood.

"Very well. We shall wait."

"Mr. Canfield, what can you possibly add?"

"Passage to Zurich."

Elizabeth understood.

The doctor left and Canfield found that he could lie on his right side. The Swiss *Geheimpolizist* walked around to be nearer.

"Sit down, sir," said Canfield as the man drew up a chair. "What I'm going to tell you will seem foolish to someone like you and me who have to work for our livings." The field accountant winked. "It's a private matter—no harm to anyone outside the family, family business, but you can help. . . . Does your man speak English?"

The Swiss looked briefly at the uniformed policeman.

"No, monsieur."

"Good. As I say, you can help. Both the clean record of your fair city . . . and yourself."

The Swiss *Geheimpolizist* drew up his chair closer.

He was delighted.

The afternoon arrived. They had timed the train schedules to the quarter hour and had telephoned ahead for a limousine and chauffeur. Their train tickets had been purchased by the hotel, clearly spelling out the name of Scarlatti for preferred treatment and the finest accommodations available for the short trip to Zurich. Their luggage was sent downstairs an hour beforehand and deposited by the front entrance. The tags were legibly marked, the train compartments specified, and even the limousine service noted for the Zurich porters. Canfield figured that the lowest IQ in Europe could know the immediate itinerary of Elizabeth Scarlatti if he wished to.

The ride from the hotel to the station took about twelve minutes. One-half hour before the train for Zurich departed an old woman, with a heavy black veil, accompanied by a youngish man in a brand-new fedora, his left arm in a white sling, got into a limousine. They were escorted by two members of the Geneva police, who kept their hands on their holstered pistols.

No incident occurred, and the two travelers rushed into the station and immediately onto the train.

As the train left the Geneva platform, another elderly woman accompanied by a youngish man, this one in a Brooks Brothers hat, and also with his left arm in a sling but hidden by a topcoat, left the service entrance of the Hotel D'Accord. The elderly woman was dressed in the uniform of a Red Cross colonel, female division, complete with a garrison cap. The man driving was also a member of the International Red Cross. The two people rushed into the back seat, and the young man closed the door. He immediately took the cellophane off a thin cigar and said to the driver, "Let's go."

As the car sped out the narrow driveway, the old woman spoke disparagingly. "Really, Mr. Canfield! Must you smoke one of those awful things?"

"Gevena rules, lady. Prisoners are allowed packages from home."

CHAPTER 43

Twenty-seven miles from Zurich is the town of Menziken. The Geneva train stopped for precisely four minutes, the time allotted for the loading of the railway post, and then proceeded on its inevitable, exact, fated ride up the tracks to its destination.

Five minutes out of Menziken, compartments D4 and D5 on Pullman car six were broken into simultaneously by two men in masks. Because neither compartment contained any passengers, and both toilet doors were locked, the masked men fired their pistols into the thin panels of the commodes, expecting to find the bodies when they opened the doors.

They found no one. Nothing.

As if predetermined, both masked men ran out into the narrow corridor and nearly collided with one another.

"Halt! Stop!" The shouts came from both ends of the Pullman corridor. The men calling were dressed in the uniforms of the Geneva police.

The two masked men did not stop. Instead they fired wildly in both directions.

Their shots were returned and the two men fell.

They were searched; no identifications were found. The Geneva police were pleased about that. They did not wish to get involved.

One of the fallen men, however, had a tattoo on his forearm: an insignia, recently given the term of swastika. And a third man, unseen, unmasked, not fallen, was first off the train at Zurich, and hurried to a telephone.

"Here we are at Aarau. You can rest up here for a while. Your clothes are in a flat on the second floor. I believe your car is parked in the rear and the keys are under the left seat." Their driver was English and Canfield liked that. The driver hadn't spoken a word since Geneva. The field accountant withdrew a large bill from his pocket and offered it to the man.

"Hardly necessary, sir," said the driver as he waved the bill aside without turning.

They waited until eight fifteen. It was a dark night with only half a moon shrouded by low clouds. Canfield had tried the car, driving it up and down a country road to get the feel of it, to get used to driving with only his right hand. The gas gauge registered *rempli* and they were ready.

More precisely, Elizabeth Scarlatti was ready.

She was like a gladiator, prepared to bleed or let blood. She was cold but intense. She was a killer.

And her weapons were paper—infinitely more dangerous than maces or triforks to her adversaries. She was also, as a fine gladiator must be, supremely confident.

It was more than her last *grande geste*, it was the culmination of a lifetime. Hers and Giovanni's. She would not fail him.

Canfield had studied and restudied the map; he knew the roads he had to take to reach Falke Haus. They would skirt the center of Zurich and head toward Kloten, turning right at the Schlieren fork and follow the central road toward Bulach. One mile to the left on the Winterthurstrasse would be the gates of Falke Haus.

He had pushed the car up to eighty-five miles an hour, and he had stopped at sixty within the space of fifty feet without causing a dislocation of the seats. The Geneva *Geheimpolizist* had done his job well. But then he was well paid. Damn near two years' wages at the going Swiss rate of Civil Service. And the car was licensed with the numbers no one would stop—for any reason—the Zurich police. How he had done it, Canfield didn't ask. Elizabeth suggested that it might have been the money.

"Is that all?" asked Canfield as he led Elizabeth Scarlatti toward the car. He referred to her single briefcase.

"It's enough," said the old woman as she followed him down the path.

"You had a couple of thousand pages, a hundred thousand figures!"

"They're meaningless now." Elizabeth held the briefcase on her lap as Canfield shut the car door.

"Suppose they ask you questions?" The field accountant inserted the key in the ignition.

"No doubt they will. And if they do, I'll answer." She didn't wish to talk.

They drove for twenty minutes and the roads were coming out right. Canfield was pleased with himself. He was a satisfied navigator. Suddenly Elizabeth spoke.

"There is one thing I haven't told you, nor have you seen fit to bring it up. It's only fair that I mention it now."

"What?"

"It's conceivable that neither of us will emerge from this conference alive. Have you considered that?"

Canfield had, of course, considered it. He had assumed the risk, if that was the justifiable word, since the Boothroyd incident. It had escalated to pronounced danger when he realized that Janet was possibly his for life. He became committed when he knew what her husband had done to her.

With the bullet through his shoulder, two inches from death, Matthew Canfield in his own way had become a gladiator in much the same manner as Elizabeth. His anger was paramount now.

"You worry about your problems, I'll worry about mine, okay?"

"Okay. . . . May I say that you've become quite dear to me. . . . Oh, stop that little-boy look! Save it for the ladies! I'm hardly one of them! Drive on!"

On Winterthurstrasse, three-tenths of a mile from Falke Haus there is a stretch of straight road paralleled on both sides by towering pine trees. Matthew Canfield pushed the accelerator down and drove the automobile as fast as it would go. It was five minutes to nine and he was determined that his passenger meet her appointment on time.

Suddenly in the far-off illumination of the head lamps, a man was signaling. He waved his hands, crisscrossing above his head, standing in the middle of the road. He was violently making the universal sign, stop—emergency. He did not move from the middle of the road in spite of Canfield's speed.

"Hold on!" Canfield rushed on, oblivious to the human being in his path.

As he did so, there were bursts of gunfire from both sides of the road. "Get down!" shouted Canfield. He continued to push the gas pedal, ducking as he did so, bobbing his head, watching the straight road as best he could. There was a piercing scream—pitched in a death note—from the far side of the road. One of the ambushers had been caught in the crossfire.

They passed the area, pieces of glass and metal scattered all over the seats.

"You okay?" Canfield had no time for sympathy.

"Yes. I'm all right. How much longer?"

"Not much. If we can make it. They may have gotten a tire."

"Even if they did, we can still drive?"

"Don't you worry! I'm not about to stop and ask for a jack!"

The gates of Falke Haus appeared and Canfield turned sharply into the road. It was a descending grade leading gently into a huge circle in front of an enormous flagstone porch with statuary placed every several feet. The front entrance, a large wooden door, was situated twenty feet beyond the center steps. Canfield could not get near it.

For there were at least a dozen long, black limousines lined up around the circle. Chauffeurs stood near them, idly chatting.

Canfield checked his revolver, placed it in his right-hand pocket, and ordered Elizabeth out of the car. He insisted that she slide across the seat and emerge from his side of the automobile.

He walked slightly behind her, nodding to the chauffeurs.

It was one minute after nine when a servant, formally dressed, opened the large wooden door.

They entered the great hall, a massive tabernacle of architectural indulgence. A second servant, also formally attired, gestured them toward another door. He opened it.

Inside was the longest table Matthew Canfield thought possible to build. It must have been fifty feet from end to end. And a good six to seven feet wide.

Seated around the massive table were fifteen or twenty men. All ages, from forty to seventy. All dressed in expensive suits. All looking toward Elizabeth Scarlatti. At the head of the table, half a room away, was an empty chair. It cried out to be filled, and Canfield wondered for a moment whether Elizabeth was to fill it. Then he realized that was not so. Her chair was at the foot of the table closest to them.

Who was to fill the empty chair?

No matter. There was no chair for him. He would stay by the wall and watch.

Elizabeth approached the table.

"Good evening, gentlemen. A number of us have met before. The rest of you I know by reputation, I can assure you."

The entire complement around the table rose as one body.

The man to the left of Elizabeth's chair circled and held it for her.

She sat down, and the men returned to their seats.

"I thank you. . . . But there seems to be one of us missing." Elizabeth stared at the chair fifty feet away directly in front of her eyes.

At that moment a door at the far end of the room opened and a tall man strutted in. He was dressed in the crisp, cold uniform of the German revolutionary. The dark brown shirt, the shining black belt across his chest and around his waist, the starched tan jodhpurs above the thick, heavy boots that came just below his knees.

The man's head was shaven, his face a distorted replica of itself.

"The chair is now taken. Does that satisfy you?"

"Not entirely. . . . Since I know, through one means or another, every person of consequence at this table, I should like to know who you are, sir."

"Kroeger. Heinrich Kroeger! Anything else, Madame Scarlatti?"

"Not a thing. Not a single thing . . . Herr Kroeger."

CHAPTER 44

"Against my wishes and my better judgment, Madame Scarlatti, my associates are determined to hear what you have to say." The grotesque shaven-headed Heinrich Kroeger spoke. "My position has been made clear to you. I trust your memory serves you well about it."

There were whispers around the table. Looks were exchanged. None of the men were prepared for the news that Heinrich Kroeger had had prior contact with Elizabeth Scarlatti.

"My memory serves me very well. Your associates represent an aggregate of much wisdom and several centuries of experience. I suspect far in excess of your own on both counts—collectively and individually."

Most of the men simply lowered their eyes, some pressing their lips in slight smiles. Elizabeth slowly looked at each face around the table.

"We have an interesting board here, I see. Well represented. Well diversified. Some of us were enemies in war a few short years ago, but such memories, by necessity, are short. . . . Let's see." Without singling out any one individual, Elizabeth Scarlatti spoke rapidly, almost in a cadence. "My own country has lost two members, I'm sad to note. But I don't believe prayers are in order for Messrs. Boothroyd and Thornton. If they are, I'm not the one to deliver them. But still, the United States is splendidly represented by Mr. Gibson and Mr. Landor. Between them, they account for nearly twenty percent of the vast oil interests in the American Southwest. To say nothing of a joint expansion in the Canadian Northwest Territories. Combined personal assets—two hundred and twenty-five million. . . . Our recent adversary, Germany, brings us Herr von Schnitzler, Herr Kindorf, and Herr Thyssen. I. G. Farben; the baron of Ruhr coal; the great steel companies. Personal assets? Who can really tell these days in the Weimar? Perhaps one hundred and seventy-five million, at the outside. . . . But someone's missing from this group. I trust he's successfully being recruited. I speak of Gustave Krupp. He would raise the ante considerably. . . . England sends us Messrs. Masterson, Leacock, and Innes-Bowen. As powerful a triumvirate as can be found in the British Empire. Mr. Masterson with half of the India imports, also Ceylon now, I understand; Mr. Leacock's major portion of the British Stock Exchange; and Mr. Innes-Bowen. He owns the largest single textile industry throughout Scotland and the Hebrides. Personal assets I place at three hundred million. . . . France has been generous, too. Monsieur D'Almeida; I now realize that he is the true owner of the Franco-Italian rail system, partially due to his Italian lineage, I'm sure. And Monsieur Daudet. Is there any among us who have not used some part of his merchant fleet? Personal assets, one hundred and fifty million. . . . And lastly, our neighbors to the north, Sweden. Herr Myrdal and Herr Olaffsen. Understandably"—here Elizabeth looked pointedly at the strange-faced man, her son, at the head of the table—"one of these gentlemen, Herr Myrdal, has controlling interest in Donnenfeld, the most impressive firm on the Stockholm exchange. While Herr Olaffsen's many companies merely control the export of Swedish iron and steel. Personal assets are calculated at one hundred and twenty-five million. . . . Incidentally, gentlemen, the term *personal assets* denotes those holdings which can be converted easily, quickly, and without endangering your markets. . . . Otherwise, I would not insult you by placing such meager limits on your fortunes."

Elizabeth paused to place her briefcase directly in front of her. The men around the table were aroused, apprehensive. Several were shocked at the casual mention of what they believed was highly confidential information. The Americans, Gibson and Landor, had quietly gone into the Canadian venture unannounced, without legal sanction, violating the U.S.–Canadian treaties. The Germans, von Schnitzler and Kindorf, had held secret conferences with Gustave Krupp—who was fighting desperately to remain neutral for fear of a Weimar takeover. If these conferences were made known, Krupp had sworn to expose them. The Frenchman, Louis François D'Almeida, guarded with his very life the extent of his ownership of the Franco-Italian rails. If it were known, it might well be confiscated by the republic. He had purchased the majority shares from the Italian government through plain bribery.

And Myrdal, the heavyset Swede, bulged his eyes in disbelief when Elizabeth Scarlatti spoke so knowingly about the Stockholm exchange. His own company had covertly absorbed Donnenfeld in one of the most complicated mergers imaginable, made possible by the illegal transaction of the American securities. If it became public knowledge, the Swedish law would step in, and he'd be ruined. Only the Englishmen seemed totally poised, totally proud of their achievements. But even this measure of equanimity was misleading. For Sydney Masterson, undisputed heir to the merchant domain of Sir Robert Clive, had only recently concluded the Ceylon arrangements. They were unknown in the import-export world and there were certain agreements subject to question. Some might even say they constituted fraud.

Huddled, quiet-toned conferences took place around the table in the four languages. Elizabeth raised her voice sufficiently to be heard.

"I gather some of you are conferring with your aides—I assume they are your aides. If I'd realized this meeting made provisions for second-level negotiators, I'd have brought along my attorneys. They could have gossiped among themselves while we continue. The decisions we reach tonight, gentlemen, must be our own!"

Heinrich Kroeger sat on the edge of his chair. He spoke harshly, unpleasantly. "I wouldn't be so sure of any decisions. There are none to be made! You've told us nothing which couldn't be learned by any major accounting firm!"

A number of the men around the table—specifically the two Germans, D'Almeida, Gibson, Landor, Myrdal, and Masterson—avoided looking at him. For Kroeger was wrong.

"You think so? Perhaps. But then I've overlooked you,

haven't I? . . . I shouldn't do that, you're obviously terribly important." Again, a number of the men around the table—excluding those mentioned—had traces of smiles on their lips.

"Your wit is as dull as you are." Elizabeth was pleased with herself. She was succeeding in this most important aspect of her appearance. She was reaching, provoking Ulster Stewart Scarlett. She continued without acknowledging his remark.

"Strangely obtained assets of two hundred and seventy million sold under the most questionable circumstances would necessitate a loss of at least fifty percent, possibly sixty percent of market value. I'll grant you the least, so I shall hazard an estimate of one hundred and thirty-five million dollars at the current rates of exchange. One hundred and eight, if you've been weak."

Matthew Canfield lurched from the wall, then held his place.

The men around the table were astonished. The hum of voices increased perceptibly. Aides were shaking their heads, nodding in agreement, raising their eyebrows unable to answer. Each participant thought he knew something of the others. Obviously, none were this knowledgeable of Heinrich Kroeger. They had not even been sure of his status at this table. Elizabeth interrupted the commotion.

"However, Mister Kroeger, surely you know that theft, when eminently provable, is merely subject to proper identification before steps can be taken. There are international courts of extradition. Therefore, it is conceivable that your assets might be calculated at . . . zero!"

A silence fell over the table as the gentlemen, along with their assistants, gave Heinrich Kroeger their full attention. The words *theft, courts,* and *extradition* were words they could not accept at this table. They were dangerous words. Kroeger, the man many of them vaguely feared for reasons solely associated with his enormous influence within both camps, was now warned.

"Don't threaten me, old woman." Kroeger's voice was low, confident. He sat back in his chair and glared at his mother at the opposite end of the long table. "Don't make charges unless you can substantiate them. If you're prepared to attempt that, I'm ready to counter. . . . If you or your colleagues were outnegotiated, this is no place to cry. You won't get sympathy here! I might even go so far as to say you're on treacherous ground. Remember that!" He kept staring until Elizabeth could no longer stand the sight of his eyes. She looked away.

She was not prepared to do anything—not with him, not with Heinrich Kroeger. She would not gamble the lives of her family more than she had already. She would not wager at this table the name of Scarlatti. Not that way. Not now. There was another way.

Kroeger had won the point. It was obvious to all, and Elizabeth had to rush headlong on so that none would dwell upon her loss.

"Keep your assets. They are quite immaterial."

Around the table the phrase "quite immaterial" when applied to such millions was impressive. Elizabeth knew it would be.

"Gentlemen. Before we were interrupted, I gave you all, by national groupings, the personal assets calculated to the nearest five million for each contingent. I felt it was more courteous than breaking down each individual's specific worth—some things are sacred, after all. However, I was quite unfair, as several of you know. I alluded to a number of—shall we say, delicate negotiations, I'm sure you believed were inviolate. Treacherous to you—to use Mr. Kroeger's words—if they were known within your own countries."

Seven of the Zurich twelve were silent. Five were curious.

"I refer to my cocitizens, Mr. Gibson and Mr. Landor. To Monsieur D'Almeida, Sydney Masterson, and of course, to the brilliant Herr Myrdal. I should also include two-thirds of Germany's investors—Herr von Schnitzler and Herr Kindorf, but for different reasons, as I'm sure they realize."

No one spoke. No one turned to his aides. All eyes were upon Elizabeth.

"I don't intend to remain unfair in this fashion, gentlemen. I have something for each of you."

A voice other than Kroeger's spoke up. It was the Englishman, Sydney Masterson.

"May I ask the point of all this? All this . . . incidental intelligence? I'm sure you've been most industrious—highly accurate, too, speaking for myself. But none of us here have entered the race for a Jesus medal. Surely, you know that."

"I do, indeed. If it were otherwise, I wouldn't be here tonight."

"Then why? Why this?" The accent was German. The voice belonged to the blustering baron of the Ruhr Valley, Kindorf.

Masterson continued. "Your cablegram, madame—we all received the same—specifically alluded to areas of mutual interest. I believe you went so far as to say the Scarlatti assets might be at our joint disposal. Most generous, indeed. . . . But now I must agree with Mr. Kroeger. You sound as though you're threatening us, and I'm not at all sure I like it."

"Oh, come, Mr. Masterson! You've never held out promises of English gold to half the minor potentates in the backwaters of India? Herr Kindorf has not openly bribed his unions to strike with pledges of increased wages once the French are out of the Ruhr? Please! You insult all of us! Of course, I'm here to threaten you! And I can assure you, you'll like it less as I go on!"

Masterson rose from the table. Several others moved their chairs. The air was hostile. "I shall not listen further," said Masterson.

"Then tomorrow at noon the Foreign Office, the British Stock Exchange, and the board of directors of the English Importers Collective will receive detailed specifics of your highly illegal agreements in Ceylon! Your commitments are enormous! The news might just initiate a considerable run on your holdings!"

Masterson stood by his chair. "Be damned!" were the only words he uttered as he returned to his chair. The table once again fell silent. Elizabeth opened her briefcase.

"I have here an envelope for each of you. Your names are typed on the front. Inside each envelope is an accounting of your individual worths. Your strengths. Your weaknesses. . . . There is one envelope missing. The . . . influential, very important Mr. Kroeger does not have one. Frankly, it's insignificant."

"I warn you!"

"So very sorry, Mr. Kroeger." Again the words were rapidly spoken, but this time no one was listening. Each one's concentration was on Elizabeth Scarlatti and her briefcase. "Some envelopes are thicker than others, but none should place too great an emphasis on this factor. We all know the negligibility of wide diversification after a certain point." Elizabeth reached into her leather case.

"You are a witch!" Kindorf's heavy accent was now guttural, the veins stood out in his temples.

"Here. I shall pass them out. And as each of you peruse your miniature portfolios I shall continue talking, which, I know, will please you."

The envelopes were passed down both sides of the table. Some were torn open immediately, hungrily. Others, like the cards of experienced poker players, were handled carefully, cautiously.

Matthew Canfield stood by the wall, his left arm smarting badly in the sling, his right hand in his pocket, sweatily clutching his revolver. Since Elizabeth had identified Ulster Scarlett with the 270 million, he could not take his eyes off him. This man called Heinrich Kroeger. This hideous, arrogant son of a bitch was the man he wanted! This was the filthy bastard who had done it all! This was Janet's personal hell.

"I see you all have your envelopes. Except, of course, the ubiquitous Mr. Kroeger. Gentlemen, I promised you I would not be unfair and I shan't be. There are five of you who can not begin to appreciate the influence of Scarlatti unless you have, as they say in cheap merchandising, samples applicable to you alone. Therefore, as you read the contents of your envelopes, I shall briefly touch on these sensitive areas."

Several of the men who had been reading shifted their eyes toward Elizabeth without moving their heads. Others put the papers down defiantly. Some handed the pages to aides and stared at the old woman. Elizabeth glanced over her shoulder at Matthew Canfield. She was worried about him. She knew he, at last, faced Ulster Scarlett, and the pressure on him was immense. She tried to catch his eye. She tried to reassure him with a look, a confident smile.

He would not look at her. She saw only the hatred in his eyes as he stared at the man called Heinrich Kroeger.

"I shall delineate alphabetically, gentlemen. . . . Monsieur Daudet, the Republic of France would be reluctant to continue awarding franchises to your fleet if they were aware of those ships under Paraguayan flag which carried supplies to France's enemies in time of war." Daudet remained motionless, but Elizabeth was amused to see the three Englishmen bristle at the Frenchman. The predictable, contradictory British!

"Oh, come, Mr. Innes-Bowen. You may not have run ammunition, but how many neutral ships were loaded off how many piers in India with textile cargoes bound for Bremerhaven and Cuxhaven during the same period? . . . And Mr. Leacock. You can't really forget your fine Irish heritage, can you? The Sinn Féin has prospered well under your tutelage. Monies funneled through you to the Irish rebellion cost the lives of thousands of British soldiers at a time when England could least afford them! And quiet, calm Herr Olaffsen. The crown prince of Swedish steel. Or is he the king now? He might well be, for the Swedish government paid him several fortunes for untold hundreds of tons of low-carbon ingot. However, they didn't come from his own superior factories. They were shipped from inferior mills half a world away—from Japan!"

Elizabeth reached into her briefcase once again. The men around the table were like corpses, immobile, only their minds were working. For Heinrich Kroeger, Elizabeth Scarlatti had placed the seal of approval on her own death warrant. He sat back and relaxed. Elizabeth withdrew a thin booklet from her briefcase.

"Lastly we come to Herr Thyssen. He emerges with the least pain. No grand fraud, no treason, only minor illegality and major embarrassment. Hardly a fitting tribute to the house of August Thyssen." She threw the booklet into the center of the table. "Filth, gentlemen, just plain filth. Fritz Thyssen, pornographer! Purveyor of obscenity. Books, pamphlets, even motion pictures. Printed and filmed in Thyssen warehouses in Cairo. Every government on the Continent has condemned the unknown source. There he is, gentlemen. Your associate."

For a long moment no one spoke. Each man was concerned with himself. Each calculated the damage that could result from old Scarlatti's disclosures. In every instance the loss was accompanied by degrees of disgrace. Reputations could hang in balance. The old woman had issued twelve indictments and personally returned twelve verdicts of guilty. Somehow, no one considered the thirteenth, Heinrich Kroeger.

Sydney Masterson pierced the belligerent air with a loud, manufactured cough. "Very well, Madame Scarlatti, you've made the point I referred to earlier. However, I think I should remind you that we are not impotent men. Charges and countercharges are parts of our lives. Solicitors can refute every accusation you've made, and I can assure you that lawsuits for unmitigated slander would be in the forefront. . . . After all, when gutter tactics are employed, there are expedient replies. . . . If you think we fear disdain, believe me when I tell you that public opinion has been molded by far less money than is represented at this table!"

The gentlemen of Zurich took confidence in Masterson's words. There were nods of agreement.

"I don't for one second doubt you, Mr. Masterson. Any of you. . . . Missing personnel files, opportunistic executives—sacrificial goats. Please, gentlemen! I only contend that you wouldn't welcome the trouble. Or the anxiety which goes with such distasteful matters."

"*Non*, madame." Claude Daudet was outwardly cool but inwardly petrified. Perhaps his Zurich associates did not know the French people. A firing squad was not out of the question. "You are correct. Such troubles are to be avoided. So, then what is next? What is it you prepare for us, eh?"

Elizabeth paused. She wasn't quite sure why. It was an instinct, an intuitive need to turn around and look at the field accountant.

Matthew Canfield had not budged from his position by the wall. He was a pathetic sight. His jacket had fallen away from his left shoulder revealing the dark black sling, his right hand still plunged in his pocket. He seemed to be swallowing continuously, trying to keep himself aware of his surroundings. Elizabeth noticed that he now avoided looking at Ulster Scarlett. He seemed, in essence, to be trying to hang on to his sanity.

"Excuse me, gentlemen." Elizabeth rose from her chair and crossed to Canfield. She whispered quietly to him. "Take hold of yourself. I demand it! There's nothing to fear. Not in this room!"

Canfield spoke slowly, without moving his lips. She

could barely hear him, but what she heard startled her. Not for its content, but for the way in which he said it. Matthew Canfield was now among the ranks in this room in Zurich. He had joined them; he had become a killer, too.

"Say what you have to say and get it over with. . . . I want him. I'm sorry, but I want him. Look at him now, lady, because he's a dead man."

"Control yourself! Such talk will serve neither of us." She turned and walked back to her chair. She stood behind it while she spoke. "As you may have noticed, gentlemen, my young friend has been seriously wounded. Thanks to all of you . . . or one of you, in an attempt to prevent my reaching Zurich. The act was cowardly and provocative in the extreme."

The men looked at each other.

Daudet, whose imagination would not stop conjuring pictures of national disgrace or the firing squad, answered quickly. "Why would any here take such action, Madame Scarlatti? We are not maniacs. We are businessmen. No one sought to prevent your coming to Zurich. Witness, madame, we are all here."

Elizabeth looked at the man called Kroeger.

"One of you violently opposed this conference. We were fired upon less than a half hour ago."

The men looked at Heinrich Kroeger. Some were becoming angry. This Kroeger was, perhaps, too reckless.

"No." He answered simply and emphatically, returning their stares. "I agreed to your coming. If I'd wanted to stop you, I'd have stopped you."

For the first time since the meeting began, Heinrich Kroeger looked at the sporting goods salesman at the far end of the room, half concealed in the poor light. He had reacted with only moderate surprise when he realized Elizabeth Scarlatti had brought him to Zurich. Moderate because he knew Elizabeth's penchant for employing the unusual, both in methods and personnel, and because she probably had no one else around she could browbeat into silence as easily as this money-hungry social gadfly. He'd be a convenient chauffeur, a manservant. Kroeger hated the type.

Or was he anything else?

Why had the salesman stared at him? Had Elizabeth

told him anything? She wouldn't be that big a fool. The man was the sort who'd blackmail in a minute.

One thing was sure. He'd have to be killed.

But who had tried to kill him previously? Who had tried to stop Elizabeth? And why?

The same question was being considered by Elizabeth Scarlatti. For she believed Kroeger when he disavowed the attempts on their lives.

"Please continue, Madame Scarlatti." It was Fritz Thyssen, his cherubic face still flushed with anger over Elizabeth's disclosure of his Cairo trade. He had removed the booklet from the center of the table.

"I shall." She approached the side of her chair but did not sit down. Instead, she reached once more into her briefcase. "I have one thing further, gentlemen. With it we can conclude our business, and decisions can be made. There is a copy for each of the twelve remaining investors. Those with aides will have to share them. My apologies, Mr. Kroeger, I find I haven't one for you." From her position at the end of the table she distributed twelve slender manila envelopes. They were sealed, and as the men passed them down, the investors taking one apiece, it was apparent that each found it difficult not to rip open the top and withdraw the contents at once. But none wished to betray such obvious anxiety.

Finally, as each of the twelve held his envelope in front of him, one by one the men began to open them.

For nearly two minutes the only sound was the rustling of pages. Otherwise, silence. Even breathing was seemingly suspended. The men from Zurich were mesmerized by what they saw. Elizabeth spoke.

"Yes, gentlemen. What you hold in your hands is the scheduled liquidation of the Scarlatti Industries. . . . So that you have no illusions of doubt concerning the validity of this document, you will note that after each subdivision of holdings is typed the names of the individuals, corporations, or syndicates who are the purchasers. . . . Every one of those mentioned, the individuals as well as the organizations, are known to each of you. If not personally, then certainly by reputation. You know their capabilities, and I'm sure you're not unaware of their ambitions. Within the next twenty-four hours they will own Scarlatti."

For most of the Zurich men Elizabeth's sealed information was the confirmation of the whispered rumors. Word had reached them that something unusual was taking place at Scarlatti. Some sort of unloading under strange circumstances.

So this was it. The head of Scarlatti was getting out.

"A massive operation, Madame Scarlatti." Olaffsen's low Swedish voice vibrated throughout the room. "But to repeat Daudet's question, what is it you prepare us for?"

"Please take note of the bottom figure on the last page, gentlemen. Although I'm quite sure you all have." The rustle of pages. Each man had turned swiftly to the final page. "It reads seven hundred and fifteen million dollars. . . . The combined, immediately convertible assets of this table, placed at the highest figure is one billion, one hundred and ten million. . . . Therefore, a disparity of three hundred and ninety-five million exists between us. . . . Another way to approach this difference is to calculate it from the opposite direction. The Scarlatti liquidation will realize sixty-four point four percent of this table's holdings—if, indeed, you gentlemen could convert your personal assets in such a manner as to preclude financial panics."

Silence.

A number of the Zurich men reached for their first envelopes. The breakdowns of their own worth.

One of these was Sydney Masterson, who turned to Elizabeth with an unamused smile. "And what you're saying, I presume, Madame Scarlatti, is that this sixty-four point plus percent is the club you hold over our heads?"

"Precisely, Mr. Masterson."

"My dear lady, I really must question your sanity . . ."

"I wouldn't, if I were you."

"Then I shall, Frau Scarlatti." I. G. Farben's von Schnitzler spoke in a disagreeable manner, lounging back in his chair as if toying verbally with an imbecile. "To accomplish what you have must have been a costly sacrifice. . . . I wonder to what purpose? You can not buy what there is not to sell. . . . We are not a public corporation. You can not force into defeat something which does not exist!" His German lisp was pronounced, his arrogance every bit as unattractive as reputed. Elizabeth disliked him intensely.

"Quite correct, von Schnitzler."

"Then, perhaps"—the German laughed—"you have been a foolish woman. I would not wish to absorb your losses. I mean, really, you can not go to some mythical *Baumeister* and tell him you have more funds than we—therefore, he must drive us out into the streets!"

Several of the Zurich men laughed.

"That, of course, would be the simplest, would it not? The appeal to one entity, negotiating with one power. It's a shame that I can't do that. It would be so much easier, so much less costly. . . . But I'm forced to take another road, an expensive one. . . . I should put that another way. I have taken it, gentlemen. It has been accomplished. The time is running out for its execution."

Elizabeth looked at the men at Zurich. Some had their eyes riveted on her—watching for the slightest waver of confidence, the smallest sign of bluff. Others fixed their stares on inanimate objects—caring only to filter the words, the tone of her voice, for a false statement or a lapse of judgment. These were men who moved nations with a single gesture, a solitary word.

"At the start of tomorrow's business, subject to time zones, enormous transfers of Scarlatti capital will have been made to the financial centers of the five nations represented at this table. In Berlin, Paris, Stockholm, London, and New York, negotiations have already been completed for massive purchases on the open market of the outstanding shares of your central companies. . . . Before noon of the next business day, gentlemen, Scarlatti will have considerable, though, of course, minority ownership in many of your vast enterprises. . . . Six hundred and seventy million dollars' worth! . . . Do you realize what this means, gentlemen?"

Kindorf roared. "*Ja!* You will drive up the prices and makes us fortunes! You will own nothing!"

"My dear lady, you are extraordinary." Innes-Bowen's textile prices had remained conservative. He was overjoyed at the prospects.

"D'Almeida, who realized she could not enter his Franco-Italian rails, took another view. "You can not purchase one share of my property, madame!"

"Some of you are more fortunate than others, Monsieur D'Almeida."

Leacock, the financier, the gentlest trace of a brogue in his cultivated voice, spoke up. "Granting what you say, and it is entirely possible, Madame Scarlatti, what have we suffered? . . . We have not lost a daughter, but gained a minor associate." He turned to the others who, he hoped, would find humor in his analogy.

Elizabeth held her breath before speaking. She waited until the men of Zurich were once again focused on her.

"I said before noon Scarlatti would be in the position I outlined. . . . One hour later a tidal wave will form in the Kurfuerstendamm in Berlin and end in New York's Wall Street! One hour later Scarlatti will divest itself of these holdings at a fraction of their cost! I have estimated three cents on the dollar. . . . Simultaneously, every bit of information Scarlatti has learned of your questionable activities will be released to the major wire services in each of your countries. . . . You might sustain slander by itself, gentlemen. You will not be the same men when it is accompanied by financial panic! Some of you will remain barely intact. Some will be wiped out. The majority of you will be affected disastrously!"

After the briefest moment of shocked silence, the room exploded. Aides were questioned peremptorily. Answers were bellowed to be heard.

Heinrich Kroeger rose from his chair and screamed at the men. "Stop! Stop! You damn fools, stop it! She'd never do it! She's bluffing!"

"Do you really think so?" Elizabeth shouted above the voices.

"I'll kill you, you bitch!"

"You are demented, Frau Scarlatti!"

"Try it . . . Kroeger! Try it!" Matthew Canfield stood by Elizabeth, his eyes bloodshot with fury as he stared at Ulster Stewart Scarlett.

"Who the hell are you, you lousy peddler?" The man called Kroeger, hands gripping the table, returned Canfield's stare and screeched to be heard by the salesman.

"Look at me good! I'm your executioner!"

"What!"

The man called Heinrich Kroeger squinted his misshapen eyes. He was bewildered. Who was this parasite? But he could not take the time to think. The voices of the men of Zurich had reached a crescendo. They were now shouting at each other.

Heinrich Kroeger pounded the table. He had to get control. He had to get them quiet. "Stop it! . . . Listen to me! If you'll listen to me, I'll tell you why she can't do it! She can't do it, I tell you!"

One by one the voices became quieter and finally trailed off into silence. The men of Zurich watched Kroeger. He pointed at Elizabeth Scarlatti.

"I know this bitch-woman! I've seen her do this before! She gets men together, powerful men, and frightens them. They go into panic and sell out! She gambles on *fear*, you cowards! On fear!"

Daudet spoke quietly. "You have answered nothing. Why can't she do as she says?"

Kroeger did not take his eyes off Elizabeth Scarlatti as he replied. "Because to do it would destroy everything she's ever fought for. It would collapse Scarlatti!"

Sydney Masterson spoke just above a whisper. "That would appear to be obvious. The question remains unanswered."

"She couldn't live without that power! Take my word for it! She couldn't live without it!"

"That's an opinion," said Elizabeth Scarlatti facing her son at the opposite end of the table. "Do you ask the majority of those at this table to risk everything on your opinion?"

"God damn you!"

"This Kroeger's right, honey." The Texas drawl was unmistakable. "You'll ruin yourself. You won't have a pot to piss in."

"Your language matches the crudity of your operations, Mr. Landor."

"I don't give pig piss for words, old lady. I do about money, and that's what we're talkin' about. Why do you want to pull this here crap?"

"That I'm doing it is sufficient, Mr. Landor. . . . Gentlemen, I said time was running out. The next twenty-four hours will either be a normal Tuesday or a day which will never be forgotten in the financial capitals of our world. . . . Some here will survive. Most of you will not. Which will it be, gentlemen? . . . I submit that in light of everything I've said, it's a poor fiscal decision wherein the majority allows the minority to cause its destruction."

"What is it you want of us?" Myrdal was a cautious bargainer. "A few might rather weather your threats than accept your demands. . . . Sometimes I think it is all a game. What are your demands?"

"That this . . . association be disbanded at once. That all financial and political ties in Germany with whatever factions be severed without delay! That those of you who have been entrusted with appointments to the Allied Controls Commission resign immediately!"

"No! No! No! No!" Heinrich Kroeger was enraged. He banged his fist with all his might upon the table. "This organization has taken years to build! We will control the economy of Europe. We will control all Europe! We will do it!"

"Hear me, gentlemen! Mr. Myrdal said it's a game! Of course, it's a game! A game we expend our lives on. Our souls on! It consumes us, and we demand more and more and more until, at last, we crave our own destruction. . . . Herr Kroeger says I can't live without the power I've sought and gained. He may be right, gentlemen! Perhaps it's time for me to reach that logical end, the end which I now crave and for which I'm willing to pay the price. . . . Of course, I'll do as I say, gentlemen. I welcome death!"

"Let it be yours, then, not ours." Sydney Masterson understood.

"So be it, Mr. Masterson. I'm not overwhelmed, you know. I leave to all of you the necessity of coping with this strange new world we've entered. Don't think for a minute, gentlemen, that I can't understand you! Understand what you've done. Most horridly, why you've done it! . . . You look around your personal kingdoms and you're frightened. You see your power threatened—by theories, governments, strange-sounding concepts which eat away at your roots. You have an overpowering anxiety to protect the feudal system which spawned you. And well you should, perhaps. It won't last long. . . . But you will *not* do it this way!"

"Since you understand so, why do you stop us? This undertaking protects all of us. Ultimately yourself as well. Why do you stop us?" D'Almeida could lose the Franco-Italian rails and survive, if only the remainder could be saved.

"It always starts that way. The greater good. . . . Let's say I stop you because what you're doing is a far greater blemish than it is a cure. And that's all I'll say about it!"

"From you, that's ludicrous! I tell you again, she won't do it!" Kroeger pounded the flat of his hand on the table, but no one paid much attention to him.

"When you say time is running out, Madame Scarlatti, how do you mean it? From what you said, I gathered time had run out. The expensive road had been taken. . . ."

"There's a man in Geneva, Mr. Masterson, who's awaiting a phone call from me. If he receives that phone call, a cable will be sent to my offices in New York. If that cable arrives, the operation is canceled. If it doesn't, it's executed on schedule."

"That's impossible! Such complexity untangled with a cablegram? I don't believe you." Monsieur Daudet was certain of ruin.

"I assume considerable financial penalties by the action."

"You assume more than that, I would suspect, madame. You'll never be trusted again. Scarlatti will be isolated!"

"It's a prospect, Mr. Masterson. Not a conclusion. The marketplace is flexible. . . . Well, gentlemen? Your answer?"

Syndey Masterson rose from his chair. "Make your phone call. There's no other choice, is there, gentlemen?"

The men of Zurich looked at each other. Slowly they began to get out of their chairs, gathering the papers in front of them.

"It's finished. I am out of it." Kindorf folded the manila envelope and put it in his pocket.

"You're a beastly tiger. I shouldn't care to meet you in the arena with an army at my back." Leacock stood erect.

"You may be bullshitter, but I'm not gonna slip on it!" Landor nudged Gibson, who found it difficult to adjust.

"We can't be sure. . . . That's our problem. We can't be sure," said Gibson.

"Wait! Wait! Wait a minute!" Heinrich Kroeger began to shout. "You do this! You walk out! You're dead! . . . Every God damn one of you leeches is dead! Leeches! Yellow-bellied leeches! . . . You suck our blood; you make agreements with us. Then you walk out? . . . Afraid for your little businesses? You God damn Jew bastards! We don't need you! Any of you! But you're going to need us! We'll cut you up and feed you to dogs! God damn swine!" Kroeger's face was flushed. His words spewed out, tumbling over one another.

"Stop it, Kroeger!" Masterson took a step toward the raving man with the splotched face. "It's finished! Can't you understand? It's finished!"

"Stay where you are, you scum, you English fairy!" Kroeger drew the pistol from his holster. Canfield, standing by Elizabeth, saw that it was a long-barreled forty-five and would blast half a man's body off with one shot.

"Stay where you are! . . . Finished! Nothing's finished until I say it's finished. God damn filthy pigs! Frightened little slug worms! We're too far along! . . . No one will stop us now! . . ." He waved the pistol toward Elizabeth and Canfield. "Finished! I'll tell you who's finished! She is! . . . Get out of my way." He started down the left side of the table as the Frenchman, Daudet, squealed.

"Don't do it, monsieur! Don't kill her! You do, and we are ruined!"

"I warn you, Kroeger! You murder her and you'll answer to us! We'll not be intimidated by you! We'll not destroy ourselves because of you!" Masterson stood at Kroeger's side, their shoulders nearly touching. The Englishman would not move.

Without a word, without warning, Heinrich Kroeger pointed his pistol at Masterson's stomach and fired. The shot was deafening and Sydney Masterson was jackknifed into the air. He fell to the floor, blood drenching his entire front, instantaneously dead.

The eleven men of Zurich gasped, some screamed in horror at the sight of the bloody corpse. Heinrich Kroeger kept walking. Those in his path got out of his way.

Elizabeth Scarlatti held her place. She locked her eyes with those of her killer son. "I curse the day you were born. You revile the house of your father. But know this, Heinrich Kroeger, and know it well!" The old woman's voice filled the cavernous room. Her power was such that her son was momentarily stunned, staring at her in hatred as she pronounced his sentence of execution. "Your identity will be spread across every front page of every newspaper in the civilized world after I'm dead! You will be hunted down for what you are! A madman, a murderer, a thief! And every man in this room, every investor in Zurich, will be branded your associate if they let you live this night!"

An uncontrollable rage exploded in the misshapen eyes of Heinrich Kroeger. His body shook with fury as he lashed at a chair in front of him sending it crashing across the floor. To kill was not enough. He had to kill at close range, he had to see the life and mind of Elizabeth Scarlatti detonated into oblivion in front of his eyes.

Matthew Canfield held the trigger of his revolver in his right-hand pocket. He had never fired from his pocket and he knew that if he missed he and Elizabeth would die. He was not sure how long he could wait. He would aim in the vicinity of the approaching man's chest, the largest target facing him. He waited until he could wait no longer.

The report of the small revolver and the impact of the bullet into Scarlett's shoulder was so much of a shock that Kroeger, for a split second, widened his eyes in disbelief.

It was enough, just enough for Canfield.

With all his strength he crashed into Elizabeth with his right shoulder sending her frail body toward the floor out of Kroeger's line of sight as he, Canfield, flung himself to the left. He withdrew his revolver and fired again, rapidly, into the man called Heinrich Kroeger.

Kroeger's huge pistol went off into the floor as he crumpled over.

Canfield staggered up, forgetting the unbearable pain in his left arm, which had been crushed under the weight of his own body. He leaped on Ulster Stewart Scarlett, wrenching the pistol from the iron grip. He began hitting the face of Heinrich Kroeger with the barrel. He could not stop.

Destroy the face! Destroy the horrible face!

Finally he was pulled off.

"*Gott!* He's dead! Halt! Stop! You can do no more!" The large, strong Fritz Thyssen held him.

Matthew Canfield felt weak and sank to the floor.

The men of Zurich had gathered around. Several helped Elizabeth, while the others bent over Heinrich Kroeger.

Rapid knocking came from the door leading to the hall.

Von Schnitzler took command. "Let them in!" he ordered in his thick German accent.

D'Almeida walked swiftly to the door and opened it. A number of chauffeurs stood at the entrance. It occurred to Canfield as he watched them that these men were not simply drivers of automobiles. He had good reason. They were armed.

As he lay there on the floor in terrible pain and shock, Canfield saw a brutish-looking blond man with close-cropped hair bent over the body of Heinrich Kroeger. He pushed the others away for the briefest instant while he pulled back the misshapen lid of one eye.

And then Canfield wondered if the agony of the last hours had played tricks with his sight, corrupted the infallible process of vision.

Or had the blond man bent his head down and whispered something into Heinrich Kroeger's ear?

Was Heinrich Kroeger still alive?

Von Schnitzler stood over Canfield. "He will be taken away. I have ordered a coup de grace. No matter, he is dead. It is finished." The obese von Schnitzler then shouted further commands in German to the uniformed chauffeurs around Kroeger. Several started to lift up the lifeless form but they were blocked by the blond man with the close-cropped hair. He shouldered them out of the way, not letting them touch the body.

He alone lifted Heinrich Kroeger off the floor and carried him out the door. The others followed.

"How's she?" Canfield gestured toward Elizabeth, who was seated in a chair. She was staring at the door through which the body had been taken, staring at the man no one knew was her son.

"Fine! She can make her call now!" Leacock was trying his best to be decisive.

Canfield rose from the floor and crossed to Elizabeth. He put his hand on her wrinkled cheek. He could not help himself.

Tears were falling down the ridges of her face.

And then Matthew Canfield looked up. He could hear the sound of a powerful automobile racing away. He was bothered.

Von Schnitzler had told him he'd ordered a coup de grace.

Yet no shot was fired.

A mile away, on the Winterthurstrasse, two men dragged the body of a dead man to a truck. They weren't sure what to do. The dead man had hired them, hired them all to stop the automobile heading to Falke Haus. He had paid them in advance, they had insisted upon it. Now he was dead, killed by a bullet meant for the driver of the automobile an hour ago. As they dragged the body over the rocky incline toward the truck, the blood from the mouth sprewed onto the perfectly matted waxed moustache.

The man named Poole was dead.

PART FOUR

CHAPTER 45

Major Matthew Canfield, aged forty-five—about to be forty-six—stretched his legs diagonally across the back of the army car. They had entered the township of Oyster Bay, and the sallow-complexioned sergeant broke the silence.

"Getting close, Major. You better wake up."

Wake up. It should be as easy as that. The perspiration streamed down his face. His heart was rhythmically pounding an unknown theme.

"Thank you, Sergeant."

The car swung east down Harbor Road toward the ocean drive. As they came closer to his home, Major Matthew Canfield began to tremble. He grabbed his wrists, held his breath, bit the front of his tongue. He could not fall apart. He could not allow himself the indulgence of self-pity. He could not do that to Janet. He owed her so much.

The sergeant blithely turned into the blue stone driveway and stopped at the path, which led to the front entrance of the large beach estate. The sergeant enjoyed driving out to Oyster Bay with his rich major. There was always lots of good food, in spite of rationing, and the liquor was always the best. No cheap stuff for the Camshaft, as he was known in the enlisted man's barracks.

The major slowly got out of the car. The sergeant was concerned. Something was wrong with the major. He hoped it didn't mean they'd have to drive back to New York. The old man seemed to have trouble standing up.

"Okay, Major?"

"Okay, Sergeant. . . . How'd you like to bunk in the boathouse tonight?" He did not look at the sergeant as he spoke.

"Sure! Great, Major!" It was where he always bunked. The boathouse apartment had a full kitchen and plenty of booze. Even a telephone. But the sergeant didn't have any signal that he could use it yet. He decided to try his luck. "Will you need me, Major? Could I call a couple of friends here?"

The major walked up the path. He called back quietly. "Do whatever you like, Sergeant. Just stay away from that radiophone. Is that understood?"

"You betcha, Major!" The sergeant gunned the engine and drove down toward the beach.

Matthew Canfield stood in front of the white, scalloped door with the sturdy hurricane lamps on both sides.

His home.

Janet.

The door opened and she stood there. The slightly graying hair, which she would not retouch. The upturned nose above the delicate, sensitive mouth. The bright, wide, brown searching eyes. The gentle loveliness of her face. The comforting concern she radiated.

"I heard the car. No one drives to the boathouse like Evans! . . . Matthew. Matthew! My darling! You're crying!"

CHAPTER 46

The plane, an Army B-29 transport, descended from the late-afternoon clouds to the airport in Lisbon. An Air Force corporal walked down the aisle.

"Please buckle all seat belts! No smoking! We'll be down in four minutes." He spoke in a monotone, aware that his passengers had to be important, so he would be more important, but courteous, when he had to tell them something.

The young man next to Matthew Canfield had said very little since their takeoff from Shannon. A number of times the major tried to explain that they were taking air routes out of range of the *Luftwaffe,* and that there was nothing to worry about. Andrew Scarlett had merely mumbled understood approval and had gone back to his magazines.

The car at the Lisbon airport was an armored Lincoln with two OSS personnel in the front. The windows could withstand short-range gunfire, and the automobile was capable of 120 miles an hour. They had to drive thirty-two miles up the Tejo River road to an airfield in Alenguer.

At Alenguer the man and boy boarded a low-flying, specially constructed Navy TBF with no markings for the trip to Bern. There would be no stops. Throughout the route, English, American, and Free French fighters were scheduled to intercept and protect to the destination.

At Bern they were met by a Swiss government vehicle, flanked by a motorcycle escort of eight men—one at the front, one at the rear, and three on each side. All were armed in spite of the Geneva pact, which prohibited such practices.

They drove to a village twenty-odd miles to the north, toward the German border. Kreuzlingen.

They arrived at a small inn, isolated from the rest of civilization, and the man and boy got out of the car. The driver sped the automobile away, and the motorcycle complement disappeared.

Matthew Canfield led the boy up the steps to the entrance of the inn.

Inside the lobby could be heard the wailing sound of an accordion, echoing from what was apparently a sparsely populated dining room. The high-ceilinged entry room was inhospitable, conveying the feeling that guests were not welcome.

Matthew Canfield and Andrew Scarlett approached the counter, which served as a front desk.

"Please, ring through to room six that April Red is here."

As the clerk plugged in his line, the boy suddenly shook. Canfield grabbed his arm and held him.

They walked up the stairs, and the two men stood in front of the door marked with the numeral six.

"There's nothing I can tell you now, Andy, except that we're here for one person. At least that's why I'm here. Janet. Your mother. Try to remember that."

The boy took a deep breath. "I'll try, Dad. Open the door! Jesus! Open the door!"

The room was dimly lit by small lamps on small tables. It was ornate in the fashion the Swiss felt proper for tourists—heavy rugs and solid furniture, overstuffed chairs and much antimacassar.

At the far end sat a man in half shadow. The spill of light angled sharply down across his chest but did not illuminate his face. The figure was dressed in brown tweeds, the jacket a combination of heavy cloth and leather.

He spoke in a throaty, harsh voice. "You are?"

"Canfield and April Red. Kroeger?"

"Shut the door."

Matthew Canfield closed the door and took several steps forward in front of Andrew Scarlett. He would cover the boy. He put his hand in his right coat pocket.

"I have a gun pointed at you, Kroeger. Not the same gun but the same pocket as last time we met. This time I won't take anything for granted. Do I make myself clear?"

"If you like, take it out of your pocket and hold it against my head. . . . There's not much I can do about it."

Canfield approached the figure in the chair.

It was horrible.

The man was a semi-invalid. He seemed to be paralyzed through the entire left portion of his body, extending to his jaw. His hands were folded across his front, his fingers extended as though spastic. But his eyes were alert.

His eyes.

His face. . . . Covered over by white splotches of skin graft below gray short-cropped hair. The man spoke.

"What you see was carried out of Sevastopol. Operation Barbarossa."

"What do you have to tell us, Kroeger?"

"First, April Red. . . . Tell him to come closer."

"Come here, Andy. By me."

"Andy!" The man in the chair laughed through his half-closed mouth. "Isn't that nice! Andy! Come here, Andy!"

Andrew Scarlett approached his stepfather and stood by his side, looking down at the deformed man in the chair.

"So you're the son of Ulster Scarlett?"

"I'm Matthew Canfield's son."

Canfield held his place, watching the father and son. He suddenly felt as though he didn't belong. He had the feeling that giants—old and infirm, young and scrawny—were about to do battle. And he was not of their house.

"No, young man, you're the son of Ulster Stewart Scarlett, heir to Scarlatti!"

"I'm exactly what I want to be! I have nothing to do with you." The young man breathed deeply. The fear was leaving him now, and in its place Canfield saw that a quiet fury was taking hold of the boy.

"Easy, Andy. Easy."

"Why? . . . For him? . . . Look at him. He's practically dead. . . . He doesn't even have a face."

"Stop it!" Ulster Scarlett's shrill voice reminded Canfield of that long-ago room in Zurich. "Stop it, you fool!"

"For what? For you? . . . Why should I? . . . I don't know you! I don't want to know you! . . . You left a long time ago!" The young man pointed to Canfield. "He took over for you. I listen to him. You're nothing to me!"

"Don't you talk to me like that! Don't you dare!"

Canfield spoke sharply. "I've brought April Red, Kroeger! What have you got to deliver! That's what we're here for. Let's get it over with!"

"He must understand first!" The misshapen head nodded back and forth. "He must be made to understand!"

"If it meant that much, why did you hide it? Why did you become Kroeger?"

The nodding head stopped, the ashen slit eyes stared. Canfield remembered Janet speaking about that look.

"Because Ulster Scarlett was not fit to represent the new order. The new world! Ulster Scarlett served his purpose and once that purpose was accomplished, he was no longer necessary. . . . He was a hindrance. . . . He would have been a joke. He had to be eliminated. . . ."

"Perhaps there was something else, too."

"What?"

"Elizabeth. She would have stopped you again. . . . She would have stopped you later, just the way she stopped you at Zurich."

At Elizabeth's name, Heinrich Kroeger worked up the phlegm in his scarred throat and spat. It was an ugly sight. "The bitch of the world! . . . But we made a mistake in twenty-six. . . . Let's be honest, I made the mistake. . . . I should have asked her to join us. . . . She would have, you know. She wanted the same things we did. . . ."

"You're wrong about that."

"Hah! You didn't know her!"

The former field accountant replied softly without inflection. "I knew her. . . . Take my word for it, she despised everything you stood for."

The Nazi laughed quietly to himself. "That's very funny. . . . I told her she stood for everything I despised. . . ."

"Then you were both right."

"No matter. She's in hell now."

"She died thinking you were dead. She died in peace because of that."

"Hah! You'll never know how tempted I was over the years, especially when we took Paris! . . . But I was waiting for London. . . . I was going to stand outside Whitehall and announce it to the world—and watch Scarlatti destroy itself!"

"She was gone by the time you took Paris."

"That didn't matter."

"I suppose not. You were just as afraid of her in death as you were when she was alive."

"I was afraid of no one! I was afraid of nothing!" Heinrich Kroeger strained his decrepit body.

"Then why didn't you carry out your threat? The house of Scarlatti lives."

"She never told you?"

"Told me what?"

"The bitch-woman always covered herself on four flanks. She found her corruptible man. My one enemy in the Third Reich. Goebbels. She never believed I'd been killed at Zurich. Goebbels knew who I was. After nineteen thirty-three she threatened our respectability with lies. Lies about me. The party was more important than revenge."

Canfield watched the destroyed man below him. As always, Elizabeth Scarlatti had been ahead of all of them. Far ahead.

"One last question."

"What?"

"Why Janet?"

The man in the chair raised his right hand with difficulty. "Him. . . . Him!" He pointed to Andrew Scarlett.

"Why?"

"I believed! I still believe! Heinrich Kroeger was part of a new world! A new order! The true aristocracy! . . . In time it would have been his!"

"But why Janet?"

Heinrich Kroeger, in exhaustion, waved the question aside. "A whore. Who needs a whore? The vessel is all we look for. . . ."

Canfield felt the anger rise inside him, but at his age and in his job, he suppressed it. He was not quick enough for the boy-man beside him.

Andrew Scarlett rushed forward to the overstuffed chair and swung his open hand at the invalid Kroeger. The slap was hard and accurate. "You bastard! You filthy bastard!"

"Andy! Get back!" He pulled the boy away.

"Unehelich!" Heinrich Kroeger's eyes were swimming in their sockets. "It's for you! That's why you're here! You've got to know! . . . You'll understand and start us up again! Think! Think the aristocracy! For you . . . for you. . . ." He reached with his slightly mobile hand to his inside jacket pocket and withdrew a slip of paper. "They're yours. Take them!"

Canfield picked up the paper and without looking at it handed it to Andrew Scarlett.

"They're numbers. Just a lot of numbers."

Matthew Canfield knew what the numbers meant, but before he could explain, Kroeger spoke. "They're Swiss accounts, my son. My only son. . . . They contain millions! Millions! But there are certain conditions. Conditions which you will learn to understand! When you grow older, you'll know those conditions have to be met! And you'll meet them! . . . Because this power is the power to change the world! The way we wanted to change it!"

The man-boy looked at the deformed figure in the chair. "Am I supposed to thank you?"

"One day you will."

Matthew Canfield had had enough. "This is it! April Red has his message. Now I want it! What are you delivering?"

"It's outside. Help me up and we'll go to it."

"Never! What's outside? Your staff members in leather coats?"

"There's no one. No one but me."

Canfield looked at the wreck of a man in front of him and believed him. He started to help Heinrich Kroeger out of the chair.

"Wait here, Andy, I'll be back."

Major Matthew Canfield, in full uniform, helped the crippled man in brown tweeds down the stairs and onto the lobby floor. In the lobby, a servant brought over the crutches discarded by the Nazi when he first ascended the staircase to his room. The American major and the Nazi went out the front door.

"Where are we going, Kroeger?"

"Don't you think it's time you called me by my right

name? The name is Scarlett. Or, if you will, Scarlatti." The Nazi led them to the right, off the driveway, into the grass.

"You're Heinrich Kroeger. That's all you are to me."

"You realize, of course, that it was you, and you alone who caused our setback in Zurich. You pushed our timetable back a good two years. . . . No one ever suspected. . . . You were an ass!" Heinrich Kroeger laughed. "Perhaps it takes an ass to portray an ass!" He laughed again.

"Where are we going?"

"Just a few hundred yards. Hold your pistol up, if you like. There's no one."

"What are you going to deliver? You might as well tell me."

"Why not? You'll have them in your hands soon enough." Kroeger hobbled along toward an open field. "And when you have them, I'm free. Remember that."

"We have a deal. What is it?"

"The Allies will be pleased. Eisenhower will probably give you a medal! . . . You'll bring back the complete plans of the Berlin fortifications. They're known only to the elite of the German High Command. . . . Underground bunkers, rocket emplacements, supply depots, even the Führer's command post. You'll be a hero and I'll be nonexistent. We've done well, you and I."

Matthew Canfield stopped.

The plans of the Berlin fortifications had been obtained weeks ago by Allied Intelligence.

Berlin knew it.

Berlin admitted it.

Someone had been led into a trap, but it was not him, not Matthew Canfield. The Nazi High Command had led one of its own into the jaws of death.

"Tell me, Kroeger, what happens if I take your plans, your exchange for April Red, and don't let you go? What happens then?"

"Simple. Doenitz himself took my testimony. I gave it to him two weeks ago in Berlin. I told him everything. If I'm not back in Berlin in a few days, he'll be concerned. I'm very valuable. I expect to make my appearance and then . . . be gone. If I don't appear, then the whole world knows!"

Matthew Canfield thought it was the strangest of ironies. But it was no more than he had anticipated. He had written it all down in the original file, sealed for years in the archives of the State Department.

And now a man in Berlin, unknown to him except by reputation, had reached the same conclusion.

Heinrich Kroeger, Ulster Stewart Scarlett—was expendable.

Doenitz had allowed Kroeger—bearing his false gifts—to come to Bern. Doenitz, in the unwritten rule of war, expected him to be killed. Doenitz knew that neither nation could afford this madman as its own. In either victory or defeat. And the enemy had to execute him so that no doubts existed. Doenitz was that rare enemy in these days of hatreds. He was a man his adversaries trusted. Like Rommel, Doenitz was a thorough fighter. A vicious fighter. But he was a moral man.

Matthew Canfield drew his pistol and fired twice.

Heinrich Kroeger lay dead on the ground.

Ulster Stewart Scarlett was—at last—gone.

Matthew Canfield walked through the field back to the small inn. The night was clear and the moon, three-quarters of it, shone brightly on the still foliage around him.

It struck him that it was remarkable that it had all been so simple.

But the crest of the wave is simple. Deceptively simple. It does not show the myriad pressures beneath that make the foam roll the way it does.

It was over.

And there was Andrew.

There was Janet.

Above all, there was Janet.

LUDLUM ON LUDLUM

Few writers have skyrocketed to popularity with the speed of Robert Ludlum, with each succeeding thriller becoming a bigger bestseller. The key to his success may lie in John Leonard's comment in *The New York Times*, "Mr. Ludlum stuffs more surprises into his novels than any other six-pack of thriller writers combined."

Some people claim Ludlum has secret sources for information found in his stories. In one, an early book, a key theme was CIA involvement in domestic surveillance. At that time the subject shocked many people. Later, of course, this fact proved to be correct. Other people suspect Ludlum was an agent himself during the years prior to his career as a novelist. Not true. For close to twenty years he was in show business—as an actor, producer, and as the "voice" of dozens of television commercials for products ranging from Tiparillos to Tuna Helper.

During his "voice" period, Ludlum's wife crowned him "King of the Toilet Bowls." As he tells it, "there was this product called Plunge. All I had to do was read three words: Plunge works fast. In spite of my off-hand delivery, they used my three words in over one hundred different commercials. The money from this put one of my children through two years of college."

Although none of Ludlum's novels draws on his show business background for subject matter, they all reflect techniques he learned in the theater. Ludlum says, "the theater man knows that he must involve the audience. He understands structure more than anyone else—the logical evolving of one event into another event without losing the audience's attention. Because if you lose their interest, you're closing Saturday night."

Ludlum admits, "I write primarily as an entertainer. But I find that whether you're writing comically or dramatically, you write from a point of view of something that disturbs or outrages you. And that's what I do. I admit to being outraged—mostly by the abuse of power by the fanatics. The extremes bother me, right or left." Yet he adds, "I disapprove of violence, that's why I show pain for what it is. When my characters get hit, they hurt. They don't jump back into action like John Wayne."

All of this—and more—can be found in the published work of Robert Ludlum. Since his first novel, *THE SCARLATTI INHERITANCE*, he has amassed an enviable record of success: *THE OSTERMAN WEEKEND*, *THE MATLOCK PAPERS*, *THE RHINEMANN EXCHANGE*, *THE GEMINI CONTENDERS*; more recently, *THE CHANCELLOR MANUSCRIPT*, *THE HOLCROFT COVENANT*, *THE MATARESE CIRCLE* and *THE BOURNE IDENTITY*.